✤ CHAPTER ONE ✤

He had a habit of regretting his purchases. He'd buy vanilla yogurt when he meant to buy plain, nylon socks when he wanted cotton, and lobster at the Chinese take-away when most people knew that a lobster plate for 70 pence was not a promising choice. And now he sat on a Pan Am airliner with his new small wife beside him. He'd had a girlfriend, Victoria. Not anymore. He'd told her, when he left for India, not to wait for him. He'd spent most of his time in India secretly hoping she would. And now he fervently hoped she hadn't.

The plan was this: to go to Madras as a visiting scholar and return with a chunk of an art history dissertation in hand. Instead, he had an Indian woman. He wasn't certain that the marriage was binding. It had been performed hastily in a temple down the road from the college, and there hadn't been a notary present. The priests hadn't worn shirts. He felt a shirtless man could have little in the way of official authority. But then, if the marriage weren't binding, what would he do with this woman, leaning trustfully against his shoulder, asleep or pretending to be? *Sorry, love,* he might say, *it seems we're not actually married. There's a letting agency down the road and a market on the corner. Best of luck with everything.* Her hair was loose and drifted onto his chest. She wore a sari and two gold bangles. From above, he studied the fringe of her lashes. No, he couldn't turn her away.

George had left for India with visions of social clubs and exclusive dining rooms that served gin and tonics and Sunday roasts. His supervisor at the university was from Exeter and would show him how to make his way through the heat and the dust. He would spend his afternoons in the cool of the English library, and emerge in the evenings for drinks at the club. There would be bridge games, played by English girls gone moist who would sit with their legs spread, wearing thin cotton dresses and fanning the heat away.

It was August 1974. Everyone spoke of the heat, the cloud of it that had smothered him the moment he stepped off the plane in Madras. But it wasn't the heat that stayed with him, not even the dust. It was the air, thick and glutinous, that existed nowhere else in the world. And swarming through every molecule of it was Madras and everything in Madras: sweaty silk, water, the curiously thin coins, tin cups, oil, frying food, groundnuts, the empty smell of boiled rice, turmeric, coriander, cumin, coconut oil, cow dung, goats in the street, naked children wearing nothing but gold chains around their waists, beggars with no legs, adobe houses, power cuts, wells, irrigation ditches, billboards, hotels, mothballs, citronella, fire. All of it rushed into George each time he inhaled. And when he exhaled, none of it came back out.

There were two English women on his course, Stella and Jo, and they didn't play bridge. They took tea in their rooms, spending most of their time studying and the rest

THE PRAYER ROOM

A NOVEL BY

SHANTHI SEKARAN

MACADAM CAGE

MacAdam/Cage
155 Sansome Street
Suite 550
San Francisco, CA 94104
www.macadamcage.com

"Hearts and Bones", Copyright © 1983 Paul Simon
Used by permission of the Publisher: Paul Simon Music
Library of Congress Cataloging-in-Publication Data

Sekaran, Shanthi, 1977-
  The prayer room / by Shanthi Sekaran.
    p. cm.
  ISBN 978-1-59692-321-8
1. Indian women–Fiction. 2. Identity (Philosophical
concept)–Fiction. 3. California–Fiction. I. Title.
PS3619.E45P73 2009
813'.6–dc22

                                          2008030006

Printed in the United States of America.
1 2 3 4 5 6 7 8 9 10

Book design by Dorothy Carico Smith

To the house on Winding Creek Road,
and everyone who once lived there.

Two people were married
The act was outrageous
The bride was contagious
She burned like a bride
These events may have had some effect
On the man with the girl by his side

"Hearts and Bones," Paul Simon

of it on "expeditions" to local temples, getting skinny and brown as natives, wearing badly wrapped saris, and maintaining a steadfast indifference to George. No club, no parties, no nights made slippery by gin. George was a student, and no different from every other student around him. He ate in the canteen with the rest of them, spooning watery lentil soup onto rice, drinking from his own bottle of preboiled water to keep off the runs. He studied in his hall library under the whir of some sleepy ceiling fans, haunted daily by the room's single resident fly. His supervisor was an effete and sweaty man who spent his days in a very large office. He could happily speak with George for three and a half hours about seventh century temple engravings. But an existence outside of his office was something he probably never risked. Days swelled like bloated carcasses and ruptured into months. George stayed and worked and was oblivious to the gift that this country was about to push, with its wide and forceful smile, into his arms.

And this was where they met: it was May, a month when bathing was useless. George stepped out of the bathroom and into a fresh coat of sweat. He put on a clean linen shirt, cool at first, until it too melted to his skin.

In the lecture hall, fans were mounted to the walls, but any air they made vanished immediately into the roomful of bodies.

Her first words: *Excuse me.* His first words: *Go ahead.*

And she squeezed past him into the crowded lecture hall. George looked after her, the first Indian woman he'd seen in a dress. The dress was white, cotton, so thin that it shaded her more than clothed her. It fell to her knees. Hers were the first brown calves he'd seen since leaving Heathrow.

He watched for her the next week and the week after, spotting her always in the back row. Legs crossed, dress creeping above the knee, showing a narrow strip of thigh. Brown skin was taking on new meaning for George. In a country with so much of it, he got to see so little. After eight months, he'd begun to forget the thighs and breasts of English women.

To look without looking was a vanishing art form. It had certainly vanished in Madras, where people gawked at him, leaned out of their windows as if they'd never seen a tall white man before. In his one and only lecture, George looked without looking at the people around him, homogenously brown, speaking an English that brought to mind neither Forster nor Kipling. He sat at the lecture hall's center and had to turn in his seat to look at her, which he did, awkwardly, three times. The man next to him stared at George each time, annoyed at the needless fidgeting. She wore her hair loose around her shoulders. Indian women didn't do this. Loose hair was intimate. He looked again and his elbow knocked his pencil to the ground, where it rolled under the seat in front of him, un-reachable, gone forever. Feeling foolish, he vowed never to look back again.

When he did look back again, Viji caught him. She stared back, her eyes wide with some mixture of amusement and surprise. The man next to him turned to have a look too, but he didn't see what George saw. Brown legs, bedroom hair.

And now, there were worse places she could be. The last
four days had been a fever dream, and this, the baggage
claim at Heathrow, was just an extension of it. Viji stood
by the carousel and watched other people's luggage go by.
Hulking suitcases, brown boxes wound desperately with
twine, a black leather bag with the tip of a shoe sticking
out. She'd had to come in through the noncitizen line;
George had said he would meet her on the other side. She
watched the clock at the far end of the hall. Ten minutes,
still no husband. His line had been shorter. He should have
been through by now. Around her glided a sea of British
people—towering, pink-hued, dressed in trousers, hair
that was brown and lighter brown and lightest brown.
They all looked like George. Which one had she married?
Next to her stood a tall Caucasian male, a few days' stubble
sprayed across his cheeks. Same sand-colored hair. Linen
shirt, linen trousers. She looked down to find sandals and
pink toes, knobbly with the lesions of a hundred mosquito
bites. This could have been her husband, but it wasn't.

✤✤✤

A month after they married, they had a honeymoon. George
felt it was only right, that after all the strangeness something
predictable was in order. They toured the Lake District,
driving around Cumbria in his father's '67 Volkswagen. They
listened to the radio, tinny beneath the engine's urgent
roar. *Cooar blimey!* was a phrase she learned, and *six of
one, half a dozen of the other, mates' rates, don't fancy yours
much, ee by gum!* Most mornings, the engine refused to

start, until George learned to bleed the radiator and seal it with his lips to blow out the air bubbles.

They had no set plans for that holiday, and they wasted a good deal of time asking what the other wanted, tossing their choices around like work colleagues on a business trip: *Shall we eat in a pub tonight or a restaurant? There's an Italian down the street, or would you prefer something light? I was going to get another pint, but I don't have to. Would you join me? You don't have to. Well, I don't mind. Whatever you want. It's fine, that's fine with me. Are you sure?* Often Viji wished George would just order for her, and George wished Viji would get an opinion of her own. Surely there were things she hated, but he had yet to find them. The only thing she'd refused was the kidney pie he'd bought from a farm shop. She'd even eaten the black pudding that came with their hotel breakfast. "So tasty." she said, stabbing the black congealed disc with her fork. "Like nothing I've tasted." She stopped suddenly. "It isn't beef, I hope."

"No," George said. "No, not really."

She resumed eating, chomping happily. "How do they make it?" A herd of sheep roamed by their window, and George managed to skirt the question.

He found that he liked her voice. They had talked some in Madras, but not much, and it wasn't until now that he truly learned how she sounded. She spoke with an accent that he recognized as educated, a voice that wrapped around the language and stretched it out like taffy. She turned words into intimate things; she spoke with an affection for the syllables themselves. The hours spent driving passed easily with her, conversations drifting in and out the car window.

From Ulverston they drove to Lake Coniston, and from there to Windermere. Everything around her was green, Hollywood green, as green as Scarlett O'Hara's ball gown, soaked with pigment by the months of winter snow and spring rain. Driving with George through the countryside, Viji felt she didn't know him at all. The few scraps of intimacy they'd collected during those hectic nights in Madras had vanished. Now he was a man with light hair who gripped the steering wheel tightly, his jaw set. He pointed to streams that ran between the fields, and to flocks of sheep and cows. He named the massive hills towards which they drove. They stopped in towns with bewildering names like Tintwhistle and Penistone, bought eggs and bread from farm shops. She felt obligated to compliment the scenery whenever possible, and took every opportunity to be awed by the land of which he— of which all these English—seemed so very proud.

Around them rolled the valleys she'd seen in paintings. They planted a warm ache inside her. Fields of tiny yellow buds spread as perfectly rectangular as if a servant had clipped them back with shears. Around her, all was beauty—fenced in, trim and sedate. Every blade of grass looked like every other blade of grass, as if they'd all had a meeting and decided how to be. Blankets upon blankets of miniature flowers, atop the greenest green. Nowhere could she see the dusty roadsides or pointless rock piles of home. The English countryside was like English desserts: custard on pudding, cream on cake, sweet smothering sweet and holding at bay the salty bits of life.

George bought a bottle of sloe gin from a local farmer.

Viji asked him how much it cost. This was a habit of hers, he was beginning to learn. He wouldn't tell her, and they had their first fight. He had his reasons for buying that particular bottle on that specific day. The price didn't matter. Besides which, it cost far more than he could afford, and he preferred not to remind himself of this. He would save it, he said, for a special occasion. It would get better with time.

They picnicked at the southern edge of a lake one muggy afternoon, after George had bought some elder-flower wine and oatcakes and cheddar. By the time they'd finished half the bottle, George's words were slurring and Viji had fallen into a warm haze. When George wandered off to piss in the bushes, Viji lay on the lakeside, her head resting on her forearm. The world was in a stupor. She watched, for what seemed like hours, the water's hot fast ripple, perfectly silent. Drunken geese flew in a teetering V over the tree line. On the opposite shore were some ducks, gliding smoothly across the lake's surface, showing no signs of the frantic churn beneath. She thought of her uncle's village house, of the river that ran past it, bordered by arid dirt and cut by a bridge. She missed the creek behind her home in Madras. She missed the fried fish her mother's cook would make. She dozed. Not even George's footsteps woke her. She woke when his lips brushed her neck and, sleepily, she unbuttoned his shirt. They made love there on the hard, grassy bank. On the main road above, a tractor rattled by but didn't stop.

It was a sordid business, this luring of females to his bedroom. It was such an obvious sort of game, mired in nervous dialogue and badly worded invitations. George wished for a way around it, but there was none. With Viji, the game troubled him more than usual—he somehow felt guiltier with her than he would have with someone English. It wasn't just that startled gasp of pain when he entered her, the sudden rigid clutch of her body under his. It was more the sense that he was a predator, and she his prey. *Nonsense*, Victoria would have said. *That little thing is more predator than you'll ever be.*

They slept in his old bedroom at his parents' house in Sneinton, a neighborhood at the eastern end of Nottingham. On a twin mattress hardly big enough for both of them, they slept against each other, locked in like pieces of a puzzle. Often he woke in the mornings with his feet on the floor and a cramp in his lower back. Viji's brown legs wrapped all the way around his waist, and her soft sheets of hair snuck into his mouth.

George felt little need for sleep. And he was glad, at least, to not have to watch her leave. No longer did he lie helplessly as she wrapped her sari around and around, carefully tucking the pleats into her waistband, her face drying into a tight mask of worry and guilt. And she was happy to be here with him, or so it seemed at night. During the days, she spent long hours gazing out the window. During the days, he wasn't so sure.

Still, there were times when the very existence of Viji—in his mother's kitchen, standing next to him at the cornershop, dreaming in a window seat—sucked the language from him, left him verbally bereft and unable to work. Sometimes he wondered what she would do if he left her somewhere, at the supermarket or the post office in town. Would she find her way home, making her quiet way down the pavement, or would she simply vanish? Would she find a job in a bakery and a flat in the city center? He could only watch her and wonder how she'd ended up here, with him, on this pockmarked strip of England. There were moments when he despised her for it, the way she'd mutely latched onto his life, wandered into his bed, then into his world, and forced upon it an outline. He'd preferred it shapeless.

One summer afternoon, she sat staring out the window, past the murky pane and beyond the rain to some point far in the distance. Her silence was a maddening static that filled the room and made it impossible to think. "What are you doing here?" he asked.

She turned to him. "Pardon?"

"What are you doing in England, here, with me? You hardly know me."

She stared at the carpet for a few minutes, thinking. Then she shrugged, "It's what I was meant to do. It's what my mother wanted." How sluggish she was, with her languid blink and her swaying foot, how like a cow. He expected her to flick a fly away with her ear. Instead she turned quietly back to the window.

He shook his head. "Rather *obedient* of you, isn't it? Not exactly twentieth century." He thought of Victoria, who would never have let herself be married off like this. It felt mean but he didn't care. "It's not something an adult would do, is it? To pick up and leave because Mummy tells you to? Mummy says, you obey, that's how it works with you, isn't it?" No answer came. "I*sn't it*?"

She whipped around to look at him. "You did it. You

married *me*. Mummy said, *you* obeyed." She looked straight into him and shook her head. "She wasn't even your mother."

He opened his mouth to argue, to pick away at the first tender scab he could find, but stopped himself. "Why did you do it?" he asked.

"No George, why did *you* do it?" The question hung between them like the mist outside, and Viji turned back to the rain.

They spent nearly three months with his parents as George submitted and defended his thesis. In that time, Viji took easily to the role of dutiful daughter-in-law, helping Marla, George's mother, with the laundry and the washing up. She liked Marla, who laughed easily and wore colorful headbands and strings of beads around her neck. Viji learned to use the kettle and made tea twice a day. She woke at seven in the morning and went to bed at ten. It was these minute scheduling points that gave her purpose during the foggy, do-nothing stretch of weeks.

In the kitchen, she watched as brussels sprouts were scored and chickens basted. The Sunday that Marla roasted a side of beef, Viji ate only potatoes and carrots.

"I'd love to taste your food, Viji. Do you cook?" Marla asked, eyeing Viji's beefless plate.

Viji glanced nervously at George.

"Viji hasn't cooked much, Mum," he said. "She had a cook at home."

"Well, fiddle-dee-dee," Stan grunted.

"Stan."

"Dad, it's just the way—"

"I can cook," Viji interrupted. She turned to Marla, who was safer than the men. "I can cook for us."

That Monday Marla found an Asian grocer. She and Viji returned, arms resplendent with yellow and crimson sachets of powder, cinnamon sticks, and sacks of onions and fresh chilies. Viji smiled freely, like a child.

She began cooking early the next afternoon. The family had left her to herself, her only companion the cat, who normally padded at the feet of whoever was in the kitchen, its head cocked in a one-eyed search for chicken-fat drippings or a crumbled corner of cheese. But today, only a thin powdering of turmeric littered the kitchen floor. The cat sniffed it, recoiled and slipped into the corner.

For dinner she was making chicken curry, Madras-style, to be simmered for hours in a thick, peppery broth. She was making eggplant raita, for which the thin slices of eggplant had been rubbed with salt and fried and waited crisp-edged on a tea towel. From the corner of the kitchen, the single eye of the single-eyed cat flashed in the passing sunlight. It kept watch over her, suspicious as a nosy neighbor. She'd never asked what had happened to its other eye. Was it gone altogether or sealed beneath the soft black lid?

It felt good to hold a knife again, to wrap her palm around its wooden hilt and use it to slice and crush. To change things completely, simply because she wanted to—this was satisfaction. George came down once and said something about a walk. She ignored him. Before her waited a bouquet of garlic bulbs. She began with the onions, fast rhythmic slicing, pulling her fingers away from the flashing blade as a hill of white grew upon the chopping board.

But it wasn't natural for her to stand at a high counter like this, her elbows splayed from her sides. A hot finger of pain slid down her back. She rolled her neck from side to side, but the ache only shifted and spread. Quickly, she gathered the chopping board, the knife, the onions, and placed them on the floor by the kitchen table. Here she sat back comfortably on her haunches.

Viji had spent her childhood on the kitchen floor, first watching Old Krishnan, then young Kuttima, chop and grind and fry. They kept the floor immaculately clean, and vegetables were kept in baskets along the walls. By the time she left Madras, she was immune to the lung assault of frying chilies and could mince six bulbs of garlic in under a minute. Soon she forgot about the ache in her back. She could no longer see the cat or hear the footsteps from upstairs. If she heard the knock at the back door, she ignored it. She'd been thinking of the first time she cut onions, how Kuttima had laughed at her, how copiously they'd made her cry. She didn't hear the door creak open or the offbeat tread of heavy footsteps that followed.

The door slammed and she dropped the knife.

"What the bleeding hell is this?" Stan's voice boomed through the kitchen. "What're you doing on the floor, you daft cow?" He leaned over, hands on knees, to peer directly into her face. "What the bloody hell y'doing?" he asked again. "The floor is not where we cut the vegetables." She could tell he was speaking slowly and clearly for her benefit. He paused between each word, as if she were deaf or old or merely stupid. "The. floor. is. not. where. we. cut. the.

ve-ge-ta-bles. The. floor. is. for. the. animals. You see?" He
pointed to the cat, who flashed past them and up the stairs.

He was wearing his shoes indoors, and from them
wafted the smell of something foul. "Do you understand?
Are you an animal? Hey?" He stepped over her with his
putrid shoes and moved to the stove.

Viji shook her head. She could only stare dumbly at
him. What swelled inside her had no words. Stan lifted a
lid to investigate the pot of yellow stew. Then he tapped
the counter hard with his ruddy old-man finger. "T*his is
where we cut the ve-ge-ta-bles.* You see?" He examined her
for several more seconds.

To his horror, she smiled. It was a feeble smile, quivering at its edges. She stood and replaced the chopping
board. Her wrist shook violently and sprayed onion pieces
to the floor. Stan sighed and picked up a garlic bulb,
turned it over, and put it down. Her vision blurred but she
managed to find her shoes. Slipping them on, she ran into
the garden and slammed the back door behind her.

The house filled with new smells that afternoon. They
were familiar to George but worried the cat, who whipped
around his ankles like an agitated ghost. The day was
warm, too warm to wear socks, and certainly too warm to
be trapped in a kitchen. Earlier George had tried to take
Viji for a walk, but she had refused to come. He'd found
her hunched over the kitchen counter, her fingers coated
in tomato slime. Her face was taut with concentration, and
when Geoge spoke to her she stared up at him, ready to
pounce, like a forest animal trapped in its burrow. For
once she didn't need him around—indeed, she didn't

want him. The feeling, however temporary, left him sour.

Now the house was silent, and the silence saturated the air. He wished for a noise to break the heat, a thunder clap or a siren. He stopped by the mirror to fix his hair and found a thin film of sweat coating his forehead. It broke away when he touched it, like the shimmering skin that formed on soup. For weeks his internal thermostat had been running off-kilter, unable to reconcile Madrasi heat with the starchy English damp.

From the kitchen downstairs, he heard voices. First Stan, then Stan again, louder. He heard a clatter and the slam of the back door. He waited a moment, and heard nothing more.

"Dad?" he called. "Viji?" The house was quiet.

The kitchen was empty. The stove had been shut off and on it sat a pot of yellow liquid, mulchy and tired. Finely diced onions littered the floor and stuck to his heels like barnacles; in the corner, half-hidden by the radiator, was a chopping knife. A wooden chopping board lay in the middle of the work surface amid a heap of onion skins. "Viji!" he called again. Her shoes, usually waiting neatly by the door, were gone.

He found her in the garden shed. She sat perched on Stan's drinking bench, hugging her knees to her chest, rocking from side to side. Behind her, a window opaque with cobwebs framed the looming dusk. "What's wrong?" he asked. "What happened?"

She took a while to answer and this, he now knew, meant that the smallest peep would release a torrent of tears. At last she began to speak, her shaky voice patting itself smooth again. She'd been chopping in the kitchen when her back began to ache; she showed George the spot. So she'd moved to the floor. Here, she said, she could chop comfortably. He saw her as she might have been at home, her body swaying in tempo with the knife, diced onion falling from the blade like snow.

"And then your father walked in," she said. George knew what was coming. The tremor crept back into her voice. "*What the bleeding hell do you think you're doing?* he said. He scolded me for putting food on the floor. *That is where the animals eat*, he said. *Are you an animal? Are you a cat, too?*" She looked for George's reaction. "What the *bleeding hell*, he said. This is how he speaks to me?" New tears streamed down her face. How alone she looked on the bench, an empty whiskey bottle at her feet. She sniffed and caught her breath. "He can keep his bleeding hell."

It's nothing, George was about to say, *that's just the way he is sometimes*. Stan was a grizzly with no claws. But clearly, to Viji, it was something. And George knew precisely how his father would have barked the words, thoughtless as an old bulldog. "That's terrible," George said. He expected more weeping as he sat next to Viji and circled his arm around her waist. Most women fell to tearful heaps at the first sign of sympathy. But when Viji looked up, her eyes were steel. She was ready for a fight. "So what did you do?" he asked.

"Nothing." She shook her head. "I did nothing. I simply shut up like a deaf-mute. Like a stupid person."

"You're not a stupid person."

"I didn't know how to answer. What could I say?"

"So you waited for him to finish?"

"Yes."

"And then you came out here?"

"I had enough. He wouldn't leave, like an old mother-in-law, sniffing and staring and lifting the lid on the pot. Shameless, wearing his dirty shoes in the house, bringing in the filthiness from the street. I promise you, I smelled some dog shits on his shoes. I'm quite certain!"

George laughed. "Poor Viji." She stiffened, but let him take her hand in his. He pulled her face into his shoulder. "You daft monkey," he said.

"He's a daft monkey. I'm not a daft monkey," came the muffled words. He kneaded his fingers into the sore spot on her back.

"Where have I brought you, hey?"

She softened in his arms, and his collar was soon wet. The tears, he realized, had little to do with his father or the onions. She wasn't crying for Stan's language, or for the smell of dog shit, but for everything that she'd wished for, and all that had been thrust upon her. "Where shall I take you next?" he asked. She shrugged, limp against his chest. "Hmm? Go on. Your choice this time."

"Hawaii," she mumbled.

In the waning afternoon light, George led Viji back to the house. In the kitchen he helped her finish the dinner, taking her instructions and chopping chicken pieces. She spoke calmly, passed him garlic cloves to crush, explained when to use fresh chilies and when to use dried. Now and then came a sudden sniff or a sigh, soft remnants of her injury.

That night they lay together on George's twin mattress. Viji drifted off almost immediately, with her head tucked into his shoulder, but George stayed awake to

count off the hours and the sounds that drifted around
them. At three o'clock, a ghostly sigh. Three forty-seven, a
sudden jerk of her legs. He wondered if she loved him. She
never said the words, exactly, and seemed to know instinctively not to. But she must have, to some degree—he
sensed it in the way she slept, her head tucked against his
shoulder, light with certainty and peace. He didn't love
her, of course, no more than he would have if they were
still in Madras, meeting in the evenings and parting wordlessly each night. This didn't trouble him. He loved her
enough. It was easy to say these things in the dark, without
the *buts* and *what-ifs* of daylight. He loved her enough for
now, and the rest could come with time.

On the opposite wall hung one desultory football
banner, red and white and pinned crookedly above his
desk. George had never liked football. When he was fourteen he'd borrowed a book on Bauhaus from the Sneinton
Library, and with a Stanley knife he'd extracted three
prints from the book's binding. He worked surgically,
leaving not a trace of the pillaged pages. And if no one had
ever searched for those three Klee prints, then no one
would have been the wiser. Two days after he hung them
on his wall, he came home from school to find them gone.
In their place hung the banner. He knew who'd done it,
and he didn't need to ask why.

He sat up. "Viji, we've got to leave," he said. "We have
to get out of here." The clock read 5:20. He woke the next
morning to find Viji already awake and studying his chin.
Often he'd wake to find her gazing sleepily at some quad-
rant of his face. It was a habit of hers that he was getting
used to.

In the end, George had a choice of lecturing posts at two universities.

The first was in a northern city called Hull, which to Viji sounded like the unusable part of a vegetable. The second was in Sacramento. "It's California," George warned. "That's far from home, you know."

"I'm far from home already," she said. The choice was made. Two weeks later, they were gone.

George Armitage bought the house on Winding Creek Road in the winter of '75. It was covered in California jungle when he first brought Viji to see it, two days after he'd signed the papers. Willows dangled their leafy dreadlocks over the kitchen windows. Camellia shrubs that had sprouted wild in the summer now sagged nakedly across the front porch and halfway down the drive. A bed of ivy that had once bordered the street now carpeted the front lawn, and between its gleaming leaves grew patches of dandelion buds. Neighbors drove past the house quickly.

Three months later, the ivy was trimmed into a tidy rectangular field. The willows were gone and the camellias cut back. The lawn was a field of new soil—by April it would begin to sprout. Eucalyptus trees rose proudly around the property, silver-dollar leaves fluttering now and then in a breeze. George spent his evenings and weekends working on the paint, supervising the carpet-layers, telling gardeners where to mow, hosing and scrubbing, bringing the old house back. Viji watched him from her spot on the sofa bed, stroking the rise of her growing belly. By summer, the house took a breath and stood taller, like a middle-aged woman who'd discovered how badly she had let herself spread.

Sometimes it seemed to Viji that she had won a prize, a sweepstakes like they had on television, the kind where a man with a giant check arrived at the door and the winner jumped up and down, screaming. Sometimes she felt that she'd been handed someone else's life to hold until they got back. How long, she wondered, before George left her behind, or did something that made her wish they'd never met? Outside, he had planted rosebushes that were sprouting their first buds now. Inside, her kitchen was new and sunny, and the carpets were clean and so very American. She'd never had wall-to-wall carpeting before. The curtains were majestic and the furniture sturdy. It spoke of decades. It was beautiful and it was hers. She'd chosen none of it.

In the summer of '82, George finished building his back cottage. It stood at the end of the property, beyond the kidney-shaped pool, a healthy distance from the main house. He called it an in-law cottage, though his in-laws had died long before. Of his own family, only his father remained, still in the house near Nottingham where George had grown up. The old man showed no signs of wanting to pack up and leave his England for a back-garden dwelling in Northern California.

For this, Viji Armitage was thankful. George had built the cottage with care and with thoughts of England. Inside, the exposed rafters were painted blue-black, the walls white. It was Tudor-style, which meant nothing to Viji, who knew just enough about English architecture to guess that Tudor was older than Victorian, and that Edwardian was not very old at all. The cottage would be her sewing shed. She had plans for a vast worktable and chests full of fabric, shelves to hold spools of thread set down in long straight rows. She would while away the afternoons here, a happy worker in her own small factory, emerging every few days with clothes for the children, curtains, pillow-cases, cotton dresses. But by the end of the summer, the in-law cottage sewing shed had become, quietly and irrev-ocably, a pool house. It would remain a pool house, hung every summer's day with damp towels that drew mold in-doors, with two pairs of swim trunks and a small bikini that dripped gray puddles onto the linoleum.

"It's a feature," George said. "It adds value to the house."

"And for this you've given me another room to clean?" Viji asked.

"I guess so."

Viji and George had three children, two boys and a girl, all born in the spring of '76. They'd expected twins, so the two boys were no surprise. When the contractions didn't stop, the nurse told Viji it was only her placenta, nothing to get worked up about. The girl had to push her way out while Viji was alone in the delivery room, before the exit door closed and sealed her inside forever. She was no bigger than George's hand, from fingertip to wrist. She was irate at having been ignored, hungry from sharing a uterus with two larger males. She wailed incessantly.

Viji was a placid new mother, despite her daughter's crying—even the nurses noticed it. Her boys were handed to her and she smiled, as if she'd always known how they would be. But then she saw her daughter and began to weep. The nurses passed this off as the mild shock of seeing an undersize infant, something they'd grown ac-customed to. George assumed Viji was just feeling what he felt—the enormous realizations that new parenthood brings. There was so much contained in this pink hospital blanket, this cawing bundle of pointed limbs. Yellow, small, and angry. Not even the blanket could soften it. It would take a while—longer than Viji would admit—before "it" became a "she."

Photos were taken. They turned out as well as most newborn pictures. No matter how George arranged and rearranged the three bodies, it was impossible to disguise how small the girl looked next to her brothers, like a larva next to butterflies. The photos were sent to family members and friends, enclosed in cards. From India, jubilant letters returned, penned on soft blue aerograms, addressed invariably to *Mr. and Mrs. G. Amritraj.*

Girls were supposed to be beautiful. They were unprepared for theirs, and it took them seven days to name her. Until they did she was Baby Girl Armitage, property of the hospital, princess of the incubator. She was still puny when she finally came out, fully baked, but her color had turned normal. Around her, hospital people smiled and wished Viji well. They were happy for her, but not with her—and why should they have been? She was only a patient, another mother with the same questions and seeping fluids as any other mother. And beside her, almost constantly, was George.

The boys, they'd named themselves, but they didn't have a name ready for the girl. Viji sent a telegram to her mother in Madras. CHILDREN BORN TWO BOYS KIERAN AND AVINASH AND ONE GIRL. PLEASE AMMA SEND NAME FOR GIRL. It was traditional for elders to do the naming in her family. It was also traditional for hospitals to not let babies leave until they'd been officially named. Viji prayed the first night for a swift response to her telegram, and for a good name. There were some awful names out there—the Aniyoras and Bishakas and Fulkis of the world. She said a quiet prayer for those little girls, but she didn't dare think of them for too long, lest the fates snatch such a name from the air and stamp it on her baby. The next afternoon, a telegram arrived. NOW YOU WANT MY OPINION. SO GOOD AT MAKING OWN DECISIONS NAME THE BABY YOURSELF. The telegram was a swift slap. That her mother would spend so much money to spite her, even now, was what pained her most.

But she was right—it had been Viji's decision to be with George, and to stay with George, and to cling to him even as her mother had tried to beg-plead-scream him out of her. George would be her downfall, her mother had said. Viji accepted this downfall, continued to sneak from the house to see him, to lock herself into George's room despite his hesitation. And when her mother saw that she had no choice, the wedding was arranged and the entire event became Amma's idea, framed for neighbors and friends as a step up for Viji's family, a prestigious match to a European scholar. This was sufficient explanation for most of their friends, a class-conscious set that still considered the English to be superior. But between Viji and her mother, the truth of the matter stayed put. George had been but a minor player in it all.

More than her mother's approval, Viji wanted to leave the hospital. So she chose Neha. It was a name that sounded like air, like a sigh released, a free-blowing life that couldn't be harnessed to the earth.

With three children and two breasts, Viji had to devise a system of feeding. First, she learned to spread cold butter on her nipples each night; it relieved the painful chafing of three greedy mouths. Second, she learned to be systematic and fair. The boys were fussy if they weren't fed first. They howled, their eyes creased shut, their mouths stretched into rectangles of fury. The noise made her daughter nervous and kept her from feeding. So she took care of the boys first, propped them onto pillows and towels, and let them feed together. They would clamp onto her nipples, small proprietary hands on her breasts and tugging at the neck of her blouse. Focused from the start, the girl would watch her brothers nurse. Their small mouths moved like machines. Their focus was impregnable.

Viji's love for her daughter broke early one morning, when she woke to the sun's glare on her bedside clock. George was awake already. He held his daughter over the bedspread so that her legs dangled and her feet lay gingerly on the bed, as if she were standing.

"Where are the boys?" Viji asked. The baby looked to her left when she heard her mother's voice.

"Asleep still."

George lowered himself to the bed and brought the baby with him. With a hand supporting her back, he propped her up to sit, legs spread, facing him. Viji watched the baby from behind, seated, looking at George. Her head rested squarely on her shoulders, her neck tucked away beneath a fleshy fold. Her fine hair whorled around the back of her head. There was barely enough of it to cover her scalp, aside from a thick, dark tuft at the nape of her neck. She couldn't look away from the girl, who sat so definitely, contented to be only what she was. Round, without pretense, open, and wholly vulnerable. If George moved his hand, she would flop to the mattress.

"Give her to me." She wanted nothing in the world but to hold the warm weight of the baby—this baby—against her body. The feeling left her tight-chested and more terrified than she'd been when the scrawny girl was first placed in her arms. For the first time in her short life, Neha possessed her mother completely, pushing the boys away and leaving Viji disoriented, unable to shake her daughter's grip. Solid and soft, with warm breath puffing from small and perfect lips, she was precisely right. From that point, Viji knew she would never love her children equally.

The children were like nothing Viji had seen before. Soon, Neha weighed as much as her brothers. The three browned gently over the first few weeks of their lives, their skin so soft it almost wasn't there. Their hair turned chestnut, with streaks of blond, a confusion of their parents' colors. To Viji they were caramel and chocolate. Sometimes, alone with them in the afternoons, she succumbed to temptation and lifted a chubby toffee arm to lick it, or stuck a baby fist into her mouth and sucked at the sweetness. Often, lying side by side by side, the triplets did nothing but look at her. They could spend an hour simply watching, sucking their lower lips and waiting to see what she would do. It made sense to Viji. She'd spent nine and a half months expecting them; it was their turn now to wait for her.

Avinash Armitage was the first boy born and the first to walk. When he was nine, he smacked his head on the edge of the pool's diving board and nearly drowned. George, who had been watching, managed to pull his son out of the water. He held his hand to the wound at the back of Avi's head, where the trickle of blood was growing sluggish. His other two children looked on as Avi squinted up at George.

"He's lost a lot of blood," Avi's sister observed.

Although Baby Girl Armitage had become Neha Armitage, Neha soon turned into Babygirl. And by this name, in certain corners of her universe, she would always be known. She had grown by this time to match her brother's height. She was the only one of the three who looked more like George than like Viji.

"Will he be anemic now?" Kieran Armitage leaned over, caramel hair dripping onto his brother's chest, and felt his wrist for a pulse.

"No, sweetheart, he won't be anemic." George held a towel to Avi's head until the bleeding stopped. He would wash the wound with pool water before Viji saw them.

Kieran kneeled and looked into his brother's eyes. "Do you feel at all dizzy?"

"I don't know."

Kieran Armitage, named after George's late uncle, quickly outgrew his brother. At the age of ten, he fell into the overweight category on his pediatrician's growth chart, and began a strict regime of diet and exercise, one that he would maintain throughout his life. He took to counting his steps and insisted that George teach him to measure his own pulse. He'd read in *Pearson's Guide to Health and Wellness* that one should walk at least ten thousand paces a day. Generally, he lost count before the day was up.

Viji was a happy mother, though she sometimes didn't know how to act with the triplets—whether to bend the rules or hold fast to them. Boundaries or freedom. Both, of course. But that didn't help either. She was instinctively gentle with the boys and Babygirl. The only time she'd hit them was when they'd wandered away from her one afternoon, out of extreme boredom, at Macy's. They were found after an hour, asleep in the stuffed armchairs of the front window display. Later in their lives, the children would remember a time when Viji got so fed up with their fighting that she pushed the three of them out of the house, wearing nothing but their underpants, and locked the door. Kieran claimed it was the middle of winter and Avi remembered that it was the front door she shoved them from, not the back. Viji remembered none of this, and resented her children for bringing it up so often.

When they were eleven, both Avi and Kieran caught the chicken pox. Babygirl stayed healthy and was banned from her brothers' bedroom. The boys spent their days in bed designing an underground nuclear shelter.

Avi bested his brother by designing a nuclear shelter camper home with brown racing stripes, to keep the family mobile in the event of global disaster. It was little more than an armored tank with enough room for beds and a kitchen.

George, on his nightly sickbed visits, examined the sketches. "What would we need a grenade launcher for?"

"To defend ourselves," Avi replied.

"I thought the armored siding would defend us."

"You never know."

"Where's the bathroom?"

Babygirl, not to be left out, sent messages to her brothers via her mother. Mostly, she sent drawings.

And the boys sent drawings back.

Two weeks later, Babygirl caught the chicken pox. Outside, it was summer; school had let out three days earlier. As she lay in bed, scratching with abandon, Kieran read the funnies aloud to her from outside her bedroom door. He wouldn't go near her, though he was immune. He'd heard about mutant strains. He knew about shingles. Downstairs, the doorbell rang, eight deep chimes with one note missing in the middle.

He was reading a *Peanuts* cartoon to her when a man walked into the hallway. He was tall and gray-skinned, with a shock of white hair and a suitcase. "What's the matter?" he asked. "Can't she read?"

Kieran knew that this was his grandfather and that he was from England. An enormous suitcase sat at his feet. Judging from the size and fullness of it (peaks and mounds poked out against the fabric, as if he'd brought someone with him), Grandad Stan had come to stay.

On the day he arrived, Avi hovered at his side and Kieran hurled questions at him. Ruben Tashima had once told Babygirl that his grandmother smelled, but her knowledge of grandparents extended no further. So the arrival of Grandad Stan didn't seem to warrant her brothers' excitement. Babygirl stayed in her room to scratch.

In England, Stan had been a cabbie. He was used to talking loud, to the point, and facing the other way. Even now, in Viji's kitchen, he spoke over the noise of a nonexistent engine.

"Well," George said, "we certainly weren't expecting you."

He hugged his father and held him until Stan pushed away. "How long are you staying?"

"How long will you have me?"

George turned to Viji, who didn't know what to say. She smiled after a moment and answered, "For as long as you can stay."

When Stan went upstairs to wash, he paused at Babygirl's room. "Catch the lurgie?"

"Pardon me?"

Stan walked on without a reply. From upstairs, Babygirl could hear Viji's knife against the chopping board. It rapped hard against the wood and echoed through the house.

She cut the broccoli with a blunt knife, sending the odd sprout leaping to the floor. It was at times like these that Viji began to think of the small injustices of her life with George. The way George left his wet towels around the bedroom and never seemed to notice that she hung them for him, used her toothbrush instead of his own and consistently appropriated the new ones she bought, greeted other women by kissing their cheeks, though Viji could never bring herself to do the same with men, refused to throw out old appliances and crammed them, rusted and oozing liquids, into the corner of the garage. The way George seemed not to think about their anniversary until she dropped a very heavy hint. How he pretended to forget that Tuesday was trash collection day, overlooked birthday cards attached to gifts, spent all his time in his study while she had never had a study to go to, and seemed always to be right, even when she knew he wasn't.

And now, probably through some fault of George's, she would have an old man living in her home. An old man who stank of tobacco smoke and looked quizzically at Viji when she spoke, always taken by surprise, as if she were a cat who'd walked up and asked him for the time. An old man who, all those years ago, had told her she was an animal. The blade nicked her finger and she gasped. The flesh beneath her nail pooled with gathering blood. Heaven only knew why he was here, and how long he would stay. Worst of all, the pool house would become an in-law cottage, and she would never, ever have her sewing shed.

Later that afternoon, Stan leaned into the pool house and sniffed. He sniffed again. He kicked the doorframe, turned to George and Viji. "Mildew," he said. "It'll rot these walls to the core. What have you been doing with it?"

"It's been our pool house," Viji said.

"But it was meant to be a cottage," George added, "for you."

"For me!" Stan stepped in, hands on hips, and kicked at the wall. "No chance of me living here now, not until something's done for these walls." Stan was right. Viji looked sheepishly at the floor's stained linoleum. She wouldn't have let her own parents live here.

And so Stan would move into the boys' room. Kieran and Avi would move into sleeping bags on Babygirl's floor, and Babygirl would resent the change. That night, the moon lit the eucalyptus trees outside her window, and haloed her brother's heads.

"Do you think Grandad ever fought in a tank?" Kieran asked. He and Avi lay on their backs in sleeping bags.

"Probably. I bet he's killed someone, too."

"That's stupid," Babygirl said. She scratched at her lesions, annoyed by the exaggeration. "Why would he have killed someone?"

Avi propped himself on his elbows. "He probably did, you know, when there was war. Practically everyone had to fight. Even the women."

"That's not true."

"Is too"

"Bullshit."

Babygirl gasped at the word, and only a blanket crammed into her mouth could stop the laughter. Then she remembered the scab on her foot and curled under the covers to pick it.

"What're you doing?" Kieran asked.

"Picking a scab."

"Grody. If you pick a scab you have to eat it, you know."

"Do not."

"Do too. Or else your skin won't heal. And you'll turn into a walking festering wound."

"Gross, Kieran."

"I know."

Babygirl placed the thin disc of skin on her tongue, felt it moisten, and thought again of the first spray of lesions to appear on her neck. Viji had seen her scratching and grabbed her hand. *Chicken pox*, she'd pronounced. *It's your turn now.*

This was exciting. A week to watch TV and eat what she wanted. And more importantly, membership in the still small group of classmates who'd had it. There were only three others in her class, not counting her brothers.

A snore, like a distant car motor, drifted from the other side of the wall. It trailed off. It swelled. It faded again. This continued until the snore reached its full crescendo and tripped over itself. There was coughing. She heard the creak of bedsprings and the boys' bedroom door softly opening. A few minutes later, she heard it close. Below her, arms crossed on their chests, her brothers were already asleep.

CHAPTER THREE

George awoke.

Where am I?

Home. Bedroom. This is your wife. You love her. Her lips are moving. She is trying to tell you something. George took out his earplugs.

"…an everyday matter, George. I think we should talk to him about it but really, I think *you* should talk to him about it."

"What was that, darling?"

Viji looked at him in quiet disbelief before starting again. "Stan. Your father. He's staying here, in this house. Do you remember? It wasn't just a dream."

George knew his father would give a reason for the visit in his own time, if such a reason existed. In the meantime, it was a bit rude to inquire directly as to *why* he had come. There were no whys or wherefores when it came to family. It was Saturday. He put the earplugs back in, smiled at the sound of nothing. He closed his eyes. He sensed Viji looking at him. He knew she was talking again; he could feel the sound waves bounce against his head. When George had hugged his father, he could smell their lounge in Nottingham, specifically the old red sofa, infused with aftershave and turpentine and Sunday dinners. Smells faded, seeped silently away before anyone knew they were gone. Like the last edge of a sunset. It must be down to natural selection losing one's distinctive smell would make it easier to ingratiate oneself into a new tribe. He pushed the thought away, wanting only to sleep. But now came a twittering sound, like a bird. When he turned to it he saw Viji, her mouth moving rapidly, the wind of each syllable pinging off his forehead.

"…not taking this seriously! We are not ready to have your father in our house!"

George pulled the covers over his head. "Why not? I think we are."

"We have no room to put him in, in case you didn't notice."

"It's a big house. He's fine in the boys' room for now."

"For now. And then? And then, George? And then?"

George threw the covers off and sat up. It was Saturday. Viji was like this on Saturdays. Always. "So what now? You want me to get up now and refurbish the guest house? Is that what you're saying?"

Viji pouted. "Go back to sleep. I'm not saying you have to do it now." With a quick twist, she wound her hair into a bun, picked up the laundry basket, and left the room. George sighed. Another morning, he might have been given tea in bed. He might have lain twisted around Viji, her soft folds melted halfway into his. Or best of all, he might have been left to wake up alone, to draw himself from the spiraling flush of dreamworld back to the pinpoint of reality. With the curtains closed, it was dark in this room. With the curtains drawn and the maroon walls and green bedspread, it was always autumn in this room, even when the outside was August. He stood. His legs were hot in their pyjamas. Curtains closed, autumn. Curtains open, summer, blinding white.

✤✤✤

America. For George, before he knew better, America was a hilly jumble of shop fronts, fire escapes, hot dog vendors and steaming potholes. America was Humphrey Bogart and Woody Allen and Diana Ross and Andy Warhol. It was lipstick and disco and blues and pizza and sex and black coffee and boys in tweed caps shouting, *Extra extra read all about it.* It was Alcatraz and Ellis Island and the reflecting pool at the Washington Monument, Hare Krishnas and flower children and that woman sticking a daisy in the muzzle of a gun. It was where people ate Chinese takeout straight from the carton and walked down busy sidewalks arguing about something esoteric with the friend they'd bedded once in college. George had stepped off the Greyhound bus expecting all of this.

Instead, he'd found Sacramento. He wasn't the first. There were the natives before him, then the settlers and the gold miners, then the businessmen and senators and civil engineers and urban developers and doctors and nurses and teachers and Avon ladies and donut shop franchisees. Its fresh pavement sank in the shimmering heat of summer and whipped up a harsh freeze in the winter months. When he first moved to Sacramento (with Viji and her suitcases and her hanging brass lamps that made everything heavy), it was a city pockmarked by empty lots. Bordering these were gray and green eucalyptus trees.

From the heart of downtown rose the dome of the state capitol, surrounded by rose gardens in a neighborhood where people never walked alone at night. Its storefronts were criminally ugly and separated from the road by vast parking lots. The closest restaurant to their small apartment was a drive-through sausage hut. The closest thing to a pub was a place called the Hard Luck Saloon.

George and Viji drove every week to the supermarket in their secondhand Impala, and on Thursday nights they watched *Three's Company*. Viji stayed home every day while George went to his office at the university. She took English for Foreigners at the city college but stopped going after a few weeks, telling George she spoke so much better than the other students that every time she opened her mouth, she felt she was showing off. Now and then, they went to the movies downtown and parked as close to the theater as possible because Viji didn't like the lonely streets or the dark. But by the time they moved out of their apartment and into the house on Winding Creek Road, things had begun to change.

And by the time the children started school, Sacramento had grown into a typical suburban city with cineplexes and shopping malls and gyms. A jazz festival came through town each May, and high school bands played at the annual Memorial Day parade. Now Sacramento had festivals and outdoor cafés that closed at seven o'clock. In the summers it had Shakespeare in the Park. There was a French café downtown for the people who preferred not to be seen at malls. Sacramento was trying to be a city other than itself. As to whether this was a bad thing, George just wasn't sure.

The neighborhood of Maple Grove was set apart from the rest of the city by an entrance of arching oaks. Its roads spread like hair through the tree shadows, dipped and climbed into hills, and sprouted, every so often, a dark and dingy creek. The *Sacramento Bee*'s real estate section called it "ritzy, rustic; a new suburban paradise." Viji cut out the article and pasted it into a photo album. There were no sidewalks in Maple Grove, only bushes and wooden fences bordering the streets. Houses stood far apart, sprawling ranch-style across acre-long yards, masking the swimming pools and cherry trees that lay behind. Every Fourth of July, the residents of Maple Grove gathered at the corner of Rockwood and Maple Glen to kick-start a parade that wound around the southern border, down Winding Creek Road, and across Ladino Lane. It never ventured into other neighborhoods. The parade ended at the house of whichever mother wanted it most, and the children ate watermelon and sang, *You're a grand old flag you're a high-flying flag and forever in peace may you wave, you're the emblem of the land I love in the home of the free and the brave.*

For the rest of the year, the streets of Maple Grove lay mostly empty, aside from the few residents who took their evening strolls and walked their dogs to poop next to other people's lawns. Only Mexican gardeners could be seen during the day. They angled leaf blowers at the road and stepped back for passing cars. At four o'clock, the leaf blowers shut off and the pickups drove home. The rumble of their engines faded, gaving way to shouts from distant swimming pools.

But every neighbor knew at least one other neighbor,

and news of Stan's arrival traveled fast. Elena Feldman was
the first to bring a cake, baked at home and smothered
with chocolate. She rapped on the kitchen window one afternoon, called *yoo hoo,* and greeted Viji as if they were old
pals. She was more than charmed to meet Stan, who kissed
her hand and followed her every movement with his eyes.
But she wasn't nearly as charmed as Marcia Fromm, whose
great-grandfather was English, who brought frosted cupcakes, and who insisted that Stan come for tea the next day.
You mustn't keep him to yourself, she scolded Viji. Viji managed to smile as she poured scalding water into a teapot.
A new neighbor, a bona fide English neighbor, was something that had to be seen. Of course, the fact that George
was and always had been English seemed irrelevant.
George had been in Sacramento so long that he was pretty
much an American. And so, when Stan wasn't smoking on
a deck chair, he was touring a neighbor's house. It didn't
seem to matter that Viji had never seen the insides of these
houses. When he returned from such visits, he had little to
say. From his silence, Viji could assume only that he wasn't
impressed, and that the efforts of the Maple Grove ladies
were wasted on a man like Stan.

Stan removed his trousers and spread them on the deck chair. The seat was hot and would burn the backs of his very white thighs if he wasn't careful. He unbuttoned his shirt, removed it, and hung it on the back of the chair. He began to take his undershirt off, but thought twice. *Easy now, Stan. Take it slow.* Removing his black leather shoes, he lined them up at the foot of the chair. He didn't wear socks. Too hot. Hot as Spain, this. The pool was kidney-shaped and clear, free of shade, a few leaves floating at one end, and bordered by cement that baked in the afternoons. He'd never been in a house with a pool. He lit a fag, settled into his deck chair, and closed his eyes. Tobacco in his nostrils, sun against his eyelids. There was nothing better. In the soft pillow of heat, he could relax. No fear of a sudden chill wind, or of a finicky sun that cooled itself on a whim or dodged behind a cloud for no reason. The weather here was like a good woman: warm and constant, never threatening to abandon a man before he abandoned her.

He thought of Marla, his wife. Marla had been an artist in every sense. She had painted frescos for people with too much money who liked to think of themselves as lords and ladies. Mostly, these people lived in the Park, the wealthy part of Nottingham. Their fathers had owned the old lace factories, then used that money to make more money. Stan's father had been a cabbie, Marla's a factory foreman. But the posh folk welcomed Marla with open arms, went on waiting lists for her, talked about her like she was the secret of the century, and all because she did some pretty drawings on their walls. Eventually, one of them got it into his head to put a painting on his ceiling. And so Marla obliged. She painted those ceilings quicker and better than Michelangelo.

Stan used to go along to help on his days off. He'd stand below Marla, handing up tint mixes, soaking and drying brushes. From below she looked like a sculpture—a tall and strong body atop a ladder and platform, one arm held high to the ceiling, the other poised beside her hip. Black hair hung down her back. Her breasts, from below, were golden pears, round weighty fruits that pressed against the cloth of her shirt. He watched her paint angels, fat and naked things with special names that Marla knew but that Stan could never remember. They had trumpets and wings, and sat on rocks next to men with long beards. Marla wouldn't eat while she painted. *Go on*, Stan would urge. *Just a quick one.* He'd hold sandwiches up to her, shake his thermos, try to tempt her with the hot tea inside. Just two ticks, she would say, I'll just finish up on this. And then she'd ignore him. She ignored the lady of the house who clopped through in high heels, bringing her friends to watch. She ignored the maid who came in to polish the wood floor. She ignored the three o'clock ruckus of children coming home from school, even though George would be reaching home that very minute, opening the door to their empty row house, dumping his

coat on the floor, and making himself a sandwich. Two
ticks turned into two hours, and then more, until Stan gave
up and, sitting by himself on the floor of the rich person's
house, opened the sandwich box and ate. He always saved
two halves for Marla.

She went up every morning tough and straight, and
came down every evening speckled with paint, eyes dark
and tired. It troubled Stan that his wife had to work. If he
could, he'd have given her her own grand house to paint.
Or he would have hired painters for her, and sent her out
with a bag of money to buy hats with her lady friends.
Eventually, the ceilings did her in. Like nails hammered into
her neck, she said. Her back burned, and she rubbed salve
into her aching arms each night. But there was only one way
to paint a ceiling. He was tempted at times to tell the posh
people to sod off, to leave his wife in peace. But two shits
don't make a shilling, and it was best to let her work. If the
Sistine Chapel was what they wanted, Marla would deliver.
In the end, she was a better soul than any of them.

He felt a pull of guilt when he thought of his wife.
Leaving Nottingham had meant leaving her. But Stan had
had no choice—memories of Marla didn't pay the bills,
and he couldn't drive a cab forever. He'd locked the windows and shoved the door shut against a rising hill of post.
They fell through the letter slot every day, those envelopes
with mean little windows. They started out white and over
the months turned pink. He couldn't pay a penny toward
the water bill, and they were threatening to turn it off.
Well, do it then, he'd wanted to say. But there was no one
to say it to. He couldn't pay his phone bill, either, but that
didn't stop it from coming every month, the number at

the bottom of the page growing like a blister. Absurd, when he thought of it, since he never used the phone—who was there to call? But when he rang to get his service discontinued (the first call he'd made in weeks), the confusion of it was too much to handle, the rigmarole of operators and the identification codes they kept asking for. Not to mention that they wouldn't cut his service until he'd paid his bill. *Well,* he said, *if I could pay my bill, I wouldn't be cutting my service, would I?* He'd also been ignoring the invoice from the furniture store that had sold him the new sofa after the old one surrendered to fleas. They told him he'd have a year to pay for it. They hadn't told him about the interest they'd charge. Bailiffs had started coming around, bald men with earrings, banging on the door in the early hours of the morning, when Stan was still naked and sipping his tea or huddled in bed with the covers over his ears. They were modern-day bounty hunters, and they had no respect for penniless old bastards like him. He could hear the neighbors open their windows and doors to see what the commotion was about. Soon the bailiffs would stop. Now that Stan was gone, the neighbors could say, truthfully, that they had no idea where he'd gotten to.

The door slid open and the boys came out. The children didn't dress in the summer, just wore swim shorts all day, every day. Into the pool they jumped every morning, first hopping and shivering in the cold water, then dunking themselves in again and coming up smiles. Stan decided he would tell them about Marla. In fact, he had a whole host of things to tell them. He watched them run past the pool and to the pool house.

Things to tell the boys about (and the girl):

MAKING ROSES GROW PROPER MUGS OF TEA HOW TO ASK A
WOMAN ON A DATE HOW TO LET A WOMAN DOWN EASY WHAT
TO DO WHEN YOU'RE LOST IN A CITY YOU'VE NEVER BEEN TO BE-
FORE HOW TO TELL IF A BLOODY LAYABOUT'S ABOUT TO VOMIT
IN YOUR CAR HOW TO WIN AN ARGUMENT WHAT TO DO IF YOU
LOCK YOUR KEYS IN A CAR THE DIFFERENCE BETWEEN A GOOD
LAGER AND AMERICAN PIGEON-PISS BREATHING UNDERWATER
(THE IMPORTANCE OF) RODGERING A WOMAN AGAINST A BRICK
WALL (THE MECHANICS OF) (WOULD PROBABLY BE BEST TO
LEAVE THE GIRL OUT OF THIS ONE) CARVING A ROAST DOING A
BACKFLIP RETURNING A PURCHASED ITEM WITHOUT A SALES
SLIP EVEN AFTER YOU'VE USED IT CHANGING A BUSTED WHEEL
THE DIFFERENCE BETWEEN AN EXCUSE AND A REASON.

"Grandad!" The boy flapped his hand, calling him
over to the pool house. "Grandad!" he called again. Stan
didn't want to get up, but he did.

Next door, at 3710, the Bauers had a real-life water-
slide. The skinny one had climbed the pool-house wall and
perched there, one hand blocking the sun from his eyes.

"What do you mean, a slide?" the pudgy one asked. He
still stood on the ground, fingers tight around Stan's wrist.

"A real slide, like at Water World. It goes straight into
the pool, and it's twisty."

"No way."

"It's true, I swear."

"Well, bloody hell, stop spying and go play on it," Stan
said.

The boys looked at each other, and then back at their
own quiet house. The sound of splashing trailed over from
the Bauer pool.

"What?"

The pudgy one shrugged. "I don't think we're supposed to."

"Why not?"

"Mom said it would be rude."

"To go without being invited," the skinny one added.

"Oh, for Christ's sake, you're only children. You don't need an invitation."

The boy shrugged. Stan sighed. He eyed the deck chair, where his clothes lay spread, sleeping in the sun.

"Come on, then. I don't have a calling card, but I think I can get you an audience."

The boys whooped, and the skinny one jumped down from the wall.

"Where's the other one?" Stan asked.

"What other one?"

"The girl one."

"She's inside."

"She still poorly?"

The pudgy one shook his head. "But Mom said she still has lesions and the sun'll make them scar."

"Well, bollocks to that."

Kieran didn't know what bollocks were, but he knew that he'd have to get Babygirl. He and Avi burst into her room, and with sun-warmed arms they pulled her out of bed. She was already wearing her swimsuit.

❦ CHAPTER FIVE ❦

A few rules: never wear shoes in the puja room. Never go in dirty, or before taking a shower. Never enter during the first three days of menstruation. Refresh the flowers and water daily. Sit with your legs crossed or tucked beneath the body, but never with your feet stretched forward. Never blow out the flames of the oil lamps—wave them or snuff them out. The left hand shouldn't be used unless absolutely necessary. Every puja room has a small bell, to be rung during prayers, a pot of vermillion and one of vibhuti, the soft gray ash that's dabbed on the forehead after prayer.

Viji had learned her prayers as a child, a stock repertoire of Sanskrit chants. She didn't always know what they meant, but she'd said the words so many times that they were part of the low, constant hum of her thoughts. Sometimes she caught herself chanting in the car, at the supermarket, while washing the dishes. These came easily to her, mouthfuls of five and six syllables that tumbled from her lips with no more effort than it took to breathe. She knew what some, but not all, of the words meant. All she really needed were the sounds, soft allegros on her tongue.

There were, of course, the other prayers she'd learned from the nuns at the convent school—weighty, admirable passages with solid words that Viji could never get quite right. With them came the memory of a sharp slap, fire across her palm, two Doloreses (Tall and Sweet), and the priest. *Kingdom come, thy will be done.* They smelled of mahogany, these words; they sang of wood resin and choking frankincense.

🙙🙙🙙

Viji was aware that she'd been standing like this for several seconds, listening to the breathing of her classmates, as loud as a cricket chorus in the silent room. It was girls' assembly, and forty brown faces waited. Viji was aware of the hand, her left hand, that gripped her right arm, worrying the scaly skin of her elbow. How many times had the sisters told her not to stand like this? She glanced over at Tall Dolores, whose face was a cloud of pretend tranquility. Sweet Dolores sat in the corner, gripping a rosary. The visiting priest sat next to her, important and old and beige and plain, a face like a canvas bag.

Her sister sat in the second row, the only smile amid the jumble of gray uniforms. She closed her eyes. *Just look at me and finish it and sit down*, Shanta had told her. She grinned foolishly now, and Viji had to curl her lips in to keep from smiling back. Before she began, she took a breath, as Tall Dolores had taught her.

"Our father, which art in heaven, hollow be thy name."

A sharp glance from Dolores to Dolores, and four eyes shot to Viji. The priest rubbed at his lips, as if brushing away breakfast crumbs.

"Thy kingdom comes,
Thy will be done, in heaven as it is in earth."

Another deep breath, and:

"Give us this day our daily bread
and forgive us our trespasses,
as we forgive them that trespass against us."

Though she could feel herself recite the words, all she heard was the drum of uncertainty that beat against her temple. The sounds trailed obediently from her, and then she was finished: "For thine is the kingdom, and the power, and the glory, for ever and ever and ever."

She thought there might have been clapping.

Only one or two of the other girls had snickered at Viji's mistakes. Even Shanta seemed not to know that anything was amiss. If everyone had laughed, if they'd gasped and cupped their hands over their mouths, at least Viji might have stopped. At least she wouldn't have continued, as she had, into the warm, foul mouth of her errors. At least she might have shut up and sat down and not found herself standing here, in front of the priest and Shanta and everyone, her hand stretched out to Tall Dolores.

Thwack. The ruler came down on Viji's palm. She felt nothing at first.

Thwuh. The ruler missed and there was quiet, hissing laughter.

"You moved your hand." Tall Dolores grabbed her wrist and held it too tightly. "You think you don't deserve this?" This time the ruler caught Viji squarely on the ridges of her palm, along the small hills that rose below her fingers. The sting shot across her heart line.

The class fell quiet, except for the rustle of the rosary. Sweet Dolores's timid fingers fondled every bead. The priest cleared his throat and crossed his legs. When Viji looked at him, he smiled.

One more rapturous *thwack,* and Viji yanked her hand away. She began to cry. She blamed it, not on the ruler or the pain in her wrist or even Tall Dolores, but on the smile that seeped across the old priest's face, at once pitying and spiteful, as if he'd expected precisely this. If he had gazed sternly at her, if he'd been as unfeeling as Tall Dolores, Viji would have been all right. But now she felt foolish and wronged, and the tears tasted like medicine. She saw herself, as if in a dream, crumple-faced, her mouth wide with weeping, her teeth bared. She knew the other girls were laughing at her and that she was weak. Nobody cried during these punishments. It was a rule among the girls: no crying during punishments.

Tall Dolores tapped her back with the ruler ,and Viji returned to her seat. She wanted to run from the room. She didn't dare. But she couldn't stop crying, either. Even after the urge had gone, she couldn't put an end to the sharp and phlegmy inhalations. Her eyes ached but the tears continued, through the assembly, during the math lesson, and into the reading activity.

At some point in the middle of English, she found herself dry. The tears had petered out without her having even noticed. Her classmates had lost interest long before, and her teachers pretended not to care. Her breath was steady, her cheeks tight and stinging slightly.

By lunchtime, her face was tired. Her parts were loose and rattled in their casings. She filed to the canteen, as usual. Here, Shanta met her and held her left hand. Viji ate with her right, and had to put her food down when she wanted a sip of water.

"I don't know what's wrong with that lady," Shanta said, her fingers gripping Viji's, "I liked your speech."

"It wasn't a speech."

"She was acting big for the priest, that's all, that's what everyone said."

"I hate her."

Shanta picked up her crispy fried vada and placed it on Viji's plate. "I hate her too." They ate in silence. "Don't tell Appa."

"Why not?"

"Don't tell him what she did. Don't tell Amma, either. She might tell Appa."

"Why?" Viji asked again.

"You know why. He'll do something. He won't act properly."

"He'll get angry?"

"He'll get very very angry."

"Do you think he would come here?" She envisioned her father's pointed face bearing down, into the orbit of Tall Dolores's wimple, the old nun glaring back and clutching her rosary.

"Okay. Shanta Akka?"

"Yes?"

Viji paused. "I won't tell."

That night, Viji found Old Krishnan, the cook, in the kitchen. She showed him the faint pink band across her palm, and he gave her a whole laddu, golden and sweet and bigger than her wounded hand. She ran with it to her room, climbed under her bedsheet, and ate it in careful bites, until it was gone completely.

✤✤✤

Viji sighed and sifted through the roses in her basket. She would find a good one for Appa. Before some of the frames in the puja room, she placed only clumps of petals. Some got whole roses, some got nothing, depending on her mood. For Appa, she would find a good one.

Though it wasn't her fault, she sometimes felt guilty that there were no photos of her father in her house. She didn't own one. Her family hadn't kept photos in their home, at least not of the people who were living in it. And why should they have? They were all there all the time, the same old faces around the dinner table night after night, the same weary backs that shifted onto beds for afternoon naps and gathered in the kitchen in the evenings. Appa's departure meant one less face, one less back, one less cup of coffee in the mornings. For those he left behind, it was easier to just forget him.

But now that he was gone, there would be a photo hanging in the family puja room in Madras, dug out of some dusty cabinet. She longed to see it, a real picture with impeccable lines: Appa's nose, his eyes, his chin. Her own memory of him was shifty and blurred.

No one quite knew when Appa died, or how. Correction: someone must have known, for a telegram had come one day, but that someone wasn't Viji. Instead of a picture, she had a rock for him, one that fit neatly in her palm, a luscious cream color with streaks of copper. She didn't know where it had come from. She'd found it outside the pool house, just sitting there, one summer morning. She'd been nebulously aware of his death, but at the time, it had passed her by like a piece of local news, something to be known but not fully felt. "Where is it that you went, Appa?" she asked the rock. But it was only a rock, and had no answers.

卍 卍 卍

All homes should have a puja room, and it should always be kept clean. Viji's was hidden away at the top of the stairs. It was more a closet than a room. And because it was small, it was easy to maintain, though dust gathered easily, especially on the picture frames. The first picture she owned sat on the middle shelf: a print of Durga, the mother goddess, sitting on a tiger's back. Her uncle had bought this outside the Tiruchi temple. The next oldest was the Nataraja statue; her dance teacher had given it to her, and she'd practiced in front of it when she was a girl. All the gods were here—Ganesha, Siva, Krishna, Lakshmi. But Viji liked Durga best, if favorites were allowed. Durga protected and destroyed. Viji had bought prints and statues of her, crammed other idols into corners to make more room for her.

A few years earlier, George had wanted to install a light fixture. Viji wouldn't have it. Instead she lit the small oil lamps that hung from the ceiling, and a few sticks of incense. She could see well enough, and the dimness helped her concentrate. After eleven years, smoke from the lamps had turned the ceiling black. Three years earlier, Kieran and Avi and George had painted half the room light blue. The paint was uneven, smudged into dark patches, like it was in her house in India. Sometimes, the children sat here with her, all three of them, usually on Saturday mornings after their baths. Though today was Saturday, and they were in the pool. It was summer vacation, so they must have forgotten.

They would cross their legs like she told them to, their hands resting on small knees. While they closed their eyes, Viji kept hers open to watch the feathery movements of their lips. She watched for signs of their growing up—the sharpening of Babygirl's nose, the thickening of Avi's hair. She watched to see if they were becoming more like her. Her face had once been a package of small glories: her hair, her lips, the hedged thickness of her brow. At school they had called her Laughing Beauty. She was so daring back then, she should have been ashamed.

Once she had children, it felt silly to pay attention to herself. The triplets became her glories, piling into the world one after the other, Kieran's head pushing on Avi's toes, Babygirl screaming to be let out. It was as if they couldn't wait to begin. But sometimes, passing a mirror or catching a glimpse of herself in a car window, she missed being the beautiful one. She used to line her eyes with kohl.

On the side wall were pictures of people who'd died. It seemed she had to add a new one every few years—now there were eleven. "Isn't this a little morbid?" George once asked. "Doesn't it bother you to be reminded of them?" She wasn't bothered. She didn't pray to them, but she could sense them watching. The pictures were a comfort, the people in them awake and ready. In a world run by Maple Grove housewives, these felt as real to her as she'd been to them.

They began about a foot off the ground, eye level when she sat down. The first she hung was a portrait of her mother. She'd been the first to die. People looked so stern in these black-and-white photos, but it hadn't been normal back then to smile. The photograph had been taken just before her mother fell ill, so she still looked plump, her skin smooth, though a worry line cleaved her forehead. George's mother was also on the wall. George had protested when he saw it.

"I don't think my father would like this, Viji. He isn't exactly open-minded."

"But your father isn't the one on the wall, George." Open-minded or not, his wife hung there in a dark dress, hands folded in her lap, a sweep of pearls across her neck, eyes dark, hair falling over her shoulders.

There were young faces here as well. Her old classmate who had died when she was twenty-two. Viji's cousin hung in a frame above her. He was grown, yes, but he would always be young. Next to him hung her friend Anjali, who'd been many years younger than she and called her Aunty. Viji had met her parents in line at a movie theater in Davis. In those days, and even now, it was always a surprise to see other Indians. Always, they smiled at each other. "Are you Indian?" they would ask, just in case someone wasn't. "Which language do you speak?" This they had to know, even before they knew each other's names.

After Viji met Anjali's parents, the families began to see each other regularly. That is, Anjali and her parents would come to Viji's house, and George would say hello before vanishing into his study. Then they would speak only in Tamil. Always, Anjali wore her hair in two braids,

like she would have back home. Western clothes were for-
bidden; she even wore a salwar kameez to school. One
night, as they were sitting at the dinner table with her parents, Anjali cut her mother off midsentence: "You're so
lucky you get to wear American clothes." She looked
straight at Viji.

"But I'm married," Viji had replied, stupidly, as if this
were a reason. She'd wished afterward that she had said
something different.

Anjali wore two braids in the photograph. It was a
school portrait, taken in the style that was popular in the
seventies. A large, well-lit Anjali looked straight into the
camera lens, while a smaller version hovered just above,
in profile, looking up and into the distance. She'd given it
to Viji the last time they'd met. "I want you to have me
forever, Aunty."

Two weeks later, Anjali was hit by a bus. She'd been
walking to school, crossing the road, and hadn't looked
both ways. One week later, Viji had tried to phone Anjali's
mother, who didn't want to speak to her. Soon after, the
parents had moved back to India.

Sad eyes. Something, a draft perhaps, extinguished an
oil lamp. Viji relit it. The flame flickered. I would have
looked both ways, she told the photograph. The girl with
braids only stared back, steady and cold.

And between Viji's legs, fire. Heat moved between her
thighs and into her bladder, which flamed urgently. She
descended from the puja room. Bathroom, door closed,
and nothing came. She strained. It had been there a moment ago. Now, only the warm air. The clock in the living
room chimed nine. It was already hot. Her hair was still

wet from her shower, dripping down her back, soaking her blouse. She left it. The urge would come again.

The house was quiet, the hallway empty.

"Babygirl!" she called. "Kieran. Avi!"

They would still be in bed. Lazy. When she was eleven, she couldn't wait to get up. Each morning she would wake at dawn to the sound of barking dogs and the *clip-clop* of a bullock cart, and run outside to find the servants boiling water in outdoor cauldrons. Old Krishnan would pour her a steaming cup of water, then stir in milk with a spoonful of chicory. By nine o'clock, she would have had her breakfast, taken a bath, prayed, braided her hair, dressed, and practiced her dancing.

"Avi!"

She opened the door to Babygirl's room. The bed was empty and unmade. On the floor, the boys' sleeping bags lay in rumpled heaps.

She wouldn't worry. They would be swimming, or eating cereal in front of the television, which they weren't allowed to do.

The kitchen was silent. There were no cereal boxes left open, no milk dribbles or scattered Cheerios on the countertop. Through the bay window, the day was bright and cloudless. And the water in the pool was still. Her mouth went dry. She pushed away the old nightmare, the thought of three small bodies floating in the pool, suddenly unable to swim. Nonsense.

She pushed the sliding door open.

"Kieran!"

Silence.

"Kieran!"

She noticed a towel drying in the sun, slung over the yellow patio chair. Stan's leather shoes waited beside it. She was about to call again, when she heard a rustle from the rosebushes that bordered the far side of the pool.

"What's going on back there? Kieran? Answer me."

The voices grew louder—giggling and hushing as she approached.

"Kieran?" She called again, then walked to the rose bushes.

Disgust. Horror. Her boys stood, pants down, pissing on her roses. Even her daughter squatted in the shade of a floribunda shrub, her hand over her mouth, eyes creased with glee. And watching all this, smugly, was Stan.

"What is this?" Viji demanded. Babygirl lowered her hand and stopped smiling.

"Just fertilizing the roses, love."

Viji glared at Stan.

"Well, you could stand by and watch these shrubs get blackspot. Or you could learn a thing or two from me."

"I don't want my children—*relieving* themselves in public."

Stan looked around, at the sky, at the eucalyptus trees that bordered the yard.

"Are we in public?"

She turned to her boys, who stood now with their swim shorts up.

"You should have known better."

Avi shrugged.

"Grandad did it first."

The trace of a pale gold puddle lingered under a floribunda bush, then sank into the dark soil. The smell of piss hung hot in the morning air. The thought of Stan's piss, yellow and frothy, made Viji gag.

"Sorry, Mom," Kieran said, followed by another "sorry." And, quietly, a third.

Her floribunda shrubs were bushy and bursting. Clusters of pink roses sprang from each stem. She looked at Stan, who stood gazing at the trees above, planning to piss on them as well, Viji assumed.

"Okay," she said. "Come eat." She turned and walked to the house. A few moments later, light footsteps followed behind.

༄ ༄ ༄

"Babygirl, sit down."

Her daughter hoisted herself onto a kitchen stool and rested her brown elbows on the countertop. It was late afternoon, and the boys were watching cartoons. Babygirl still wore her swimsuit, and her skin was darker than ever from that morning's swim. Her hair, by contrast, was nearly blond, toughened into ropes by chlorine. Instead of showering, she'd gone to her room after swimming and put on her new bracelets. Viji brought her a pudding pop from the freezer and stroked her head, smoothing down the stray hairs.

"You have fun with Grandad, don't you?"

Babygirl nodded and tore the wrapper from her popsicle. "He's nice."

"Is he nice to the neighbors? When he goes to visit?"

Babygirl shrugged. "I guess so."

"When you went to the Bauers' house, was he nice

there?" Viji imagined Stan trickling urine onto their rosebushes.

"Yes."

"And did Mrs. Bauer talk to him? Was he nice to her?"

Babygirl's eyes grew wide. "Sure. But you know what?"

"What?"

"If Grandad was nice to anyone, it wasn't Mrs. Bauer.
It was Loopy."

"Who's Loopy?"

"The maid."

Lupe, the Bauer's housekeeper, cleaned houses around
the neighborhood. George had offered to hire her, but Viji
didn't want a stranger cleaning her home.

"And what is Loopy like?"

"She's Mexican, I think. That's what Erin Bauer, told me
anyway. And when Grandad was talking to her, he was, like,
leaning against the side of the house." She jumped off the
stool and left her popsicle on the counter to demonstrate.
"And Loopy was standing kind of like *this*." Babygirl leaned
against the kitchen wall, one leg crossed over the other, her
hip cocked comically to one side, her flat chest stuck out.

"How do you know he liked her." Viji asked.

"Well, he was leaning over, sort of, and talking really
close to her. Which is what a man does when he likes a
woman." Viji hid her surprise and let Babygirl continue.
"And I don't blame Grandad. Loopy is way prettier than
Mrs. Bauer, and plus she isn't married or a mom—at least
that's what Erin Bauer told me. And she wears red lipstick,
even when she's working. And you know what else? She
wears purple jelly sandals, the exact same color as my jelly
bracelets." She held her hand out proudly and jiggled the

purple rubber rings around her wrist. Melting chocolate began to pool across the counter. Babygirl clicked her tongue, picked up her pudding pop, and licked the line of chocolate that was trailing down her arm.

🌱🌱🌱

Of all the things Stan brought with him—stinking cigar smoke, talky neighborhood ladies, alfresco urination— Viji was glad for one of them. One Sunday morning, washing crusty pots from the previous night's dinner, she saw something she hadn't thought existed in Maple Grove. Walking up the long cement drive, wearing a red jogging suit and sneakers, with painted nails and a satisfied smile, was another Indian woman. Viji froze midwash and stared. She was unmistakably Indian, even with her tidy short hairdo. In her hand was a plate, covered loosely by a napkin.

The sides of the yellow napkin flapped in the breeze, threatening to fly off and reveal what the plate held. Viji continued to stare, even as the woman rang the doorbell. She'd always felt like an elephant who'd moved to the city; she'd never dreamed she would see another of her kind again. But here one was, on the doorstep like a dream, holding her plate, tapping on the kitchen window, smiling at Viji, calling *yoo hoo* and laughing. Viji threw the pot down and ran to the door. She wiped her wet hands on her trousers.

Kamla Mehta had lived in Maple Glen for eight years, in a house on Ladino Lane that couldn't be seen from the road. Viji remembered it now from her evening walks: the snaking driveway that led to invisibility, bordered on both sides by dense oleander.

"And what does your husband do?" Viji asked. Kamla's face grew cold and still. Her husband had been an anesthesiologist. He was still an anesthesiologist. He was no longer her husband. They'd divorced three years earlier, and Kamla had kept the house. He now lived in Arizona with his new wife, a nurse from his old hospital. They had one child, a daughter, who lived with Kamla. She would have to come over sometime to meet the triplets.

Though Kamla had come to meet Grandad Stan, she stayed to drink tea with Viji. Stan was away, off somewhere with that maid, and Viji was grateful for it. Kamla laughed a great deal, sometimes over nothing detectable. But Viji liked this. She wanted a friend who laughed, and who would make her laugh. She liked the way Kamla leaned against the kitchen counter and crossed her ankles. She liked her pretty face—the sharp Gujarati nose, the wide smile and lips that were clean and neatly formed, free from the fleshy excesses of Tamil mouths. Kamla had skin that glowed from beneath. Strange, Viji thought, for a divorced woman to be so happy. It must be the exercise.

George walked into the kitchen as Kamla finished her tea. "Why hello!" he said.

"Hello there!" she replied. They both glanced at Viji.

"I'm glad you finally stopped by," George continued. "I've been wanting you to meet Viji." So they knew each other. Viji looked from one to the other, wanting to know how this had happened, not wanting to ask.

"I heard we had a visitor in the neighborhood, so I wanted to stop by." She reached over and squeezed Viji's hand. The questions subsided.

"You must come over again," Viji said. She knew her

voice sounded plaintive. "Would you like to stay for lunch?"
And Kamla did.

George was acting shy. Viji found it funny and strange
that he came in from his study, made himself a sandwich
from the items strewn on the counter, and disappeared
again. But with Kamla in front of her, she didn't want to
think about George.

Where do you come from? What language do you
speak? How long have you been here? Why did you come
here? Are you ever going back? They ran through the usual
questions, setting down the details to finalize their bond,
tilting their heads for yes, biting on cardamom pods for
their tea. Kamla was from Gujurat, and knew little of
Tamil Nadu. Viji was from Tamil Nadu and knew nothing
about Gujurat, except that Gujus were good businessmen
and Gandhi was from there. And really, how long could
they talk about Gandhi? But it didn't matter. By the time
they'd finished their sandwiches, Kamla held Viji's hand
across the table. They were like lovers in a restaurant,
minus the dripping candle, minus the plate of spaghetti
and the man with the violin.

In bed that night, the question came back.

"So you've already met Kamla?"

She crept into the dip between George's shoulder and
chest.

"I have. I'd guess about five years ago. She and her
husband were out walking."

"She's pretty, isn't she," Viji said.

"Sure."

"More beautiful than me?"

"Of course not."

"You're lying."

George laughed and scooted down to bring his face level with Viji's.

"How could I be lying?"

She shrugged.

"Look at your eyes. They're ludicrous." Coming from George, this was flattery. "Pools I could fall into and drown. And your hair. Who has better hair than you? And this mole here, below your eye. It's ever so slightly raised, so that even in the dark I know it's there. And your belly. What in the world could be better than your belly?"

He kneaded, with his palm, the two soft mounds of her belly. They'd been there always, even before she'd had children. He ran his finger along the line of fur that trailed from her navel. His fingers moved softly around her.

"She had a divorce, you know."

Viji still said "dye-vorce" rather than "divorce." But she knew George would never poke fun.

"You seem to like her," he said.

"Yes, I do."

She felt him smiling in the dark. A long silence followed. Viji thought George might have fallen asleep.

"Maybe you should spend more time with her," he said.

"*Yes*, George."

In an attempt to find Viji friends, George had set her up with other wives in the neighborhood, for tea parties and craft days, for afternoons volunteering at the local Loaves & Fishes, all of them long and torturous affairs. No playdates this time. Kamla would be her friend alone.

There might have been jasmine, Viji thought, gazing from the family room window to the rosebushes at the end of her yard. They were still full and tall, but fading from fuschia to pink. They were losing their vigor, tired from staring into the fierce summer sun. Soon their petals would detach, spinning like propellers to the ground or falling in a single swoop, a silent rose-voice calling *Geronimooooo*, like Avi when he jumped off the diving board. It was jasmine she missed, such a heavy scent from the most delicate petals. Why had she so thoughtlessly planted roses?

Regardless, American jasmine was no good, the way the flowers poked from their stems like daggers, petals rolled so tightly, never to open. Pink-tipped. Thin and stingy. She wanted real jasmine, the kind you find in temples and market stands, strung together to be pinned into hair. That jasmine was luminous, with full round bulbs, pure white petals that let the sun shine through. Precious and plentiful.

She went out without her slippers, forgetting to take a basket or scissors. The cement around the pool burned her feet, and she had to step quickly and leap onto the grass. Only the best roses could be taken—no brown spots or wilting petals. Without scissors, she had to use her fingers.

Thorns bit her, no matter how carefully she avoided them. She wasn't supposed to smell the roses; until her morning puja was over, their scent belonged to God. But the perfume was pungent, almost alcoholic, and it sprayed the air every time she pinched a rose from its stem. She couldn't help but breathe it in. She inhaled deeply.

There had been jasmine that night, looped around her braid and hanging a few inches past it, brushing her bare neck when she moved, like cool fingers on her skin. There had been a few white students at the reception, like the young man with brown-blond hair—golden under the lights, dark when he stood by the piano. He wore an Indian kurta with trousers. It was a strange combination, but the material skimmed his chest and he looked almost regal. She recognized him from her History of Art lecture. She tried not to stare.

A professor at the University of Madras had published a new book, and this was why they had gathered—not to sip gin or whiskey or whatever it was that sloshed in her glass and was making her thirstier. Mostly there were old men in suits, their faces clean-shaven. She didn't know why she'd come. The book, the celebrated book, sat forlornly on a corner table. Opened, flipped through by half-distracted fingers, and left alone to gape at the ceiling. Viji stood next to it and turned its pages. Slick photographs of temple sculptures, some writing, but not too much. Not enough to distract from the black stone women with V-shaped grins, breasts like coconuts, hips twisted at comical angles, plump thighs and feet jumping, dancing. She felt it was more important to look at art that she couldn't find around the corner at her local temple.

She'd come to university hearing of Manet and Monet and so many others. Yet they always returned to this, didn't they? Indian sculpture, Indian paintings, Indian everything. India had invented the world, it was generally understood. She wondered if the white students knew. Everything comes from nothing, everything returns to nothing, her mother liked to say. India had invented nothingness, and then filled it to the brim.

"You must be bored with those." He stood beside her, not looking at her, looking at the page between them. She couldn't decide what to say. "Yes" would be inaccurate. "Well, I'll never tire of them," he said. His voice swaggered and the liquor scent was faint on his breath. But when she looked up, he seemed nervous. He stared intently at the page. If she had been in a film, she would have glanced up and said something clever.

"You like them, then," was what came out.

"Very much."

"Is that why you came here?"

He didn't answer, only sipped at the drink in his hand. She sipped hers. She could feel the heat off his shoulder. If this were a film, he would have touched her hand and they'd be dancing now in Kashmiri hills, him chasing her around patient trees until it started raining and she slowed to let him catch her, to let him hold her at the waist and guide her dripping to the shelter of a willow. But this was no film. They stared at the sculptures on the page. Suddenly, the breasts were too big, the smiles hysteric. Viji had said the wrong thing, or the boring bland thing, and he was disappointed. She closed her eyes and sipped her drink. He was going to walk away from her. She would be alone again with this book.

"This one's from the Madurai temple, isn't it?" He hadn't gone. He looked at her now. When she spoke, his gaze hovered on her cheek, and she could tell he wasn't listening.

ॐ ॐ ॐ

Viji was glad for the house's cool. It was late August, and still the sun was ruthless. The children were swimming at the Bauers' and the house was empty. In the puja room, she gathered yesterday's flowers and put them on a separate tray to be thrown out. She lit the small oil lamps on each shelf. After she recited her prayers, she dabbed her finger in the pot of vibhuti and pressed a dot of the gray ash to her forehead. She did the same with the pot of red powder. Then she turned to her mother's picture. This one always came first. She pressed red powder to the photo's forehead, where years of morning pujas had left a dense crimson stain.

"You were thinking about that night again, weren't you?" the photo asked. Viji was startled but not shocked to hear her mother's voice. She tried to ignore her. "There's nothing wrong with reminiscing, my girl."

Viji closed her eyes and nodded.

And then her mother did something she'd rarely done when she was alive. She giggled. "How frightened you were! How surprised!"

Viji smiled in spite of herself. She pressed red powder to the foreheads of other photos: her uncle, George's mother, Anjali.

"Like a guilty little girl, caught stealing sweets from the kitchen."

It wasn't that night, Amma.

"Whichever night it was. That night, the next night, who knows how many nights there were!"

When her mother died, so many miles away, the news tore through her like a firestorm. She hadn't known at the time that people came back. Now, sometimes, she wished they'd leave for good.

"So stubborn you are. You never listened. No! You listened very carefully, and then you did exactly the opposite."

When her mother died, grief took over, as it was expected to. But even stronger was the slow-brewing realization that home was just a house now, tucked into a corner of Madras, containing tables and chairs and beds. It also contained two aunts and her sister, Shanta, stubborn-lipped, slant-nosed, and very far away. The letters between Viji and Shanta never stopped, no matter how long Viji stayed away. They coursed with empty reassurances that all was well. They contained nothing but the scant news of daily comings and goings, talk of the weather and the triplets' progress at school. Shanta had no family of her own, so her letters spoke mostly of their aunts, spinsters themselves with little besides arthritis and resentment to fill their days. Gone was Shanta's teasing, her unsolicited advice. Sterilized by time were Viji's probing questions, her demands for gossip. But as years passed and the oceans widened between them and the continents stretched long and dry, the letters continued, proving to each of the sisters that the other still existed.

Viji spooned water from the silver cup into her palm and sipped it.

"I suppose you're happy with the way your life has turned out."

From Amma's death had grown the first tendrils of a birth: there and then her life with George began. It started as a collection of cells, sewing themselves together inside her, forming systems, organs, transparent limbs. Before this, she had loved George in frantic climaxes. Now her love was a growing thing.

Viji looked straight at her mother. *I think I should be happy. Shouldn't I?*

Between her legs, up inside her now, fire. Her mother didn't answer.

That night. She'd called it this ever since it had happened, because she didn't know what else to call it. That night had been full of everything Viji had never known before. Uncertainty, when George offered to refresh her drink. She'd looked at the drained glass of ice in her hand. "What are you drinking?" he'd asked, expecting her to know. Uncertainty again, when he asked her if she wanted to meet his classmates, and brought her over to speak to the others. She had nothing to say, but they spoke and smiled at her, apple-cheeked. Embarrassment, when an old Englishman stumbled forward, peered into her face, and told her she looked like a goddess sculpture from the Kusana dynasty. Guilt, when George asked her if she wanted to come to his room for a cup of tea, as he had some books on Manet. She'd told her mother she'd be home by nine. Extreme guilt, when she accepted his offer. Weightlessness, as they walked across the campus green to his hostel. Silence, as she relinquished every voice, followed him upstairs, past staring male eyes, and into his room. An unexpected rush of blood to the head when she sat on his bed and he sat next to her, flipped through an art book, his arm pressed against hers. An unbearable, shrieking, ecstatic rush of blood through her entire being when he closed the book in her lap, slid his arm around her waist, and kissed her. Freedom, when she let go and felt herself plunge into the mattress.

She had felt other things as well. But she preferred not to include them in her list. Calm, for example—a solitary, inhuman calm, as she gathered her sari from the floor and wrapped it around herself. The calm turned to shaking fingers that dropped the folded pleats and forced her to start again, two times, three times. Fear, walking downstairs with George, past staring male eyes, and into the night. Fear again, when she saw that it was ten o'clock and knew she would have to run home. Tingling, warm pain between her legs, where his hands had been, as she ran across the campus green. Relief, when she got home and found that her mother was still at the neighbor's. And leaden fatigue, when she undressed herself, picked the mangled jasmine buds from her hair, and fell into bed. The evening was still hot on her skin; it rode against her neck and through her belly. She had smiled all night, in spite of everything, and kept herself awake, replaying every minute, until the first blue of dawn.

If Viji had looked out the bay window that afternoon, she would have disapproved. Stan stood by the pool house, fishing hat cocked over his eyes, mug of tea in hand. The children, still in swimsuits, knelt by the bushes that clustered at the far end of the pool house, digging into the dark earth with their fingernails.

"Hold on, I'll get a stick," Avi said, and ran toward the eucalyptus trees at the back of the property.

"A stick won't make a difference; we can dig better with our hands." Kieran's cheek and knees were smudged black, and a pile of soil collected at his feet as he raked palmfuls of mud out of the hole. Slowly, the mound grew higher.

"How'd you manage to bury it in the first place?" Stan asked.

"Dunno. I think we had a shovel then."

Babygirl leaned on one arm and scooped soil with the other. Avi returned.

"Here it is!" Kieran shouted. He snatched the stick from Avi's hand and struck into the hole with it. The stick thudded.

Twenty minutes later, the treasure chest was freed from the soil. It was really just a shoebox, with a thin line of rope tied around it in a bow.

HOW TO TIE A REEF KNOT HOW TO DIG A REFILLABLE HOLE HOW TO TELL A REAL DIAMOND FROM A FAKE ONE SOLD BY A DODGY MARKET JEWELER

"It's actually a time capsule," Kieran said, "so scientists in the future will be able to see what life was like now."

"It's not a time capsule, Kieran."

"Yes it is."

" It's a treasure chest."

"We voted, two to one, remember?"

"Well, go on, then, don't matter what you call it," Stan said. "Show us what's inside."

In the time-capsule treasure chest: two AA batteries,

a pair of earrings, a purple jelly bracelet, a book of word-search puzzles, Babygirl's fourth-grade school photo (wallet-size), a calculator with a cracked display screen (stepped on by Avi), a white handkerchief, a rusted miniature racing car (thrown in the pool by Kieran), a square of Bazooka gum (dehydrated to the point of snapping in two), a *Peanuts* comic, a single silver cuff link, a napkin ring.

"What's this from?" Stan asked. He picked up the earring, a blue gem stud.

"It's the buried treasure," Babygirl said, and snatched the earring from Stan's palm.

"I've seen it before, though. Is it your mum's?" Babygirl ignored him. Avi looked at him and shrugged. She placed the earring between the napkin ring and the cuff link.

"It's just an earring, that's all."

Behind them, the sliding door hushed open and George stepped out. He wore yellow swim trunks. His chest was bare and white, his arms brown from the elbows down. He nodded to Stan and walked barefoot to the pool, wincing with each step on the scorching pavement. When he jumped in, water splashed out, sizzled on the cement, and dried.

"Let's put this away," Babygirl said, "Now! Before we lose something."

"But we haven't showed Grandad yet."

"Yes we have." Babygirl grabbed the calculator from Kieran and chucked it back into the box. With shaky fingers she wrapped the twine around it and tied a bow.

"What's going on over there?" George called from the pool.

"Hurry," she urged, "he can't see." Her voice trembled.

"She's right," Avi added. "It was supposed to be secret."

Stan stood. "I'll tell nobody," he said. "Gentleman's code."

The triplets pushed the soil back into the hole until the gathered mound was gone. Hurried hands smacked the dirt into place. When Babygirl turned to look, her father was underwater.

It was Labor Day Monday, the only day of the year that George remembered to swim. The next day, the triplets would start school again. They had bought their supplies the week before—notebook paper, pencil cases, sharpeners, fresh pink erasers. They would have to use last year's pencils. The sun still hung high, but the air cooled slightly as evening settled in. The end of summer always came too soon. From surrounding backyards wafted other people's Labor Day barbecue:, the relentless aroma of grilling meat, the smell of woodsmoke, distant splashing. The triplets squatted over the pool and dipped their fingers in, flicking the soil from their nails. They watched George swim a length, sifting currents through the water, slowly and rhythmically, never pausing. And then, slick as tadpoles, they dove in after him. Circling him, breathlessly treading water, they were as comfortable in the deep end as in the shallow. Babygirl slung her arms around George's neck and swung onto his back. He glided across the pool with her. And then, of course, it was Avi's turn, then Kieran's, and then the *again-agains* and *the last-time-I-promises*. But George didn't mind; he liked to feel the weight of them, the underwater slipperiness of their hairless skin, the ownership of their arms around his neck.

They carried on until the sun squinted meekly through the trees and dimmed the lights on their game, and when they could no longer deny that it was dark, they toweled off, shivering, and went inside.

Viji dipped a cotton ball in oil and rolled it between her fingers into a wick. This she arranged on the rim of the second oil lamp. Match hiss, flame. The room and the house were utterly quiet. She began her prayers, mumbling to herself, a tentative melody dipping and rising again.

"'Sing louder, girl, I can't hear you." Deepa, light of her younger days. Deepa, who had taught her how to braid hair.

"Come on, now. You sing like a drowning mouse." Deepa had come from the West Indies to Viji's school in Madras. She was Tamil, but spoke like no one Viji had ever known.

Leave me alone, Viji said. *I'm praying.*

"Praying. You won't get nothing praying like that. What you got to pray for, anyway?"

None of your business.

Viji smiled, her eyes still closed. Deepa clicked her tongue.

"Hmm. Keeping secrets from me. You praying for a boyfriend, I bet"

Nonsense.

"You praying for a new dress or something? A lovely sari with gold zhari?"

Yes, Deepa. That's it. That's what I'm praying for.

"What you want a sari for? You can't wear the thing round here, you know. Who you know that wears a sari?"

I know someone now.

"Who's that? That Kamla? She trouble."

You're just jealous.

"She trouble, all right."

What do you know?

"What do I know? What do I know? I know everything, that's what I know. And what you going to do, put on your saris and drive to the Arden Fair Mall? Buy some frozen yogurt in your pattu silks?"

Viji opened her eyes. Deepa vanished. Viji missed her immediately. It was leukemia that had taken her, or something like it. Diagnoses in those days were never very clear. After school ended, Deepa was married to a Tamil doctor and sent back to Trinidad. She wrote Viji a letter every week, and Viji wrote back as often as she could, but university took up most of her time. And somehow, with all she had to tell, her letters were never as wonderful as Deepa's. Her friend told her what it was like to be married, to live with a man she hardly knew, getting to know his sounds and smells and the minute mechanics of his mind. But behind the jokes about her husband's penis and demands that Viji visit her, Deepa was speaking of something else: loneliness, wanting things to be as they once were, the vertigo that comes from living someone else's life. After two years, the letters slowed to a trickle. After the third year, they stopped.

Downstairs, the house spread silently before Viji, dark inside despite the sunny morning. Breakfast had already been tidied and the trappings of lunch boxes put away.

Through the sliding glass door she saw Stan, roasting on a deck chair by the pool. Viji had never seen such dedicated sunbathing. Every morning he went out, oiled his saggy chicken legs, and lay back with his eyes closed. Where was the need for such things? Already the old man was dark as that girlfriend of his. Who, Viji noticed, had left her sweater on Stan's bed. The woman had been in his room the previous day when Viji had returned from the supermarket. Correction: the woman had been in Kieran and Avi's room, sitting on Kieran's or Avi's bed, giggling loudly enough to be heard through Kieran and Avi's wall. Dirty man. Sitting among his grandchildren's toys, defiling the memory of his wonderful wife with the likes of a low-class cleaning lady.

"What do you mean, defiling?" George had asked.

"You know what I mean George. Carrying on with this woman as if your mother had never lived."

"Viji," George said, "I'm sure if my mother were still alive, there would be no Lupe. But since she isn't, he's trying to get on with his life."

"And to do this he has to defile your mother's memory? You have nothing to say about it?"

"No I don't." George was firm. "And this isn't the first time he has *defiled her memory*."

"Well, I hope when I die I won't have to come back as a ghost and see you fooling around with other women."

"My guess, darling, is that you'll have to do nothing of the sort."

She didn't like this smile of his. "Fine," she hissed. "Then I hope I do come back .so I can haunt you until you stop."

George laughed.

"I'm not joking. I'll stand at the foot of your bed."

"Fine, Viji. You have it your way, my mother will have it hers. I reckon she isn't spinning in her grave."

Viji winced. "She's a pretty lady, this Loopy."

"Lupe'" George corrected.

"What?"

"*Lu-pay.*"

"That's what I said."

"Short for Guadalupe."

"Lupe?" she asked.

"Yes. Lupe."

Plumper than the other women in Maple Grove, this Lupe had two dimples and a wrinkle-free complexion. But she laughed louder than she needed to and talked too much. Viji didn't like women, or men, for that matter, who spoke pointlessly. But most of all, most of all, it was the way the woman smiled at Viji. Knowingly. As if the two of them shared some hidden purpose, some sisterly bond. Viji was the daughter of a magistrate, the wife of a professor. What did she have in common with a Mexican housekeeper?

"She's Guatemalan," George corrected.

"Then what is she doing here?"

George paused, looked confused. "Working here. What else?"

Viji hadn't considered that Guatemalans would want to come to California as well. She really had no idea where Guatemala was, but she assumed it was close to Mexico.

It seemed to be coming at her from all sides, this pretend solidarity. Just the other day, she'd taken the children shopping for school supplies (never mind that they still had a box full of pencils and notebooks only half used from the previous year). At the checkout counter was a black woman, hair in tight braids with small beads at the ends, like that blind singer on television. She'd paused when Viji had handed her a check. She looked tenderly at the triplets, then smiled at Viji. "You black?" she asked. Viji thought she'd misheard. "You black?" she repeated. Her name tag read: Yolanda.

"No," Viji said. "I'm Indian."

"Oh, yes'" Yolanda sighed. "Indians. *Beautiful* black folk." Avi giggled first, and then Kieran and Babygirl. Viji held out her check.

"Thank you," she said.

"*Beautiful* black folk!" the triplets mimicked, once they'd left the store. It became the chanted refrain of the car ride home. *Beautiful black folk! Beautiful black folk!* They were children. They had no idea what black meant, or Indian or Chinese or Mexican or *Guatemalan* or white. This was what Viji told herself as she drove home, trying to drown out the triplets' ruckus. The closer she got to her neighborhood, the more white people she saw in shiny sedans. Among them were dusty pickup trucks with lawn-mowers piled in the back. These were driven by Mexicans or maybe Guatemalans—who knew? She saw no black people, though she could picture the cars they drove—long, like roving gazelles, with gleaming paint and wide fenders. She wondered if other people thought she was black. She wondered if her neighbors thought she was black. Or Mexican?

She would speak to George that night. She was curious to know how long, in fact, his father planned to live with them. She was curious to see whether George knew the answer, or even cared to know.

"Why don't you talk to your father?" she'd asked the night before.

George was brushing his teeth at the time. Suds dripped from his lower lip when he spoke. "About what?" He was using her toothbrush. Hers was the purple one, his was the orange. But he was using the purple one. Always the purple one. If she switched to the orange, he would switch, too.

"About what? About anything. I never see you talk to him."

George shrugged. "What's there to talk about?"

"I don't know. What does anyone talk about? The children. England. Cricket. Beer. That girlfriend of his. When he plans to leave."

"We don't really talk like that."

"Like what?"

"Like…*that*." He spat out a final strand of foam and saliva, hunched over the sink like a sick person.

"Can you please ask him how long he plans to stay? Can you do that for me, my love?"

"Yes, darling. That I can do."

"Thank you."

"Thank *you*." He leaned over to kiss her, but the white lather was still smeared across his lip and she backed away. "Hmm," he said, dabbing at the wrong side of his mouth. "Sod off, then." He tapped her bottom, pleased with himself for a reason Viji couldn't fathom.

Viji felt a faint thread of guilt work its way through her. Stan was an old man trying to be happy. He was the father of the man she loved, the grandfather of her children. If sniffing after Mexican maids made him happy, it shouldn't bother her. If roasting himself like a turkey made him happy, she should be glad for him. If it had been her father, she would have let him stay forever. But her father would have acted differently. This much she knew.

✿ ✿ ✿

Kieran made a point of collecting his eraser shavings in a pile at the corner of his desk. This way, when Anisha Mehta looked over, she would see that he, unlike the rest of the class, was not your average slob. Kieran Armitage would not sweep his rubbery shreds to the ground for someone else to pick up. Nor would he slump down with his chin on his desk, blowing at the shavings, like Jason Schaffer, who spent most class periods digging the wax from his ear. Nor, worst of all, would he let them lie scattered like massacred insects.

They'd placed him in seventh-grade reading because he read too fast for sixth grade, which meant that Avi and Babygirl would be reading *Old Yeller* that year and Kieran would have to read *Ivanhoe*. But it also meant that he'd get to spend an hour each day sitting next to Anisha Mehta, who smelled of strawberry candy.

Kamla Aunty had brought her to the house two days before school started. The triplets had been out front, helping Viji turn on the sprinklers. Anisha Mehta was taller than the triplets, a year older, and stood with her hip cocked to one side. She looked them over, one by one, up-down, up-down, up-down. She turned to Babygirl. "Have you got a pool?" She had a raspy voice, like she had a cold and too much mucus in her throat. Without another word, the two girls walked around the house and to the backyard, leaving Kieran and Avi squinting into the sun.

Kieran wondered if Anisha Mehta had just sucked on a strawberry candy, if she was in fact always sucking on strawberry candies, or if the way she smelled came from a glass bottle with a spray nozzle attached. Maybe, like Marcia Brady, she brushed her hair a hundred times each night. She was almost taller than Kamla Aunty. This Kieran could tell even when she was sitting, particularly when he dropped his pencil by her desk and had to stoop to pick it up, as he did now, bending down past the length of leg that flowed from her navy skirt, and rising up again. He glimpsed her knee, pinker than the rest of her leg. He wondered if she shaved her legs, or if they were just naturally smooth as caramel chews. They weren't the legs of a girl. They made him think of the woman in the cigarette ad, the one who kicked her bare legs into the air while smoking. He slid *Ivanhoe*, opened to the third page, from his desk into his lap.

Pervert. She looked at him now. *Creepy perv. I'm gonna tell on you.*

Kieran looked to the front of the room, where Mrs. Valentine was drawing lines across the board.

Did you hear me? she whispered.

Kieran nodded. He glanced over. She wasn't reading *Ivanhoe.*

You're sick, you know that? she said. Her text was in her lap, but open within it was another, smaller book. Someone had brought *Are You There, God? It's Me, Margaret,* and it was making a round of the classroom.

He whispered back, *I'm gonna tell on* you.

Pervert.

I know what you're reading. You're the pervert.

As if. He wished she would just clear her throat. He raised his hand. *Freak*, she whispered. *Quit it.*

He actually had no idea what the book was about, only that it had been inciting intense discussion and significant gazes from a huddle of female classmates in the lunch yard, and that the cover featured a teenage girl sitting on her bed and smirking into the distance. This image alone suggested all kinds of dirty possibilities. Mrs. Valentine's behind jiggled busily as she wrote. *You'd better put that hand down.*

Kieran shook his head and kept his hand up. He was breathing hard now, the weak wind of his nostrils scattering, particle by particle, his mountain of eraser shavings.

Stop it or you'll be sorry.

Mrs. Valentine turned around. "Yes, Kieran?" The class turned to look at him. He normally never spoke. Jason Schaffer blinked. Someone's chair was creaking.

"Nothing."

"Are you sure?" She smiled at him like he was a baby.

"Yes, I'm sure."

The teacher looked at Anisha, then turned back to the board.

Anisha kicked him hard. Then again. And again. Kieran didn't move his leg. He felt a bruise warming to the surface, and moved his foot closer to hers. She kicked him again, softly, and then stopped.

Kamla came for tea the next Wednesday, and by the following Monday she and Viji were old friends. Kamla smacked her on the shoulder when she laughed, grabbed Viji's forearm to make an urgent point.

"You need to get out more," Kamla observed one day, as she watched Viji pick the crusted food off her potholders. "Come walking with me." And so Viji and Kamla began their daily walks. Viji would walk to Kamla's house on Ladino Lane, broaching the winding walk that led from the street to the door of a bungalow, white, with dark green shutters and a small porch, a tree swing hanging from the oak out front. It was smaller than Viji's house, but big enough for Kamla and Anisha. There was no hint that anyone but an American lived inside.

One afternoon, when they both returned to Viji's house, Stan stood at the kitchen window. He wore his fishing hat. He held a banana in his hand, a chunk of it still in his mouth, puffing out his cheeks and upper lip. Kamla laughed, and Viji couldn't help but smile.

"Oh, pretty laaaaaaady," Stan called in a nasal American accent, as they walked through the front door. "Oh pretty laaaady."

Viji felt the heat rush to her cheeks, and smiled. "Silly man," she said to Kamla. When they entered the kitchen, he said it again— "Oh, pretty laaaaaaady"—and wrapped Kamla in an exaggerated hug, swinging her slim frame from side to side.

"Oh, Stan!" Kamla laughed and slapped him on the chest. "You big joker."

Viji walked silently to the fridge and took a bag of grapes out of the fruit drawer.

"Jerry Lewis!" Stan said. "You must know Jerry Lewis, he's American."

"Silly man, I'm Indian."

"Let's see your passport."

"I'm Indian, just like your daughter-in-law."

"Yeah, but you're gorgeous."

"Stop that, now."

"I can't help myself, love."

Kamla walked over to Viji, who held a colander of the grapes under the running tap. She picked a grape off its stem and popped it into her mouth.

"Shall I make you tea, darling?"

"Marry me," Stan answered.

"I was speaking to Viji," Kamla cooed.

"No," Viji said. Which sounded rude. She looked at Kamla and smiled. "No, thank you. Can I make you some?"

George walked in barefoot, glasses crooked, his hands folded sleepily across his chest. He had been working. He fell into a daze when he spent too long in his study, and it often took him at least an hour to return to normal conversation. This, Viji reasoned, was why he forgot to greet Kamla. He made his way to the freezer, took out a pudding pop she'd bought for the children, and shuffled back into the hall.

"George," Viji called, "sprinklers."

Outside, George watched a spray of water shunt across his lawn. Slowly at first, then a rapid tattoo. *Shoop, shoop, shoop, shoop, ratatatatatata.* He'd fallen asleep in his study, and now his brain was sludge. His mouth was thick with afternoon sleep and he felt slightly sick. The episode in the kitchen struck him as unusual, but he didn't know why.

"Goodbye, George." Kamla, in blue shorts. She turned to wave as she walked away.

"Bye." He waved. The afternoon light cast her in its buttery glow, and she smiled at him. She walked past the sprinklers. A hop to the left to avoid a spray of water. Down the street, out of sight.

༅༅༅

George had a secret: he liked art, all of it. Hotel-room abstracts, landscapes of Provence, Norman Rockwell soda shops. Anathema to an academic. At weeping clowns he drew the line, but even poker-playing dogs amused him. More specifically, they reminded him of Edward Hopper.

This may have been why he'd never risen through the ranks of Sac State's art history department. Victoria was at Cambridge now, on her way to professorship. While George mooned over Renoirs, she worked her way through conferences and art journals. It was a rare month that he did not see her name in print in some journal or other. The truth was, George hated the idea of dissecting art, separating intention from execution, influence from inspiration, laying it out on the operating table for theorists to autopsy, like doctors pondering so many sinew-dripping limbs. He knew what it was to make art, how physical it was. Like birth, it was a process of tearing, destruction in the interest of creation. Like birth, it was a tiny shred of death. Sacrilege, then, to bend a painting to something Lacan had once said. Further sacrilege to write an article about it.

More than anything, George hated the language of ac-

ademia, its pointless "ologies" and "ifications." The only
function of such words was to increase the page count of
the millions of feckless PhD theses that burdened library
stacks across the country. There was certainly no place for
such language in the world of art. Like a mother, he loved
it simply because it had been created. It was beauty solid-
ified, priceless in at least one person's eyes, however
worthless in someone else's.

In every work of art there lurked a woman. All of it,
no matter what an artist insisted, was made for a woman,
about a woman, because of a woman. Sometimes, it
worked the other way around. In his mother he'd seen
Klimt. In Viji, he'd seen the *yakshi*, the ancient fertility
sculpture. But in Amaré, his assistant, he saw nothing.
Proof that he could find a woman in every piece of art,
but couldn't find art in every woman.

Amaré crouched by his desk. "Sign this," she ordered.
Here were globes of soft skin, rolling from a V-neck
sweater. Brown. Placed there for his benefit. Above them,
a face of smooth planes. Not at all unattractive. For a moment, he was taken. But then she stood and it was gone. He
grimaced. There was little George could do to distract himself from her behind, the way her ass sprawled ungraciously
in a pair of pink corduroy trousers. If he were more fashion-
savvy, he might have been able to formulate some general
rule about the incompatibility of womanly curves and lum-
berjack fabrics. But he was not fashion-savvy, as evidenced
by his own sloppy chinos and untucked shirt. The hip retro
appeal of his glasses was a fluke, more a product of a per-
sistent shopgirl than of George's fashion sense.

No, Amaré wasn't for George. She was, however, just

the woman for Stan. Something to take his mind off the Bauers' maid. A way, perhaps, to make Viji happy again. It was an unwritten (and probably untested) rule in Maple Grove that neighbors did not covet each other's house-cleaners.

"Just a moment, Amaré." His assistant stopped in the doorway and looked back at him. He looked down at his papers. "Oh, just—nothing." This wouldn't do.

"What?" She turned around, facing him now, her hand on her hip.

"Forget it."

She leaned forward. "*What?*"

She frightened him sometimes. Now, specifically. It wasn't just her exceedingly long nails, or the pugnacious set of her jaw. Or the fact that her hairstyle could change from day to day. *Out with it, George.*

"Well it's just that—I know that I don't know you particularly well…" He lost what he was saying. She frowned. "Ah—I don't know you very well, but I thought it might be worth sort of exploring certain social options."

She looked mildly interested. "Social options?"

"As in the possibility of perhaps expanding the scope of your duties, heh heh. No. What I mean to say is—"

"Dr. Armitage?"

"Yes?" He was sweating now, but smiling bravely.

"I gotta go."

"Oh. Right."

She paused in the doorway. "You *are* married, aren't you?"

"Married? Ha! Yes, of course I'm married. I can see where you thought this might be going." He rubbed his palms together. *Wrong. Very awkward.* "What I meant to say initially, Amaré, is that I know somebody who might, if he should be so lucky, spark your interest."

She cocked her head.

"Ah, of course, I wouldn't presume to know anything or *assume* anything of your…status, in that respect, but it was just a passing thought, really, that perhaps might have interested you, were you interested in this particular gentleman—"

"Let me get this straight. Are *you* asking me out?"

"No."

"Then who is?"

"I am. On behalf of somebody else."

"Who?" Nothing but questions.

"Stan."

"Stan?"

"Yes."

"Is he black?"

"White."

"Does he have a job?"

"Retired. Taxi driver."

"Age?"

"Sixty-seven."

"Hair?"

"Yes! Plenty."

"Married?"

"No. Of course not."

"Single?"

"Sort of, yes."

"Let me get this straight. You want to set me up on a blind date? With a man who's *sort of* single, twice my age, drives a *taxi*, and isn't black?"

"Well, yes." He could sense that the idea wasn't catching on.

"Dr. Armitage?"

"Yes."

"Don't do that again."

She slammed the office door, and the *click* of her shoes faded down the hall. There, done. He had tried and failed. Viji would have to handle this on her own. George smiled weakly at the closed door, opened his desk drawer, and gathered up a cluster of pencils. Outside, the campus clock chimed four times. Already the sky was dimming, though the day stayed warm. These were classic pencils, yellow with pink erasers and green metallic rims, the number 2 stamped neatly on their hilts. They smelled of fresh wood. He arranged them on his desk by ascending length. There were twelve remaining. They'd come in a box of one hundred, a happy family of them, provided free by the department. Some of the leads were dull. He considered asking Amaré to sharpen them, then thought better of it. He rearranged the pencils by descending lead length, and placed them, one by one, back in their drawer.

As a teenager, he'd taken a school trip to a pencil factory outside Nottingham. The whole building had smelled of fragrant wood with soft undertones of rubber. He remembered the machine that hadchurned out the fresh pencils, naked of yellow paint or numbers or labels, still missing their pink erasers. They had rolled onto a conveyor belt, a sea of smooth wood, and George had felt an overpowering need to put them in his mouth and chew on them, to feel the sweet crunch between his molars.

Around him stood his classmates, bored, whispering and slouching, chewing on their sleeves. All George could think of was the feel of the pencils. If he had a roomful, he would bathe in pencil wood, feel it cool and solid against his bare skin, pressing into him like a thousand small rolling pins, filling the crevices between his legs.

And then, before he could stop it (as *if* he could stop it), a string of saliva gathered force on his lower lip, dove from his mouth, and plummeted to the factory floor. *Plip.* It even made its own sound. And of course, because this was how things worked, tall and beautiful Felicia Watson was the first to see. It was too late to wipe his mouth, though he sensed the dewey droplets still perched on his chin. He wanted to vanish. He wished he were a wood slab, to be fed into a splicer, to be sliced into a million slim rods, never to be seen again. But it wouldn't have made a difference—within seconds, the whole class was staring. Felicia Watson's mouth hung open, her eyes squinting with disgust. Even the factory tour guide cast a swift glance, grimaced, and looked away. From that day, the names rained down, from the obvious (Pencil Perv, Spit Twit) to the more obscure (Lead Licker, Factory Wanker, Rubber Johnny).

But here, in the privacy of his office, George could do as he pleased. At times like these, he relished being an adult, getting to close his door and waste time, knowing that instant gratification was easy. From the drawer he picked a single pencil, ran it under his nostrils like a cigar, placed it sideways between his lips, and chewed. The office slipped away. So did his father, the maid, Viji, the triplets, the female student who'd been haunting his office hours.

Eyes closed, he gnawed away and fingered the eraser. He lost himself in the pleasure of it and gave up the earth. His was a world of wood and graphite. The wood gave way beneath his canines and crunched between his molars. He was the pencil king.

When the bell in the tower chimed again, George sat up. The pencil was covered in bite marks. He ran his finger over the toothy Braille, sighed, and chucked it in the waste basket. The afternoon was over. He'd have to ask Amaré to order more pencils. For a lingering moment, he stroked the few that remained. Then he closed the drawer, stood, put on his coat, and left.

❦ CHAPTER EIGHT ❦

July 1975. So much depended on a fast phone call from an airport terminal amid the jostling of baggage and elbows. *Victoria? I've made a terrible mistake.* This would win him immediate sympathy, but it wasn't entirely honest. He dialed. *Victoria? You won't believe this.* Flippant. Too flippant. Perhaps, he almost hoped, another man would answer. *Ah...could I speak with Victoria, please?* The phone rang twice.

"Hello?"

"Victoria?"

Victoria took herself quite seriously, as most young ladies in academia had to at the time. Even her classmates called her Miss Banks. To all others, she was Victoria. Never Vicki or Vic or Banksy. George liked to call her Sponge on occasion, and when the mood took her, she let him.

"Hello?" she said again.

"Hello."

"*George.*"

"Victoria? I've made a terrible mistake."

Silence.

"Where are you, George?"

"Heathrow."

"*Heathrow?* You could have told me you'd be back. I

could have given you a lift—"

"Victoria—"

"But I suppose you've sorted it, anyway. When are you thinking of getting back to Nottingham?"

"Victoria?"

"Yes?"

"I don't think I'll be seeing you soon."

He felt the silence this time. It rushed through the phone line and cracked the receiver, stormed through the terminal, and hushed the world around him.

"George."

He swallowed audibly.

"What have you done?"

"I've married someone."

"What?"

"I've got married. In India."

A long, terrible pause.

"To whom did you get married, George?" Her voice was dry-ice vapor. He preferred the silence.

"A woman I met there. She's called Viji—"

A click and a dial tone. He continued to speak, pouring the story into the cold receiver—for those few minutes, his most intimate friend.

George, it could be said, had difficulties with women. Based on a single glance, they expected great things of him. From what he understood, this didn't happen to other men. He could only speculate that these expectations stemmed from something physical—his aquiline nose, or the fact that he showed no sign of balding. Victoria would have blamed them on something Freudian. A wife was supposed to signal an end to the difficulties, a final settlement of the whole romantic mess. But Viji only made things messier.

George's mother was elated to learn that her son had found a wife, not to mention a beautiful, spiritually advanced, Indian one. And so were her friends. He hated them for it. What did they know of Viji? She could have been a cannibal. She wasn't, of course. (The truth was, she grew lovelier every day that she spent in this strange cold country, her skin glowing brown against the gray Nottingham sky, the shape of her softening every hard brick building she walked past. The city seemed to sigh when Viji walked through it. But George knew this could have been his savior complex playing nasty games with his id.)

His mother threw a party and they came, the friends-of-Marla that George had suffered his entire childhood. Sculptors, painters, writers. All of them certifiably imbalanced, the kind who saved their placentas and danced around fires at pagan harvest festivals. As expected, the friends-of-Stan were less prevalent. His father didn't have much need for friends or for lengthy explanations, and so his end of the guest list had been brief. The regulars from his pub were not in attendance. Barney from the taxi firm did show up; he took one swift look at Viji, another at the coterie of goateed and silk-swathed artists in the garden, and vanished to the shed with Stan and a bottle of whiskey.

Victoria stopped by, briefly. She found George in the kitchen.

"You didn't need to come, Victoria."

She gazed coolly at him. "Your mother invited me."

He looked out the window at the garden party. It was

summer, still light at ten o'clock. "I'm sorry about all this," he said.

"Is that all?"

"I'm…really very sorry about all this."

"Shut up, George."

"Well, what am I meant to say?"

She picked at the chipping paint of the windowsill. "Why did you do it?"

For this, the question he'd dreaded, he had no actual answer. If he'd been a playwright, like the mustachioed man now plying Viji with glasses of rum punch in the garden, he would have organized the facts thus:

Setup: Our hero is George, a university student. A few weeks of aimlessly ogling a young Indian woman finally give way to seduction. The seduction leads to further seduction. Viji visits his small student room two days after the first time, and then the day after, and the day after. This continues peacefully for a period of two weeks.

Turning point: Viji forgets, one night, to get dressed and scamper back home by nine.

Rising conflict: Early morning, barely light, and a banging on the door. They are discovered by Viji's uncle. Viji is taken away and George is threatened violently. He neither sees nor hears of Viji for four days.

Crisis: After class on the fourth day, he is met at the entrance to his dormitory and taken to a house in the Eggmore district of Madras. An older woman receives him. This is Viji's mother. She asks him to do the honorable thing. There is a large man standing behind her, and a larger man, who seems to be an idiot of some description, sitting on the divan next to her.

Resolution: The lovers reunite. Our hero marries for honor, if nothing else, and spirits his bride to his kingdom in the West.

But this was no answer for a woman like Victoria. It answered the wheres and whens, but not the hows. A poet would have spoken of the early dawn that broke that fateful morning, the way light had spread over his lover's breasts. The lizard on the wall above the bookshelf that had watched them every night before scooting into an invisible breach in the ceiling. The unwrapping of the sari, yards and yards and yards of it, a silk ribbon tied too many times around a gift. The bedsheet the next morning, rumpled and dull with sleep, held tightly around Viji's chest, clinging to her buttocks when she stumbled into the corridor. A novelist, like the one now rubbing his mother's shoulders, would have mentioned that she'd never complained about his grubby student room, or commented on the water stains in every corner. He would have remembered that George had answered the door in a towel and then followed the angry uncle into the corridor, holding Viji's sari out to her. An artist, like his mother, would have seen the bouquets of brown faces clumped around the stairwell and poking out of doors, staring, talking, craning for a glimpse of the half-naked woman.

If he were a poet, if he were a painter. But he was neither. And here stood Victoria, waiting for an answer that lay somewhere at the invisible juncture of his body and his heart, andthat bore no connection to his feeble, dog-paddling mind.

"It just happened."

"It just *happened*?"

"I told you not to wait for me. We weren't together, were we?"

Disdainful eyes. "No, George. We weren't. Apparently."

George felt like a bigger fool than ever. "It's getting dark out, finally. I missed the English summer." Silence. The party outside was growing looser, fuzzy around the edges. "Victoria, maybe we could talk about this some other time."

Victoria leaned in close. "There's not much to speak of, George, is there?"

She vanished around the door, and her footsteps faded down the hall. A week later, a package arrived for George and Viji. The card read, *To George and Viji. All best wishes for a very happy marriage. Victoria and Beckett the Cat.*

"What is it?" Viji asked, on tiptoe to see what George was staring at.

"It's a bag of shit."

"What?"

"Kitten shit." Curled black feces rested at the bottom of a paper bag. "I presume we can use it for the garden." George walked past his stunned new wife and into the garden, where a light summer rain had begun. His father's roses winked and blushed from the corner of the lot. Here he scattered the droppings beside each bush, crumpled the bag into a tight ball, and headed back inside before the rain could soak through his shirt.

The doorbell rang. Kamla's eyes, perched above a teacup, darted to meet Viji's. Both women trembled on the verge of laughter.

On the front porch stood two young men, rosy-cheeked, in black suits. They wore name tags.

"Hel-*lo*"' Kamla cooed.

"Yes?" said Viji. "Can I help you?"

"Well, to tell you the truth, we want to know if *we* can help *you*! We're from the Church of Jesus Christ of Latter-day Saints. This is Elder, and I'm Jonathan."

"Are you lost? Do you need directions?"

"Actually, ma'am, we're not. Far from it, in fact. We were wondering if you had a minute for a chat." His cheeks were so red, Viji wondered who had slapped him. She wanted to reach out and pinch one. How Kamla would have hooted.

"Come in, then," Viji said. She knew what these people wanted, but she didn't feel like turning them away; she'd been having a good day. Having Kamla there made her brave.

"I've heard of this church," Viji offered. These ladder-day saints, Jesus Christ and the Ladder-Day Saints. She envisioned a rock 'n' roll group, Jesus Christ on vocals, the ladder-day saints behind on drums, guitar, tambourine…

and ladders. They sponsored soft-focus commercials that played between Saturday morning cartoons—this was where she knew them from. Always some boy turning down a cigarette or visiting his grandmother, or helping a blind man to cross the street. "I should tell you, I have my own religion and I don't intend to switch. Would you like some tea?"

"Oh, well, we're not trying to convert you," said the one named Elder. "We're just spreading our message of faith."

"Mm-hmm. Did you want some tea, then, or some water?"

"Water, please. It's a warm one today. Can I ask— sorry, I haven't asked your name—"

"Viji."

"Viji?"

"Viji."

"Can I ask," he hesitated, "Viji, what your current faith is?"

"I am a Hindu." She resented his word: "current". "And so is Kamla." The two boys looked up and smiled at her. This felt suddenly like a blind double date, a pickup scene in that diner on *Happy Days*.

"And do you believe your faith will lead you to an afterlife of salvation?"

"Are you talking about heaven?"

He grinned. "So you've heard of it then!"

"Really, we care more about reincarnation. You see, if we live in this life well, if we do our duty, then we are reborn in a good life next time, a better life maybe, unless we are very naughty, in which case we come back as a rat."

Kamla spit her tea back into its cup.

The one called Elder looked nervously at his companion. "Well, have you considered, maybe, another approach to the afterlife?"

"I thought you didn't want to convert me," Viji said. She liked these boys; she didn't want them to leave.

"Well, no, we don't really—"

"I know that book you're holding. I know it's no Yellow Pages."

Elder won back his grin. "Well, in a way, Viji, it's a Yellow Pages of the blessed!"

"Let me ask, do you know about the Hindu religion?"

"Well, we do make a point of learning about all the world's religions."

"So that you can know why they are wrong, is it?"

"Maybe if you gave us a chance, Viji—"

"Let me tell you, Elder, I know about this Christianity. I went to a convent school."

"Actually, the Church of Jesus Christ of Latter-day Saints—Mormonism?—we're a unique branch of Christianity. Perhaps you'd like to—"

"Oh *ho*, I see, so you're very different from Christians, are you? Do you have a monkey god?"

The two boys gazed at each other.

"Because we have a monkey god. In fact, he's a flying monkey god. He helped Lord Rama to rescue Sita. That was his wife, who was kidnapped by the demon king Ravana. In fact, Sita was born from a seed in the ground. And do you know Garuda? He is an eagle. Who else, Kamla? Oh yes, Brahma. Brahma has many heads. Seven, I think, or maybe nine. I don't know—I always lose track. And Ganesha? He's an elephant—well, actually, he's a man with

an elephant's head. That's a long story. He rides a rat. And
who else? Kamla?"

Kamla only gaped at her.

"And you know? We get to eat sweets after praying.
Do you get sweets? Also, with Siva, we bathe him in milk,
though I'm not sure why. Siva can burn you with his third
eye. Burn a hole right through you! Can your God start a
fire with his third eye?"

The Mormon did not falter. "Our God is a righteous
God, Viji. Do you know the story of Noah?"

"With his animal twins? Oh, yes. And speaking of
floods, ours can make floods, too—no big deal. Ours can
send heaven to hell and hell to heaven. Can yours send
heaven to hell and hell to heaven?"

"Viji, I am not going to debate whose Almighty can
do what." He spoke slowly and clearly, like a harassed airline employee. "Here's some reading material for you. I'll
just leave it on the table, and we'll be on our way."

"Would you like to see my puja room?"

His eyes widened. Gingerly, he set some pamphlets
down and, holding his briefcase over his groin, backed out
of the kitchen. The other one, crimson-cheeked, followed.
"Okay, now, you have a nice day."

"Thank you!" Viji called, waving to them from the
door, waiting for them to run. Instead, they crossed the
street and walked toward the Fromm house. "Goodbye!"

She closed the door.

"Lady," Kamla sighed. "You are cukoo."

Kamla's wide eyes made Viji laugh. The kitchen filled
with laughter—the house swelled with it—and it stopped
onlywhen she hurt too much to go on.

An earring, blue crystal with a burnished-silver backing: to Babygirl, it was a beautiful thing, to be held up to a window and gazed at, an offering to the sunlight. An earring didn't belong in a box, in the dirt, underground. A man gave earrings to a woman to show that he loved her—or, if he was a very rich man, to show that he liked her. In return for the gift, the woman kissed the man or hugged him, but usually kissed him. Then he swept her into his arms, and at this point, the bedroom door always closed, or the scene, like magic, faded to black. This much she knew.

She also knew that, inevitably, a man would give her earrings. And when he did, she would be tall, wearing jeans and red high heels, with a mane of hair that flew high off her head like Christie Brinkley's. She had little idea of what he'd be like. She sensed there would be large dark eyes, a soft nose, and warmth. Like the Bauers' golden retriever.

Anisha Mehta, on the other hand, knew for sure. "Blond" she'd said. "The blonder the better. Like Almonzo from *Little House*." But rich. Rich enough to buy her diamonds, not just costume jewelry. "I won't accept costume jewelry," she'd said.

"Why not?"

"My mom said to never let a man give me costume jewelry."

"Why?"

"I don't know, it's just a rule."

Costume jewelry was anything big and ugly, Babygirl guessed, something you would wear to a costume party. Anisha Mehta had turned her nose up at the blue crystal earring.

"*Definitely* costume jewelry," she'd said. "There's no such thing as a blue diamond, anyway."

"So what?" Babygirl replied. "It's better than a diamond." Her ears burned. She wished she hadn't shown Anisha Mehta the treasure chest. She should have left it buried.

But this earring was too lovely to be buried, too small to be costume jewelry, too precious to be kept where she'd first found it, in the back of her father's dresser drawer, hidden under a pair of balled-up athletic socks. Her mother's, then. But why were they hidden away? They were a surprise for someone, no doubt.

George had been startled to see her in his room. Rough hands, hardly her father's, had snatched the earrings from her. A voice, a slightly shaky voice that didn't sound like his, explained that yes, yes of course they were a surprise; she mustn't tell her mother, or she'd ruin it for everyone. And a silence that she'd never heard before had descended as her father watched her leave the room. Standing in the hallway, she heard the dresser drawer open, and after some shuffling, she heard it close again.

ॐॐॐ

Three, in total: the number of conversations George had had with Stan since his arrival in California. Three more than he'd had the year before, or the time Stan had visited for Christmas. Probably three more than he'd had in a very long time. Then came number four.

"Fancy one?" Stan asked, as George shifted his weight on the deck chair. A cigar, unlit, already odoriferous. George smiled.

"Is it Cuban?"

"So it matters to you, then? If it's Cuban or not? Got it down at Blom's shop before I left. Does that meet your exacting standards?"

"Sure, Dad." George took the cigar and stuck it between his lips. He leaned to reach the flame that sprung up between Stan's fingertips.

"Is it Cuban," Stan muttered, shaking his head and shaking out the match, "Bloody hell."

The cigar was wrapped in a Stark's Finest label, which George peeled off. He sucked gently at the tip, coaxing out the first striated fumes. The stink of it rushed through his nostrils, filled him with the Turk's Head pub, its fake-wood paneling and green paisley carpet, the Saracen's sword that hung above the bar, the incongruous giant fish mounted and hung next to the dart board, its frame scarred by decades of lager-addled aim. The silt of the place used to hang on his father when he'd come home in the evenings, teetering in the doorway of George's bedroom, asking, every night, if he'd done his studies. Every night the same question, as if he'd spent hours at the pub pondering George's study habits, as if this were his only real concern—not the lager or the drawling, directionless talk, or the lady behind the bar who bent straight down from the waist when someone ordered a bottle from the small refrigerator. *Where's your mother?* was always the second question, though Stan had to know where she was—in her studio, door closed, as always.

But now, watching Stan work the cigar so diligently, George could only smile. Stan swept him a sideways glance but said nothing.

"How do you like it here, then?" George asked.

"Not bad, actually. Those kids of yours are all right."

"Yeah, that'll be Viji's influence."

"You reckon so?"

"I would say most definitely so."

The sheen of summer had worn away, and the moon cast its pallor more completely, drawing the deck chairs into shadows, yielding to the dance and fade of smoke trails. It was only October, but already the cold had brought the hearths back to life. Woodsmoke, the smell of idle evenings, wafted in from a neighbor's yard.

"What do you think of this earring, then?" Stan asked, assuming, as always, that George knew what he was talking about.

"What earring?"

"It looked familiar to me, is all. And I'm not one to remember earrings."

"What earring?"

"The kids have this box, don't they? Buried over yonder by the side there; they showed it me a few days ago."

A cigar flake caught in George's throat and made him cough. "And what's in it?"

"They haven't shown you, then?" Stan snickered.

"Well, there's not much to it, really. Some old rubbish, like what you'd imagine a kid wanting to keep, and then this earring. The girl kept it there. She was dead serious about it and all. You'd think if anyone found it she'd have a catastrophe on her hands."

George's heart began to drill against its case, a rabbit's thump of warning. "What does it look like?"

"Blue, and like a diamond. Small."

"Well, I don't know, Dad, you can't tell half the time where kids come across these things."

"But I'd swear on your mother's grave that I've seen it before. And you know me, I'm not one to think about earrings and the like, not to mention remembering it this long. I forget about it, but then it keeps coming back. That means something, that does.

"And it wasn't your mother's, that's for sure. Too small. Not that I know much about that sort of thing, but you know what I mean. She liked those big hoop things, didn't she? The bigger, the better with her. Like a bloody fortune teller."

"Dad."

"Don't get me wrong, son. She was a cracker, the crème de la bloody crème. I just couldn't fathom her taste sometimes."

"Uh-huh." There was a long pause. George feared his father was thinking too much about the earring. "Hear anything about the football?"

"It's the color of them, you see. It was, it was…one of a kind."

This was true, George remembered. It was one of a kind.

George had insisted on sending all three of them to private school, no matter how expensive. So the triplets went to the Whitman School. "We educate the whole child," its brochure proclaimed. To promote intergenerational understanding, the school invited parents to attend and take part in classes, especially if they were experts in certain fields. Viji had studied art and home economics in college, but had little experience with French, math, biology, or Greek mythology, so she was invited to attend Avi's Holistic Movement class.

To the class Viji wore a sari, though most other mothers dressed in clinging things that looked more like bathing suits, some stretching from their shoulders to their ankles. The teacher played tapes of drums, animal sounds, and the familiar cawings of village bulbuls that Viji remembered from her uncle's house. Interpretive dance, it was called. Viji wasn't sure what they were interpreting, but she liked the idea of taking a class with her son. The sixth graders stood next to their mothers. Blond mothers brought blond children; the woman with ginger hair stood next to a thin ginger boy. Only Avi's hair stayed stubbornly singular, amber brown with a few light streaks, an ambivalent mixture of Viji's black and George's mousy blond.

"Dance!" the teacher shouted. "Close your eyes and move with your senses! Commune with your physicality!" Viji shut her eyes and forgot to watch her son. "Feel your arms! Are they heavy like rocks or limp as willows?" The thin yards of her sari brushed easily around her body as she waved her arms, letting the music move her elbows and knees. The sound flowed from her joints and limbs and into her hips. She raised her arms and felt her pelvis gyrate to the round yowls of killer whales. She thought of Elvis. The insistent clang of a metal drum jerked one buttock, then the other, and her chest twitched to the rhythm. With her eyes closed, Viji never saw how the other mothers danced. Nor could she see Avi skitter away from her to hide himself behind other bodies. "You move so well in your dress," an astonished blond mother told her. Her clavicles pushed up against her skin, her body taut as a rubber band. "I'd be a wreck if I had to dance in that!" Viji only smiled back, and tried not to look at the fabric that pulled so tightly between the woman's thighs.

She began looking forward to these classes. Even when she wasn't there, she could close her eyes and feel the spinning, round and round. In her head, behind her eyes, there were no walls to crash into or half-naked ladies or children tripping against her legs. There was only the rush of wind against her lashes, the smile that crept across her face, and the split second of panic when dizziness threatened to topple her.

"Avi, do you enjoy the dance class?" she asked during a sullen drive to school one morning. Avi shrugged.

"How come you don't come to my classes?" Kieran asked.

"They haven't asked me, chellum." She turned back to Avi. "You don't like to dance?"

"I dunno."

"Do you want to take a different elective?"

"No."

"Ceramics, maybe? I was good at art."

"No. That's okay."

Viji was glad. She was communing with her physicality.

After a few weeks, Avi asked her to stop coming. She could still remember the morning, dropping him off in the parking lot. His brother and sister had already launched themselves into the schoolyard. "I'd like you to stop coming to my classes." He said it quietly as he lowered himself out of the car. The sun shot through the window and set his profile ablaze.

"Why?" Viji asked. She cupped his elbow with her fingers and wiggled it playfully, but he yanked his arm away.

"I would just prefer it if you didn't come." He spoke like an adult, a courteous stranger, and kept his eyes on the cement lot before him.

"Are you embarrassed?" she asked. Avi didn't answer. He turned toward a shriek from the playground. "Okay. Fine."

She said it lightly, as if it didn't matter to her. She waited for him to walk away, backpack swinging from his shoulders, before she started the car's engine. Humming something tuneless, she began to pat the steering wheel to calm herself, a steady tapping that grew faster, lost its rhythm and crescendoed into an outright beating. She couldn't stop herself, no matter how she tried. At a stop sign, a cyclist slowed down to stare into her window. But she went on whacking the steering wheel, relishing the sting of it on her palm. It was only at home, in the cool cave of her garage, that she could be still. There, she halted her hands and switched off the engine. She placed the keys on the passenger seat and sat for several minutes, until she felt like going in.

Viji shut the puja room door and exhaled. In here, freedom. Out there, an old man who thought he was some kind of ladies' man; who watched *Donahue* in the mornings at full volume; who cleared his throat after each meal in great hacking coughs, as if his food had gone down his lungs; who left careless yellow drops on the toilet seat and refused to lift the lid; who ate beans for breakfast and then stank up the guest bathroom every morning between eleven and eleven-twenty a.m.; who poked with his fork at the food she made, always muttering something about heartburn, heartburn, though it certainly wasn't heartburn that made those sounds whenever the maid came over, was it?

"*Chih*! Have some respect," her mother chided. "Who taught you to talk about your elders that way?"

Viji knelt before her mother's picture, picking a crusted fleck from the corner of the frame. "You should be making him breakfast now, girl. What's wrong with you? Leaving him hungry and alone like that, looking through the cupboards like a wild animal. No wonder he eats beans. You don't make him anything else."

"He won't eat what I make him, Amma."

"Nonsense. Is that any reason to stop? Who raised you? Disgraceful." She called to Mrs. Müller, "Isn't it disgraceful, Mrs. Müller?"

Viji turned to the dour-lipped portrait of the German headmistress, of whom she was no longer afraid. "Who said this was your business?" she asked.

"You know who, my liebling," Mrs. Müller replied.

Viji started preparing for her morning prayers. She threw yesterday's damp petals in a brown paper bag that stood in the back corner of the room, and placed this morning's roses around the collection of deities. One per frame or statue, with the extras before Durga. She poured oil in the lamps, rolled wicks out of cotton, and lit them. She recited her prayers in a half whisper, her hands clasped at her forehead. "Have some respect," came her mother's voice, echoed closely by Mrs. Müller's. It was just like them to gang up on her.

Mrs. Müller had been her mother's great friend, the headmistress at St. Mary's. She'd never wanted to live in India, and she'd made no attempt to hide it. Viji attended St. Mary's for just one year, so she only had to suffer Mrs. Müller when the lady visited for tea.

Mrs. Müller was as brittle as an old coconut husk. Her voice was the crunch of dry leaves, her hair a net of cobwebs. Once when Viji came in to greet her, the woman stroked her hair and said, "She's not a very pretty child, is she?" Viji's mother sniffed, held herself in. Nobody, as far as her mother was concerned, called a child ugly, no matter how true the statement was. Even the scrawniest, most bug-eyed servant's child was a ravishing beauty; even the boy down the road with the harelip was fine. Children were princes and princesses by default, until maturity proved otherwise. But to Mrs. Müller, children were as human as anyone else.

Both women had lost their husbands—Viji's father had gone away when she was ten, and Dr. Müller had banished himself to his study, emerging only for the students that descended on the Müller home every week. Dr. Müller had the chin and shoulders of a romantic hero. His hair leapt off his forehead, as if he'd been running in the wind. Viji had seen him only once, when he came in from the car to collect his wife, but she hadn't forgotten him.

"He asks me to join in," Viji once heard Mrs. Müller complain, "o watch him, I suppose. With his hangers-on, his admirers. He does like to be admired. Funny that his admirers are all young women." Every time the coterie gathered, Dr. Müller, perhaps out of guilt, sent a female student to knock on his wife's door. "No thank you," she would sometimes say. "I'm in purdah this week." Other times she would return the knock with a knock from her side of the door, which invariably brought on another knock, followed by a lengthy exchange of fruitless knocking that continued until confusion overcame the student and she went back down.

"Be kind to her," Viji's mother would order, "she isn't a happy woman." But often Viji heard peals of raucous laughter coming from their visits, hands slapping furniture in delight, joy that rustled against her bedroom door, urging her out to see what had happened. But whenever she walked in, she found the women in quiet conversation, any sign of the earlier ruckus tucked neatly behind a sofa cushion.

There were other women, Viji learned. "I don't have your father anymore," her mother once said, "but every day I say thank you to God that I don't have a cheating scoundrel." There was always a student who lingered after these tea parties, and Mrs. Müller could hear the delicate footsteps that followed her husband's to his bedroom. "It's the hypocrisy," she once said. "Why should I have tea with them? Why should I suffer the company of that ridiculous man? Not to mention his student whores."

"Maybe," Viji's mother once suggested, "you should go back to Germany."

"Nonsense. We're married, you know, and that's that."

Viji tucked a rose into the top of Mrs. Müller's frame. Marriage was for life; this she'd learned from Mrs. Müller, not from her mother. Viji had always held this thought proudly, as a guiding principle. The downside, of course, was that marriage was for life. Inescapable. This, she guessed, was how Mrs. Müller must have felt that final day. A student had been sent that afternoon to knock on her bedroom door; when there was no answer, she'd opened it to find a woman hanging from a silk scarf tied in a noose. A note on the bedside table read, *Please tell Dr. Müller that indeed, I would rather hang myself than come down and join you for tea.*

Viji finished praying. She kissed her fingertip and pressed it to her mother's portrait. Eyes closed, she knelt and touched her forehead to the ground. Here, again, the cramping pain. She ran to the bathroom, where the urgent tingle came out as a thin, painful trickle. Daggers inside her. She shut her eyes, waited for the throbbing to cease. Downstairs, the teapot whistled. If Stan wanted tea, she would make it.

❦ ❦ ❦

"Go ahead, darling. Scream. It's good for you sometimes."

Viji screamed again. How she'd ended up by the pool house, where Kamla found her shrieking until her chest hurt, provoked by no obvious terror, was unclear. She knew only that she'd come outside to hang the laundry, wishing she'd worn a sweater to protect herself against the heavy November afternoon. The three o'clock loam had begun to settle, frosting the lawn in ashen mist, when she noticed how overgrown the bushes were at the back of the lot. It was no wonder Babygirl feared the tigers that lurked behind them. She'd surveyed her yard. The shoddy deck chairs of summer, overstaying their welcome and littered with crumbling leaves. The patches of mud that bruised the lawn. The shuffleboard court, hardly ever used, faded now with a disc and two sticks lying at skewed angles on the ground. The house was her territory. She looked after it, saw to it that towels were washed and put away, carpets vacuumed, shelves dusted, and towels stacked in the linen cupboard. She made sure that three children left each morning, bathed and fed and combed, and that three re-turned each afternoon. But the yard, with its vast plains of grass and weeds and brambles, its insect galaxies, was foreign territory.

She had her roses, dead now until May. The thought of flower corpses rotting in the soil made her faintly nau-seous. Whose responsibility were they? Night would fall before she even finished hanging the laundry. The clothes would never dry, only drip in the dark and grow colder. The asphalt sky leaned in, close and frigid, gray cement clouds pouring into her mouth, into every crevice, stopping her up and boxing her in like a grave dug into a wall and hissing *this is yours this is yours this is yours* until she screamed.

"We all do it, you know."

"You do it, then," Viji said. Kamla clenched her fists, squeezed her eyes shut, and shrieked, open-mouthed. It was such a shocking thing. Each scream was as jarring as the last. And yet how intimate.

"Again," Viji said.

Kamla screamed again. And Viji screeched. They shouted and barked, the two of them, screaming until they laughed. Sometimes the screaming scared Viji. If it boiled up from this—her life, her home, everything and everyone around her—then there was a chance it would never stop. Other times, the screaming felt like something that could be good for everyone. She wondered if the other neighborhood ladies did it, in their kitchens and pantries, surrounded by their houseplants and cookie jars. She wondered if they could hear Kamla now as she kicked at the pool house wall, shrieking and laughing and shrieking. Maybe they would join in, Gail Bauer and Marcia Fromm and Connie Pimsky with her thin lips, or that skinny one, that Attenborough lady who speed-walked every evening. That tight-buttocked walking wonder in Viji's pool house, screaming. Maybe Abby Butler would come, and Elena Feldman with her cakes. They would be the Maple Grove Screamers, the Maple Grove Domestic Banshees. The Winding Creek Wailers.

But nobody came. Only Kamla and Viji stood in the pool house, that week and the week after, screaming into the still afternoons, thinking that someone might hear them, but not caring when nobody did.

⚘ ⚘ ⚘

"Screaming, darling, is all well and good." Kamla opened Viji's closet door. "But there are other ways to address your problems."

Viji looked over Kamla's shoulder to the shirts and dresses packed in.

Kamla asked, "When was the last time you cleaned your closet?" Stacked on a shelf above the clothes were shoeboxes, empty, lids askew or missing. A pink straw hat teetered at their peak. A bundle of old pantyhose poked out of the corner. "So much wasted fabric," she sighed. "So much polyester." She poked at a pair of green trousers and pulled her hand away, as if she'd touched acid.

"Shall we make a parachute and escape?" Viji asked.

"Indeed."

Viji grabbed an armful of hangers from the closet and flung them on the bed. Kamla opened the drawers. Viji watched her gingerly pick out a pair of old panties, the ones with the torn seam that had gone gray in the wash years and years ago, the pair all women, even Kamla, kept in the depths of their dressers. Kamla flung the panties onto the bed, then scooped an armful of clothes from the next drawer and tossed them onto the rising pile. Each piece, at one time, had felt essential. Now they grew into a mountain of scrap that dimmed the room's walls, swallowed the bed, and threatened an avalanche that would suffocate them both.

Kamla asked for trash bags.

"Really?" Viji asked. "Just throw them out?"

"You weren't serious about the parachute, darling."

Viji returned with black garbage bags and they dug in. Kamla gathered an armful and flung them into the air, where they floated and fell like autumn leaves: ill-fitting trousers and horizontal-striped cardigans that had looked jaunty in the shop, skirts with uneven waistlines, and blouses stained for eternity with turmeric.

Kamla froze. "What's this?" She was blocked by the closet door. When Viji found her, she was holding up a dress. The white cotton dress from her college days, hidden away since that night, forgotten until now.

"I know, it's so old," Viji said. "I just didn't bother throwing it away."

"Darling, no," Kamla gasped. "It's lovely. This is lovely." Kamla pointed out the lace fringe, how the work was obviously done by hand, how rare such detail was these days. She pushed past Viji to the large mirror above the dresser, held the dress against her own body, pulled the waist close against her own. Her bust pressed against the top of the dress, filling it, giving it life again. Viji felt suddenly possessive. She clutched a handful of the flouncy skirt, rubbed the soft cotton between her palms.

"It *is* lovely, isn't it?" she said. "I never really appreciated it when I had it." She remembered now—the dress on George's dorm room floor, kicked halfway under his bed by hurried feet to mingle with the dust and dead flies. She pulled at it, but her friend held tight.

Kamla spoke whimsically, gazing at herself in the mirror. "Do you still want it, darling?"

"Of course I do," Viji snapped. She softened. "I do. Though I don't think it will fit me anymore. Triplets, you know." She patted the mound of belly that rose against her trousers. Still, when she imagined how her friends and cousins back home would have bloated once they'd married and had children, she knew she was slim in comparison.

From behind, Kamla wrapped her arms around Viji and held the dress to Viji's shoulders. Viji pulled the fabric against her waist, and remembered. There was so much to remember. Even the smell, unchanged after years in a cedar-lined closet, brought back more buried visions than Viji could process. She grew breathless. She wanted to be alone with the dress, to crush it against her face and stare into the oracle of its faded folds. She glowered at Kamla's hand, still clutching at her dress. She wanted Kamla out.

But Kamla hugged her instead, gently, from behind. "It will fit, I'm sure of it. Wear it now, go on."

Viji stepped away. In the mirror, Kamla met her gaze intently, as if she understood. "All right, when you're ready, darling." She released the dress to Viji's grasp. "Shall we finish with these drawers?"

That night at dinner, the triplets pushed their plates away, even Kieran. Viji couldn't blame them. She'd cooked with little interest and could only bring herself to nibble at the cut of roast chicken that tilted drily onto the mound of mashed potatoes, lethargic and yellow, beside the green beans. George had asked for this.

"Go on, Viji," he'd said that afternoon, kneading the sore crevice between her shoulders. She liked it when he did this; it may even have saved him from explaining his request. "How about a good old-fashioned Sunday roast? Hey? Yorkshire puddings not required." He'd wrapped his arms around her, and she'd fallen back into him; it was a luxury not to hold her own weight. Viji did not make Sunday roasts—it had never been asked of her; it had never occurred to her to cook the equivalent of a Thanksgiving dinner just because it happened to be Sunday.

Viji took George's challenge, and raised him. "I'll do it if you help me."

"Deal." George did the shopping, dodging the Maple Grove ladies who populated Bel Air market on Sunday afternoons, picking over the produce aisles and gossiping over cold cuts. He bought a whole raw chicken. At home, he plopped it proudly on the counter and unwrapped it. It was unctuous, yellow, and very still.

"There you go," George said. "Ready and waiting."

"What do I do?"

"What do you mean, what do you do? It's just like a Thanksgiving turkey."

Viji always made turkey curry for Thanksgiving. The children liked it, and there was little chance of her poisoning anyone. She crouched down to the level of the turkey's hole and jabbed her finger inside it. Out came something like a pinto bean.

"It still has its kidneys," she announced.

"Those are giblets; you use them to make gravy."

Gravy. When had she ever made gravy? Gravy came in green packets with yellow writing. She sighed, turning from the chicken to her husband, who looked slightly worried now. He refrained, for the moment, from mentioning the Swede mash and brussels sprouts.

"George," she said, "this is not how I make gravy." She opened the drawer below the stove and pulled out a green packet. "*This* is how I make gravy." She could have been in an instant-gravy ad, for all her confidence. She picked up the chicken kidney. "This, I suppose, is how *you* make gravy. However, you have always eaten the gravy from the packet. So tell me," she peered into him, "why does it matter so much that I make it from these internal organs? Which brings another question to my mind—why a roast dinner tonight, of all nights?"

George shrugged. He fingered the counter's edge. "I just thought it might be nice, you know, for Dad."

It didn't occur to Viji to be annoyed by this. Her resentment would collect slowly. It would build into a sedimentary wall of minute, almost untraceable offenses.

"Okay, then. I will do my best."

The result was this, a meal that could only be apologized for. Meat that called for intrepid feats of chewing. Gravy, made by George in the end, tasting more of chicken kidneys than he'd hoped. Mashed potatoes that served their function, which was limited. Carrots and broccoli made by Viji that, fortunately, had come off well, but only underscored the chicken's shortcomings. Stan took a last swig of wine to wash down his last bite of chicken and sat chewing, his dentures clacking, for several minutes. When he finished, he asked, "What's for pudding, then?" Ice cream and watermelon, mercifully. There had been no attempt at spotted dick.

After dinner Viji returned to the bedroom. She wanted to show George the dress, to see if he remembered it. She neared the kitchen but stopped at Stan's voice.

"I suppose so," it said. "Can't go far wrong with a Sunday roast either way, can you?" (HOW TO BAKE YORK-SHIRE PUDDINGS HOW TO KEEP A CHICKEN MOIST HOW TO MAKE A PROPER GRAVY HOW TO CARVE A ROAST)

"I'm glad you liked it, Dad."

"You know who *could* do a Sunday dinner, though?"

"Yeah."

"Do you remember?"

"Yeah, I remember."

"If I didn't think it'd get me in trouble, I'd go so far as to say that her roasts were better than your mother's."

Viji stood outside the kitchen and listened.

"Mum's were pretty good," George said softly. She could hear that he was smiling. "But you know? You may be right. Victoria's may have been better."

"You're damn right they were." The two men laughed. Stan continued. "She was some woman, wasn't she? What happened to you two?"

"Well, you know."

"I don't."

"Course you do. I met Viji, Dad." Viji leaned against the wall, listening closely. George's tone had taken on a lilt that she vaguely recognized, the accent he'd still had when she met him.

"Is that all?"

She pressed her ear to the wall and held her breath.

"What do you mean, is that all?" George asked. Viji exhaled.

"Nothing, nothing at all. Forget I spoke." A heavy pause, then, "It's just that…I don't want to be awkward, you see, son. It's just that I would hate to see you plodding along in life, doing as you're told."

George sat back. This was the most his father had said to him about anything, ever. Why now? Three children, twelve years. Why not the first time he'd brought Viji home? His mother had been thrilled, and George had taken this as confirmation that he'd made the right decision.

"Do you have a problem with Viji, Dad?"

There was a long silence. Viji placed a hand over the ache in her chest.

"No. She's a good wife. The thing is, are you happy, George? I was happy with your mother. As different as we were, I was happier than I knew. I hope, in the end, that you'll be able to say the same."

Viji screwed the white dress into a ball and hurried up the stairs, shutting the puja room door behind her. She hated that man for trying to poison her husband's mind. He must have been crazy to like that classless, feces-gifting Victoria. He'd probably found her wedding present funny. She hated George by extension and wished passionately that her own parents were still alive, so that she could exact some kind of revenge.

She wished they were alive, period. Beneath Amma's portrait, she kept a rock. It was about the size of an egg, a luscious cream color with streaks of copper. The rock, because she had no photo, was her father. In some ways it was better than a photo, this rock, for she could cup it in her hands and hold it to her chest. She could wrap her fingers around his absence and feel its cool weight.

🌱🌱🌱

A dream passed through the house that night like a specter, morphing as it wound its way past puffed-up pillows, blowing smoke into the ears of those who slept. It wrapped itself around Babygirl's bedpost and whispered flocks of black-shadowed birds that flew against her, all beating wings, before they vanished. For Avi and Kieran, who often dreamed alike but didn't know it, there was a tower of cake, frosted chocolate and teetering, bending at its center, threatening to bury them both in sweet crumbled frosting. For Stan there was Marla, Marla in his taxi with wide red laughing lips, arms squeezed across her chest, body squeezed between two others, black eyes that caught his in the rearview mirror and held them there. Down the hall, the dream slipped into George and buried him in a field of flowers, brightly colored, too bright, rotting stamens, hairy anthers, obscene and sweaty marigolds, rhododendrons, and great bushy things that opened and closed their petals, opened and closed their petals, chanted the sibilant *it's hot it's hot it's hot it's hot.*

Beside him, Viji lay coated in fever, dreamless. She opened her eyes. Sleepless. Earlier, from the heavy warm black, she'd dreamed of a baggy trench coat lined with knives, which she put on and couldn't take off—searing, febrile blades that she knew were real because she knew she wasn't sleeping. Knives grew and retracted, grew and retracted, glinting in the starry sky and screeching like a fork on a china plate, no matter how she thrashed to get away. She'd woken up whimpering.

Beside her, George was still asleep, his lips working around something in a dream. She thought of going to the pool house for a scream. But then she wouldn't be alone.

This thing growing inside her, the collected bundle of her life with George, had begun to go limp, as if malnourished, as if it hadn't been fed in weeks. She felt a mother's panic and pulled herself out of bed.

There was a new chill in the puja room when she entered. It was the only place she could go. The cool brought coarse fingers to her skin, raised goose bumps as it passed. Her dress lay sprawled in the corner where she'd left it that night. She picked it up, dabbed at her forehead. Between her eyes, a stinging ache. She was glad for the dark. Around her the walls perspired, patches of grime littered the pure blue. A sheen of dust covered the hanging portraits, and her statues gazed drearily from their shelves. Viji set to work. She would use her dress. No, she would use the dish towel that lay in a shamed heap in the corner. Piece by piece, she polished the dust from the brass bowls, from the miniature bell she dingled every morning to begin her prayer, and from the peacock-shaped vermillion holder, which sat covered in fine red powder. With her fingernail she picked the black soot from the oil lamps and the crust from the edges of the frames. The carpet, littered with dried rose petals, soon wasn't. She found the hammer and started fixing the crooked nails behind the picture frames.

"There's a good girl," her mother cooed.

"I was wondering where you've been."

"I was on leave, had to take a break from this slum."

"Ha ha, very funny."

"Nothing funny about a bad housewife, my girl."

"So you've been talking to Stan?"

"Stan, Stan, what is this Stan? Who calls their husband's father by his first name?" Her mother clicked her tongue. "Americanized," she muttered.

Viji gave her mother's nail a sound whack.

"Krish-*na*, don't get angry with *me*. I did nothing."

"Easy to be dead, isn't it?" Viji whacked another nail in.

"Well?"

"Well *what*?" Viji cried.

"You'll wake everyone up, crazy. What do you want me to say?"

Viji let the hammer drop to the carpet. She rubbed her eyes and said nothing.

"I know," her mother said. "He's not your father. Things would be different with your father."

"It's true. He would stand up for me."

"Of course he would, kanna. There would be a duel to the death for your honor."

"That's not what I mean."

"It doesn't matter what you mean or what you don't mean—there is no father for you. Only me. Simple me. Simple fat me. Simple fat dead me—"

"All right." Her mother would whip herself into a frenzy if given the chance.

"You think he's some kind of great man, don't you? *My father the magistrate.* A real hero, a real Pandava prince."

"I never said that."

"I'll tell you one thing—he would have gambled you away if he could. Pandava prince, all right. If he didn't gamble you, he would have gambled me or your sister—"

"*Okay.*"

They sat silently for the rest of the hour. The pain had started, coursing now through the tangled circuits of her thighs. She ignored it.

"It's not so terrible, this life of yours."

Viji whispered a small prayer, snuffed the oil lamps, and went to bed.

✤✤✤

This, then, was beauty. Viji looked placidly into the bedroom mirror. Behind her, Kamla beamed. It made sense now. Beauty didn't lie in the eye of the beholder. Beauty lay solely in those women who believed that they were right. Just right.

Kamla had sheared off at least seven inches of Viji's hair, which lay like a black gash on the bedroom's pale carpet. What was left of it hung now just below her shoulders and curled inward at the bottom. Eyebrows, waxed. Mustache, waxed so completely that her lip looked comically bald. Down there, waxed, though not completely, of course—she hadn't seen the need. Then came eyeliner, mascara, lipstick. Not the bright pink lipsticks that came free as samples from cosmetics counters. On Viji's lips, Kamla's chocolate brown turned burgundy.

"There," Kamla said. "That's better. Definitely better."

But for Viji, something was not quite right. She'd almost asked Kamla about it on their drive to the salon. Then, lying on the treatment table, she'd almost asked the beautician. Her name was Lisa, with hair so blond it was almost white. She'd felt close to the woman, who shifted her limbs gently before ripping the wax away. One bare leg bent to the side, panty seam pulled in to reveal her bikini line, hot wax creeping into the dark spaces, she'd felt she could speak to Lisa.

"This is my first time," Viji said.

"No way, really?" Lisa paused. "Don't worry, honey, I'll be gentle." Viji grabbed the side of the table and gasped at the first rip of the wax strip. Lisa worked quietly for a moment. "That would explain the bush, though. No offense."

"Thank you."

"So what made you take the plunge?"

"My friend made me."

"Well, that's a pretty good friend. You want a special shape, honey? I could do a heart?"

"No, that's all right."

In the end, she hadn't asked Lisa, though it would have been so simple and anonymous. Lisa would have known about these things, privy to confessions from woman after woman, day after day. She would have answered frankly. Moreover, Viji was quite certain (from the moment that first strip of wax zipped down her crotch) that she would never see Lisa again.

But now it was too late.

"What's the matter, darling?" Kamla asked. Her face dropped beside Viji's in the mirror.

"Nothing's wrong."

"You don't like the makeup?"

"No! I like it very much. I do."

"Tell me."

Viji gripped the sides of her seat and told her. The cramps, the burning, how it all disappeared when she tried to pee. How they began, inevitably, in the puja room.

"They must be menstrual."

"No, they can't be—they happen during the whole month."

"It must be a yeast infection."

"It isn't."

"How do you know?"

"I just know. It always—it always seems to begin just when I think about it."

"What do you mean?"

"Well, it's as if, if I don't think about the pain, it isn't there."

"And if you do think about it?"

"Then it's everywhere."

"Everywhere?"

"It starts—down there—and then I can feel it, I can *really* feel it, in my belly and my throat and my chest and my stomach—"

And in my heart. Viji couldn't bring herself to say it. She didn't want to alarm Kamla or make the problem bigger than it was. It was pain *of* her heart, not *in* her heart. But that didn't make sense, either.

Kamla took her to a woman doctor, a small, pale lady with the teeth of a mouse, who showed Viji into a room with pink walls. On one side hung a painting of playful tiger cubs, and on the other, a diagram of a cervix. A cork board was crammed with photos of newborn babies. Viji's knees poked bald from the paper smock; her bare feet rested in stirrups. "When do the pains usually start?" the doctor asked.

Viji didn't want to explain about the puja room, so she said simply, "Not until I think about them."

"Come again?"

"They start, usually, when I think about them, and then it's hard to make them go away."

"Mm-hmm. Then I suggest that you don't think about them." The doctor asked Viji probing questions as she gelled her gloves and slid her fingers inside. She used the term "STD" and even implied that George had been unfaithful. She finished swabbing and asked Viji to pee in a cup, then said she would phone with the results.

"No," Viji said, "please don't." The doctor tilted her head. "Don't call my house, I mean." The doctor pushed her glasses up her nose.

"So you'd prefer to call us?"

"Yes, please."

"I'll make a note of it."

"Thank you."

"There, darling," Kamla said in the waiting room, "was that so terrible?"

"No more than I expected."

⚘⚘⚘

Two women. One seated, fresh and expectant. One standing, proud of her work, beaming. George gazed at Viji, who fingered the edge of her seat and looked down shyly from his eyes. The after of the before that he'd married. He looked over Viji to Kamla, caught in a film of hazy evening sunlight, and smiled at her. She smiled back, incandescent, and he had to look away. That evening, Stan noticed the difference too. The old man whistled when Viji entered the kitchen, rubbed his eyes, and looked her up and down. "Ah-*oo*-ga! *Oo*-ga-*oo*-ga!"

"Dad, please," George intervened. But later, when they were alone, George pawed the ends of her hair, traced his finger along her eyebrow, and touched her lips as if they were new. "It's like," he whispered, as his lips dandled the curve of her neck, "it's like you're another woman."

Indeed. Afterward, she slipped her nightgown on and walked down the hall. In Babygirl's room, the triplets were asleep. She laid extra comforters over the boys' sleeping bags because the night was chillier than usual. It was time to buy extra beds. Imagine a mother who made her children use sleeping bags, like vagabonds or squatters. She took a shower and dried herself. Even days later, it would surprise her to feel the tidy ends of hair curling in just below her shoulders, ducking smugly from the phantom mane that had been chopped and thrown away and mingled now with last week's newspapers.

Two days later, Viji phoned the doctor for her test results.

"Are the symptoms persisting?"

"No," she lied.

"Well, there's nothing wrong with you." But there was. In the background she heard an instrumental version of that Michael Jackson song. The doctor waited. Viji pressed the hang-up button on the receiver and held it there. Never mind. She had lived with this so far, and she would live with it until it left.

His mom had had what they called a makeover, which to Avi suggested a do-over, as if she hadn't been done quite right the first time. It happened in tennis, when the served ball hit the net but still landed in the half-court box. In any case, they were going to dinner, and Babygirl said it was to celebrate Viji's makeover, her new look. Kamla Aunty came to the door with Anisha, and they drove in two cars to the restaurant.

Kieran raced him through the parking lot to the great red-and-white-striped awning, which made Avi think of a candy store and an ambulance and a carnival all rolled into one. He beat Kieran easily and was the first to open the building's heavy door, the first to step into the warm and wonderful cloud of onion rings, red meat, sweet cherries. There was a traffic light in the middle of the restaurant, and banners for sports teams hanging at nutty angles on the wall. Here the waiters wore red vests pinned all over with funny buttons, which Avi thought was a great thing to do. They wore straw hats, sang "Happy Birthday"—*loud*— to whomever was having a birthday, and refilled sodas for free as fast as he could drink them.

The triplets got to order mozzarella sticks, which were sticks of fried cheese and, in Avi's opinion, as brilliant an idea as the vests with the buttons. He and Kieran had a burping contest after the sodas came. Babygirl snarled at them at first, until Anisha joined in. The grownups didn't seem to notice; they were too busy talking and talking and talking, as always. The triplets and Anisha sucked urgently on their straws and traded gas, with little thought of the food that lay waiting. Avi thought he was the clear winner until Kieran, who'd been quiet for several minutes, came out with a momentous *braap* that shook the walls of the restaurant.

"*Kieran*," Viji hissed. She stared openly at him. At a table nearby, a group of teenagers gazed over for a moment, then broke into snorting laughter.

"Avi started it."

Viji said nothing, but gave Kieran an empty sort of look that Avi had never seen before. Viji went back to cutting her chicken breast, slowly, as if she were thinking about something else.

"Sorry," Avi mumbled. He turned to Stan, who was just then stuffing into his mouth the largest chunk of meat Avi had ever seen a human attempt to chew. He'd seen a show about lions once, and remembered the way they ripped huge swaths of flesh from the side of a gazelle. Stan managed to wrap his cheeks around the meat, and in a few swift chews it was gone. His mother sat staring at Stan, her fork in midair. She often told the triplets not to stare. Avi picked up an entire mozzarella stick and crammed it into his mouth. He picked up another, found space between his cheek and gums, and coaxed it in with his finger. But the cheese was piping hot. It began to burn his mouth and he couldn't, try as he might, chew fast enough to make the food swallowable. Something made him gag and he had to release it all, half-chewed into an ecru paste, lumping lazily onto his plate. He forced himself to peek across to his mother and, again, was unable to explain the look he found there.

To Avi's relief, her gaze moved quickly to Kamla, who was slicing off a piece of her steak and placing it on George's plate. Her eyes were hard and her brow furrowed, as if it hurt to think. But she said nothing.

And then Babygirl: "Mom. *Mom.*"

Viji seemed to wake up. "Yes?"

"You've got lipstick on your teeth." Next to her, Anisha Mehta snickered into her shoulder.

"What?"

"You have *lipstick* on your *teeth.*"

"Oh." Viji licked her teeth once, then again. "There."

Babygirl covered her face in her palms. "It's *still there.*" She shook her head.

"Uh." This time Viji lowered her head and scraped her finger over her teeth. The girls leaned into each other and giggled. Something about this was not right. First of all, Avi had seen Babygirl do the same thing, only with toothpaste, when she couldn't find her toothbrush. And secondly, he didn't see why they had to laugh. He looked to his father, who had noticed by now.

"Just a little smudge," George chuckled. "You'll have to give her lessons, Kamla."

"Hang in there, chuck." Grandad Stan winked at Viji. "You'll get the hang of it soon enough."

Kamla smiled sadly at Viji and didn't respond to George. The smile on his mother's face was one Avi had never seen before. It was a lips-curled-in smile, and she didn't look up at anyone, but seemed to focus on smoothing down her skirt.

Behind Viji, at the table full of teenagers, a birthday broke out. A flock of waiters jogged to their table and began clapping in the air. There were a lot of them, and they crowded around Viji's chair, their behinds like so many cushions around her head. She did not look like she was having fun, not like the teenage girl whose birthday it was, not like someone who'd been given a nice haircut and a chance for a do-over.

Grandad Stan joined in the singing. And soon the rest of the table did, too, George clapping and a little embarrassed, Kieran kneeling on his chair with his fork in the air, everyone singing but Viji. Stan's voice grew louder and louder, until he was outsinging the waiters, banging his fist down with every word. *Happy*—bang—*birthday*—bang—*dear Eshhicaaa*—bang bang bang…. Grandad Stan was enjoying himself.

Viji was not. It was at this point that she started to rub away her makeup—at least, that was how it looked to Avi. With her fingertips she rubbed at the black lines below her eyes. Her cheeks flamed pink and she tried to rub this away, too. She pawed at her face and looked at the table, brushing at her cheeks and then her chin and her nose. George's clapping petered to a halt. Avi watched him swallow hard, then place a hand on Viji's arm. A runaway tear sprang down her cheek. She was absolutely silent. And within seconds, everyone at the table was silent, all except for Stan, who carried on with the especially long birthday song, clapping in the air now, like the waiters.

Once, when Avi was in fourth grade, his reading teacher had started bawling in the middle of class—real sobs, loud and jagged. She'd run from the room immediately, her shoes clip-clopping down the school corridor, her cries audible until she reached the bathroom. After five minutes, she came back and picked up her piece of chalk, and it was as if she hadn't been crying at all.

But Avi's mother didn't run from the table. She sat where she was, fenced in by the buttocks of waiters, wiping wordlessly at her cheeks. He looked to Kieran, who stopped singing and sat back down. He looked at Babygirl, who toyed with her fork and stared into her lap. The seconds passed slowly and erratically, like drips from a leaky tap.

"Looks like it's someone's birthday," George said, finally. "That's nice, isn't it?" He cleared his throat. Nobody responded. Only Viji tried to smile, that alien, curling smile that took away her lips. In the din of the restaurant, their table alone floated in silence. It was a thick silence that filled Avi's mouth and nose. It reached down into him and fished around with its imbecile hands.

He pushed his plate away and felt sick. If he could throw up, really vomit, this might bring her back, she might scold him or clean him up and become his normal mom again. He pushed down hard on his stomach, but nothing came. So he sat and watched with the rest of them, hoping, more feverishly than he'd ever hoped for anything, that the tears would simply stop. Behind Viji, the waiters shouted something, and threw their fists in the air, and then were gone, scattered back to their stations, refilling drinks and taking orders, their buttons gleaming in the light of the ceiling lamps.

Clichéd to the point of nausea, George thought. Lecherous professor, rakish young academic with flexible office hours, a sofa by his bookcase, and a lock on the door. Evening seminars for his most promising students, extra supervision in the name of research. *Wine, splendid.* Buttons undone, glasses off, massaging tired eyes. *It's getting late, but.* Tired shoulders. *If you have any other ideas you'd like to discuss.*

His university office. Before him sat a wood sprite of a girl, black hair, Asiatic eyes, and a jawline that could slice butter. A muse. Amuse. Her last name was something hyphenated and Italian. She sat cross-legged on his office chair, arms wound around the back of it, chest thrust forward. This was her modus, then—the feet-on-the-table approach. Irreverent and sexy, plan C from the teen magazine. She'd been arguing the drawbacks of sculptural uniformity, but George was fuzzy on the details, distracted by the triangle of white that peeked out from the tightly pulled fabric of her skirt. She had a large head, as did a number of his female students. It must have been a specific birthing method in the late sixties that produced such croquet mallets. He wondered if it affected their posture, caused headaches or neck aches, or if their muscles

adjusted as they grew. Surely fellatio was a brutal physical ordeal for such girls.

How many of his colleagues would take advantage of
the situation? It was almost an unwritten obligation, like
chairing a student group. How many men in general?
Probably all, at least once. More, if they were Stan. Like so
many sons, George saw his father and wanted to be different. He used to hear the ladies behind the post office
counter. *She seems all right with it, actually. It's an arty
thing, isn't it, to be all right with that sort of thing. Takes all
kinds.* He used to smell the perfume in his father's cab, too
pungent to be just a passenger's, heavy with a significance
that went beyond a lift and a fare. *She's an artist, you know.
Different strokes and all that.* Wild cackles when they discovered the pun.

But she did mind, George knew she did. He saw it
where her head met her neck, in the tilt of her long, sad
hair as she waited up for Stan, reading at the kitchen table,
sketching her next sculpture. If only he could have made
a sculpture of her.

The nymphet nattered on, smiling now at the sheer
wickedness of her latest theory. George was in a funk. He
wasn't going to listen. Like a VCR on search, he watched
himself in backward hyperspeed. Backing out the office
door, ass-first into the car, in reverse through town, past
traffic that didn't seem to mind, spitting out his breakfast,
getting back in bed, a night of fluttering eyelids, brushing
the food back into his molars, down the hall to the kitchen
and back to the table where his father sat waiting. *George,
happy you are, is thing The.* Let Stan ask again. This time he'd
have an answer. He'd have a list. What I Love About My Wife.

"Anyway," she said, propping a foot, right on cue, upon his desk, bare leg gliding into open shadows. "I guess that's all I have to say. What's your research been like lately?"

George slumped back. "It's been smashing," (here he paused, forgetting her name). "Plugging along, as always," he lied. "But must needs! Time to get on with it. Thanks for coming in," (*Andrea!*) "Andrea." He stood and she stood. Slow turn, a gaze back over her shoulder, heavy lids. He watched her until she was halfway down the hall, then closed the door and turned the lock.

It might have been the weather, the rain stammering against his office window. He watched the empty glistening street outside, its only companion a rusty Honda. Rusty cars. He never saw rusty cars in Sacramento; it never snowed enough. It never snowed. The car must have come from the East. Maybe from New York or Connecticut. He imagined this automobile setting off from a brick row house in Brooklyn, driving across the plains, the salt flats, the low rumbling ranges, to end up here, in Sacramento. He watched the rain some more, and it hit him that his life would never, ever be anything like a Woody Allen film. No chance encounters on a busy sidewalk, impromptu cups of coffee, or wandering in dusky, cramped bookstores. He would never have dinner in a cluttered loft apartment, or say *I read a poem of you and thought of his last week.* He would never have a chance or a reason to say anything like it. Outside, the streets of Sacramento stretched wide and barren, the sidewalks pristine. He welled up with longing, the sort of heartache that autumn often stirred in him.

The door opened and Amaré walked in. She looked him up and down, as she always did, and sniffed. "Your wife called," she said. The hand on the hip made it known that she did not intend to function as an answering service.

"You could have put her straight through?" George ventured, regretting the words even as he spoke them.

"Mm-hmm," she said, "I could have, except that you were in a meeting with that student." She flicked her head toward the door, making it obvious enough how she felt about such meetings.

It was a Friday. Fridays meant television for the children, and sometimes pizza. There wasn't much to do on a Friday in Sacramento, aside from a movie or a trip to a restaurant to eat basket after basket of free bread until everyone was too full for the main meal. As soon as George got home, he retreated to his study.

ᘺᘺᘺ

At four that afternoon, the doorbell rang. Nobody answered it, though he heard footsteps and voices all over the house. The bell rang again. He growled, words even he couldn't decipher, and got up from his armchair.

It was the Mehta girl.

"Hi there," he said.

"Hi."

"Where's your mum?"

"I walked over."

"It's a little dark out there, isn't it?"

She shrugged. "Can I see Babygirl, please?"

Upstairs, Anisha sifted through Babygirl's stack of

jelly bracelets. She tied them into a chain as long as the bed. "Jelly bracelets are out," she announced.

"What do you mean?"

"I mean no one likes them anymore."

"I like them."

"I don't."

"Then why are you playing with them?"

Expertly, Anisha rolled her eyes. "That's not the point."

Babygirl picked up her chain of purple bracelets and began to undo them. "So what do you want to do, then?"

"Are your brothers home?"

"Yeah. They're just doing Legos or something. I don't know what they're doing."

"Oh." Anisha perked up and stood. "Want to go for a walk?"

Babygirl didn't see the point of going for a walk. She wanted to stay home and draw. She hadn't invited Anisha over, though clearly someone had. Probably her mother. "We can draw pictures if you want." She knew this made her sound like a child, but it was what she wanted to do.

"Think your dad would drive us to the mall?"

"Um…no."

The girls sat and looked at each other for a long time. Babygirl willed Anisha to leave. "I have to stay here tonight," Anisha said, as if she'd overheard. "I don't really have a choice."

"Oh. That's okay. I'm not allowed to share my towel, though."

"Oh." Anisha cast a long glance sideways.

"But we have more towels."

"Okay."

"How come you have to stay over?"

Anisha shrugged. "My mom's having dinner. Or something."

"Oh."

"She was, like, making this big dinner. And she cleaned the whole house all by herself."

"Maybe she's having a party," Babygirl said.

"Some party." Her eyes flickered then, and a smile climbed up her face. "I guess your parents weren't invited."

"So? They probably didn't want to go." Clutched in Babygirl's palm, the stack of purple rubber rings grew moist. She stared at the wall and felt bad. She felt bad that her parents weren't invited to Kamla Aunty's great party, that jelly bracelets were no longer desired, and that she'd have to spend the rest of the day and night with Anisha.

"What's the matter?"

She shrugged, and silently cursed the tear that was collecting in her lower lid.

"Don't feel bad," Anisha said. She moved to the bed, sat next to Babygirl, and fingered the stack of bracelets in Babygirl's hand. "I think—I think it was a really small party," she said quietly. "I think it was only for two people."

"Oh. Okay." The tears retreated and leaked into Babygirl's nose. She sniffed them back in, storing them away for some other time.

❧ ❧ ❧

Then it was Saturday. Saturdays meant waking up very early to watch cartoons at a very high volume. If there was a sleepover, Saturdays meant pancakes. Which meant that

George was making breakfast at seven in the morning, because George, as a rule, was the maker of pancakes.

"Could I have chocolate chips in mine, please?" Anisha asked.

"We don't have chocolate chips."

"My mom does them with chocolate chips."

"We don't have chocolate chips."

"Oh. What do you have?"

"We have syrup," he said. She cocked her head, not impressed. "And we have butter."

Avi perked up. "Hey, remember the time Kieran sneezed on his pancake and this big fat string of snot was hanging out of his nose and mixed in with his butter?"

The table exploded in laughter and George grimaced. His children were disgusting. He wondered how they could eat around themselves. There had been a time, when he was young, when butter was a delicacy. It was kept in a butter dish, and to him it tasted as sweet as any chocolate chip.

The kitchen sounded like a monkey cage as each child yelled over the next, clanging on their plates for attention, talking with their mouths full of masticated pancake. He had given them platefuls of syrup-drenched carbohydrates with large glasses of sugary orange juice. Their voices rose, booming through the room and against the cavernous walls of his aching head.

And then silence fell, broken only by the tinging of Viji's prayer bell, far away but unmistakable.

"What's that?" Anisha asked. The triplets looked at each other.

"What's what?" Kieran said. He shot a sly glance at George.

"The ringing sound?"

"I don't hear a ringing sound."

"It must be the neighbors or something," Babygirl said.

"Yeah, I think it's definitely neighbors," added Avi.

"No, it's here inside the house. What is it?" Anisha began to squirm in her seat. Her brows rose with growing anxiety. She turned to George. "What is it?"

"Hmm? Oh! Nothing. Just my wife."

"What's she doing?"

"Just…" He looked at his children, their pleading eyes. "…testing the smoke alarms."

"Oh." Anisha Mehta considered this. "Do we have to do a fire drill?"

"No, no fire drill."

"Oh." She jabbed at her pancakes. There, done, a conspiracy concocted without words. If they were embarrassed by Viji, they hadn't admitted it before. George flipped a pancake. Inside, a small, runny bit of him sank.

And then, spurred on by who-knew-what, Babygirl spoke up. "But really it's my mom praying." The boys stopped midchew to look at her. "Doesn't your mom pray?"

Anisha shrugged. "She doesn't make noises like that."

"How come?"

"What do you mean?"

"Doesn't she ring the bell?"

"I guess not."

"Oh." Babygirl stared openly at her friend. Anisha was obviously like her. She was brown, after all, browner than the triplets and with black hair. But neither Anisha nor Kamla Mehta were like any of the Indians she'd seen before: the man at the gas station who tried to speak to Viji in Hindi, or the lady with the hair down to her knees who ran the Baskin-Robbins, or the very very dark man at the park who slammed his tennis racket to the ground and yelled, *LIVING SHIT!*

Kamla Aunty put chocolate chips in her pancakes. And she let Anisha shave her legs, and Babygirl was sure, *sure,* that Anisha was allowed to wear lipstick. Babygirl believed she would never be allowed to wear lipstick. Kamla Aunty wore high heels and had red and blue and green cereal bowls. And she'd *sent her husband packing,* or so Babygirl had heard her tell Viji. And, most certainly, she didn't pray with a bell.

CHAPTER FOURTEEN

This was the night that would change things.

A white cotton dress, packed away for twelve years, developed brown lines along its creases. She was half-sorry that they vanished in the wash. Slowly, she ironed the dress, smoothing away any traces of the past, careful not to burn any new lines in. The dress was a relic of a time before things were so very certain. Warm, creaseless, supple as age, willowy as chance. She wore it over a slip, brushed her hair, and waited for the doorbell.

Oblivious to what would set this Thanksgiving apart from all others, aside from the fact that the children had made hats, Viji tipped a colander of cauliflower into a pot of boiling water. Cauliflower was acceptable at Thanksgiving, she assumed. They must have had cauliflower in Vermont or Massachusetts or wherever that first one was. Viji had never been to the East. She held a can over a serving dish and waited for the pull of gravity to coax the purple cylinder from its home. It plopped down. She sliced along the depressions left by the can. Cranberry sauce.

It was hard to say what, precisely, set off the events that would become that night. It might have been the cranberry sauce. It might have been the pilgrim and Indian headwear the triplets had made at school, or the

record heat, eighty-one degrees on the third Thursday of
November. It might have been the effect of the record heat
on the gravy from the green packet or the mashed potatoes from the box of powder. It was more likely the four
brimming glasses of wine that Stan sailed through, or his
Guatemalan girlfriend sucking politely at her fork, or the
doorbell, an eight-note melody, its fifth note missing, a
chime pulled off by Avi and never reattached, that now
coaxed Viji from the kitchen.

Around the table: Stan and Lupe, resplendent in his-
and-hers tracksuits (an early Christmas gift), the triplets,
each wearing a headband with a feather poking from it.
"We'll be Indians," Kieran said. "And obviously Dad and
Grandad are pilgrims," handing them two pyramids of
black construction paper with buckles painted across the
front. "Lupe's a pilgrim too," Avi said.

"But she's not white," Kieran argued. (From here followed a lengthy debate about the whiteness of Lupe,
whether she was more Indian or more pilgrim, made
longer by a lesson on colonial history from George. In the
end, by virtue of being Stan's girlfriend, she became a pilgrim.) Next to Kieran sat Anisha Mehta, just then scraping
her toe up the side of his shin, making him wish for a
genie that could make him disappear. Then came Kamla:
Indian, Viji: Indian.

"Mom, you get to be Squanto," Babygirl said.

"Thank you, chellum."

And finally, George, one of three pilgrims. "I'm beginning to feel surrounded."

On the table: the cauliflower, sulfurous and warm. The
cranberry sauce that spread across its plate like a vivisected

slug. The mashed potatoes, a mountain of fluff in a bowl. Kamla had picked up the box of potato powder when she came in, and made a joke about laundry detergent. George had laughed and offered Kamla a drink. Salad. Wine, nearly half gone. Bread rolls, store-bought. Stuffing, from a pre-made mix because it tasted better that way. Gravy, *au paquet vert*. Overseeing all was Lupe's bounteous bust, propped on the table, sitting attentively between her knife and fork. And finally, the turkey waited solemnly at center stage. Tom Turkey, Viji had named him after a children's cartoon she'd seen. After she'd reached up his behind for the giblets, she had felt the need to apologize. *Tom Turkey,* she whispered, *I'm sorry.*

Under the table: Nine pairs of shoes, some of which barely touched the ground. Viji's bare feet, planted firmly in the carpet. Anisha Mehta's, now returning Kieran's kick with more kicks. Kamla, short dress, shorter than Viji had ever seen her wear, crossing and uncrossing her legs. Hands. Stan's right hand on Lupe's left thigh. Fingers.

George stood and fastened onto the turkey, plunging his knife and ripping off a wing, holding it forward—*who's first?*

Knives scraped on plates, and the remains of Tom Turkey hung in threads around his bones. Like the good housewives on television, Viji had made for him a bed of lettuce, bordered by potatoes and tomatoes. She had a glass of wine and George had two. Lupe held a fat paw around hers, with red nails that hid the swishing claret. Stan had drunk four, at least, and now stood opening a third bottle. Kamla, on her second glass, raised it to Viji and smiled. Suddenly shy, Viji looked down and fiddled with the lace on her dress.

My God, George had said, when he first saw Viji in the dress. I can't believe you still have this thing. I can't believe it still fits you! Viji hadn't known if this was a compliment. But since they were alone, she let herself sidle up and press against him, body-cloth-cloth-body. She felt, not in her gut but against it, that it was indeed a compliment. She looked up at him now, across the table. He was watching her. The two sat suspended, for those seconds, in a flush of warmth. The room around them hushed. This was them—this room and everything and everyone in it. It existed purely because George had met Viji twelve years earlier. She wondered what he could be thinking.

Her hair, he was thinking, *the dip at her throat, the way she grips that wine glass by the stem, the two neat lines on either side of the bridge of her nose, earlier today when I caught her talking to the turkey, how she curls her lips in when she chews.*

A fork catapulted across the table and crashed down against the turkey platter.

"*What* the bloody hell was that for?" Stan boomed.

Kieran, head down, muttered, "*Sorry.*"

"Dad," George warned.

"*Sorry,*" Kieran said again. "It was hard to cut the meat." There had been much concerted chewing at the table that night, but the truth was that Anisha Mehta's hand had crept down Kieran's thigh and tweaked his knee, tweaked it in a way that made his elbow jerk out.

"Kieran," Viji said. "Say sorry."

"I did!"

"Will you behave, then?"

"It wasn't me, it was the meat. It's tough and hard to cut."

So, Viji thought. Her meat was tough and hard to cut. And here was her child, her light, her world, announcing the fact to everyone.

"It's true," Anisha Mehta cut in. "This stuff ain't easy to cut."

"Anisha," Kamla scolded.

"That's all right, Kamla." Viji's voice was cool. You couldn't blame a child for what she learned at home.

"I think the turkey's excellent, Mom," said Avi, whose mouth flew open with every chew.

"Thank you, Avi."

Everyone had had too much to drink besides the children, but even they glowed with the table's giddy mist. George spoke boldly, goading and teasing. Viji wasn't used to this and she despised him slightly for it. Stan winked at her twice, a flirtation she hadn't invited, and Kamla seemed to run at the mouth. Her carefully planned dinner was out of her hands now. Only Lupe was soft and womanly and proper, despite her tracksuit, despite her glass being thrice refilled, and for the first time Viji admired her. Her hair was beautifully done, pulled into a bun with silken wisps that hung by her ears. And she wore three rings, not the sort of rings you'd wear to scrub toilets. They were simple jewels, and old, the kind passed down and kept in teakwood chests, the kind Viji had left in her own home in India, locked away and gathering tarnish. Back home, in her own country, Lupe might have been a doctor's daughter, a lawyer's wife...who knew? Nobody here seemed to care about lives that lay abandoned, molted skins shed at the borders of this new land. A mother, a husband, a chest full of other jewels—what had

Lupe left behind? She'd rescued these three rings from her mother's drawer, Viji imagined, chosen in favor of others that sparkled more but meant less. Or maybe they'd been pressed into her palm by an ancient aunt, to sell as needed or to wear when she went to a show.

Lupe had the sort of grace, sitting next to Stan, that Viji had seen only in women who were wealthy and wronged. Somewhere beyond this life of Lupe's was a withering mansion, a courtyard with cracked tiling and a fountain at its center, grown swampy with disuse. Viji re-membered the time she'd seen Jacqueline Kennedy in fuzzy black and white on the neighbors' TV, sitting so still while that Monroe woman sang to her husband. That sort of composure was quite definitely beyond Viji. She would have climbed over seats, her knees knocking into statesmen's heads, her fingers reaching for the hussy's throat. She almost loved Lupe then, though she suspected the affection was only a symptom of her own drunken exaggeration.

Later, in the kitchen replenishing the bread, Viji caught a glimpse of herself in the window above the sink. A dinky feather stuck cockeyed from her head, and wires of hair strayed from the band. Her face, her new face, was a hollow, painted red on the mouth, heavy makeup on the eyes. She'd put on blush, not visible in the shallow dark reflection. George's child bride. She was a small child, with heavy makeup and a small child's dress, a child prostitute. She looked like a child prostitute.

The dining room was silent, and then she heard soft laughter. Silence then laughter meant they were talking about her.

Back to the dining room.

"Viji," Kamla said, "these vegetables are so lovely."

"Yes," Lupe chimed in for the first time that evening, "everything's so delicious."

"I made the bread rolls," Babygirl piped up.

"No you didn't, you just heated them up," Kieran said.

"Same thing."

"Is not."

"Well, the bread rolls are very good too, Babygirl," George said. People seemed happy with what they had before them. This was all Viji asked. She picked up her wine glass and took a bigger swig than she'd planned, trickling liquid down the side of her mouth. Nobody saw.

"*Victoria!*"

Everyone turned to Stan. "Victoria!" he announced again. George stared at his father. A flake of turkey meat clung to Stan's cheek. He pointed at George with an unsteady fork. "*Victoria.* That's where I last saw those earrings."

"What earrings?" someone asked.

"The blue earrings, the blue earrings in—"

"Grandad!" Babygirl squealed. "You weren't supposed to tell!"

George froze. He peeked at Viji, who looked defiantly back at him. *What is the old man talking about?* her eyes hissed. An afterthought: *And must he have meat stuck to his face?* Finally, a glance at George's wine glass: *And you'd better watch how much you drink tonight, Mister Like-Father-Like-Son.*

George looked down at his plate. *I have no idea what he's talking about,* he eyed to Viji. But his heart was hammering and the old man was opening his mouth to speak again.

"Stan, here Stan, have some water," Lupe interjected. Thank heaven for Lupe. Stan gulped at the water and helped himself to more potato mash. That night, George swore to himself, he would dig up the box in the backyard, throw the earring into the squalid depths of the garbage bin, or fling it full-armed over the neighbor's fence. Evidence destroyed.

"So what's for pudding, then?" Stan asked. Viji rose abruptly.

"I'll just get it ready. Kamla, no, sit, everyone sit." She fled to the kitchen, where the Thanksgiving preparations lay strewn across the countertop and littered the floor. It was as if someone had walked in, thrown armfuls of food into the air, and walked out. She would have to clean this. Before *pudding*, before anything, she would have to clean.

In the dining room, the party sat quietly amid the sounds of Viji—the hysterical running of the tap, water pinging off metal vessels, pots clanging. "Maybe," Kamla said coolly, "we should go around and say what we're thankful for."

"I have a better idea," George said. He crouched before a cabinet in the far corner of the dining room, and two minutes later he rose, holding a dusty bottle. A cobweb clung to its neck. "I bought this," George said, "twelve years ago. I thought I'd save it for a special occasion." He caught Kamla's eye, not meaning to, and sent her a wide smile. She, by equal accident, beamed back.

"That's sloe gin," Stan announced. "Sloe gin only keeps for ten years, eleven at most. That'll be off by now." *Bloody useless*, he thought, and added to his list: HOW TO AVOID LIVING WITH YOUR HEAD SO FAR UP YOUR ARSE THAT YOU

LET A PERFECTLY GOOD GIN GO TO WASTE.

George lost his smile. "Why don't we crack it open and give it a go?"

"What's slow gin?" Kieran asked. George poured a glassful for the adults, and a half glass for the children, then called to Viji, who was still running the kitchen tap.

"What is it?" she asked, wiping her hands on a dish towel.

"Sloe gin!" George held her glass to her. "Remember, Viji?"

She gazed at her children's half-filled glasses, then turned icily to George. "No, thank you, I don't want any now."

"Oh come on, darling, give it a go."

"I don't think the children should be drinking, George. Their brains are still developing."

"A little won't hurt, darling," Kamla chimed. "Come join."

Viji looked at the pickled faces that circled her Thanksgiving table. Lupe, wide-mouthed, the color smudged upward from her lip. Stan, the scrap of meat fallen from his face, at rest now next to his spoon. Kamla, her cheeks on fire, her eyes brown opals. Anisha Mehta, chewing on the end of her hair, her eyes half closed. Her children, looking first at her, then at their glasses, then at her, then at their glasses. And George, the man in the Lake District who could name all the hills, who had bought farmhouse cheddar and elderflower wine and given her, on the bank of that lake, a family to call her own.

She took the glass from George and sipped from it before anyone could toast. It was worth waiting for, worth the argument they'd had on the drive home, fiery and sweet. For the second time that evening, she wished she could have George to herself.

The group dispersed, Viji back to the kitchen, the children to watch the *Peanuts* special. As far as Viji knew, the rest of them could have been anywhere. She felt at peace for the first time since pulling the turkey from the oven. *Victoria,* ringing like brass from the lips of her husband's father, was now a soft and faraway memory. The dishwasher gurgled and belched a trail of steam onto the floor. She would get a new one for Christmas. Either that or a microwave. She'd seen Gail Bauer's new microwave through her kitchen window when she'd gone walking with Kamla. It was a nifty robotic ally, ready to heat at the press of a button. Viji would have one soon.

She heard a thud from the living room, a muffled laugh. Unmistakably Kamla, who seemed rather jolly that night, for no reason Viji could surmise. Surely Thanksgiving for a divorcée was a sobering occasion, which was why Viji had invited her in the first place. She stepped into the dining room. And this, Viji thought, was how the divorcée showed thanks. Kamla and George sat on the carpeted steps that led down to the split-level living room, thigh to thigh, crouched together over an encyclopedia, her face just inches from his, both their hands holding the page down, George reading in almost a whisper.

"What is it?" Viji blurted. George looked up. What, exactly, she was asking was unclear even to her.

"Sloe gin!" he announced. "We're looking it up, but it isn't in here." Kamla grinned at the page, like a schoolgirl who'd caught the giggles in class.

"I see," Viji said, and crossed the living room without a word.

She closed the bedroom door behind her and threw the dish towel on the bed. The idea was that George, sensing her disturbance, would follow. He would ask her how she was and place his arms gingerly around her shoulders, until he sensed that she wasn't going to push him away, at which point he'd pull her into a devoted embrace. A minute passed. She didn't like this feeling— jealousy and aimless anger, seeping through her like liquid bleach. Another minute passed, and another. She'd been fixed to the spot with her knees clenched, until she grabbed the dish towel from the bed and tried to rip it in half and, when it refused to tear, hurled it at the mirror.

She flung open the bedroom door. The house was still, oblivious to what boiled inside her. The plunking and tinkling of a Charlie Brown piano trailed from the television. She passed the living room, where Kamla sat with George, a stack of encyclopedias now at his side. In the puja room, she would find peace. She moved without sound, so that she would not be spoken to.

What happened then, at the top of the stairs, would never be discussed, explained, or apologized for. There was Stan, there was Lupe. They filled the puja room with red faces, excessive hips, hands on Lupe and hands on Stan. There they stood, pointing to her photographs, picking up her figurines and turning them over in their fat, oily hands. Stan held her small silver pot of vermillion, the red powder she dabbed on her forehead when she prayed. He dipped his finger in it, sniffed the powder, tasted it. They were obscene.

"Get out," Viji ordered.

They were wearing their shoes. *They were wearing their shoes.* "Get out!" she shrieked. With small hands she pushed Stan, slapped at his shoulders. "Get out get out get out!" She had never touched him before. She was producing noises that weren't words. They were nothing but words that had fallen from her lips and shattered. Stan and Lupe hurried past her, bumping her farther into the room and stumbling down the stairs. She kicked the air behind them and felt burning tears. At the foot of the stairs stood George, holding the banister and looking up. His mouth hung open.

"What in the world, Viji," was all he said.

"They can't go in there," she wept. Stan stood with George now, who stood with Kamla. Lupe was a form in the shadows. The children, four heads in the kitchen doorway, were very still. Everyone waited.

"Don't go in there," she gasped, pointing behind her to the lit room. A searing ache gripped her now, the pain from the puja room, moving up her inner passages, encircling her womb. She held her stomach in. "You mustn't—" she began. The banister slid from under her hand, the floor leapt to meet her, a rush of movement, and the room went dark.

꽃꽃꽃

Nighttime. Viji awoke. She couldn't remember the sun setting or climbing into bed, or taking off her clothes. She lay naked now between the warm sheets. The house was dark and silent, dinner put away, the children asleep, or at least in bed. There was something about physical weakness that created physical need. Even in her fragile state, lying limp and bare in bed, her ears still buzzing with her cries, Viji reached for George. It surprised him—she could tell by the way he held her forearms, nearly restraining her, before he pulled her in. "What are you doing?" he asked sleepily, as she slid open the buttons of his pajamas. But his questions ended there. They made love wordlessly, lying on their sides, facing each other, as if love were just an episode of sleep. He'd waited all evening for this, from when he first saw the ardent head of her nipple press against the cloth of the dress. He was grateful for her now.

After, Viji lay quietly with George, his arm across her chest, his other arm wrapped tightly around her waist, his leg bent over hers. He held her close, as if to keep her from seeping across the covers, off the bed and into the carpet. She was calm now, and could hear her own breath billow faintly, with only the smallest rattle.

She woke again. It was almost morning. Something was wrong. Viji lay stark and frigid.

Something had happened—not that night but another, long ago. The feeling was faint, like a vanishing headache. She still felt flashes of it, blinding white behind her eyes. She looked at George. Something was not right. She had been breathless in her sleep, pinned down, her own flimsy hand covering her eyes.

She still felt the warmth of his body from earlier that night, his bear-hands that cupped her breasts and massaged the flesh of her hips. She still felt him wet against her, his weight pushing against hers. She realized her hand was around her throat, her grip lax, as if she'd been protecting herself from something in a dream.

Beside her, a mountain range beneath the sheets, George began to snore. He shifted onto his stomach. Once, he opened his eyes and looked at her. She waited for him to say something, but he just closed his eyes and slept again. Through the window, moonlight drifted like steam and settled over the dresser. A pile of white caught Viji's eyes—her dress, folded clumsily, stained with crimson powder. When she slid out of bed, the cold electrified her skin. She picked up the dress and, still naked, walked out of the bedroom, across the house, and to the laundry room. Here she laid it in the sink and watched as water gushed into the vermillion stain, turning it bright yellow. It would stay that way forever. She switched off the tap and left the sink full of soggy cloth, forever blemished.

The bedroom clock read 4:12.

After the night's series of battles and defeats, Viji fell into a fever. She spent six days rolled into bed, covers pulled to her chin. To get out of bed would have meant exposing herself to the raw elements of daily living, and this she could not bear. For comfort, she tried to imagine a time before worry. But none of it helped—neither her mother's kitchen nor the summers in her uncle's village, neither the swims in its tepid river nor the thought of being a swaddled infant. She went, once, into the puja room, where Thursday's flowers had dried and shriveled into cheerless crumbs. She tried to pray, lit an oil lamp, but her words felt empty. And when she listened for the voices, nobody came, not even her mother. So she retreated to bed again, where she tried to imagine death, cool soil pressing down on her eyelids, the heavy smell of

peat, resin from a coffin, her body and lips and hair a pile
of ashes blown by the wind and fluttering, at last, into an
ocean, a river, away. She tried to imagine life as a fetus,
floating in a womb, free from the demands of earth and
air, amniotic fluid glugging past her eyelids, into her ears
and back out, a time before joy or disappointment, before
she'd fallen in love or walked down streets or tasted water.
At times she sensed her children moving through the
room. A clammy hand on her forehead, the after-school
sounds of vinyl backpacks and Velcro. Once she felt the
soft rake of manicured nails running through her hair:
Kamla.

George cared for her. He brought her soup on a bed
tray that she hadn't known they owned. He lifted water to
her lips, and sometimes sweet fizzy drinks. He took her
temperature at night. She cared for none of this. This sick-
ness, this care, was just another cobblestone on a path that
led the wrong way. What was she doing here in Sacramento, married with three children? She hadn't asked for
this. Her marriage she hadn't wanted. This house she
hadn't seen until after the papers were signed. Even her
children—she had wanted one. Who'd asked for three? All
three at once. What next? Kamla. George would take
Kamla away from her. She would become his friend, he
would kiss her on the cheek, and they would laugh in *that
way* together. He'd taken everything from her.

Several times a day, she wondered if she'd ever managed to make a single good decision. A sign that she had
done at least one thing right, at one juncture of her life,
and she would have gotten out of bed. No sign came. But
on the seventh day, there was a letter.

Now and then, with little regularity and no warning, an aerogram made its way west across a continent, over an ocean, past highways and state borders, and into the mailbox at the end of their drive. It was always the first piece of mail visible, its garish blue jumping from the stack of bills and junk mail. The sketch on the back of the aerogramme varied from year to year. This time it was Jawaharlal Nehru, in high collar and soda-fountain cap. Babygirl ran into the bedroom with it, her backpack still swinging from her shoulders. "Can I do it?" she asked, already clutching the mail opener. Often these letters came from Viji's cousin Meera or her aunt from the village, asking for a wire transfer and complaining about her uncle's gout. But this one was from her sister. *Sister,* it said. *We are all fine. When will you come to see us again? It's been so long.* As if she'd thought twice about it, she added: *You need to come back and take care of things.*

What there was to take care of, Viji didn't know, but if she could have left that night, she would have. However, a woman with three children can't flee overnight, dragging them behind like fugitives. There were visas to obtain, and airplane tickets for four people. Shanta was locked into Viji, hidden like a secret passageway inside her. Never had her sister asked her to visit, not once since Viji had left—not even when their mother had died. She wondered why the call for her to return had come so suddenly; but then she realized that it wasn't sudden. It had, in fact, taken twelve years. She could picture her sister, sitting and looking out from their veranda, deciding all at once that Viji had been gone too long, then charging inside to pick up a pen and write this letter. Her patience had worn thin, or maybe the realization had set in that Viji might never be coming back. Either way, Viji was going for the Christmas holidays. George said he would have to stay behind, though Viji never did ask him to come.

She didn't talk much those days, because any question that left her lips threatened to fly out of control. She would have to act as if things were normal, or else he'd never let her go.

"Why do *we* have to go?" Kieran wanted to know.

"Why not?" Viji had just hung up on a travel agent who couldn't find Madras International in her database. The kitchen was hot with afternoon sun, though it was early December.

"I thought we were going to Santa Cruz for Christmas."

"I have family, Kieran. Surprise, surprise. Do you know how long it has been since I saw them?" Viji asked.

"No."

"Twelve years. And how old are you?"

"Eleven."

"I haven't seen them for as long as you've been alive. Imagine that."

"How come we're going now?" asked Avi.

"She told us, dummy," Babygirl cut in.

"Don't call me dummy. Mom!"

"Don't call names, Babygirl."

"But how come we never went before?"

Viji turned to Avi. For this she had no answer. Or rather, she had too big an answer. Where to begin? *Because going back was always too much. It was too much.*

"They live so far away, chellum. But they're our family, and they want us to come."

"Like who?"

"Like who?" Viji was losing patience. "Like my sister."
She gazed at her children. "My sister sends the three of you
cards every year on your birthday. Not one card, three
cards. Do you know what that costs from India? One for
each of you. And do you ever write back?"

"No. How come she doesn't just send one with three
names on it?"

"Have you ever sent a thank-you note?"

"No."

"And yet she continues to send them."

"When are we going?" Kieran wanted to know.

"As soon as we can. Christmas."

"We're missing Christmas? That's BS."

"Kieran."

"Why do you care if we miss Christmas?" Babygirl
scowled at Kieran from the kitchen counter.

"What's your problem?"

Viji turned to the next travel agency listed in the
phone book. By dinnertime, it was settled. They would fly
for eleven hours, land in Malaysia, and spend a day in
Kuala Lumpur. They would book a hotel, and even take a
city tour if they felt up to it. Or just sleep, which was probably what the triplets would want to do. The kids could
have their last real shower in the hotel bathroom. Viji
hadn't told them about Indian bathrooms yet. She hoped
everyone would just squat when they needed to. She, on
the other hand, began to crave an Indian bucket bath. To
scoop hot water from a bucket, pour it over her head, and
let it run down her back. A bath felt real only when she
could hear the splash of water on stone.

In her own bathroom, Viji turned on the shower. Cold water gushed out. What happens when cold water turns warm? Viji couldn't say, exactly; she knew only that the frosty spray that hit her fingertips wasn't changing at all, though she'd been standing patiently outside the shower, naked, arching her body away from the solitary bullets of water that leapt off the tub and nipped her belly and legs. And then it arrived. Softly, on her palm, the needles of chilly water melted away, a cushion of heat and steam growing around her. Warm, warmer, hot. Hot enough to boil rice. Like showering in a cup of tea.

George used to bathe with her while she showered, sinking lower and lower in the tub as the pool of water grew. There were no children to watch yet, though Viji grew more global each day, her belly swelling into a ripening pod. They lived in a small apartment downtown. It was the time, in that first year, when she was beginning to open to him. She let go of her shyness gradually, let it float away from her like a balloon let loose. It was not long before she let him see her naked, in full light, with nothing to cover her. He liked the way water rained from her hair and onto her buttocks, forming two small streams that ran down her thighs and vanished when they reached her knees. Her game was to cup her hands to collect the water that ran off her belly, then throw a handful of it at George, letting it splash a pattern in his chest hair. Sometimes she'd let him soap her breasts, and they'd both watched the lather scatter like ocean foam, drawing rivulets down her hips.

In the house on Winding Creek Road, the master bathroom was large, with shag carpeting and a mirror that covered an entire wall. There was no tub, only a large flat-bottomed shower. It had two showerheads, so they could have showered together, facing each other, but they never did. Viji leaned against the shower wall and let the spray bounce off her shoulder. Steam filled her lungs like happiness until she could hardly breathe. But it was a pleasant suffocation, and it passed when a gust of fresh air blew into the bathroom. She soaped her upper back, scraping the skin and coming away with gray grime beneath her fingernails. She sipped water from the showerhead and spat it out, then let the spray rinse her nails clean. Around her, the ceiling and walls vanished in a tranquil fog.

"Viji."

She jumped. The air was opaque, and all she could see of George was a shadow in the doorway. Her breath was coming fast. She closed her eyes to the rush of steam.

"Viji, it's soaking. How hot is that shower?"

"I'm fine," she gasped.

George's face, now at the shower door.

"Viji."

"What?"

"Turn off the shower."

Leave me alone. She didn't say it. Instead she turned off the tap. The ceiling dripped.

"What do you want?" she asked.

"Are you okay?"

Of course not. "Yes, why?"

"So you're going to India, then?"

She stood dripping. The glass door was clearing, revealing her nakedness to George. She hugged herself. "And you're taking the kids?"

"Yes," she said.

"There just seems to be a lot you're not...talking about."

"My sister asked me to come, and I'm going."

"*Right.* Exactly. Your sister calls, and you go. As you should do." George stopped short. He sighed. "But why now, exactly? Do you know? Is she sick?"

The glass was clearing, and she could see George's head and shoulders. "I don't think so," she shrugged. "No. No, of course she isn't sick." She opened the shower door and reached past him for a towel. He caught her arm and held it. "Let me go."

"Viji—" As she struggled from his grasp, he wrapped his arm around her. "Viji, come here." She pushed against him. He wanted to hold her. He pulled her in so that her head was on his chest.

George's arms were around her now; water soaked through his shirt. This body that held her, her husband's, felt empty to her, no more human than the sleeves of a bathrobe. Weakly, she began to cry.

"What happened?" he sighed, as if he knew.

What she felt for him—what she used to feel—had grown inside her for twelve years, fluttering, kicking, feeding. Now it floated with its limbs adrift, listless.

A towel. George swaddled her in it, binding her arms to her sides. George could be forceful. Sometimes he got his way without even seeming to ask for it. He was a quiet and vigorous wind.

She let herself go limp, and he held her close. His shirtfront was soaked now, and her hair dripped onto his trouser fronts.

"What is it, darling?" he asked. "What's going on?"

"I have to leave."

"For India. Of course you do." That wasn't what she meant, but she said nothing.

The morning came, mid-December, when Viji and the children would leave. Thinking was futile amid the rush of zipping suitcases and frantic runs from bedroom to kitchen, last-second grabs for a book or colored pencils. George listened to the racket of the triplets as he shaved. They'd been up since the dark hours before dawn, abuzz with the adventure ahead. Standing before his closet, he paused. He rarely thought of what to wear. But that morning, feeling dull, he wanted something bright. Feeling murky and edgeless, he wanted something crisp and clean. He chose a newly laundered shirt that hung in its plastic cover, and a bright green sweater that he'd never worn before. He was, after all, sending his wife away. When she looked back at him from the departure gate, he wanted her to see a handsome man.

And then they were in the car on the two-hour drive to the San Francisco Airport. They'd left Stan at home; there wasn't room for him in the car. His version of goodbye had consisted roughly of an observation: *So you're off, then*, and a warning: *Careful of them snake charmers, now.*

The children filled the car with questions. How long will it take to get there? No, to India? How come so long?

How many miles is it? How are we going to eat? How do you cook food on a plane? Who's going to take care of us when we get to India? How are we going to have money there? Can we see the Taj Mahal? Why not? How come Dad isn't coming? Why not, though? Can he come after? Why not? Why? Why?

Viji fell asleep with her mouth open somewhere past the Davis exit. The engine's rumble gave her a peace she hadn't felt in weeks, and for once she slept dreamlessly. She woke, two hours later, to the careening of the car across the highway, through lanes and lanes of honking cars, and onto the airport entrance ramp.

George sighed as he craned his neck to see over a passing motorbike. Airports, like funerals, were designed to distract from what was truly happening—painful departures, goodbyes, and hellos to be followed by lengthy stays. Three terminals to choose from—who knew? He chose the first. He wound through narrow lanes with arrows pointing hopefully, knowing that an incorrect turn could draw him to the wrong side of the terminal or spit him back onto the highway. And then there was parking: short stay, long stay, shorter than expected but too long for some, longer than short but not worth taking a shuttle, satellite, hotel, delivery, and rental. He looked longingly at the drop-off curb, then winced with guilt.

Twenty minutes later, George stood watching his wife and three children file toward the check-in counters. From where he sat, distanced by a sea of suitcases, they were four heads in a crowded airport, one larger with black hair, three smaller, of uniform height, with hair the color of chocolate. Not a single person there knew that they were his. The evening before, he'd been grading papers in his study when he felt a movement at the half-open door. "Kieran," he'd said to the side of head he saw hovering by the doorway. It was Avi.

"Hi," Avi said.

"Hi."

"What are you doing?"

"Marking some papers. And what can I do for you, sir?"

Avi only shrugged.

"Here, help me with this, then." George gave him the grade register and showed him how to record the students' grades next to their names. Avi worked quietly with George, kneeling on the chair by his desk. Soon, George knew, Avi wouldn't have to kneel. Nor would he bother with George or his office, and neither would the other two. They were well on their way to the sad and necessary end of childhood, the period of disenchantment, of falling hopelessly out of love with one's parents, of looking for bigger, better, and brighter things than family and home and food and love. For the moment, though, they were still his—and here he was, sending them away.

They were halfway to the front now, maybe two-thirds of the way. George counted the number of people in front of them, the number of people behind them. There was much lifting and putting down of suitcases as passengers filed along the guide ropes. He closed his eyes and rubbed his lids and waited for the comedian in the queue to make bleating noises. He watched them reach the front, greeted by a woman who ran her tongue over her teeth compulsively. And then they were finished, turning, coming back to him once more.

At last, the slow walk to security. Slow because they had time, slow because George couldn't bear to hurry. And all at once, they were hit by the inevitable—the pervasive, ruthless smell of cinnamon and sickly-sweet sugar. Every airport had one of these stands. It was a monopoly, designed to entice travelers and coax them into a docile state of diabetic coma. George hated them.

"Mom!" Kieran began.

"No," said Viji.

"Please? Come on." The other two joined in, *please please please please*, hands clasped in prayer, suddenly religious.

"Momm-y-y-y," Babygirl whined. "Please can we have some? We're starving!"

"No, they're bad for you."

She scrunched her eyes in desperation. "I *beg* you—"

"Never beg!" Viji barked. George was startled. Babygirl fell quiet, scratched her cheek, and stared at the wall. George sought Viji's eyes but she snapped them away. It was the stress of traveling—three children, suitcases. The triplets with their backpacks looked up at him.

"Come on, you three," he said. "Come with me." He headed to the stand, Viji's eyes hard on his back as his children trailed after him, hopping in anticipation. He bought them each a bun, and a fourth to share with Viji.

"They'll be sick on the plane now," Viji said, fixing her eyes on the departure screen.

"No we won't, Mom," said Avi. "Promise."

"Food takes forty minutes to digest, and we have two hours," Kieran added. He had his tongue out, trying to lick the syrup that had crusted on his cheek.

"It's good," George ventured. He held the bun out to Viji. "Try some." Without a word, Viji pinched a piece off the bun and watched the white icing break away. How sad she looked. "Viji," he began, but didn't know what else to say. She shrugged in response, looked up with a weak smile. "I will miss you, darling."

"You'll be fine," she whispered. "I'll be back soon." This wasn't so much a lie as a thoughtless promise. She'd left a note for George to find when he got home.

And then they were at security for the kiss goodbye. The triplets looked at the ceiling, at the people in line, at the metal detectors, at anything that wasn't their parents kissing. It was a lingering kiss. For George it was redolent of temporary separation, cinnamon icing, and unspoken promises to keep the house clean, water the lawn, and call on Christmas. Viji's lower lip quivered.

George gathered the children in a single embrace, then stood quickly and chuckled. He was terrified that he would cry, and the peril of it crept up his throat and threatened to fly loose. "Goodbye, darling," he said to Viji.

"Goodbye." She looked intently into his eyes, as if examining his pupils, then turned to go. He caught on her face that last flicker, when her eyes switched off, grew dim, and retreated back into themselves, when the ties from a moment before were severed and she became, once again, a single solitary person. He could have chased after her, pulled her back and into a final embrace. Or she could have turned and run to him, leaving the triplets behind and bewildered. But she didn't, and neither did he. So he watched her pass through the metal detector and walk farther and farther away, until she was no more than a troubling memory.

PART II

✿ CHAPTER ONE ✿

"Mom. *Mom*."

"What?"

"That man has no legs."

"Don't stare, Kieran."

"What happened to his legs?" The man sat on a make-shift cart with wheels and pushed himself along with his knuckles. Dreadlocks fell down his naked back.

"Was it from the war?"

"What war?"

"You know, the Vietnam War."

Viji laughed out loud for the first time in days. "What are they teaching in that school?" They followed their porter, a boy no older or taller than the triplets, as he carried one suitcase on his head and pulled the other along behind him. They passed a wall of brown faces, eager, staring, smiling, looking past them for relatives who were due to file out of the arrivals hall. "Hurry," she urged. She wanted to get home, but the children moved so slowly, gazing around, stopping, staring, wasting time. She hurried to the waiting taxi to make sure the porter didn't "accidentally" leave one of their suitcases on the ground. A five rupee tip for his services. What could anyone possibly do with five rupees? Fifty rupees. The porter locked eyes with her and grinned, then galloped away before she could change her mind.

Madras after midnight. They drove past black-and-white-striped barriers that divided the city's main avenues. Low huts lined the streets, and trees sprouted from piles of debris. Atop the piles women squatted, sorting through the rubble, while men hacked at the larger rocks with pick-axes. It was cool after midnight, a better time to work. Lanterns lit the piles around them, and from the car Viji could see the mosquito clouds that gathered around each light. They sped by ghostly gray skeletons of buildings, great gaping beehives still missing their windows and doors. Around them, spindly towers of scaffolding rose like scarecrows into the sky. She was in a world half-finished. Billboards flashed past as the car picked up speed: cinema heroines with fair skin and dangerous eyebrows, hair thicker and blacker than the ocean. Heroes with mustaches, villains with mustaches. The children had fallen asleep.

As soon as they were on the outskirts, freed from the nocturnal throat of the city, the quiet residential areas began to look familiar. Even under the haze of night she recognized the signposts, the low walls that lined the road, plastered with cinema posters and government warnings to POST NO BILLS. Yes, this signpost was familiar, this house with the Ganesh carved into the side; she knew that stone walkway, this fenced-in park with the grass and coconut trees. She recognized the rhythm of the bumpy road, the groaning tires told her she was close to home. Verandas and high balconies in green-pink-beige-white-yellow, houses like frosted cupcakes.

The taxi slowed to a halt. She knew this house. This

was hers. A bare lightbulb over the veranda switched on when the driver turned off his engine. Elsewhere on the street, veranda lights switched on and people emerged in doorways and stood in clusters to watch. She shook the children awake and pulled them from the car. They walked hunchbacked with sleep, whimpering.

The door opened and Shanta emerged. Viji ran down the walkway and dropped her bags, pushed past the children, and forgot to pay the driver. Her sister stood waiting. Warm arms, home.

With dawn came the first drumbeats of the day, the clopping of a bullock cart, the squeak of the neighbor's gate, the perpetual bark of a local dog. The shrieking dog was still alive. She'd heard it every day growing up, a cry that shredded the mist like a woman's scream. Now Viji heard it in her dream. She opened one eye to the hazy morning. The bark came again. She opened the other eye, this one crusted with sleep. The digital clock on the dresser flicked over to 4:23. She was wide awake now and still swollen from the flight. Around her, the bed was littered with triplets. Kieran and Babygirl on either side, Avi at the foot. They'd wandered in during the night and now they lay with arms outstretched, making the air even muggier.

This was her bed, though it seemed smaller now. This was the bed she'd fallen into every night of her life, the same bed she'd tossed on for hours after those first meetings with George. She'd lain hot and wide-eyed between these sheets, content that she'd escaped another punishment, happy to sacrifice another night's sleep to her wandering thoughts.

George. George would have found her note, would

have read it once and then again, then sat down and read
it again and then looked around the room for clarifica-
tion the way he always did. He would want to phone her,
to demand to know what was going on, but he wouldn't
have a number. She'd said that she would phone him as
soon as she could. She would put this off and put this off,
not wanting to look through the neighborhood for the
STD, the international calling center. But when she did
speak to him, his voice would be calm and measured. He
would ask her questions and expect to be answered. She
felt ashamed now, and childish for running away. A grown
woman would have told him the truth of what she felt, in
person and eye to eye. A grown woman would have at least
bid him a proper farewell.

But really, given the opportunity, what would she say?

Over the past few weeks, every time she thought of
speaking frankly, she stopped herself. Words were liabili-
ties, capable of skidding out of control and giving things
away. Like the fact that she was going to India and wasn't
sure about returning. Like the fact that as she kissed
George at the airport and felt his confidence course
through her, she wanted nothing more than to shatter it.
How could she tell this man, who stood before her
clutching half a cinnamon bun, that she might be leaving
forever? There'd been a quiet moment, just after dawn,
when Viji would have liked to say goodbye. But he had
been asleep, and all she could do was brush the hair from
his eye. How soft he had looked while sleeping.

Now she rose and navigated her way past sleeping
arms and legs. Stone stairs cool and ashy beneath her feet,
Viji went down to the kitchen.

Kuttima was a servant lady who'd been with them since both she and Viji were children. She'd come to them motherless, shorter than the broom she held, with arms as thin as blades of grass. She stayed with the family through her teenage years, through learning to read and write, through her marriage and motherhood and widowhood. In this time she'd graduated from sweeper to errand girl to kitchen helper to head chef. She was the central cog that held their house together. Now, she sat on a straw mat spread over the kitchen floor, chopping plantains with what looked like a Saracen's sword.

It had once belonged to Old Krishnan, the cook Viji's mother had hired when the family had enough money to hire such people. It had chopped leathery mutton and potatoes for curries heavy with starch and ghee. But when Old Krishnan was found drunk and dead outside a city brothel, the knife had passed over to Kuttima. And there lay the secret of Kuttima's rise within the household   not in the knife, but in the wonders through which it sliced. With Old Krishnan went the stodgy sameness of local food, and into the void he left, Kuttima brought the gentle cuisine of the Kerala coast. It came from her without instruction, as instinctively as dancing or laughing. For breakfast, there were banana curries and spongy coconut pancakes with thick middles, chewy and faintly sweet, the frenzied patties of vermicelli noodles, steamed and soaked in coconut milk and sugar, sending up hot vapors before they cooled on the table. Kuttima could tell which fish vendors sold good meaty pieces, and which sold the gritty bracken from the bottom of the net. She used to say she could tell by their faces. *See him,* she warned Viji, *Mister*

Smiley-Smiley? Selling shit, that one. Him with the beady eye? Look at him, how greedy he is, he doesn't want to give it up. Let's go to him. Viji thought of Kuttima's fried chili fish, and her stomach twisted with longing.

"Well, well," Kuttima chimed. "Sleeping Beauty's decided to join us, I see." She looked around the empty room for agreement. "Had a good sleep, Sleeping Beauty?" In the distance, the dog shrieked.

"Yes, good enough." It felt strange to speak Tamil again. Either sleepiness or lack of practice had turned Viji's tongue thick and foolish. Kuttima barely looked at her, just chopped away at her plantain, as if Viji had always been in this house, hadn't married a foreigner, hadn't disappeared for twelve years and then turned up with three children and suitcases, wild-eyed with jet-lag, too groggy even for a bath. "Where is everyone?"

"Asleep in their beds, like you." She hacked at a plantain and the tip went flying. Viji picked it up for her. "Only Kuttima gets up this early. Only Kuttima makes the breakfast and boils the coffee and reminds the rooster to crow."

Viji smiled. "Without you, we'd all be eating street snacks."

She grunted. "There was a time when you would have liked that. Home food was never good enough for Sleeping Beauty."

"That's not true!"

"It is. Street Goat, that's what we called you. Always coming home with a belly full of fried stuff and no room left for dinner."

Viji studied the woman, trying to work out if she was younger or older than Viji. Kuttima had always been miniature, hence her name. Her doe eyes and crooked teeth gave her the air of a small girl. But now she was hunched and graying. Fatty hills of flesh peeked from the back of her sari blouse.

"And what would Sleeping Beauty like for breakfast?"

"Anything."

"Anything. What do you eat over there? Hmm? *Cawn fa-lake*?" She tried the words and hooted, shaking her head. "Go sit," she ordered. "I'll bring your coffee."

"No, I'll do it." From a pot clattering on the stove, Viji poured boiling water into a steel *cafetière*. She could smell the chicory in the coffee as she waited for it to filter. Behind her, she could feel her mother, ready to shout an order, filling the kitchen with her voice and her belly and her loud laugh. Hot breath whispered against Viji's neck and she turned. Nobody there, but her ear still tingled.

With a cup of milky sweet coffee, she passed from the kitchen to the sitting room. Above her a ceiling fan ticked over slowly. Low divans stretched along the four walls, covered now in clear plastic. She sat, straight-backed. She felt formal, a guest in her own home with no host to receive her. The plastic groaned when she slumped back and let her knees splay open. How they would have scolded her, if anyone could see.

The room hadn't changed at all. Its scant array of objects still hung in the same places—the cuckoo clock above the door (brought from Switzerland by her uncle), her grandmother's framed needlepoint, a weathered calendar of painted flowers that changed every year but always looked the same. On the wall behind her was an oil painting of a village woman, her sari draped over her hair, a brass pot resting on the dramatic curve of her hip. It was painted in shades that were typically Indian, mustard and brown and wild, muddy green. She turned away. There was a television in the room now, with a doily and a small clock on top of it. That was the only change.

The clock on the television clicked to five. Her sister would be up soon. Her two aunts still lived upstairs as well. Viji drank her coffee and waited for them to come down, to fill her world and make it recognizable. The ceiling fan released a sigh, then ticked louder. It stirred no air at all.

"Vijaya," her sister's voice came softly from the stairs. She stood like a painting, hand on the banister, in a crisp blue cotton sari. Shanta came to the divan, sat down with Viji, stroked the hair on her sister's temple. In her eyes Viji saw love, yes, but beyond this, in the dense black of the pupil, lay more than she could read, eyes ponderous with truth and age. Shanta had never married, and, of course, by this point she never would. She was of this house, born here and sewn into it forever, like the nuns in their convent school who'd been wed to the musty classroom walls and the cool wooden pews of the chapel.

Shanta had softened in some way, like newspaper left out in the damp. She didn't crackle the way she used to. Old Shanta would have been in the kitchen, shouting orders and clanging pots just for the noise of it, and calling Viji a dirty dog for having not bathed yet. New Shanta sat heavily on the divan and stroked Viji's arm, two fingers from wrist to elbow, purposefully, as if trying to smooth away the years of their separation. Sleep washed over Viji and she rested her head on her sister's shoulder. The ceiling fan ticked off the seconds.

Shanta found a gray hair on Viji's temple and pulled it out. Viji squealed and rubbed the itch away. Shanta giggled, "Krishna, see what happens when you leave us so long?" The gray hair sprung giddily from between her fingers and landed somewhere on the floor. "What shall we feed you first, *ha*? Some idli?" Viji shook her head. Shanta grasped her wrist. "Something sweet, then?" Viji looked down and smiled. Her sister shook her wrist. "Something sweet. Still the same."

"*È* Shanta!" Kuttima called from the kitchen.

"*Ha*," her sister called back, eyes fixed on Viji's face. Shanta's face had grown plump around the bend in her nose, the depression in her cheek. One eye was half-closed, stuck in the middle of a wink, at the start of a sneeze.

"*Shanta!*" Kuttima yelled this time.

"Sit," Shanta whispered. "We'll make you something sweet."

Viji was upstairs again, shaking the triplets awake. Avi whined and swatted at her when she stroked his head. Kieran didn't react at all, but lay heavy and limp and silent. Babygirl scooted away before Viji could even touch her and cocooned herself under the bedspread. The room was marshy with the smell of breath, a miasma of airplanes and upset stomachs. She watched them sleep and wondered if they had any idea where they were. They must have been imagining themselves at home in their beds, surrounded by white walls and carpet, the stark valley winter waiting at the window. What a shock it would be when they opened their eyes and saw this room, with its chalky blue paint, lacquered-wood furniture, and stone floors. How strange to discover that outside of this bed and their mother, they knew nothing and no one. Not even where the bathroom was, or how to get a glass of water, or where the road led that stretched past the veranda, or what that shrieking bark was, or who these women were, populating this house, old and older and oldest. She would let them sleep. And when they woke she would guide them through this world, infants again, showing them what to eat and where to walk and when to sit and how.

A second later, she was being shaken awake. Shanta stood over her. "What happened?" Viji asked. Shanta laughed and slapped her on the bum. Babygirl stirred, sat up in the swirl of bedspread. She looked at Viji, at Shanta, at the boys, and then at the cloudy mirror on the wardrobe.

"Good morning," Shanta sang. Her English was bold and clearly pronounced. It was the English of the convent-school nuns. At the boom of her voice, Kieran kicked his feet, smacking Avi in the head, and both boys flailed awake. The clock read 12:15. Shanta pulled the triplets out of bed and sniffed affectionately at their foreheads, then grimaced at the smell. Bewildered and looking back to Viji, they were bundled out of the room and down the stairs. Shanta would wash them in the big bath downstairs, with the thoroughness of a mother. She would think nothing of seeing them naked, or letting them see each other naked. Viji didn't stop her. They would see how things were done in her home. More importantly, she wouldn't have to show them the toilets and watch their little American mouths fall open. Oh, the toilets, those hole-in-the-ground toilets that even the best houses had.

The triplets wouldn't understand that these were clean, cleaner than the Western kind. She lay back on the bed and dozed a while longer.

♧ ♧ ♧

The bathhouse was in the garden, a small adobe hut with a thatched roof and gaps at the top of the wall where a very tall person might spy on whoever was bathing. The triplets followed Shanta like a trail of ducks. From the balcony, an old woman stood and watched them, rubbing her belly and thumping her cane. "Come on, come inside," Shanta said in English. Avi looked at Babygirl, Babygirl and Kieran looked at Avi.

"All of us?"

"Come, come in."

The bathing hut was dark and humid. Along its wall ran a stone bench, and beneath their bare feet the marble was veined with mud trails. They could still hear the old woman's cane, *thump-thump-thump*ing to the beat of the dripping tap.

"Where's the shower?"

Shanta turned a tap in the corner, and water thudded into a large tin pail. She gestured to them to remove their clothes.

"What?" Avi asked.

"She wants us to take our clothes off."

"For real?"

"I think so."

"*Ha*, yes," Shanta coaxed. "Take the clothing off."

Because her voice was gentle, Kieran obeyed. Shirt off,

shorts off, underwear off, he hung them from the hook on the door, then stood pale and soft in the shadows. Avi shrugged and whipped off his T-shirt and dropped it on the wet floor. Shorts off, underwear off, he looked thin and dark next to his brother. Now both boys were naked and holding their hands over their crotches, which made Shanta laugh when she saw.

Babygirl stood in the doorway, still fully clothed, watching the water gush into the pail. Behind her, the door opened and Kuttima came in. She carried a cauldron of steaming hot water, freshly boiled.

"*Everyone* is in here." Babygirl murmured to her brothers.

"I know. It's weird."

"*Neha*," Shanta called to Babygirl. She gestured to her to remove her clothes. Babygirl shook her head vigorously, waved her arms across her chest.

"*No*," she said, "Uh-uh."

"Just do it," Avi urged, shifting from foot to foot. "It's getting cold."

Kieran looked sleepily at her. They were resigned to this, it seemed. "We won't look, promise."

"Cross your heart and hope to die?"

"Stick a needle in my eye."

Kuttima mixed the hot water into the cold and stirred it like a witch's cauldron. And then, across the room came Shanta, impatient, with big hands to undo Babygirl's buttons, to pull down her shirt, big hands dripping cold water.

"No!" she cried and ran out the door. She escaped. The boys heard her slippers slapping on the pavement, until they faded to silence. For a few minutes, the only sound in the yard was distant splashing and the trickle of water from a hole in the corner of the bathhouse.

❧ ❧ ❧

Shanta bustled in now, her face a map of worry, and banged the first vessel on the table. This was normal, Viji knew. Brought up with servants they could no longer afford, Shanta didn't fill the gap well. But she wouldn't hire new servants, either, no matter how many times Viji offered to send the money. She said servants couldn't be trusted anymore. The room buzzed with her sister's anxiety, and Viji felt the old house returning. Eventually there would be difficulty, but it would build slowly at first. Viji would light the fuse with some small offense, and then each new, minute tangle would lead them further away from the harmony of that morning, closer to an explosion twelve years in the making.

Viji followed her back into the kitchen, and a rush of memory swept over her. The smell of mustard seeds needled the corners of her mouth. The chilies had burst in their frying oil, releasing themselves into Viji's nasal passages and making her sneeze. When she closed her eyes she could feel her mother again, just behind, and hear the *clank* of her bangles as she unscrewed the money jar to send Kuttima for sweets. She opened her eyes to a gush of steam that poured from the stove, the smell of new-boiled rice. Shanta spooned it into a serving dish. She watched her sister, bending and reaching and stooping for this pan, that serving spoon, shuffling to the fridge for the stainless steel vessel of yogurt. She had softened and sweetened, like an overripe plum. Too old to pickle, too tender to pucker the lips of those who dared to bite.

"And Uma Athai and Pushpa Athai?" Viji asked.

"What of them?"

"I haven't seen them yet. Where are they?"

"Sleeping. That's all they do now. Sleep, eat, sleep, eat. Like babies."

"They're old."

"I'm old. They're mad."

Viji clicked her tongue and smiled. The boys entered the kitchen, smelling of sandalwood soap. Babygirl followed, still wearing her clothes from the airplane. They examined the black stone floors, and stared up at the brass pots that hung from the ceiling, and the dark shelves crammed with jars collected over decades. Seeing Babygirl, Shanta grabbed her hand and kissed the thumb. "Naughty one, hmm? *Sweet* and naughty, just like your amma!" Babygirl twisted away, embarrassed to smile, and scratched her nose.

Kuttima spooned fish from the frying pan into a colander, where the oil would drip away. "Go sit," she ordered.

The family dining table was set now with four banana leaves and stainless steel pots that steamed from beneath their covers. Banana leaves were for special lunches. Shanta worked fast while the food was hot, spooning onto each leaf precise and modest mounds from every vessel. She would eat alone, a dutiful hostess, after the others had finished. Six different dishes, then seven, then eight. Viji tried to remember the last time she had cooked this much. Nine dishes in the end, the auspicious number. There were green beans fried with mustard seed, curried plantains, a dollop of homemade yogurt, tomato chutney, eggplant fried and swimming in cashew-nut gravy, a mound of fresh rice, a crispy puppadam, a teaspoon of garlic pickle, and finally, laid gently in the center, a chunk of fish fried in chili and coriander, swaddled in a crumbling crust. A feast for a daughter who'd been away too long. "Eat," Viji heard her mother say from somewhere in the room. The *clank* of her bangles. But it was Shanta's voice, and Shanta who poured boiled water into their glasses.

Viji peeled the flesh from the fishbone. Her hands trembled and, she felt short of breath, as if unfastening the buttons of a long-lost lover. A ball of rice, a pinch of fish, dipped just so in the garlic pickle, tinged lightly with the sour yogurt. The first morsel passed from her lips to her tongue. She began to cry.

"What's wrong? Is it too hot?" Shanta asked. "It's too hot. Kuttima, you made it too hot."

"I made it the way I've always made it—stop talking nonsense."

"It's not too hot," Viji said.

"Living there, isn't it? Living there and eating hamburger-french-fries. You've lived so long with the oatmeal people and now you can't eat your own food. Isn't it?"

"It's *not* too hot," Viji tried again. "Kuttima, it's excellent."

Kuttima humphed. "And what about the oatmeal children? Too hot for them too?"

The triplets perked up at the word "oatmeal". "Nothing," Viji said to them.

"They have oatmeal?"

"No. Do you like your food? Is it too hot?"

"It's good," Kieran answered. "But what's this runny stuff?"

"That's yogurt."

It quivered under Kieran's prodding finger. "It doesn't taste like yogurt."

"That's because it's homemade."

"How come you don't eat regular yogurt?" Kieran asked his aunt.

Shanta looked at Viji. "What is it?" she asked. "He doesn't like the yogurt?"

"He likes the yogurt."

"Is it too hot? We can make him something else."

"It's yogurt, Shanta, how could it be too hot?"

"Too hot, Kieran?" Shanta asked him in English. "Would you like toast and jam?"

"No thanks."

"It's fine, Shanta, not too hot."

"Kuttima? Go buy some bread."

"It's *fine*, Shanta!"

The fuse was lit. Her first offense. Shanta fell silent. She pinched a few stray grains of rice from the tabletop and passed wordlessly into the kitchen.

There was a tree in front of the house now, a single tree just before the veranda. They used to chop it down whenever it began to grow because a single tree at the front of the house brought bad luck and death. But it had continued to grow, no matter how often they chopped it. They'd hired a gardener to pull out the roots, but he wasn't able to, not even after Viji's mother threatened not to pay him. He wouldn't accept payment, he said, for something he couldn't do. The more they tried to kill the tree, the harder it tried to grow. But now, Viji saw, they'd decided to leave it alone. Death and luck had found them, tree or no tree. It was taller than she and sprouted young branches, as knock-kneed and feeble as the legs of a fawn.

Behind the solitary tree stretched the veranda, held in by a low adobe wall. Viji felt something release inside, some tension drip off like candle wax, as she opened the gate from the road, her arms full of marigolds. This was home. She knew every corner of it—the sitting room beyond the veranda, behind that the kitchen, and to one side, the formal dining room. To the other side, behind heavy mahogany doors, lay the puja room. She hadn't been in there yet. Nobody had asked her to go, and something made her stop at its door every time she tried. But now she'd been to the flower lady, her arms were full of offerings, and Shanta was waiting for her to begin their Saturday prayer.

Inside, Viji hesitated at the puja room door, leaning in to smell the wood, the dark resin that curled from it like smoke from a forest.

"Go in, baby." The old aunt's voice made her jump.

"I haven't had a bath yet," she lied.

"Go anyway. Who's going to care?"

"No, I shouldn't."

"What, do you roll in shit every night? You're clean enough. Go in."

"No, later."

"Go!"

"No."

"Go, I say!" She rapped her cane on the ground. "Ungrateful girl!"

"Athai?" Shanta called. "Leave her alone."

Pushpa Athai glared at the kitchen. "Queeny bitch," she muttered. "Bring my tea!" Viji stood still, hoping her aunt would leave. "Bring my tea, girl!" She beat the floor even harder with her cane. "Deaf! Are you deaf? Bring my tea!" She gawked at Viji with bewildered anger. "Tea! Tea! Tea!" Viji scurried to the kitchen, her arms still full of flowers.

Shanta laughed when she saw her. "Don't look so scared. I told you they were mad." She poured a long stream of milky tea from cup to vessel, vessel to cup, cup to vessel, to cool it down. It grew frothier each time. Then she placed the cup on a saucer, leaned over, and whispered, "We're next, sister." Viji left her cackling, and took the tea to her aunt.

At last, they were alone again. The aunt had gone up for her morning nap.

"Come," Shanta took Viji's hand and grabbed the fistful of marigold strands. Viji started toward the mahogany doors. "Not there! This way."

Up one flight of stairs, up the next, was a room that had once been used to store the wedding trousseaux of the women in the family. The great wooden chests towered against the wall, stacked high in the shadows, filling the room like boxed prayers. Their only use now was to block the light from the single window. To lift their lids would bring up a torrent of moths, the oaky smell of old silk, the softly rustling memory of cloth on cloth from the last time they were folded and locked away. In Viji's trousseau would be three saris: one Kancheevarum silk, one Benares silk, one pure crepe silk, the very minimum for a bride. They'd had no time to shop, and besides, her groom wouldn't have known the difference. There were no in-laws demanding a dowry, and George had no sisters to pick over the trousseau and sniff at her jewels. It was easy to marry a vellakaran; they had no demands aside from beauty and intelligence and personality. Still, Viji's mother had acted like she was doing George a favor. She called him Horlicks behind his back, her malted-milk son-in-law.

Shanta lit the oil lamps, and in the tepid haze Viji could see the shelves of idols, statues, and framed paintings, a small stone lingam. The dark flickered when she exhaled. Along the wall, the photographs—her cousin, a great-aunt, and so many others who'd receded to the corners of her memory, whom she hadn't thought about in years. Busily, Shanta arranged the marigolds around the picture frames and idols.

"Why here?" Viji asked.

"Hmm?" Shanta was dotting red ash onto the foreheads of the photographs.

"Why is the puja room here? What happened to the old one?"

"The aunts pray there."

"And?"

"And?"

"Why can't you use that one?"

Shanta turned to her, her forehead furrowed. "You don't like this one?"

"No—*yes*, but why have a separate one?"

Shanta considered her languidly, then returned to her tasks, humming. Silently they sat for several minutes, cross-legged on the floor, contemplating the shelves of deities, not uttering a single prayer, not even to themselves. At last, Shanta spoke. "This is mine," she whispered. "That is theirs."

Four women who never left a house instead claimed every corner of it, scurried to its edges like roaches, and slipped under its walls. Women in a house together went to great lengths to stake out their territory. Shanta couldn't bring herself to pray in the same room as her aunts, yet she fed them and dressed them and listened to their barmy demands day after day, knowing that only death would bring an end to it.

"Sister," Viji whispered. "Come live with me." But Shanta was deep in prayer now, her eyes closed and her lips tripping over the silent words.

๛๛๛

That afternoon in the library, Viji picked a book off the shelf, an old schoolbook of poetry, and pressed the open pages against her nose. This was the smell of books in India. If she took this book home with her, she'd be able to smell it whenever she wanted, for a time, until the scent faded and smelled like nothing, like everything else in Sacramento. She closed her eyes. Very nearly, she could hear the susurrations of the pages piled high around her. *Remember*, they said.

She remembered a swing—a solid mahogany platform that hung from the ceiling by heavy chains. It was high, and

had no back or side supports. It wasn't a swing for children. She'd tried to hoist herself onto it once and ended up
stuck, forearms clamped against the hard wood, knowing
that letting go would send her crashing to the marble floor.
Yet she wasn't strong enough to thrust her legs onto the
seat. She was stuck. Her elbows stung. She called out for
her mother, but nobody came. Soon she was crying, with
no free hand to wipe her tears or her dribbling nose.

This was her first memory, the first thing she knew
had happened, that wasn't told to her by someone older.
She couldn't remember if she eventually fell to the floor, or
if somebody found her and helped her down. She asked
her sister about it.

"What swing?" Shanta said. "We never had a swing in
this house." And then, "Swing, there was no swing. Only
fancy people had swings in those days."

Viji remembered it was brown as syrup, and that it
smelled of resin. She knew that its chains were made of
shining brass, and that the floor below had black and
white checks. And as she hung there damp-faced, the blunt
wood digging into her belly, a breeze through the window
had coaxed the swing into a gentle sway. She was rocking
through the air at last, legs clenched, swinging just slightly.
She had stopped crying then, and held on tighter.

That afternoon Viji came upon her sons hurling
themselves onto the divan and laughing uncontrollably at
the obscene *blurp* of the plastic sofa cover. "Mom," Avi
squealed, "the sofa's farting."

"Yes, ha ha," Viji said. "Where is your sister?"

"I dunno. She made it fart first and then she got mad."

Babygirl stepped into the room then, still scowling at

her brothers. This set them off again, pouncing and laughing and *blurp*ing and getting louder and louder. Such a commotion sounded devilish in the yawning old house.

"*Kieran, Avi,*" Viji called over the din. "KIERAN, AVI." They stopped and waited. Well-behaved. "Do you have any homework?" They blinked at her. "You didn't bring any?"

"It's Christmas. Our only homework is to write about our holiday heritage."

She sighed. She hadn't a clue what this meant, this holiday heritage. When she was the triplets' age, she was doing geometry. "Let's see the house, then." She took them all over the three-story building, into former bedrooms that held only broken bits of furniture, into the game room stacked with dusty carom boards and domino sets, to the library guarded still by sentinel rows of forgotten books, as faded now as the wallpaper, rubbed into silence by years of neglect. Her father had loved this room. She used to find him in here, sitting silently, gazing at a far shelf or running his hand over the long, cool table. When he left, nobody else ventured in—not even Viji dared to enter with her books.

She found Babygirl and took all three of them to the rooftop, crisscrossed with clotheslines. On the ground Kuttima had spread sheets of newspaper, lined with row upon row of fat chili peppers and lemon rinds, drying in the sun to be stored and pickled. From here they could see Madras, hung with power lines and clotheslines of white dhotis flapping in the wind. The palm trees were pregnant with coconuts. Surrounding them were rooftops of tidy terraces and ceramic tiles, and further out were the putty-colored roofs of the slums, kneeling to one side, warped by heat and faded by repetition. A wind blew through the city and swept up the smell of rain. Viji's nostrils filled with sky, pink as cotton candy and thick with moisture. She thought suddenly of the blue, blue California sky, a color she would never see in Madras.

"See there." She pointed to the local temple with its carved stone tiers, stacked like a charcoal wedding cake. Beyond it rose the brown crosses of the Episcopal church.

"Mom, what are we doing for Christmas?" Avi asked.

"We're not having Christmas, Avi."

"What?" He gaped at her in disbelief.

"In India only the Christians have Christmas."

"But we're Christian. Dad's Christian."

"Daddy's a compassionate atheist."

"What?"

"How come we can't do Christmas?" Babygirl accused.

"I told you. What do you want, a Christmas tree?"

"Yes!"

"They don't have them here. Shall I send you to the church?"

"No! We want Christmas!"

"They don't do it the same way here, Babygirl. You wouldn't like it." She'd always felt sad for the Christians she saw, singing off-rhythm songs about Jesus, not even in their own language, making childish chalk drawings of Santa Claus, decorating their verandas in gaudy foil, members of a club that no one wanted to join.

That evening, Viji woke from a nap to total darkness. Not even the streetlamps outside her window were on, nor were the veranda lights. The power had gone. "Shanta?" she called. "Avi? Kieran?" She felt her way downstairs, careful not to slip, though she knew these steps by heart. The street outside had fallen quiet, as it often did on Sunday evenings, and the house was perfectly still. Only a cloud of light glowed from deep within the kitchen. Theirs had been the first house in this district to have electric lighting. Now all the houses had it, but the current was sure to fail at least twice a day. Viji cursed the darkness softly as she entered. "I'm here," she announced to the empty front room. If her sister heard, she didn't respond. They were in the kitchen, Babygirl seated on the floor by Kuttima, peeling a ginger root with her fingernail. The boys sat next to an oil lamp on the ground and played cards with a deck from the airline. The darkness calmed them. When she was young, the family always came together at these times, gathering around a candle to wait for the lights to come back. Shanta sat on a chair against the wall, eyes closed, focused on a tune she was humming. She fanned herself with a magazine, released by the dark from her evening tasks. Work stopped when the current went. Only gnats churned silently, charmed by the flames. The children, with nothing more to do, began to count them.

George was on a train that clattered and shook all the way from London to Nottingham. A swift punch to the side might have jogged its parts into place. The side of his head rattled against the windowpane and went numb. He didn't know how the cold seeped through trains, but it always did. He wished he were back in London, in the cheerful anonymity of St. Pancras, where the people were too busy to be sad, and not on this train that hurtled toward his old town and his father and their small, dark, terraced house. A woman sat next to him. She was pretty and young and wore a skirt with a slit up the side. He considered speaking to her, but the moment passed and she got off at Milton Keynes. Now there was nothing left but to sit back and watch the high phone lines that stretched past the window. They danced against the gunmetal sky, leapt off each pole and dipped and dodged and leapt again. He watched them for an hour or maybe more. Then, with his ear pressed against the cold shuddering window, he fell asleep.

George awoke. *Where am I? Home. Bedroom.* He looked to his right, where the pillow was smooth and the sheets pulled flat. She had made the bed, leaving not even the lopsided impression of her head. She was gone. Not even her smell lingered, not even the ghost of her. It was as if she'd wanted to disappear from him completely.

Beyond the spot where she would have been lying, a crack of light winked through the curtains. He hoisted himself out of bed. Curtains closed, autumn. Curtains open, blinding white. George squinted against the sun, radiant and perfectly round, its edges sharpened by cloud. All color had leaked from the sky. In the yard the roses had tumbled from their bushes and the trees were bare. The pool gaped dumbly at him.

She'd left a note. *Dear George.* He'd found it on his return from the airport, folded on the dresser. *I have to stay awhile with my sister, and I have to decide what to do with myself.* He'd wondered what it was that she might possibly have to do with herself. *Because I might not come back. I am not happy and I don't know if I ever was. I never had the chance to even ask myself this.* He grew cold, something inside him beginning to drip. *You once asked me why I was here, with you. It was a good question. I ask myself this question now because I have to, because I'm not sure anymore of why I am here, in this place, with you. Because I found myself in a life that was not mine.* He wondered when she'd had time to write this note, whether she'd written it while he was sleeping or in the shower or at work, whether she'd written it last-minute that morning, or on some previous day, saving it in a drawer or tucked beneath her pillow. The paper was soft, as if it had been sweated on, the creases slack with refolding. *Because maybe I should never have left my home. Because I hardly knew you. Because I never knew myself, or if I did, then I must have forgotten. The children will be back by January in time for school, but I may not. I hope you understand and can forgive me.* Well,

no, George thought. No, he did not understand. He'd
found the note yesterday evening. She had positioned it
carefully on the dresser, perfectly aligned with the edge of
the drawers. The paper whispered between his shaking fingers as he read.

So that was it, then. She was leaving him. Ground-
locked, helpless, he wanted to find Viji, but she was on an
airplane gliding peacefully away. He wouldn't even be able
to phone her once she'd landed, not until she phoned him.
He crumpled the paper and tossed it on the table. He
kicked the wall, and kicked it again, then backed up a few
paces, ran up, and kicked it again. His big toe screamed
with pain. It wasn't enough—he snatched the note back
up and tore it and pinched it into the smallest possible
shreds. He wouldn't miss it. The words were burnished
into the backs of his eyes. Poetic drivel. *Because because
because.* That wasn't his wife speaking, it was a sad woman
novelist writing something from a sad novel for women.

Because I might not come back. The enormity of what
Viji had said punched into him, specifically into his gut,
which began to tremor and unravel and sent him running
to the toilet to release an avalanche, stinking and shameful.
He rested his head on his bare knee. He was weak—
nothing he did would change that.

And then he waited for her call. The first day, he
checked his watch at eight a.m. and calculated that she
would just be landing, sweating her way through Madras
International, climbing into a taxi for the short drive
through the nighttime streets. The children would be itchy
and exhausted from the flight. At ten a.m., he guessed
she'd be lying awake, listening to the sounds of shadows in

the house from which he'd rescued her long ago. That first day inched along painfully. His morning, her night, his evening, her dawn. And still she didn't call. Maybe it was a holiday; the STDs would be closed.

The second day, he got up early and went to the university and was utterly unable to work. The third day, he packed a sandwich, so he wouldn't miss her call on his lunch break, and left for work before dawn. He was liquid with fatigue those mornings. There was nothing he could do but hold his head in his hands to keep it from flopping to the desk. He tried to imagine the small events of Viji's days but found that he couldn't. "You don't look so hot," Amaré observed.

"I'm waiting to hear from my wife. She and my children are in India."

"Oh yeah? That's nice for you, a vacation from the family."

He'd never before seen the inside of the washing machine, not even at the shop where they'd bought it. A filter of some sort rose up from inside, a narrow metal volcano. The whole thing looked like a doughnut and made him want one. It was Tuesday evening, and George was in the laundry room. They had an entire room for laundry. At home in Nottingham, his parents had had, luxury of luxuries, a so-called washer-dryer crammed next to their fridge, just to the right of the kitchen sink. So-called because it washed, but never properly dried. It was impossible to expect the same machine to both wash and dry a garment. Still, it roused the ire of their neighbors, who trudged to the launderette with their netted sacks of dirty clothing, then trudged home again to hang their damp clothes on the line. Here, the dryer was a colossal thing. He could have climbed inside and tumble-dried himself.

At his feet sat a plastic basket full of clothes, brimming with the innards of his father's hamper, and with his own collection of dirty underwear. He'd separated Viji's clothing and left it in the bedroom. He feared he would ruin it with some sort of bad decision.

"No way around it" he whispered, "may as well get stuck in." With that, he grabbed a handful of Stan's underwear and chucked it in the washer, followed by another and another. His father had more underwear than he'd expected. He was well stocked with underpants, though they'd been battered and stretched with time. Holes, apparently, were no reason to throw out a pair of underpants. And then, from among the sad gray flags emerged a pair of bright pink panties, as shocking and beautiful as a butterfly on a rubbish heap. They could only be Lupe's—Viji didn't own lace panties. These were finely woven, and surprisingly small. For a moment he let himself imagine the fabric peeking from Lupe's folds, lost between her belly and her thighs, a rhapsody of silk and flesh. And then he felt sorry for Lupe, that this delicate web of hers should be handled by the likes of him, that she should have found her round and well-meaning hips in the rough hands of his father. Women were spider silk, so easily torn. Men were clamoring children.

It occurred to him, before long, that Viji could have done the laundry herself. It was really the least she could have done before leaving him forever. God knows she'd had the time, those hours and days spent staring at the

bedroom wall. She might as well have turned her gaze to
the clothes hamper, to the dial on the washing machine, to
this box of blue and white powder. She might as well have
turned her listless hands to sorting and folding. But eventually, he would have had to do this himself. There was no
way he could have lasted until after Christmas on the
clothes he had in his closet, not even if he wore the same
clothes and underwear several times a week. With a prayer
for the pink delicates, he threw a cupful of detergent in,
closed the washer door, and pressed the button that
looked most faded—surely this would be the setting that
Viji used most. The machine hummed and whirred
through the night, and by the next morning, it was done.

By the fourth day, he'd stopped calling her Viji and
started calling her "that woman." Why hadn't that woman
called? Why hadn't she bothered contacting him? His student visited, chatting and spreading her legs and even
winking at him once. He was unresponsive and spoke in
monosyllables until she got up to leave. He fought the urge
to throw a pen at her large head as she walked out of his
office. He glared at Amaré when she brought him a syl-
labus to sign. Amaré glared back. He had a feeling that
women worked in collusion. They worked in covens, cov-
etous, capricious, complicit, and covert. There were other
words he could think of.

That evening George hovered in his father's doorway.
Stan sat upright in bed, eyes closed and silent. *What if he's
dead?* George thought. *What if he's dead and I can't reach
Viji and I have to throw him a funeral on my own, with no
one to invite but Kamla and Lupe and maybe the neighbors?*
He would have to choose a coffin himself and order the

small triangular sandwiches.

Just then a glorious snore erupted from Stan and woke him, startled and blinking. He shifted position, farted, then leaned back and closed his eyes again.

"What is it, son?" he asked with his eyes closed.

"Did you want dinner?"

"What's on?"

In the cabinet, a box of macaroni and cheese awaited the children's return. "Pasta?"

It wasn't until George emptied the packet of yellow powder over the boiled macaroni, fingering the remnants that hid in the foil corners, that he realized the meal wasn't big enough. He didn't feel much like eating, but Stan would demolish his serving in two mouthfuls. In the fridge were two tomatoes and a gallon of milk, plus several Tupperwares that had crusted over with time. Viji could have cooked and frozen some meals for them. It was the least she could have done. He sighed and picked up a tomato. He hadn't wanted dinner, hadn't even wanted to make Stan dinner, but it was all that had come to him when he'd stood in his doorway.

What he really wanted was a little fatherly counsel. But how to ask Stan for advice? *Dad, I think my wife left me. What would you do?*

He emptied the entire pan onto a plate, chopped some tomato, and set it before Stan. George would eat later, or maybe not. They sat together as Stan chewed thoughtfully and without complaining about his macaroni. His father was the last person George would normally have asked for relationship advice. He'd spent his life despising Stan's ways with women, but now he had no one else to turn to.

"Dad," he began. "Dad—" Stan looked up, chewing. "What would you have done if Mum had left you?"

"If she'd what, now?"

"If she'd left you. If she'd got up and left and said she wasn't coming back."

"Are you saying she should have left me?"

"Would you answer the question, please?"

"Probably gone down the pub and got pissed."

"Really?"

"Then I'd have topped myself."

"Hmm. Romantic."

"Aye, that's me. Dead romantic."

Stan scraped the last of the cheese sauce onto his fork. "Not bad, son," he said. "Not a bad meal at all." He patted George on the back, got up, and headed out the front door. It was nearly freezing outside—frost already coated the bushes, and Stan wasn't wearing a coat. Never mind, he was only going next door. He had a woman there, warmth enough for a still winter's night. Warmth and skin and hair. George left the kitchen adrift in dinner mess, a dusting of yellow powder on the countertop, a plate abandoned on the table.

Day five, and Viji hadn't called. By now she'd become "that fucking woman." That fucking woman had run away to hide. That fucking woman had taken his kids. That fucking woman should have called to let him know that they hadn't been massacred or kidnapped, that his children weren't lying in the middle of a godforsaken rice paddy. It occurred to him briefly that his children could indeed have been lying in a rice paddy or a sewer or the dark hotel bedroom of an international organ dealer. And soon he began to fear that even Viji, that fucking woman, could have fallen in harm's way. Indians in a crowd couldn't be trusted not to riot. There might have been a crush at the airport, a stampede at customs. Or a customs officer who took her into a back room. Or a drunken cabbie, his rheumy eyes seeping over her bosoms as he opened the car door. She might not have made it to her family's house at all. They might have been looking for her themselves, sick with worry and unable to phone him. Six servants, no telephone. Not even a pencil could make him feel better.

He passed the minutes and hours in his office, one hand holding his head up and the other punching keys as the words streamed through him. K-I-N-G-D-O-M-C-O-M-E-T-H-Y-W-I-L-L-B-E-D-O-N-E-I H A-T-E-T-II-I-S-M-I-K-E-Y-L-I-K-E-S-I-T-T-H-I-N-G-S-W-E-S-A-I-D-T-O-D-A-Y-T-H-A-T F U-C-K-I-N-G-F-U-C-K-I-N-G-W-O-M-A-N He was starved for her. She'd never done this to him before.

The phone rang.

"Hello."

"It's Viji." A pause. "Hello?"

"Darling!" He felt dizzy. "Darling, where are you? Where have you been?"

"I'm in India."

He began to laugh weakly.

"George? George, what's wrong?"

"You didn't call, Viji. Why didn't you call?"

"What?"

"I *said*, why didn't you call?" But the phone line crackled and hushed.

"We're fine here. The STDs were closed."

"Oh."

They fell quiet and let the precious international seconds tick by. George's thoughts snuck away from relief and clung greedily to Viji's note. *Because because because* and the final verdict: *I may not.* His head flopped to the table and he listened with his nose smushed against the desktop.

From Viji's end he heard the dinging of bicycle bell. And all at once he saw her, the folding chair on which she sat, the damp-stained walls of the STD office, the rolled-up garage door that framed the street. Just outside the door was a woman at a cart piled high with white and orange flowers and hulking garlands for the temple. Auto rickshaws, round and dusty, black as woodlice, *putt-putt*ed by. Cycling past were men with grasshopper legs of pure bone and sinew, their calves yellow with dust.

"George?"

"Ypsh?"

"Are you still there?"

"Ypsh." He lifted his head. "That note you left—" The phone bleeped three times. Their time was running out. "Call again, Viji, please. When will you call again?"

"I will soon. Next week."

"Darling, we need to talk about that—"

A loud click, followed by silence. Not even a dial tone to tell him the call had ended—just the cold suspension of sound.

✿ ✿ ✿

It was time for home, and for Stan, assuming that Stan was even home.

When George was fourteen, a psychic had come to the house, invited by his mother. She dressed normally, in brown trousers and a baggy white wool jumper, the sort that sheep farmers wore. She had an enormous bust, boring hair and a boring face, and glasses that made George think of his lettering teacher. She asked for a cup of herbal tea and proceeded to tell George's mother that she had strong eyesight, a possible termite problem, money in her future, not long to live, and a daughter with green eyes. The prediction of the non existent daughter didn't soften the blow of his mother's imminent death.

"Don't fret, my love," his mother had laughed. "In cosmic terms, "not long" could mean a hundred years!" But some fragile bud of psychic ability told George that his mother would not live for another hundred years. And from that day, he began to dread her inevitable absence. His dread took on different forms and set at last, like quivering jelly, on this. The scene that trundled before him now, on this Tuesday before Christmas, was exactly and precisely what he'd feared his life would come to: a wordless dinner with his father; dreary evening rituals of nursery food followed by hours of television. Only this evening, Stan would disappear to join his girlfriend, and George would be left with the television. Or a book. Or his flaccid pink member in his hand. He would read half-heartedly the book of Cheever stories he'd bought earlier that year, and ponder how he might make better use of this time, this vacation from his family.

Before he left for university, his mother had taught

him the principles of cooking forhimself—how long to
fry an onion, the dangers of raw garlic, the proper consis-
tency for chicken stew, the beauty of rare beef, the travesty
of allspice. Every dish, like every person, had to have a
dominant flavor. Texture was as important as taste.

To his credit that evening, George created a plate of
fish fingers that tasted predominantly of breaded cod, peas
that tasted primarily of pea, and mashed potatoes that
tasted first and foremost of mashed potato. It was probably identical to the last meal he'd ever cooked, in his
student flat in Exeter, before Madras, before Viji, before
dinners cooked daily without fail and placed faithfully on
his table. Fish fingers were easy enough to find in Sacramento, though they were a food meant for children,
judging from the cartoons and word jumbles on the box.
He wondered why he'd never thought of them before now.
Stan chomped appreciatively at the meal, coating fish in
potato and jabbing happily at the peas.

"Christmas soon," he grunted.

"Yep"

The evening spread between them like a thick paste.
Outside, the screeching of brakes.

"Ten days away," Stan said.

"Yep."

"Any plans?"

"Plans? No, not really." There was a department holiday party the next night, but George never went to those.
"How 'bout you?"

Stan shrugged and stabbed a stick of cod.

"I suppose you'll be with Lupe? Going to church,
maybe?" George couldn't help grinning at the thought of

his father kneeling, standing, kneeling, standing, at a Catholic Mass. It didn't occur to him that Stan would spend Christmas with his son.

The kitchen fell into silence, save for the clacking of Stan's dentures. When he'd finished, George collected the empty plates and stacked them in the dishwasher.

"I'm off," Stan said. He held his down coat and pulled his fisherman's hat over his eyes, as he'd done every evening after dinner for as long as George could remember, before heading out to the pub. This time he'd be going to Lupe's, maybe to the movies with her, maybe to her house, maybe someplace George hadn't even thought of, like dancing or bingo or church.

"Is someone picking you up?"

"Yep."

"See you later then, Dad."

Stan seemed startled by this pleasantry. "Aye," he said. George wiped fish-finger crumbs off the table and watched as Stan stood straight-backed on the front porch, hands in his pockets, waiting for the flash of headlights.

When one was on vacation from one's family, what did one do? George sat in his study to consider. He could very easily:

Order a pizza.

Watch television until his eyes teared.

Buy a dirty magazine.

Start that journal article he'd been meaning to write.

Hire a stripper. (He'd done it once before for a college friend's bachelor party. A mistake from the start—she'd been squat and pigeon-breasted, chewed gum, and chatted through her performance: *So where ya from, then? So when's the wedding, then? So wot's it ya do, then?)*

Call someone, anyone, and speak without interruption.

Write a letter to Viji. He missed her. She filled up his evenings, even when they did nothing.

Walk naked through the living room.

Walk naked from the waist down, through the living room and into the kitchen, out the back door, through the shriveling cold of the yard, around the pool, along the thorny bushes, around the shuffleboard court, back inside, past the television, back through the living room, up the stairs down the stairs, up the stairs down the stairs, his nudity waggling between his legs like a giddy earthworm for all the world—or in his case none of the world—to see.

The doorbell rang, eight deep chimes, one missing in the middle. Hastily, he bundled his thoughts and shut the dishwasher. He opened the door.

"I was driving by and saw you in the window," Kamla said.

"Oh," he replied. "Okay." His cheeks were flushing.

"Can I come in?"

"Of course. Of course!"

She stood in the entryway. "The house is quiet." The only sound came from the final fading reverberations of the doorbell. Then thesy, too, melted into silence. George and Kamla turned together and looked at the split-level living room, now a well of shadow.

"How about some tea?" Kamla asked.

George inhaled sharply. "Yes. Okay. Come in. Sorry. Come in." Tea George could do. Once during exams, he wanted to tell Kamla, he'd risen in the middle of the night, made a pot of tea, and left it in the kitchen undrunk, with no recollection of it in the morning. Tea he could do in his sleep.

She pulled the sugar from the cupboard. "Do you have cardamom?"

"No. I'm not sure. That's more Viji's department."

She turned to him and tut-tutted. "Really, George, you're useless!" Then she reached over and squeezed his hand.

"Viji's not here," he blurted before he could stop himself. Kamla blinked back at him. "She—she's out of town. With the children"

"Oh—I know." She bit her upper lip. "I know she's not here. Is that all right? Are you busy?"

He was a fool and a cretin, and all he could do was say that of course, of course it was all right. They stood in silence and listened to the tea brew.

"So" Kamla began, and stopped. She leaned on the counter. She carried the talk almost single-handedly, with an ease that made George grateful for every word she ut tered. It was she who fed the conversation, he who rode its gentle wave. They spoke about the children the car the weather the malls the highways the university the cost of heating Ronald Reagan Ronald McDonald Christmas Hanukkah this new African one and Diwali.

George was aware that he'd been tapping his finger on the counter and laughing at every pause, like some sort of mental degenerate. He wondered how much longer he'd have to keep this up, this charade of being a normally functioning person, a witty and social and likeable adult. When Kamla smiled and looked directly into his eyes, he choked a little on his own saliva.

When he was a child, he'd been unable to speak to his

friends in front of his parents. It was intolerable to be
watched in conversation, to be observed for later com-
ment. His parents weren't here now, but Viji was. She was
everywhere in the kitchen, crouched in the cupboards,
swinging from the refrigerator door, riding the slick sharp
wheel of the electric can opener. She lurked in every slurp
of tea, nuzzled her way into the pauses.

"Have you spoken to Viji?" Kamla asked, at last.

"Hmm?" He feigned nonchalance. "Oh, yes, actually.
Just the other day, in fact."

"And she's fine?"

"And she's fine," he nodded judiciously.

"It must be nice for her, you know, to be back home
again. After so long."

Of course—Kamla knew nothing of the note, of Viji's
silence, of that fleeting troubled glaze over her eyes when
he had bid her goodbye. Or did she?

The words he wanted lay somewhere between his tes-
ticles and his stomach. They quivered: "Did she say
anything to you? Ever?"

Raised eyebrows. "Like what?"

"Like why she left, or—"

Kamla looked at him quizzically and smiled. That
smile meant something. "Not really," George stood in silence, unsure of whether to push on. "She didn't *leave*
George, did she? It's only a holiday. I could use a
holiday" She smirked. "You men. Such babes in arms. Always struggling to be independent and then when it
comes, you don't know what to do with yourselves."

"But surely—I mean, it was a bit sudden, you know,
surely she must have said something."

"Hmm, no. I was thinking of taking Anisha to the beach. She likes the beach, you know, more than the mountains. Her father was a mountain person. A mountain man." He felt her watching him. "She wasn't very happy, you know, George. I think she needed to see her family again."

But I'm her family, he wanted to say. "Right. Right. I suppose I don't miss my own family in quite the same way."

"Well, your family's here." She nodded at the pack of tobacco Stan had left on the counter.

"I suppose you're right."

"*But* you must miss England, don't you?"

George shrugged. (Of course he missed England. But he missed more than England. If he acknowledged the void, really looked down into it, he'd see that it would take more than a landmass to fill it.)

Kamla sniffed at the air. "Smells fishy."

"Fish fingers."

"Oh. You don't know how to cook?"

Forty minutes later, George saw Kamla to the door. She tucked her hair behind her ear and said goodbye. And then, because men on vacation from their families often did things they couldn't explain, he said, "I have a Christmas party tomorrow."

"Oh, really?"

"Well, a holiday party, Christmas, Hanukkah."

She waited.

"Fancy going?"

She considered, hand on doorknob, then smiled that inscrutable smile. "No. Not really. But thank you."

George nodded.

"Goodbye."

"Bye."

He closed the door and shoved his face into the cold fragrant wood. "Shit," he said. "Buggery."

❧ CHAPTER THREE ❧

Shame on you, Viji scolded herself. *Shame, shame, shame, behaving like those teenagers on television.* She'd hung up on George, and now it embarrassed her to think of that letter she'd written. She looked around at the street that tumbled and wheezed around her, a cacophony of storefronts, a train wreck. The STD office keeled into the sari shop, which butted against the sweet shop, which rammed into the grungy teahouse, which crashed into the tailor's. She flapped her feet, yellow with silt from the crumbling road. She would wash them before she entered the house. What was once just ground, just normal inevitable dust, was now dirt.

On the veranda, three small pairs of shoes waited, which meant the children were inside. The day before, they'd wandered into the streets and gotten lost. They had become things of fascination for the local children, who'd fingered their hair and left grubby marks on their clothes. They'd been brought back by a secretary from a doctor's office around the corner.

Inside, the house was dark, the only sound the whip of the ceiling fan. Then, from the kitchen, familiar voices, the *clank* of a pot. She slipped upstairs to the library to be alone.

But when she opened the door, someone was already in there. She gasped and closed it. He was shoulders and a head and sat in a shadowy corner. "Shanta," she called, but not loudly enough, because nobody answered from downstairs. Maybe they had a visitor. Maybe they had a visitor and she'd just rudely shut the door in his face. She prepared a smile and opened the door again. There was nobody. "Hello?" she asked. "H*ello-oooh*," she cooed, like a true-blue Maple Grove housewife. Nobody. Her heart tripped over itself and she had to breathe slowly to calm down.

"I'll sit down," she said, out loud, because it helped to hear real sound. She did sit down, in the chair opposite her father's favorite. Arms on the armrests. She sat for several minutes, until at last she decided there was nobody in here, it was all in her head. She sighed once, then again, hoping it would help her relax.

This was her father's safe haven. He'd surrounded himself in here with books. Did they hold the answers? They were other people's words. They had little to do with her. Words, in general, had little to do with the impulses and mysterious flashes of sound and sight that made up daily living.

She remembered him as a man with a massive face and a vast plane of a forehead. He was clean shaven, except for the thick sideburns that cradled his face. His eyes were wide. His body, in comparison, was thin and feline. He was kind. He angered easily.

She'd always known he was something of an outcast. A magistrate, yes, but a stranger everywhere he went. Maybe that's why he liked it in here. Books didn't require him to say anything or be anything. She'd once heard him called an idiot. She hidn't remembered it until just now, and the thought of it pained her. It was the word her mother's mother used, and not in the way most mothers-in-law used it. What she meant was that Appa was subpar, recallable goods.

Every day he swallowed pills that resided at the bottom of a silver cup. Viji used to poke at them with her fingers. They were smooth like beetles, red like rust, blue like Krishna. He would point to things. Yes, she remembered now. He would see things before anyone else did, so quickly that when she looked, they'd be gone. He once saw a well in the courtyard, and a girl with red hair.

What she remembered best was the large, warm presence of him, the way he'd turn her upside down and hold her by the ankles and swing her like a pendulum. And yet gnawing inside of him had been something that was invisible to her, a small girl hanging by her ankles, trying not to laugh because laughing made it harder to breathe, her mouth tight with glee and gasping. In the hanging-from-her-ankles world, everything had been born anew, from the upside-down gate to the upside-down tree stump that grew from the dirt sky, to the upside-down dog across the street, barking into the ground. Somewhere in there, something must have happened. Something in that upside-down world of theirs had made her father want to leave, to stay away forever.

༈༈༈

"You can't go there." The guard had stood before Viji. He wasn't much taller than she was, though she was ten and he a grown man, but the thick khaki fabric of his uniform, the cap pulled low over his eyes, gave him a certain authority.

The marble floors cooled the courthouse. They were polished to a shine, but still the building smelled of stagnant water. Beyond the guard was a reception desk, and beyond that, an occasional adult roaming past. Shanta stood a few feet behind her, poised to step forward and drag her away.

"I'm looking for my father, sir."

"Who is your father?"

"A magistrate, sir. He works here."

"Do you have an appointment?"

"No."

"Then no entry."

"Please, sir—"

The guard barked an order at a man who squatted against the wall. The man scurried to his feet and ran from the building. In less than a minute, he returned with a steel tumbler of tea. The guard held it a few inches above his lips and poured it in a stream down his throat, glugging rhythmically, steam rising from his lips.

"Go away." He clicked his tongue and hissed at Viji. "Off with you, or you'll end up in this court for real."

The courthouse was a day away from crumbling. Every afternoon felt like the last day of the building's life. She had been here three times already, standing outside of it after school, fingering the cracks in its giant pillars. Appa had left more than a week before, and now she was stuck living with the neighbors, in the big house that grew cold at night, in a bedroom whose wardrobes were too tall for

her, so that she had to wait for a servant to bring down
her uniform each morning. She wanted Appa home again
so that she, too, could return.

The courthouse was the color of age and death, bled
pale by the perpetual loss and gain of inhabitants. Along
the courthouse wall sat a row of men, squatting in the dirt,
their dingy shirts hanging loose from their necks. Their
clothes were not in tatters, nor did they have begging
bowls. They simply sat and waited for orders. They com-
pleted the orders and returned to the squatting position.
This was their job. They ignored Viji and Shanta.

Next to one of the columns sat a bull with horns
painted red and yellow, flicking flies away with its tail. If it
was waiting for its owner, its owner never came. It was a
homeless bull.

Beyond the pillars, the street ran with its own wor-
ries, too crowded and hot to bother with the two girls, one
small and short-haired, in a gray uniform, peering into
the building's entrance; the other taller, impatient, with a
violet bruise burgeoning over her eye.

"He's not coming," Shanta said. She prodded the
cushion of her bruise.

"Yes he is. He has to."

"I'm hungry."

"It's only four o'clock." Viji was hungry too. On the
street corner a man was selling crunchy, salty spirals of
murukku. A few people had left the building already, men
in brown suits and narrow ties. Through the arched entry,
she could see the guard, leaning against the reception desk,
his baton a lazy pendulum.

"He never shows up," Shanta said.

"He might this time."

At five o'clock, as people left in thickening clots, Viji ventured back in. The guard shifted his weight and cocked his hip. "Please, sir, can I see my father now?"

"Not possible. No children." This sounded to Viji like a made-up rule. He eyed their gray uniforms. "Why aren't you in school?"

"Excuse me, sir, school is dismissed."

"And who is your father?"

She said his name. He shook his head and said, "No such man."

He seemed to be saying that no such man existed, that her father—magistrate, pill taker, ankle swinger—simply wasn't true.

Viji stayed outside the courthouse until dark, when the trickle of lawyers and secretaries had slowed and finally stopped. The two girls watched as the guard pushed the door shut. They listened to the latch bolt into its lock. It didn't matter to Viji that Shanta was right, that Appa wouldn't come out of the courthouse. And to Shanta, who never left Viji's side but kept quiet, fretful watch, it didn't seem to matter, either.

❦❦❦

Later that afternoon, the kitchen boomed with laughter. "Again," Kuttima called, clapping her hands. "Again, again!" Viji shook her head and held her aching belly, the room blurring behind tears of mirth.

She grabbed another plate and turned to the two washbasins filled with water. "How American ladies wash dishes." She dipped the plate jauntily into one basin, dipped it into the next basin, and set it aside to dry. It was crusted with rice still, and dripped brown suds. She turned to her audience and beamed.

"Again, again!" Uma Athai thumped her foot for more. Viji had done this little sketch four times already, alongside "American lady speed-walking," "American lady winning money on the radio," and "American lady in a sanitary-pad commercial."

A scream. Upstairs. Babygirl.

"Babygirl?" Viji called. The room fell silent. No answer came. "Chellum?" Viji swept up the stairs and Shanta followed. They found Babygirl in the bedroom, her back against the wall, in horrified silence. "What?" Viji asked. "What?" She followed Babygirl's gaze to the wall above the bed. There, a green lizard, no bigger than a finger. It was thin, utterly harmless, almost transparent, possibly malnourished.

"Pshh! That's it? This is why you screamed?"

Babygirl glared. She scowled at Shanta, who leaned against the wall panting, still breathless from the stairs.

"It's just a lizard, Babygirl, it won't do a thing to you."

"What's it doing here?"

"They live here. They kill mosquitoes and flies. There's probably one in every room!"

"Nuh-uh."

"Yes."

"No."

"I'll make a bet," Viji ventured. Her daughter's eyes brightened.

"For what?"

"Ice cream."

"They have ice cream here?"

"They have ice cream here—of course they have ice cream here." She looked sideways at Babygirl and sighed. Her children thought this was a barbarian country—no toilets, no showers, no pizza, no ice cream. *I'll pee in America,* Babygirl had said that first day. India was the seat of civilization, the home of mathematics and poetry and science—but none of this mattered to children who had to squat to shit.

"Okay! I bet you."

"Let's go." In the library, a yellow lizard clung to the wall above the bookcase. In the game room, it scurried past the carom board and came to rest next to an old, dusty vina. In one bedroom, above the bed; in the next, above the dresser; in the next, above the lamp—this one was smart, waiting for gnats that gathered around the light. In Shanta's puja room, a small green lizard waited just beside the door, which made Babygirl squeal and run into the hall.

"See?" Viji said. "Every room."

"We haven't been to every room yet, though."

"Yes, we have."

"What about downstairs?"

Before Viji could speak, Babygirl ran down the stairs, nearly slipping in her hurry. Viji followed her down the stairs, through the sitting room, and watched her burst open the puja room doors.

"What's this?" Babygirl stopped abruptly in the doorway. Cobwebs hung from the ceiling like streamers, and a thick layer of dust coated the frames on the wall. Viji sneezed six times. "Gosh," Babygirl said.

"You know, Babygirl. You know what this room is."

"This isn't like ours."

"No," Viji agreed, "this one isn't like ours."

Proof at last that the aunts had wholly, indubitably, 101 percent lost the plot. Viji held the end of her sari over her nose and mouth to block the dust. Inside, what had once been the house's centerpiece, shown proudly to guests, cleaned faithfully every day, was now a sepulcher, a relief map of death. On its far wall, a heavy blanket of silt covered the photographs of Viji's mother, three uncles, great-uncles, great-aunts, grandmothers, grandfathers, four cousins, the old neighbor.

It was incredible that the aunts could pray in here, the dust was so thick and aggressive. It pierced through the cloth that covered her nose and mouth and made her cough until she retched. "*Kuttima*," she called. "Bring water. A bucket of water."

Kuttima, mumbling, brought her what she asked for. There was only one way to do this, and Viji wasted no time. With one swoop she flung the bucket over the room, the water rising in a great arc and splashing down over everything. Dripping pictures, streams coursing from the statuettes, the black stone lingam glistening. It would take many buckets more and a merciless scrubbing. But now, after days of rattling aimlessly in the old house, Viji had a purpose.

❧ ❧ ❧

"How come," Kieran began, spitting over the side of the balcony, "there are so many poor people here?" The dollop of spit dropped lazily to the pavement below and splattered next to the veranda wall. From above he watched a half-dressed family ragtagging down the main road. The little boy wore a dingy brown shirt and no underpants; his smaller sister wore a skirt with no shirt, her soccer ball of a belly swelling over the waistline. They'd had to split their only outfit, Kieran guessed. Their mother, or maybe their grandmother, had dark reptilian skin and a bun of thin hair.

Babygirl and Avi were stretched out next to the carom board, stacking the round pieces in their corners. Viji had taught them the day before how to play. The board was a square the size of a Twister mat, with pockets in the corner, from end to end almost as long as Babygirl. An expert already, Avi shuttled his red piece into a corner pocket. He whistled triumphantly.

They'd been on the street the day before. They'd wandered out on their own while Viji was taking a nap. There were no sidewalks here.

"How come everyone's staring?" A man leaned out of his shop to watch them pass.

"Maybe we should go back." But before they could go anywhere, they were surrounded. Children their height, with worried eyes and older faces, crowded in around them. Fingers reached out to rifle through their hair. Some wore school uniforms, like the Whitman uniforms, but light blue instead of navy. They pushed in around them until the triplets stood trapped in a shrinking circle. Avi looked at Kieran and both boys turned to Babygirl, who stood slapping at the hands, twisting away from the children, exhaling sharply. "Stop it," she grunted. "*Stop* it!"

After what seemed a very long time, a lady from an office came out and shooed the others away. She didn't have to ask them who they were, she just brought them back here, back to Viji.

The evening before, Viji had taken them to a temple. It was a dark place, with a roof that climbed into the sky. Inside was airless and wet and smelled of burning oil. The ceiling dripped into a puddle on the floor, but no one seemed to notice. No one put a bucket underneath it, or rags. Men with no shirts, only a thread looped diagonally around their chest and white cloth tied around their waist, loitered next to pillars, or strolled toward the ringing of puja bells. He thought maybe they prayed for a living. Like priests. Kieran wondered who would pay someone to pray for a living.

He worried that his shoes would be stolen. They'd had to take them off outside, and beneath his feet the stone was worn into smooth ripples. If he were poor, he would've waited outside temples and chosen the best-looking shoes. Then he would've taken them and sold them to other poor people, or to bargain hunters with lots of money. If he were poor and had no legs, like the man at the airport, he didn't know what he'd do. It wasn't as if a man with no legs could steal a pair of shoes unnoticed. *What do you need those for?* someone would surely ask. The only other person he'd seen with no legs was in his history book, a man in a wheelchair with a mustache like a broom, whose jeans closed off neatly at the knees. At least he had a wheelchair. Then he'd skipped even further into the book to look at the photographs of tall, wild, bushy jungles and helicopters in the trees.

"Turn back to the Iroquois nation, Kieran. We won't be studying that," his teacher had said. When he'd asked why, she'd said, "It's not history yet."

"But it's in our history book." He was bored of the Iroquois and their five nations and their longhouses.

"Yes, but it's very recent, Kieran. We need to look at what's come before."

Before what? But he'd turned back without protest, to look at what had come before.

When they'd first arrived in America, George and Viji were no different from any other two immigrants. They'd searched, like truffle-seeking pigs, for the something-in-the-air that every immigrant wanted: a sense of normalcy. That warm, bread-in-the-oven certainty that seemed to cleave to everyone around them. From their first steps on American soil, that long ride from the airport, their descent into the Sacramento Valley, they yearned for a normal, ten-fingers-ten-toes life. This house, these pots, this parking space between the two white lines, this mailbox where mail appeared abracadabra every afternoon. In hopes of attaining this normalcy in their small rented flat, furnished for them by the university, they began to make offerings: a houseplant purchased from Emigh Hardware, a trip one Sunday to the International House of Pancakes, a tablecloth with matching yellow place mats, a blender with six settings from Sears. But still, normalcy was no more than a taste on the backs of their tongues. Like the elusive truffle, it burrowed deeper into

the earth and farther away from them. To dig for it would
be to dig clean through the earth's core, straight through
to Madras, to Nottingham, emerging black-snouted, tri-
umphant, and back where they had begun.

Even when the wish for ten-fingers-ten-toes turned
into the reality of thirty-fingers-thirty-toes, the pungent
cloud of difference followed them, weighed them down
like jet lag. Which diapers? Which brand of mashed-up
food in tiny glass jars? Which schools? Which friends for
the children—this four-year-old with the grandfather's
eyebrows? That blond girl who picked her nose and
rubbed the harvest on her tricycle? The runtish boy on
growth hormones? Whom to trust? Whom not to trust?
For Viji, this last question was easy: black people, Mexicans, anyone who seemed to be struggling or worse off
than she was, anyone who didn't pop fresh from the pages
of a JCPenney catalog. For George, more bent on actually
using his judgment, the decision was harder, but he finally
settled on a few equally obvious choices: Girl Scouts
frightened him—they seemed far too competent at too
young an age. Car salesmen, particularly the ones who
said, *What've I gotta do to get you to walk outta here with
a*—. Game-show hosts, not that he would ever conceiv-
ably encounter one. And real estate agents.

Theirs was named Marcia, pronounced Mar-see-ya.
She wore yellow stockings to match her yellow high heels.
She showed him a haunted-looking gray house with col-
lapsing shutters, a "fixer-upper" near the capitol, a row of
tract houses in the middle of a field, and a green stucco
nightmare with pokey holly bushes growing around the
porch. She showed him a number of houses that made

him consider moving back to England. But finally, Marcia with the yellow stockings redeemed herself. She brought him to the house on Winding Creek Road. Perhaps because of what he'd seen before, perhaps from a sense of urgency at the thought of Viji's swelling belly, George saw the house once, kicked a wall to make sure it was sturdy, and said, "I'll take it." He signed the papers, and that was that.

Viji and George had done their best to turn the big bushy place into a bastion of normalcy. And they got close, close enough to catch a whiff of it occasionally, in the peace of a warm Sunday or the reliable hum of the water heater. House-job-car—they had all they needed. So they did what every immigrant eventually did. They said to themselves, *This is it. This is where we stop.* And they settled, somewhere in the middle of the deep dark earth, close to the truffle, or very far away.

Somewhere in the pool-house soil, perhaps not far from that truffle, nestled among the tentacles of sprinkler systems and sewage lines, level with the cement foundations of Maple Grove's houses, was the box. And inside the box, the shrapnel of George and Viji's life together, guarded lovingly by their children. A cufflink, a handkerchief. A pair of blue crystal earrings.

It was night. Stan returned after George had gone to bed, his footsteps muffled by the hallway carpet. George hadn't slept yet, hadn't even come close. He got up and stood at the sliding doors. The pool in moonlight winked at him. *I know what you're up to,* it rippled. As if in response, the security light by the pool house snapped on. Nothing but a cat. George saw its tabby coat as it clawed a eucalyptus tree.

The earrings were safe underground. Only the children knew where they were. Except now Stan knew, too. And, he sensed, so would Viji one day. How silly he'd been, holding on to those. How sentimental and wholly unlike himself. The earrings were, he was absolutely certain, not safe underground. Too many others were privy to what had once been his alone, and the realization of it left a sour coating in the back of his throat, a cocktail of bile and worry. He would have to dig them up.

The sliding door opened with a *hoossssh* and he was outside, barefoot. The late-December frost turned his toes to pellets of stone. When he kneeled beneath the glare of the security light, his pajamas went soaked and brown. He dug with his bare hands and didn't get far. From the pool house he fished an old handshovel that he'd bought for Viji's roses. Yarns of cobweb stuck between his fingers and clung to his face. He raspberried a sticky strand from his mouth.

With the shovel he cracked the frost. This was the spot, he was sure of it. He could still see the children kneeling here that Labor Day afternoon. The dirt flew in fast and meaty clumps. He was strong, even at this slack hour of the night. And within seconds, yes, he hit the box.

His fingers turned fat, swollen with cold. They shook when he opened the lid, scattering dirt over the children's treasures as he fished out the earrings. A quick toss into the swimming pool or over the fence to the neighboring yard, and he would be free of them forever. But of course he wouldn't do that. He sat, his ass a block of ice now, and fondled the twinkling stones.

A flash in the window. He looked up and yelped

aloud. Stan stood at the sliding door, backlit by the family room. Hands on glass, he peered out at George. George didn't know what to do. He waved. Stan did not wave back. George waved more deliberately. Stan only stood there, as if he hadn't seen. In his sleep, his hair had flipped the wrong way and hung like an awning off the side of his head. "Dad?" George called. Stan pawed at the glass, then turned around and walked back into the house. George would bury the box, go inside, and get in bed. He looked down at the earrings, glinting prettily in his grubby palm.

❧ CHAPTER FOUR ❧

1980. George woke as the train slowed into Nottingham station. He'd forgotten how all English train stations looked the same, with their squat platforms, that brick dome, and the façade of arches caging a circular drive. Weak-kneed with sleep, he stepped off the train. The chill slapped him awake. This kind of cold happened only in March, when the skies blushed blue and the clouds scattered, leaving the freeze to unleash itself on the earth below. Down south, among London's buses and high buildings, it was warmer and damp. In Sacramento, the buds would be popping forth. He looked around expectantly, trying not to look expectant, to see if anyone had come to collect him. Of course his father wouldn't be there. But he looked for the old fishing hat anyway. How lovely it would be to see his mother, in her silly disco sunglasses and green coat. Up the stairs he lugged his suitcase, over the platforms to the station lobby. He would take a taxi home, or maybe just walk.

George! The voice came from his head, a distant call that he attributed to being home again after nearly four years. It came once more, *George!* It was an apparition, born of a need for familiarity, the same urge that made him think he recognized the strangers who milled around the lobby, checking arrival times and holding up newspapers. And then he heard, "George!" This time it was real, a clarion call, unmistakable. He turned, and by the newsstand in the distance he saw a red glove waving. And then she was there, in the middle of the station, running and smiling and looking so much like home that he wanted to sweep her up and roll her to the ground.

Victoria grabbed his forearms before he could wrap them around her. She beamed, and for several seconds they stood looking at each other. Then her smile fell. "All right, George?" she asked.

"All right, Victoria."

She sped ahead of him, and he had to jog with his suitcase to keep up.

"I didn't know you'd be here," he panted.

"Your dad called me."

"What? He did? When?"

"Last week. I suppose when he knew you were coming." She stopped abruptly. "Well, don't look so worried, George, you know how he is."

"Right."

"It doesn't mean anything."

"Right."

"Listen, it'll be fine."

"I know."

She placed a gloved hand on his arm. "You must be shattered."

"I could sleep."

"Well hold on for the taxi ride and then we'll get you to bed."

The drive to Sneinton was two miles long, but rammed

with traffic. Hindi film songs filled the car and a Ganesh pendant hung from the rearview mirror. The driver spotted George's gaze and turned the volume down.

"No, it's all right," George said. "Turn it up if you want."

Victoria smirked.

"What?"

"Nothing at all."

They stared silently out of opposite windows until the taxi stopped. Together, they walked down the row of terraced houses until they came to 38.

"The door's unlocked," Victoria said. And so it was. Inside, the house smelled of old sausage. The radiator hissed its welcome and a television tinned from the other room.

"Hello," he called, but no one seemed to hear.

Victoria shouted, "We're back!" and the television switched off.

"Hiya, George," his father said. He looked worn, his hair more white now than blond. George went to hug him, but his dad skimmed away from him and headed down the corridor. "She's been asking for you," he said. "Excited and all sorts."

The house was even smaller than George remembered, and darker. He'd forgotten how much furniture was packed into the small rooms, sideboards pushed against bookshelves and sidetables, as if too much space would cause a person to come unmoored and fly off the face of the earth. There was one window overlooking the sunless street; the others looked onto their neighbors' walls. In the days he spent there, he wouldn't get used to the narrow kitchen, smaller than his pantry in Sacramento. The knocks and voices from the neighbors adjacent would keep him awake at night.

"George," his mother said as he sat down on her bed. "You caught me napping."

"Hi, Mum." He hugged her awkwardly, leaning across her chest, squeezing her shoulder. She wasn't thin or wasted, neither skeletal nor hollow-eyed, not at all the way he'd imagined his sick mother. Her face was full, swollen from painkillers, he would later find out. Her voice was strong, nothing like that choking whisper they used in the movies. Her hair was black still, with the streaks of gray she'd had for years and years. She was pale, but her skin had always been milk white.

"How are you, Mum?"

"The rebel armies are advancing, darling." He didn't know what to say. "Hand me my tobacco, will you?"

"Tobacco?"

"What?" she shrugged. "What harm could it do me now?" The tobacco packet held a row of ready-made spliffs.

"Who rolled these for you?"

"Never you mind, George." She lit a fag, and the smoke she blew into his face was rotten with marijuana.

"What's that, then?"

"It helps me relax. Now put the kettle on, will you? And take a shower, please—you smell of airplanes."

Later: "Is it so shocking I would be here?" Victoria sat on the carpet by the fireplace, holding one palm up to the flames. The light sharpened the lines around her mouth.

"It's shocking you would come when I was here," he replied.

"I know. I behaved horridly. I shudder to think of it."
She shuddered physically then.

"You talk different," he said.

"I talk *different*? *You* talk different."

"Nonsense."

"You sound like John Wayne."

"You sound like the Queen."

"There's an unlikely pairing."

He laughed.

"And?" she asked.

He knew what she meant. And what of his life now, over there: wife and three children who had just turned three, fragile and frightening and as packed with latent destruction as eggs balanced on the lip of a spoon. On the opposite end of a twelve-hour flight, his future awaited him. Here, in stocking feet, was his past.

She didn't have to ask the questions, he knew them already. Was he happy? Yes, of course. And his wife? She has a name, you know. And yes, he could only presume she was happy, though she had cried when he'd left for the airport, but she was prone to such leaps of emotion and he knew how fond she was of his mother. Victoria went upstairs and George lay awake on the sofa until after five, when he finally drifted off, and was woken an hour later by the kettle.

He stayed for three weeks, and so did Victoria.

"You don't have to stay, you know, Victoria."

"I want to, George. It won't be long now, will it?"

"I suppose not."

His father disappeared in the mornings and returned at dinnertime. No one knew where he went. "You'd think he'd want to be here now, of all times," George said. He didn't care that he sounded bitter.

Victoria shrugged. "It may be easier, you know, for him to not be here."

In the afternoons George took walks with his mother, slow, creaking walks to Sneinton Dale, each day's walk a more stringent exercise in perseverance. It felt strange, at first, to be back on his old street after six years away. He recognized the crack in the pavement that he'd leapt over every day, running for the bus stop, his toothbrush in his back pocket and half a mug of tea sloshing in his hand.

Marla was young still, too young to be acting so old. He tried to urge her a bit further each day.

"A bit farther Mum, to the lamppost."

"I'm not feeling up to it, George."

"Sure you are, I'm certain you are."

"I'm tired today."

"Never mind that, you can do it! I'm sure you can!"

"Stop acting so American, George."

The walks grew shorter. Soon they moved from Sneinton Dale to their short street, then to the front door, until at last they extended only between the bedroom and the bathroom. She was stubborn, more stubborn than ever now that she saw the end. It was clear that she'd decided to die, and there was no one to talk her out of it. But George pushed her anyway, not because he thought she'd recover, but because he couldn't bear to see her give up. The painkillers gave her terrible wind, an embarrassing rumpus that she couldn't control. But George found it comforting. In those last days, it was the only vigorous thing that came from her.

Tea bags, Stan thought. She would want tea bags in the kitchen for whoever stopped in, and Victoria sponge, she'd told him to buy Victoria sponge, and her pearls, she would want to wear those bastard pearls, and her shoes—where did she keep her shoes, and what shoes did she wear? What shoes did she even wear? And there was a book, wasn't there? A book about a girl that she had wanted put in with her, or was it a book of poems—*yes*—a book of poems from that bloke who lived by the lake and didn't pay his council tax—was it poems or just words?—what was his name and where was that book? Of course in her bookshelf, where else, and then there was the pipe she'd shownhim wasn't there, someone or other—the Egyptians—they'd been buried with their pipes. It was in here somewhere in this drawer it was in this drawer where she kept those sorts of odds and ends, oh hell she made a list and what did he do with it? What did he do with that list?

❦❦❦

George woke to a distant shriek, fading, and the memory of a fat black hand pushing out from his closet door. His dreams had a dark edge now. This had begun, he supposed, with adulthood. He slid out of bed for a piss. Through the bathroom's square window the night was still blue. An owl called, its voice a cool bassoon.

It was hunger that woke him. His belly muttered with hot indignation. In the kitchen he found a banana. He poured himself a glass of milk. This had been his mother's cure for insomnia. He opened a jar of peanut butter and dipped the banana in, dipping again after every bite. He left pale yellow threads behind, banana film squashed like mucus into the jar. His nerves had settled. He cherished this time of night, when he managed to cross its path. A single lit room in the middle of a dark house, the domain of jet lag, of final exams and midnight snacks. He crammed the last bite into his mouth and swallowed the milk down before he'd even finished chewing. This was satisfaction.

At that hour of the night, hearing was easy. The clink of shades against the sliding door, the clear rustle of dried leaves. He blinked, and peered from the kitchen into the family room. A breeze moved through the house.

"Hello," he called, quietly, in case he was being foolish. The screen door was open. His breath caught in his throat. "Hello," he called, louder. "Who's there?" It could have been a ghost or a strong raccoon. There was no answer, and hardly a sound. He picked up a whisk. No, too airy. He found a potato peeler in a drawer, good for gouging the eyes. Stepping out of the kitchen, he felt for the television and skirted the coffee table, making his way through the blackened family room. He moved wincingly, expecting at any second to be seized and smothered. He raised the potato peeler. "I'm armed," he called.

And then he saw. The backyard was a shallow well of

moonlight, and at its center was the pool. It lay tranquil despite the breeze, unblinking. It turned to gaze back at him, a subterranean eye. Beyond the water, lit by a quivering reflection, he saw his father. "Dad!" he shouted, but Stan didn't hear. George stepped outside. "Dad!" The sound fell into the night. As George drew closer, he could see that it wouldn't matter how loud he shouted. Stan squatted in the dark soil by the pool house, wearing only his pajamas. His hands shook with cold, his fingers rifled through the dirt, as if he were sifting it, searching for something. He worked busily, now and then throwing a bit of dirt over his shoulder. George stomped toward him. "Dad!" he called. Stan looked into the distance, but his eyes never settled on George.

George jogged to reach his father and put his hands on his shoulders. Never wake a sleepwalker, he remembered—the shock could kill them. He stepped away quickly. Stan's shoulders shook and the tremors reached his voice as he mumbled.

"Marla?" Stan said, the name rising like a question. The syllables rang clearly, there was no mistaking them. "Marla," he said again, growing impatient. He began slapping at the dirt, bare-fingered punishment for not yielding his Marla. George stood up and watched. He had seen this before.

Marla was buried in Sneinton Cemetery. George had always assumed she'd be scattered at sea, or buried in a grassy dale in the sun, somewhere in Devon or on the southeast coast, where it was sunny, where gulls cried and swooped. "Rubbish idea," she'd said. "This is my home." It was a rainy and gray day, and they were black-clad, moving slowly through the burial ground. It was a funeral from a film, George had thought, looking at the people around him. Even the hippies and the artists had put on their funeral costumes, even they knew how to mourn. George did not know how. He was numb, watching through a looking glass. The others threw clumps of dirt on the pale polished wood of the casket. His father threw the last clump, and then it was George's turn. Stepping to the middle of the group, where the preacher held a basket of earth, he scooped up a respectful handful, just enough to cover his palm. A moment later the wind picked up and swept some of the soil from his palm. He watched the brown granules race off his hand, scattering in the wind and landing nowhere near his mother's casket. He was aware that the others were watching, waiting for him to do something normal. But there seemed no point in it; it was just as good to stand there, letting the dirt fall through his fingers, like hourglass crystals. When the breeze died down, a few large clumps remained in his hand. These he threw onto the casket, where they landed and broke into sand.

He closed his eyes, counted to five, and then walked back to stand with Stan. The preacher said some words, a woman in a hat with black netting sobbed audibly. He hadn't seen her before. There was a shell around him, and off it pinged the light drizzle, the preacher's words, the hymn sung by resolute voices, the shadow of the gravedigger who stood nearby with his shovel and waited for them to finish. But like any shell, his was meant to crack. A few people George vaguely recognized walked up and hugged him. They didn't hug Stan, who stared without blinking at the stone slabs of the church.

It began when the first person left, walking off with
that steady slow gait that was meant to show respect. *Leave
them alone*, it said, *let them say goodbye.* Others followed.
The group dripped away, like black water from a faucet.
And with each empty space, Stan's eyes grew wider until
he was looking wildly around, at the trees, at the sky, at
George. "No." He said it calmly, as if someone had asked
him a question. No, this wasn't happening, was what he
meant, and George agreed. "Not yet," Stan shook his head
frantically and then he was down on his knees, stooping
far into the grave and scooping out the dirt, throwing
handfuls of it over his shoulder, undoing what had been
done. He didn't stop, not when George pulled at his sleeve,
not even when the gravedigger stalked over or the priest
murmured useless platitudes. Dirt flew and covered them
all, it landed in Victoria's eyes, powdered George's shirt
and did not stop until George wrapped his arms around
his father and pulled him away, tackling him to the
ground. They lay together for a few seconds, their heads
resting in the peaty grass, both of them as close to Marla
as they would ever be.

George had heard his father cry then, for the first and
only time. Stan had been rigid and bulky in his arms, and
he remembered how holding him hurt his elbows. The
shell around his father, hard and blemished, had finally
cracked. George's breath came in winded gasps and above
them, Victoria stood and waited. The priest walked away,
the gravedigger chewed and waited. Then they were in a
car, driving home, and it was done.

Now, beyond the pool, the bushes sat like sentries
bearded with leaves. Stan's pajamas were soaked. There

was nothing for George to do but watch. He brought Stan's coat out and draped it over his shoulders. The deck chair scraped on the pavement when George sat down. It was a warm night for December, and a still one. The air was sharp, waiting for wind, waiting for something. It lasted five minutes more and then Stan rose, teetered on his heels, and let the jacket slip from his shoulders. He walked back inside and left the sliding door open. George picked up the potato peeler and followed him in, closingthe door and locked it.

Victoria had stayed with them for a week after the funeral, though no one had asked her to. Stan barely noticed she was there, but as she told George, she hadn't come to be noticed. George was due to go home himself, and he looked forward to the flight, to those long hours in the air when nobody would know what had happened to him.

He had to go through Marla's possessions, Victoria said. Stan would never get around to it. Two piles, she said: keep and throw. In the throw pile: Marla's shoes, old boots and sandals that were faded and stiff from not being worn. Her clothes, most of them. George was sorry to see them go, the rainbow caftans, the faux-fur collars, the shapeless crocheted concoctions. Viji would wear none of these. He couldn't imagine who would. He kept a blue cardigan that smelled of Marla.

"It smells of patchouli," Victoria said, sniffing deeply. "And potatoes."

"Stop that." He snatched it from her. "You'll use up the smell."

In the keep pile: her leather gloves, buttersoft. A cameo brooch that she had never worn but looked expensive.

Most of her jewels were old junk, and had taken on the rancid smell of aging metal. And then, of course, there were the earrings. They twinkled sadly in her box, blue stars in a moonless sky. He slipped them into his pocket.

From across the room, "I'm sorry, George."

"What?"

"I'm sorry." She stood with her arms hugged around her chest. "This is really awful, isn't it?"

He shrugged, "She was ill, Victoria."

"Well, of course she was." She kneeled next to him, on the throw pile. "But it's awful, isn't it?" He shrugged again. There was nothing to be done about it. Women needed to say things aloud. She began to cry then, meekly at first, then in racking half-sobs, improperly formed. "It's fucking awful, this." She picked up a bracelet, dropped it.

"It's rubbish," he agreed. "It's the shittiest thing I've ever had to do."

When she moved into his arms, it felt natural. She had been there before. There was nothing exciting about Victoria. To him she was home. She rubbed his edges away. He wanted to tell her he disliked her hairstyle. She'd gotten one of those perms, and it frayed her hair, made it dry and frantic at the ends. He distracted himself with this as her arms braceleted his waist, as her hands slid up to his chest. She was unbuttoning his shirt. And he was letting her.

"I don't like your hair," he said.

"I don't care." He tangled his fingers into that mess of hair, and found it surprisingly soft. His fingers slid down to pull up her sweater and she shrieked. "Your hands are cold."

"Sorry."

He knew the ridges of her spine and the plains of her back; they were as familiar to his fingers as a relief map of England. He knew the circumference of her waist. It had stayed the same over those few years. And here were the small nubs at the ends of her shoulder blades, the ones that fit neatly between his lips. He didn't need to touch her breasts, he knew everything about them from their warmth. And her small, feverish mouth. This was Victoria. George was a blind man who didn't need to see.

For a moment he feared that Stan would walk in, but Stan had gone to sleep in George's old room, not wanting to come back to this bed, not tonight.

Soon they lay without clothing, pillowed and blanketed by piles of old cloth, the crumbs of his mother's life. The two piles had seeped into each other, and among them were strewn George and Victoria's clothes. He could see that her lips were swollen and red. He pawed at the raised red speckles around her mouth. "Sorry," he said, "I haven't shaved." She felt her own face, then looked into his and said nothing.

When she sat up, her breasts dangled onto her stomach. She surveyed the room. "It's buggered now," she said. "We'll have to start all over again."

✿✿✿

Back, now, to George's office, the smooth leather armchair he'd bought with department funding. Outside the office, the noisy Christmas party trailed from the hallway to the faculty lounge, where an open bar had been set up. A ruckus of music and yelled conversation—why people had to yell at parties, George would never understand—students excited by the free booze and the chance to see their professors drunk, anonymous rock 'n' roll rattling from the department's sound system. But George could hear nothing but the calm susurrations around his earlobe, moving now into the spiral, and a voice.

Oh, George. George what are you doing? It was Victoria's voice in his ear, or so he imagined. In reality, the only thing in his ear was the slim, slippery laugh of a sylphlike female student. It was she of the office visits, she of the crossing and uncrossing legs, of the heavy eyes and large head and flipping ebony hair. He wasn't composing an ode—he just couldn't remember her name. *What are you doing, George?* The answer: George was doing nothing but sitting in an armchair, his world turned to a carnival after five Ketel One martinis, four of them drunk in hasty succession, courtesy of the art history department. She stood across the room, but close enough to ensure that she would see him. She was wearing fishnet stockings, of all things, running the toe of her high-heeled shoe up and down the inside of her leg. She was speaking to another female student—this one in jeans and a T-shirt, she hadn't even bothered to brush her hair—and casting lingering glances his way.

"Keep your knickers on," George muttered to nobody. "You think a pair of fishnet stockings is all it takes? I've seen fishnets in my time." He leaned forward and squinted in her direction. She remained oblivious. "You don't know the fishnets I've seen." She laughed at something the other girl said—it looked like a genuine laugh, not staged for his benefit.

She didn't belong in fishnets. She belonged in a gossamer bedsheet, wrapped across her chest and tumbling over her bum, down her legs, swishing across the floor when she walked.

What are you doing, George? The voice felt real this time. In the distance, he spotted Amaré, next to the bar, looking directly at him and shaking her head.

He awoke the next afternoon feeling like someone had yanked out his organs, swirled them in a sewage tank, and crammed them back down his throat. The pain was a knife in the back of his head. He hobbled to the bathroom, bent over at the waist, turned on the shower, and threw up in the bath drain. *Bad form*, he scolded himself. Bad form, through and through. Fortunately, he'd invented a cure at university. He switched the shower to cold and tried not to yell as the ice water missiled his back. A cold shower, the coldest shower possible, followed by a naked sleep, without sheets, to freeze the misery out. It was the only way.

Around them, the puja room dripped. Kuttima quavered in the doorway. "Be careful, you. It's not respectful."

"Keeping it so dirty," Viji snapped. "*That's* not respectful. What's wrong with these women?"

Kuttima hissed, "They're crazies, you know. You know what crazies they are."

"Yes, mad, crazy, that's what everyone says. It's no excuse for this." She waved a limp arm around the room, where picture frames seemed to trail tears, where the dust-coated lingam thirsted for more water.

Kuttima shrugged. "You want to clean it? You're here now. So clean it"

Here, in the corner, was a picture wrapped in plastic. It was caked with an age of dust that covered the image like concrete. But Viji knew what it was. She remembered the old fingers that had held it, dark and dry as vanilla pods. She remembered sitting in his lap, Krishnan the cook, and listening to the story of Kama.

The earth and heavens were terrorized by a demon named Taraka, who'd gained great powers through meditation.

"What kind of powers?" she'd asked.

"Great powers. The power to burn things. The power to take whatever he wanted, to control anything, to run the rivers dry or make them flood."

"To take whatever he wanted? Like what?"

"Sweets from puja meant for other gods: gold, jewels, land, water, fire—"

"Any sweets he wanted?"

"Yes."

"Even pista kulfi?"

"Yes."

"And gulab jamun?"

"Yes."

"And kesari?"

"Yes."

"And what about chocolate?"

"Any sweets."

"Whenever he wanted? How did he get them?"

"Listen! I'm telling you a story. There was one reason only that Taraka could make such mischief. Siva, the great destroyer, the master of fire, the holiest of holies, was mourning the death of his beloved."

"What's mourning?"

"He was sad."

"Why was he sad?"

"Wait. To escape such sadness, Siva retreated to a mountain grove and fell into a very, very deep meditation. Because of this, only Taraka could use his powers. And so Indra, the king of heaven, came up with a plan. What Siva needed, he said, was a woman, to bring him back to the world."

"But why?"

"Sometimes, my little grapefruit, it simply works that way. But Siva, he was a great sage; another woman would never interest him. Oh no, not even Uma, daughter of the mountain king, reincarnation of Sati, Siva's lost love."

Viji remembered fingering this picture while Old Krishnan spoke. It was shiny then, and new, and showed a sweet-faced man holding a bow and arrow made of flowers. She'd bent the corner of it, back, forth, back and forth, until Krishnan slapped her hand.

"And she was a beautiful woman, this Uma," he continued.

"She was?"

"Oh yes! My *god*, how lovely! Her hair itself was an ocean, her eyes were the eyes of a fawn. Her voice was the melody of Govinda's flute! Bees hovered at her lips, thirsty for the sweetness of her breath. And such bosoms! Each one was as swollen as the earth itself!"

"That's not possible."

"Nothing is impossible. Now listen. They hatched a plan. Uma would go with Kama, the god of love and fascination, to find Siva in his mountain abode. And *tuk*! Kama would shoot his arrow, Siva would open his eyes and fall hopelessly in love with Uma. All would be well again."

"That's a good story."

"Patience, child, I've not finished. You see, this Kama, he went to Siva's mountain home, and what do you think he did?"

"What?"

"He got so frightened, he couldn't do a thing!"

"Why was he frightened?"

"Girl, I will tell you. This Siva was covered toe to head in ashes from puja. His hair was filthy and long and slithering with snakes."

"No!"

"*Yes*. A cobra circled his neck, scorpions crawled at his knees, and lizards ran round and round at his feet. He was a real fright, I tell you. So terrified was Kama that he dropped his bow and arrow, and di-*shum!* It fell clattering to the ground. What a sound it made!"

"And what happened?"

"Siva awoke. Before him, he saw Uma, draped in golden sun, sweet like a pot of milk."

"And did he love her then?"

"No, he did not love her. He was not happy to be disturbed. He said to himself, *What is it that has woken me? Surely not this woman?* Siva looked around, he scanned the whole world, and—"

"How did he do that?"

"Siva can see anything with his third eye."

"Third eye? He has three eyes? That's not real."

"It *is*. The third eye of Siva is all-knowing, all-seeing, all—"

"But how does someone have three eyes?"

"He did, just like that, okay?"

"But it doesn't make sense."

"He is Siva."

"But where is the third eye?"

"Just *here*," pressing a finger to her forehead.

"But how come he needs three eyes?"

"So that he can see everything."

"But how come—"

"F*inished!* Too many questions from you. And why? And how? And when? Enough!"

"But what happened?"

"I'm trying to tell you, aren't I? Now listen. Siva saw Kama, Siva grew angry, Siva killed Kama with a lightning bolt from his third eye."

"A *lightning* bolt!"

"*Shu*! Quiet. Kama was dead, gone, so-long, a pile of ashes on the ground. And Siva resumed his meditation. There. End of story. Finished farewell goodbye auf Wiedersehen that's it!"

"That's it?"

Her father had come to the doorway then and Krishnan, jumped to his feet, tumbling Viji from his lap to the ground.

❦❦❦

Now, with the edge of her fingernail, she picked away the layers of soot. She dripped water on the picture to loosen the sticky residue and soon he was visible again—Kama, with his bow and arrow, the god of love and fascination. She stuck him in Krishnan's picture frame. It was unusual to have a cook's picture in the puja room, but here was a young Krishnan, moon-faced, his hair combed back like a movie star's. He stood proudly in some photo studio, his hand slotted like Napoleon's under the buttons of his jacket. The photo had been with him when he died, and Viji's mother had put it in this frame. The frame now hung on the bottom row, close to the ground and toward the back of the room; he was, after all, only a servant.

She remembered that young face. It wasn't so different from how Krishnan had been when he had died. In fact, the only thing old about Old Krishnan were his fingers, shriveled by the juice of onions and lemons, a hundred times burned by frying oil, scraped and peeled by knives. How strange, she thought, that she should remember sitting here with him, in this puja room. Family puja rooms weren't for servants. Servants were meant to have their own.

It was one of the few times in her life that Viji noticed irony: Krishnan, a mere cook, stared down by her father on many occasions and shooed from the puja room whenever he ventured in, hung securely on this wall. But her father was nowhere to be seen.

"Shanta, what happened to Appa's photo?"

"Which one?"

"In the puja room, downstairs."

Shanta shrugged, "We never put one up."

"What?"

"We just didn't." Her sister pressed down on the rice grinder and filled the kitchen with its metallic din.

She asked Uma Athai, who laughed gleefully but would not answer. She asked Pushpa Athai, who looked sharply into her eyes and whispered, *Don't tell the children.*

"Tell them what?"

"Tell them this. Yes, exactly." She nodded sagely and would say no more.

"Shanta," Viji returned to her sister.

"Yes, *Viji,*" she answered in English. She sat at the dining room table and polished forks that they never used.

"There's no photo of Appa in the puja room."

"Yes, Viji, this I know."

"And why?"

"It was decided that we wouldn't have one, that is all."

"Who decided?"

Shanta cast tired eyes over her sister. "You ask so many questions. Why these questions now?"

"There's something somebody isn't saying."

"Isn't there always."

"Stop it, Shanta."

Shanta stopped, laid her dustcloth on the table, and pointed her fork at Viji. "What is this Shanta-Shanta? What happened to Shanta Akka? How about some respect? Are we twins? And what is this Viji-Biji business? Is that what they call you there? What happened to Vijaya?"

"That's beside the point."

"Oh *ho*. Beside the point, is it, madam professor?"

"Please listen to me," Viji said. She sat with Shanta and placed her hand on the dustcloth. "I simply noticed that the picture of Appa was missing from the puja room. This seems like quite a strange thing, don't you think?"

"Something strange, is it?" Shanta looked at her intently now, and Viji grew nervous. "Coming from America to tell me there is something strange in my house? Well, listen to me, Sherlock Holmes. There are things you might not understand, and who could blame you? You've been away too long." She paused. "Forget it. Tell me what you want to eat."

"Understand what? Understand what, Shanta?"

Shanta leaned close to Viji and whispered, "I'm not going to tell you."

Viji laughed at the absurdity of it, but Shanta's face stayed blank.

"Tell me!"

"No."

"*Shanta.*"

"Enough! Who are you, coming here and asking me about these things? Don't you know? Don't you re- member? Or did you forget like you forgot us? Hmm? Polish these forks!"

Shanta scraped her chair back and was gone.

After so little time, Viji was sick of this house. She'd had enough of the old women who coursed through it, day after day, eating away at it like termites, giving nothing back to the world.

Later that night, she spied on the children as they watched television, a Tamil soap opera that Viji had never seen before. It tinned through the house, unrelenting drama, tears, shrill violins, and the ubiquitous funny man: short, dark, and fat with a nasal voice that could be heard from any point in the house. The funny man never changed. The children sat fixated, though they couldn't possibly have understood a word of it. How long their bodies were growing, Avi lying on his belly over the plastic-covered sofa, Babygirl sitting on her feet, Kieran hunched and cross-legged, with terrible posture like George's, his chin jutting and eyes half-closed. How obliv- ious they were. How oblivious everyone was, even George. Only Viji had known she was taking the children away, perhaps to send them back alone. And if she wasn't coming back herself? What would she do then? She had no illusions of being able to live without them. The very thought of it set off sirens. She ached.

When they were younger—watching television, sleeping, riding in the car, Babygirl and Avi used to climb onto Kieran, as if they knew he could cushion them. Viji used to have to nudge them apart, lay them neatly aligned in a single crib. Later, as toddlers, they abandoned their own small beds and piled into Kieran's. Viji would find them, a hillock of limbs in the morning. It didn't seem to matter then, where Kieran ended and Avi began, where boy gave way to girl, whether or not her daughter's hair melted onto her son's forehead. It didn't matter to them, it didn't matter to her. Now they slept separately, still innocent, she assumed, of how their bodies would change.

But one day soon, Babygirl would come to her with a quiet announcement, and Viji would react accordingly. She would speak calmly, as if the event were hardly worth mentioning. There would be few words on the matter, only instructions. She wouldn't cry or poke fun or act like the day was some momentous occasion. She'd avoid those oily pronouncements that she'd had to suffer from her mother and her aunts: *You're a woman now, things are going to be different.* And by no means would she go around to her friends' houses, as her own mother had, to spread the happy news. *My daughter is a woman!* her mother had announced in every sitting room. She imagined Gail Bauer's eyes, saucers of surprise, were she to knock on her door and announce, *My daughter is a woman!*

Viji remembered when it had happened to her, how she'd felt sticky with the news, how it had made her skin crawl to know that people knew, and to know they knew she knew. Her mother had hounded her away from the puja room: *Never while you're unclean! You know better.* Her aunt had taken her aside at her ceremony, tight crow-hands around Viji's arm, and instructed, "Men will look at

you now, Viji. Their eyes will be everywhere. Cover up!"
Viji only snatched her arm back and slunk upstairs. The
men didn't look—she was a stick figure still, a stick figure
seeping life, hiding in bed. It would take a few years for
the men to start looking. And when they did, Viji would
know what to do.

But then again, maybe Babygirl would be excited—
maybe she would strut down the hallway and burst into
Viji's room. *I'm a woman now!* Maybe she would even
want a ceremony. If she didn't, Viji wouldn't make her sit
through one. She wouldn't do that to Babygirl.

"No ceremony?" Amma started the second Viji entered, not even waiting for her to light the first lamp. "No
ceremony at all? Hmm. Doesn't matter. She can live
without blessings. She can live without luck."

I'm not listening.

"Ho ho, big surprise."

*There's no need for such things. Why so much galatta
for every little thing?*

"Correct, correct. Who needs blessings when you live
in America? Life is one big blessing, isn't it?"

Yes, maybe it is.

"Big house, big car, big professor father. Isn't it?"

Viji's ceremony had taken place on the third day of
her first period. Spread across the sitting room floor were
bowls of fruit, a brass pot on whose mouth was balanced
a coconut, and trays of jasmine. For the first time, Viji was
allowed to wear a sari.

"I can only thank God that you had one—or else who
knows where you would have ended up."

Are you saying you approve of my marriage?

"Don't talk so fresh."

I'm very lucky. I have a good life.

"Yes, you do."

And not because I sat in front of a coconut.

"Wretched girl. Don't talk to me. I don't even want to see you." But her mother didn't leave the room. She stayed to seethe where Viji could feel her, first in her belly, then in her womb, then as a clenching ache in her thighs. She bent over and clutched her abdomen, breathing through the pain. She was used to it by now.

Thinking back to how she was, she understood her mother's fears. Viji had been wild, wearing her hair down like a demoness, using her Diwali money to buy dresses and lipstick, pulling Deepa into her bedroom to practice filmy dances, and deliberately practicing again outside the convent school, opposite the corner tea shop, where the boys from the boys' school gathered in the afternoons. Maybe this wasn't wild by American standards; Viji didn't know anymore. Parents always seemedshocked by the things their children got up to. If Viji had danced in front of boys, what would Babygirl do? If she bought lipstick secretly, what would Babygirl buy? But her daughter, playing now with the end of her braid, wasn't interested in lipstick or boys. It was too early. It would always be too early. Maybe, Viji thought, the ceremony wasn't such a bad idea. Maybe, when the time came, she'd have one after all.

There were things about this place, this country she had once called hers, that surprised her. The multitude of eyes, for instance. Had they been there before? Eyes all over, the women staring harder than the men. Their eyes slid like tentacles over her hair-nose-chin. Her own eyes she cast to the floor in public, fixed on the sidewalk or a triplet. They watched her chest her hips her knees her feet as she walked, her shoes her bag her fingers that gripped the leather handle. She wished she had eyes in all these places so that she might stare back at them. Once she had blended in here, with the rickshaw driver and the men at the tea shop and the woman with angry eyes who held a mangy-haired child on her hip. She'd been a Madrasi who scowled into the sun, her nose and mouth twisted against the city's solar glare. For twenty years she'd shared the air with these people, but America had left its indelible mark. She passed a woman in a dirty sari, sitting behind a wooden cart piled high with jasmine buds. She tried to imagine this woman with sunglasses and a purse, and the thought of it made her laugh.

Even worse was the way they stared at the triplets, cutting into them with their eyes in search of an explanation for these creatures with the caramel skin, molasses hair, and cherry noses, stocky American legs and straight strong teeth. How much dishti, evil eye, must have been piling up around her children. She would have to take them to a priest.

Because she didn't scrunch her eyes and scowl, because she was inexplicably a thing of wonder, Viji was deprived of what she wanted most: to look, to soak up all that had dripped away from her. As she walked around like this, eyes downcast, the streets around her faded like an overexposed photograph, until only the thick and obvious structures remained.

So, because there was no other way, she went undercover. She coated her hair in coconut oil and wound it into a poor, sprouting bun. From Kuttima's room she stole a worn-out sari. On her cheeks and forehead she rubbed turmeric paste, which the local women wore to keep their skin soft, even though it turned their faces yellow. She screwed up her nose and eyes, cocked her head, and bared her teeth as if she were carrying a hundred-pound weight on her back. And soon, with very little effort, she walked the streets unnoticed, a well-oiled and shining example of anonymity.

At the end of a lane, a house waited. At its crown, was a weather vane, at its foot, a swing. For years it had lingered at the end of its death, waiting for Viji's return before it let itself crumble to the city street. She wouldn't remember it initially; it would only seem familiar. But it had something to show her.

And then, with little idea of where she was going, she turned into a lane. A woman at a jasmine cart picked her teeth and watched Viji approach the house. With nothing to hold her interest, the woman turned away. And then, the weather vane. Viji knew this house, but only vaguely, like a relative she'd met once at a wedding. They called it the big house. But she didn't recognize the pink-stained veranda or the Lakshmi carvings on the door or the heavy iron lock, busted open now so that the door stood ajar. Inside, the house had faded to gray, covered in the fine soot of neglect. On the ground, a carpet of broken glass. But Viji knew this house. She blew at the wall and the charcoal dust scattered to reveal sky-blue paint. She scraped her toe along the floor to find the black-and-white tiles. Emerging colors scattered the clouds. *See*, the house whispered, but it was only the creak of the door. She didn't know why she knew this house, she didn't know what it meant to her.

She wasn't used to this. Life with George was a series of answers. She knew the questions to ask and he knew how to answer them. She wanted him now, his logical conclusions and solidly stacked surmises. Here, questions seeped into each other. Answers blended into the walls like lizards.

Look, the house seemed to say (but it was only the snap of glass beneath her sandals. *Here*, said clacking mouse feet in the corner. *No, here*, whispered the brush of her sandals on the floor. *Through that door there*, said an insistent shadow, beckoning. She obeyed. Over a meadow of broken glass, white with collected dust, hung a hefty length of brass chain, broken in the middle, fat enough to have once held a swing. Her swing. *Only rich people had those.*

Viji had been here. Viji had lived here. Like honey from a pot, the memory dripped back into her.

Shanta had been here, too. They had stood on the veranda of the big house. The lady and man of the big house had been there. In fact, the whole street watched from windows and doorways—everyone but Viji saw what happened. All she had seen was a hand, Shanta's, a sticky, flesh-smelling palm clamped over Viji's eyes and nose, Viji prying at the fingers so she could see. She wanted only to see.

I hate Amma.

Why should you?

She made him go away. She made him want to leave, didn't she? And where has he gone?

How should I know?

But Shanta had only two hands, so Viji heard everything: new voices, hard shoes on the street, the slam of the car door. How she longed to see the car! She had seen only a few in her life, monuments on wheels, chariots for men in dark glasses.

Appa had left them—of this she was certain. Where he was going, no one would say. She imagined that he'd simply gone to another house, the way she had, that he'd wake the next morning and wash his face at a different tap, spit water into a different hole, walk down a different street to the same office in town. The house may have even had other children—two small girls, like Viji and Shanta, but wholly unlike them. Or perhaps, like Viji, he'd be staying with a kind old couple in a house with a swing. Whether he deserved to go away, Viji would never know. Like most children, she came into the world assuming everyone was good, and spent the rest of her life discovering otherwise.

"*Shanta!*" Viji bolted through the kitchen. Shanta's

eyes grew round with fear.

"What's happened to you, woman? Why are you dressed like a beggar?"

"I found it. Where the swing was."

"Which swing? Oh, that swing. What are you up to? What is all this?"

"*What is all this* is what I want to know." She paused. "Appa's picture—is it because he left us?"

Shanta sighed. "In a way, yes."

Viji plopped to the ground. "But why did he leave, Shanta?" It had never occurred to Viji to ask anyone this, though for years the question had darted around her like a nosy fly. It had never occurred to her that an answer existed.

"He left because we sent him away. You know that."

"He was sent away," she repeated. "But why was he sent away? What did he do?"

Shanta laid down the knife. Her eyes searched Viji's, and, finding nothing, she replied, "That's something I thought you would know, more than any of us."

And Shanta would say no more. Her half-closed eye turned its gaze to the vegetables, and there it would remain.

Like she'd done so many times in her life, Viji closed the puja room door. Her partial cleanup had progressed. Kuttima's work. The aunts wouldn't have bothered. The statues were again lined neatly on their shelves, the floor swept and clean. There was fresh water in the offering cup, and new vermillion had been dabbed on every photograph.

Her mother stared out of her frame, from the same photo that Viji had at home. A tepid wind sailed through the room, raising the remnants of dust from the floor. Beyond the door, the house was silent.

Her mother spoke. "I died in this house," she said. "Don't you give me any trouble."

I'm not.

"And why should you be surprised? My house, my room. What else?"

Nothing else.

The photo of Old Krishnan still lay dog-eared on the floor.

Amma.

"Don't ask me."

Please.

"Don't ask me."

Viji cocked her head to the side to get a new view of the picture. "But what is there to ask?" she said. "What exactly is the question?" George was closer to her than she thought.

"Keep that vellakaran out of this. Mister professor. Where is he now, tell me?"

Never mind.

"Close your eyes and pray," Amma ordered.

Why? What's the use?

"Close your eyes," she repeated, "And pray."

Viji did not pray, but she closed her eyes. And when her eyes closed, her throat opened, the hidden grotto of anger and love, where the tears hurt the most, where emotion could swell and burst without warning. And there, in the back of Viji's throat, the fetus of a feeling was born. Curled inside her it grew head-tail-eyes, and like a tadpole it knew to swim, swishing and leaping, then coursing upstream to her head, where at last it unfurled: a memory.

The kitchen. A mound of chapati dough sits smugly

on its wooden board on the floor, waiting to be divvied into balls and rolled flat. Amma, young Amma, pinches a fingerful and dabs it into her palm. Old Krishnan, young Krishnan with moonface and almond eyes, does the same. He looks straight into Amma's face, as if he's searching. They both look up at Viji. Amma continues to ball the dough. Krishnan begins to roll, forearms tensing then releasing. Viji sees paper and green and yellow pencils. She draws a house, coloring more busily than she ever has. She wishes yellow weren't so close to white. And looking without looking she sees: hands on dough, one ball, two balls, Amma placing a ball in Krishnan's hand, Krishnan's fingers closing around the dough. Then she sees the beaten fingers of a cook and, laced gently through them, the soft fat fingers of a wife. This was all Viji needed, though other visions followed: the dark coarse finger sliding a trail up her mother's arm, her mother shying away, Krishnan smiling, gazing at her as if he were singing a love song, her mother glancing sharply at Viji, then pulling away, pulling Viji's arm, *Come, chella-kutti, it's time for your reading, isn't it time for your reading?*

Shanta was a vault. And Viji couldn't explain what she was looking for. Not then, not in the daylight. She would wait for the night, just before dawn, when the high fences built in the afternoon had fallen away, when the world was unreal and truth could be coaxed from sleepy corners. She would sneak out of her room and into Shanta's. Her sister would sit up at first, startled by the presence of another in her bed, something she had never known. And then she would scoot over to make room for Viji. Viji would lie next to her sister, pillowed by the bosoms that reminded her of

Amma. She would stroke Shanta's nose that curved to one side, and try to push it back the other way, as she had when she was young. There's something I'm not remembering, she would say. There's something about this house that I've lost. And now I come here and I see these things, like Krishnan's photo and not Appa's. And this swing. And that house. And I think that something is not right, but I don't know what it is. And Amma, what was she doing with Old Krisnan? What were they up to? And Shanta?

Shanta did not answer. Not in the daylight, not in the privacy of night. And Viji returned to her room and packed her suitcase. In the morning, things would be real again—the screaming dog, the clouded mirror, the smell of coffee and the sizzle of dosas in a frying pan. But most real would be the suitcase, packed in the corner of the room.

"We're going," Viji said.

"Where?" Kieran looked at Babygirl, who looked at Avi, who looked at Kieran.

"It's Christmas tomorrow, you know."

"I *know*."

"Are we going home?"

"No, Avi." The children looked up with gray faces. What a mother she'd been, bringing them to this dreary house, with only a rooftop to play on. How serious she'd made them. She wanted badly to see them smile.

"Come on, long faces, cheer up!" She forced a laugh. "We're going to the beach!"

A chorus of yells rose from the rooftop. In the distance, atop the big house, the weather vane swung around in the wind, as if it shared their joy.

The next day, on a bus brimming with strangers, Viji regretted leaving. More accurately, she regretted leaving on a bus. Already Kieran had thrown up once and Avi was looking green. Heat rash had spread an army of lesions along Babygirl's arms. "One hundred degrees!" Viji scolded her. "One hundred degrees every summer in Sacramento, and now you get heat rash? Now?" She felt a twist of guilt when Babygirl shrugged and looked at the ground. She was a terrible mother.

Goodbye, she'd whispered to the house with the single tree, to the women in the doorway who never ventured beyond the gate, their lives crusting around them.

She wanted to ask the man next to her to move. His hand was wedged against her thigh and she sensed that he didn't mind it so much. But already his arm was hanging out the window, his hand flat against the outside of the bus as if he were holding the walls together. The ride was twelve hours long. A sack with vomitous drippings sat at her feet and its fumes grew stronger as the day grew warm. Four hours had passed.

And at last, at last, the bus spewed them to the pavement at the Trivandrum station, where under white porticos the light coastal wind nudged her back to life. The children, armed with backpacks, looked accusingly at her. But here in the sea air, she found it easy to smile.

George needed a fried egg. An egg dripping with oil, crispy around the edges, on well-buttered toast, was the final step in obliterating a hangover. In the kitchen he heard voices and a sudden laugh. Stan, Lupe. No. Stan and Kamla. A quick check in the hall mirror confirmed his suspicion that he looked as if he'd died, partially decomposed, and come back to life. There was nothing to be done for it but retreat back to bed. He pushed on.

Dogfaced, he entered the kitchen.

"On the mend, then, son?" Stan observed, shoving a hand in his pocket.

"Why are you so happy?" George asked.

"Hello, George darling, feeling better?"

He lamented his bloodshot eyes and blue skin. He remembered he was wearing a yellow bathrobe over sagging underwear. He sensed his sorry chest hairs sprouting weakly, and couldn't bring himself to answer.

"Eggs," he said, and fished a frying pan from the cupboard below the stove. Cracking the egg (slamming it too hard on the edge of the pan, splattering yolk over his fingers), he watched Kamla, looking without looking. She was natural in their kitchen; she leaned against the counter and held her cup of tea as if she owned the counter and

the cup and the tea bag that floated inside it. He watched
her drum her fingernails and move her hand to her waist.

"Have you heard from Viji, George?"

"No."

"Not at all? Really?"

"Once. One time."

"Is that all? I would have thought—"

"The STDs were closed!" he snapped.

There was silence, and he could feel his father looking
at him.

"I'm sure you'll hear from her soon, though," she said
quietly. "I'm waiting for *my* postcard."

*You of all people should know that no one sends post-
cards from India*, he wanted to say. What would they send
pictures of? The broken sewers and beggars and mysterious pools of liquid in the street? The Taj Mahal? Sure,
why not—nowhere near Madras, but who cares? But he
said nothing.

"Well, I should get going," she said. "Anisha will be
home any minute." She paused. "She takes the bus. But you
know that."

George focused on his frying egg and heard Kamla say
goodbye to Stan. The door closed on her, and she walked
quickly down the drive and disappeared around the corner.

"You're a right bloody bastard," his father announced.

"Why?"

"You know why, talking to a woman like that."

"You're right, Dad," George muttered. "Guess I'm not
as good with the ladies as you are."

"I'd've thought if nothing else, I taught you how to
speak to a lady."

"Yes, I'd've thought as much, too."

"I don't know what that means," Stan grumbled. "I'll leave you to yourself now, you daft sod."

"Thanks, Dad."

Later that evening, George found himself walking down Winding Creek Road and turning the corner onto Ladino. A couple walking their dog said hello to him, and he nodded back. He'd never seen them before. A man jogging alongside a helmeted boy on a bicycle with training wheels stuck his hand up in greeting. George hesitated and then waved back.

The door opened. Kamla's daughter stood there, looking up at him.

"Yes?"

"Hi there!" George kicked at the ground and tried to seem casual. From inside the house, Kamla called, "Anisha, who is it? Did you ask who it was first?"

Breathless, Kamla came to the door. A smile blazed across her face. She invited him in. But the girl stood in the doorway, staring up at him, and didn't move. He found it hard to squeeze by her. She didn't budge, not even when his hip grazed her shoulder. She was like a robot.

"I was just walking," he explained.

"It's a warm night, isn't it?"

"You want to walk with me?" he asked.

He could tell she was about to say yes, but then she stopped. "I was going to have some tea. Would you like some?"

Yes, tea he could do.

It began then, a period that George would think about often and never be able to explain. George had tea with

Kamla that evening. He apologized for how he'd spoken and she laughed his words away. She smiled too much and punctuated her sentences with pensive, meaningless shakes of the head. He left an hour later, knowing he would take a walk again the next day, but wondering if he should. Kamla, standing at the door, said, "Come back anytime," and the words wrapped around him like two warm arms.

He returned the next evening.

"Do you like to read?" he asked, noticing Kamla's bookshelf. It was empty, except for a dictionary and some coloring books.

"My husband was the reader," she said. "I used to read a lot, but then Anisha came. It would be a good thing to do, though, wouldn't it?" George picked up a coloring book with a red fox on the cover. The pictures were poorly filled in, with little attention to tonal harmony. He saw no evidence of any attempt to stay within the lines. His children would certainly have done better.

"Would you like to start reading again?" he asked. "I could lend you a few things."

She paused with her teacup in midair. "That would be lovely. That could be my project now, to fill that shelf."

"Yes!"

"But I should fill it with my own things, really."

"Like what?"

"Like *books*."

"Right."

"Do you know where I could buy some books of my own?"

He leaned in and surprised himself with a grin. "I know just the place."

✤✤✤

The smell of woodsmoke trailed through Maple Grove, as it did every winter when the temperature dropped to freezing. Houses down Winding Creek Road glowed with hanging lights. The Fromms hung theirs sloppily, the bulbs multicolored and large, drooping from their rows, an electrical chord trailing visibly from roof to wall. Across the street, the Attenborough willow tree dripped with light, and next to their mailbox stood a cardboard sleigh pulled by plastic reindeer. On their door was a wreath of tiny white bulbs. Next door, the Bauers had invested in the new kind of light, small white fairy bulbs that clung with desperation to the eaves of the house, straight stark lines of cheer that winked into the dusk: on-off-on-off-on-off-on-off-on. The twinkling was keeping George awake. He snapped his curtains shut, muttering. Every Christmas had its Scrooge.

The Armitage house was a puddle of darkness, broken only by the garden lanterns that shone every night, every month, every year. This was normal. What was not normal was the hacking sound that trailed from the far end of the lawn. George listened to it for several minutes, a pillow over his head, before he realized that it wasn't right.

He opened the front door.

"Dad!" he called to the stooped figure at the end of the yard. "What the hell are you doing?"

His father didn't answer. It was happening again, but this time he had to be stopped. The sound: Stan with an ax, chopping at a pine tree. George had never liked pine trees.

Stan wielded the ax with wild strokes. Where had he

found it? Could sleepwalkers rummage?

"Dad," George said firmly, "put down the ax." Stan, of course, paid no attention. Gingerly, George stepped in, reaching for the ax handle. Stan raised it over his head. George grasped the handle. Stan slammed the ax down and millimeters—millimeters—stood between the blade and George's foot.

A dense wind swallowed the shake in his voice. "Put it down. Put it down." Stan dropped the axe. Heavily, he fell into his son's arms, his head over George's shoulder. George held him in the cold. He was like a sleeping child. He was like a sack of flour.

🌱🌱🌱

The next time he met Kamla was late on a Thursday afternoon, a week before Christmas, in a cramped and murky bookstore on J Street. There was hardly enough light to read, and the shelves rained dust each time he pulled a book down. It was run by an old man who sat stooped on a stool and never moved. He wore glasses with square black frames, the sort the NHS used to give out for free. George piled his arms with books, and the old man began to watch him suspiciously. He chose Carver, Cheever, Bellow, and Roth, but worried his choices were too masculine, so he put down Roth and picked up Woolf. She would never get through Woolf, but she could try. He worried that his choices were too obvious, but Kamla seemed happy with them. The books towered in his arms and threatened to avalanche.

"That all?" the old man at the counter sneered. "Sure

you got enough there?" He sighed when George handed
him a credit card, and made a show of blowing the dust off
his mimeograph machine. "Come again," he said, handing
over the purple-shadowed receipt. He ladled a slow, thick
gaze over Kamla, and nodded to George before handing
over the plastic bag.

They went for coffee. There was one café in the area,
with pink tablecloths and Toulouse-Lautrec prints, which
seemed to serve only almond croissants. They shared one.
And then they drove home, separately. They returned to
that café the next time. It was close to his office, and easier
than walking the streets of Maple Grove. They met in the
evenings and then, always, drove home in separate cars.

I could show her my office, George thought one dark
afternoon, as he gazed at her headlights in his rearview
mirror. But then, *why would she want to see my office?* And
then he remembered Amaré, who'd taken it upon herself
to guard his marriage like a bulldog. She scared him more
than the neighbors did. He'd passed the man and woman
with their dog in front of Kamla's house the week before,
and found himself feeling guilty. He could very nearly hear
the crinkling questions from the woman to the man—*who
do you think—isn't he—maybe they*—the sort of questions
a man on his own wouldn't bother with, questions it took
a woman to ask. If his neighbors knew he went to Kamla's,
would they care? Would Stan say anything, or Lupe? It was
nobody's business in the first place, and secondly, there
was no business to discuss.

There were places they could go, away from Maple
Grove, where they would be highly unlikely to see anyone
they knew. There were dozens of other neighborhoods

outside of his own leafy hamlet. And if they left in separate cars every time…but George was thoroughly certain he was doing nothing wrong. He could ask her if she'd seen the park. Land Park lay across from the children's school, a vast and grassy pasture with nothing but trees and rambling shrubbery, where the school held its annual picnic. So of course she'd seen it. But had she really seen it?

This was the sort of thing George thought about while lying in bed alone. This was what he thought about when he sweated into his pillow, one hand working beneath the sheet. He hated himself afterward, without fail. This was what he was thinking about, one late night, when the phone rang.

"Hi," said the voice. "It's me."

"Viji."

"Are you okay?"

He sat up. "Hi, yes, I'm okay. Are you okay?"

"Were you worried about me?"

"Of course I was," he said. He realized he was lying. He'd finished worrying. His aim now was to look past the hole she'd left, as if it weren't there, as if she hadn't left him. "Are the kids okay?"

"We're in Kerala now."

"Kerala? How on earth did you get there?"

"A very long bus ride. George, are you all right? You sound strange."

"I'm fine. I'm in bed."

"Oh."

"How are the children?"

"They're happy, very happy now. They like it here. The beach, you know."

His throat stuck a little when she spoke of the children. He imagined them, bellies jutting, jumping into the ocean as if it were a swimming pool.

"Be careful with them. Where are you staying?"

"At a hotel. But there's no phone in our room."

"Oh. All right."

"Have you been eating?"

"Of course I've been eating. Viji?"

"Yes."

"Why did you go?" He was asking because he'd promised himself he would. He heard how uncommitted his voice sounded, and wondered if Viji heard it too.

"I couldn't stand it at my sister's anymore, you know, it was just so—"

"No—what I mean is, why did you leave here? Your note…"

A silence. "I know. It's hard to explain. I needed to get out of there for a while, just to come back home. You understand that, right? You understand that I needed to come back here for a while?"

"But are you coming back *here*?"

"I don't know. I think I am."

"When?"

"I don't know. I'll send the children back in time for school, like we planned."

Like we planned. He hadn't planned on anything but having a normal Christmas with his family.

The phone clicked its signal.

"Time is running out."

"Have a good Christmas," he said. "Will you call on Christmas?"

"I'll call, and you can talk to the children."

"Give them my love?"

"Okay."

"All of my love," he added. The phone clicked off, and she was gone.

ψψψ

They met in the bookshop later that week. *I read a poem of you last week and thought of his.* He wanted again and again to say those words, but never found a chance to. He and Kamla didn't discuss the fact that they were meeting, because there was no need to explain something that didn't mean anything. He asked himself what they spoke about and how they managed to fill so many hours with so much talk and so little in common. It was a question Viji would have asked, and that George, truthfully, could not answer.

CHAPTER NINE

It was Christmas, and George and Stan were alone.

"Are you going to church today?"

"Am I, bollocks. Have I ever gone to church on Christmas?"

George shrugged.

"I've got my lady coming to dinner. Is that all right with you?"

"Really? Yes, of course. I hadn't thought about dinner, though." He didn't even know if the shops were open. He'd never planned a Christmas, not once in his life. He bought presents, he was present, and that was always enough. He knew about some dried pasta in the cupboard and a chicken leg in the fridge that was due to go off the next day. There was a dusty bottle of wine in the pantry. And his students had given him, among other things, a box of chocolates. "We don't have any vegetables," George said. Stan strolled to the pantry, opened one cupboard, then another. He returned to the kitchen with a potato in each hand. "Potatoes aren't vegetables."

"Like hell they aren't."

"They're not real vegetables."

"Well they don't have feet, do they? If they were good enough for me, they're good enough for you."

Potatoes done three ways—boiled, roasted, and mashed. These had constituted the major part of his parents' Christmas dinners. Before his father's arrival, George hadn't eaten a potato since he had left England, not even a french fry. And he hadn't spent a Christmas with his father since 1975. Christmas was his mother's game.

🌱🌱🌱

The morning after the night of the ax, George had asked Stan if he knew what happened.

"What are you getting at?"

"You were outside, Dad, with an ax, chopping a tree. You were sleepwalking."

"No. I snore. I'm a snorer. I don't sleepwalk."

"You were chopping at a pine tree with an ax."

"You know my brother Charlie? Now, *he* was a sleepwalker. One Christmas Charlie got himself up dead in the middle of the night, went over to the neighbor's yard and killed their hen. Just snapped its neck with his bare hands, like he was taking a piss, then turned back home and went to bed. We only knew he'd done it from the bloody feathers in the kitchen thenext morning."

"Did you hear me? You were up last night, chopping a pine tree with an ax."

Stan shrugged. "It's Christmas, anyway. We'll be needing a tree."

George stared at his father.

"You do do Christmas in this house, don't you?"

Beneath their Christmas tree were four presents: a wrapped box of fruitcake from the art history department, and three small boxes for the children. Viji always bought their gifts, from the long lists they drew up in October. Sometimes she got the discounted imitation versions of what they wanted, and their faces fell just a little as they tore the wrapping away. But still, *Wow, thanks!* they would cry, and, *Hey, this is what I wanted!* This year George had stopped into an antique store. For Babygirl he'd bought a silver and mahogany jewelry box with tulips engraved on the lid, and for each of the boys, an antique model roadster, hand-painted, with a moving steering wheel. None of these had been on their lists, but he'd wanted to get them the best things possible.

♧♧♧

The only store open on Christmas was Super-Duper, the sort of gigantic supermarket that had begun to spring up around the outskirts of town. It was as large as the Sacramento airport, a florescent beacon on the valley landscape. Its warehouse shelves were stacked to the ceiling with bulk-buy crates of potato chips, screwdrivers, and chicken nuggets. Who, George wondered, would need eighteen screwdrivers?

Later, George pressed his nose to the window and watched the steam from his breath condense and drip down the pane. In the kitchen, his father was frying steaks. In one pot, potatoes were boiling. In another, they sat mashed. And in a punch bowl on the counter, he'd emptied a two-pound bag of Super-Duper-brand potato chips. George groaned into the window when he heard Lupe arrive.

Early that afternoon, Viji had phoned. He'd spent most of the call speaking with the children and less than a minute with Viji. It hurt his neck to pretend to be cheerful, but he did it anyway. He told Viji about the potatoes and she laughed. He was proud, for a moment, to hear her. But when he hung up, he felt he'd been speaking only to a pleasant acquaintance. Now he had nothing but the day to cling to. It stretched before him, vast and dry.

"Hello?" Kamla answered.

"Merry Christmas," he said.

"Merry Christmas," she said softly.

"How's it been?" In the background he heard a girl's wail, angry words. "George?"

"Yes?"

"I can't talk now, maybe tomorrow?"

"Right. Of course."

"Bye."

"Bye."

"Thank you for calling."

"Bye, Kamla."

George's mother once took him to see a pianist. He was playing in an underground tavern, with heavy air and barrels stacked against the wall. Aunty Dona was there with a man he'd never seen. At first the adults stared at George, but then they lost interest. Do you see what he's doing? Marla whispered. He was playing with two hands, she explained, but one hand played a full bar ahead of the other. The sound felt groundless at first, like a rowboat on a turbulent sea. It made him shake his head. But then it began to sound fine. Never beautiful, just fine. It was something to get used to. George was one of those hands, Viji was the other. On the day George married Viji, she loved him, or at least he thought she did. He did not love her. When she had the triplets, his love for her hit him like a speeding truck. But she was too distracted by those three new lives to remember that she loved him. And then, saying goodbye to her on Christmas morning, he loved her desperately and suddenly.

❦❦❦

She might have felt the same way, for just a moment, if she hadn't turned and seen what she saw: wide cheeks, eyes like half-moons.

The children had spoken in high excited voices to George. He had gifts waiting for them. They stood in the STD office, sun-dried now, the boys in their swim trunks and Babygirl in her bathing suit. The man who ran the office stared at her. Viji wanted to hiss at him.

"Come on," she said.

"But we didn't get to talk to Grandad."

"Other people are waiting, Avi. Next time we'll talk to Grandad." Behind them a line was forming, white tourists phoning home for Christmas. She herded the children out the narrow door and looked back, instinctively, to make sure she hadn't left anything. A man stared back. He was young. He didn't stare like an Indian. His eyes were soft. When he smiled, she could only blink before turning out the door and following the triplets home.

She saw him twice that day. It wasn't clear if he'd followed her, or if they'd found each other by chance in the lobby of the Sea Rock Inn. Something was pulling at her sari. She looked down. "What is it?"

"I have to go number two," Kieran whispered. She handed him the room key.

What kind of life was this, which could be knocked off its tracks by a child's need to poo? But it couldn't be blamed on this, not solely.

He walked toward her purposefully, as if they had business to discuss. "Merry Christmas," he said.

"Merry Christmas." She could hardly breathe the words. She didn't know why.

"Can I ask where you're from?"

"India. Madras. Well, America."

His eyes shifted to the bindi on her forehead. "Do you celebrate Christmas?"

"Yes," piped up Babygirl.

He looked down and grinned. "Well, great, 'cause we're having a very special visit from *you know who*."

"I'm too old for Santa Claus," grumbled Avi. "Mom, can we go to the beach?"

Her child was rude. She looked up at the man and had nothing to say.

"There's a service also, in the chapel. You're probably not interested, but…"

"No," Viji said, "I'm not."

"I'm from Michigan," he said.

"I see."

Kieran was back, tugging at her wrist.

"Did you wash your hands?"

"What?" the man asked.

She looked down at Kieran and repeated the question. "Yes."

"Come, let's go." She gathered them hastily and began to run with them once they hit the sand. The lobby had been stifling; she'd barely been able to breathe.

✿✿✿

"Mom?"

"Hmm."

"I want to see Daddy."

"I know, chellum." Babygirl lay on the towel beside her, her small, hot head pressed into Viji's armpit. She wore heart-shaped sunglasses from the Country Club Mall and her child belly rose like a muffin top.

"When is Daddy coming?"

"He isn't coming."

"Oh." She considered this. "When are we going home?"

"Next Wednesday. After New Year's." In so much sun, Babygirl had turned into a negative of herself, her light skin now dark brown, her chestnut hair almost yellow. Viji didn't tell her that she and Avi and Kieran would be flying alone, or that a nice stewardess would sit with them and give them games to play.

Later, Viji felt herself falling asleep in the shade of an aged catamaran that lay halfway up the beach. The splintered logs of the boat blocked most of the wind, and only a coy breeze ruffled the pleats of her sari. No bathing suits for her, not like the white woman sunbathing in the bikini, ignoring the fishermen's stares as if they didn't matter to her. From beneath, the sand warmed Viji's towel. The children were on the shore, digging a hole. Each day they dug a hole. Their only goal was to make it as wide and deep as possible and then let it fill with water, their very own swimming pool. As if the ocean weren't enough. She sighed, and soon she was asleep.

The mind wanders when released from wakefulness. Hers tried to act casual, sauntering over to that place it wasn't supposed to go. Amma's kitchen, Old Krishnan, chapati dough, and a heavy granite rolling pin. There is police tape around these memories; the door that leads to them says *emergency exit, alarm will sound.* She hears heavy footsteps—it is only her father. But he ignores her when she speaks, he pounds past her toward the kitchen. And then he stops, looks back at her. He takes small steps now, kitten steps, moves like a phantom to the kitchen door. Viji wants to shout, she knows now what is happening. Amma's voice, Appa's. Appa roars. Alarm bells. The heavy granite rolling pin, Amma screeches *no-no, no-no,* like a wild nocturnal bird. Krishnan wails and holds the back of his neck. Appa pounds his own head against the wall, and Amma escapes to the puja room. When Krishnan cries out, he sounds like the shrieking dog.

The alarm was wailing now.

She woke to the distant hammering of church bells. It was Christmas. The sand was warm. On the shore, with the froth of the ocean lapping at their ankles, her children were digging a hole.

That night, they ate fish on the balcony, chili-fried barracuda, a Christmas treat. Only an hour earlier, she'd seen a fisherwoman carrying a stack of the wide, flat bodies in a vessel balanced on her head.

The children were in bed, asleep, murmuring fish dreams, when Viji rose and opened the balcony door. Below, the ocean rose in steady black waves.

Then she was on the beach, her nightgown whipping around her legs. There was so much in it, this peaceful roaring thing. It had a power that frightened her. It could rise up at any moment and come crashing down, wrecking the dry world, swallowing her and the triplets whole.

Her mind swirled. Thoughts of Krishnan and Amma, of the squelching sound of broken flesh, the canine cry of pain, of George. What would her father have done to George?

She hadn't prayed for three days. In her suitcase waited the dusty picture of Kama, god of love and fascination. This was all she cared for now. He was all that

mattered in the end, wasn't he? She'd left the others behind. Ganesha—let the obstacles come. Lakshmi—let her
be poor, who needed money? What did it buy besides
hotel rooms? Saraswathi—knowledge only brought more
questions. Better to have none of it. And Durga—mother
goddess, protector. It was the moon's decision. If the moon
wanted to stir the ocean into a frenzy, it would. Nothing in
Viji's measly ant prayers would change that.

A meadow of moonlight spread over the children. It
didn't wake them the way sunlight did. They hadn't asked
for gifts this year; they hadn't said a thing that morning
when there were no packages to open, no wrapping paper
to tear into or ribbons to strew over the hotel room floor.
She held her chest and swallowed a sob. It rose suddenly
from within, like a wave of nausea. Children found ways
to protect their parents. How kind hers were to her.

With sunrise came new thoughts of breakfast, ocean
air, hole digging on the shore. She sat in the sand and
watched the boys with shovels, her girl at her side.

He found her again. She knew from the tremor of
sand around her that he was approaching. *These Christians*, she thought. Would they never give up? She thought
of the poor Mormons, how brash she'd been with them.

He sat in the sand beside her. He was wearing long
shorts and his chest was bare.

"Are you a priest?" she asked, before they even knew
each other's names.

"I'm Aaron," he said, "And you are?" He was avoiding
the question.

"Viji."

"Viji?" He gazed at the water long enough for her to

wonder if their conversation was over. "I'm no priest, Viji."

"If you're not a priest, then why are you at the church?"

"I guess you could say I'm a missionary."

She clicked her tongue. Babygirl, on the other side of Viji, stared up at him.

"And why have you chosen to come to India?"

"Well, I didn't choose, exactly. I was chosen. Spreading the word, I guess. You know."

"Yes," she said, "I know." He had a lazy way of talking, as if he knew the words would come and felt no need to push them. They were silent for a while. It was difficult to speak to someone without a solid, predetermined reason for speaking to them. "Do you know many people here?"

He shook his head. His skin was baked, and the sun had trodden lines as fine as spider trails into the corners of his eyes. Twenty-five, at the oldest. Or thirty. Viji had forgotten what twenty-five looked like.

"Mom? I'm going."

"Okay, chellum. Stay on the sand."

She felt a twinge of guilt, dismissing her daughter so she could speak with this man.

"I was wondering," Viji said, "why you didn't wear a priest's collar."

He laughed aloud. "That'd be kinda weird. Swim shorts and a collar? I'd look like a stripper, actually." This shocked her slightly. "We know about strippers, you know." He winked.

"Are you from the Mormon church?" she asked. He grinned to himself, though she couldn't think what might be funny, unless he too imagined Jesus bebopping with the Ladder-day Saints. "I met some missionaries once," she said, shyly. "I think I was quite rude."

"Don't worry about it." He nudged her with his elbow. "Chances are, they had it coming."

Really, a priest shouldn't be nudging and winking like this, she wanted to say. *Not even a missionary.* The truth was, she wanted to be alone. It made her uncomfortable to have a man next to her, here on the beach, acting friendly like this and winking.

"I'm not trying to convert you, you know."

"Oh no, just spreading your message of faith, is it?"

"I detect a hint of sarcasm. Listen, if you do want to come to the church, just to see—"

"You never know," she said. "You might like to be a Hindu." She stood up. "We have a flying monkey." With that she turned and headed for the ocean, the thick sand turning her tread inward, so that each step nearly spun her around.

She could still see him from the ocean, his chest browning slowly in the sun. He'd smelled of sunscreen, which reminded her of the triplets. She saw him in the hotel lobby that night, but he didn't see her. He was sitting in an armchair, his hands folded, and thinking deeply about something.

"Who's that man?" Kieran asked. His voice was flat.

"You met him, no? He's a priest. He works for the church over there. You remember? The bells were ringing?"

"How come you were talking to him?"

"He was talking to me," she said, suddenly on the defensive. "Grownups talk to each other, Kieran, no big deal."

"Yeah, *Kieran*, no big deal."

Viji glanced down at her daughter.

"How come he's here?" Babygirl asked.

"I don't really know. He's trying to get other people to join his church, I guess."

"Are you going to join his church?"

"Of course not."

"Why not?" Avi asked. "We could have Christmas for real, then!"

"Yeah!"

"Don't be stupid," Viji scolded. "He's a nice man, anyway."

"He's boring," Babygirl muttered.

"Yeah, he's boring," Kieran said.

Babygirl whispered into his ear and he shrieked with laughter.

"What?" Viji asked.

"Nothing!"

"*What?*"

Bubbling with giggles, "Babygirl said he has hair coming up from his butt."

"He doesn't! What do you mean?" Viji scolded. "What's wrong with you three?"

That night, she lay in bed, stroking the sand-whipped softness of her neck. From above, she was a ghostly sculpture beneath her sheets, casting her own shadows in the moonlit room. How silly she felt, thinking of him. She wondered what it would be like to be alone in a room with him. Minus the triplets, minus the church and the watchers on the beach. She thought of his bare chest and wondered if the sand made his skin as soft as hers, or if it had that rough clamminess of men.

From beneath her pillow she pulled out the picture of

Kama and smoothed its corners down. This was what
she'd come to, without her puja room, hiding the picture
like a teenager smitten with a movie star. What a sight he
must have been, burned through the core by Siva's rage.
Was there a hole through his middle? Did he burn first
around the edges like a piece of paper, the rest of him
charring away in black crumbs? Did he disappear *poof* in
a cloud of smoke, like those villages in Japan? Was there a
crater where he had stood?

There had been craters, fleshy depressions, in Krishnan.
Viji had watched from the upper balcony as he stumbled
from the kitchen to the courtyard. He'd looked up to find
the sun. He wasn't crying. His cheeks were crushed plums.
His eyes swelled against their sockets in permanent surprise. When he bent over, the blood dripped from his lips,
like syrup, to the earth below. He gagged, but nothing
more came. To the bathhouse he stumbled, to wash the
blood away.

She sat up in bed. This was when she went to the big
house, the house with the swing. She was sent to stay with
them. A family, she remembered clearly now, a woman
with gray hair at her temples. A man with a massive wart
on his cheek. The wart made Viji gag once at the dinner
table. These were the big-house people. She flushed with
heat. There was no air in the room.

At Kovalam Beach, the sands were white, even at
night, and the sea was wise old indigo. On that television
show, the one with the island and the small man who
shouted, "The plane! The plane!" she'd seen seas that were
clear and turquoise like the water in a child's wading pool.
Not so here. Here, the ocean was opaque with secrets. And

at night, dark blended into dark. She could sense, for the first time, that the world was a sphere.

The wind was stronger on the beach than it had been on the balcony. Her nightgown wrapped around her calves and clung to her belly and breasts. She was walking down the beach, on the wet sand because it held her weight, shoeless, so she could grip with her toes. She was nearing the church.

The big-house people had taken her to church. The convent nuns—Sweet Dolores, Tall Dolores—had gazed approvingly at her. *We knew you'd find us*, their smiles had seemed to say.

At Kovalam Beach, the church was round and squat, like the old mission buildings in Sacramento. The walls were perfectly white. Dark beams held the corners of the building, and a bell hung from a tower in the front. It was a church that could have been made from clay, shaped by a giant's hands.

Sand swallows sounded. She didn't hear the footsteps approaching; she didn't know another soul was awake anywhere in this bottomless night. She saw him, at last, in the scant light that cast itself off the church wall. He held a walking stick, like a prophet.

"How do you always find me?"

"What do you mean?" But he smiled as if he knew.

"Why are you awake?" They could speak directly at night, free from constructs and reason.

"Jet lag," he said.

"How long have you been here?"

"Three months."

"And still you have jet lag?"

"I've kept it. I like it. I like being awake at night." He shrugged. "Will you come in?"

"Yes." She gazed at the heavy doors. Inside the smoky silence, everything meant more. Their footsteps echoed. She could smell the incense that had once been used to hide the smell of dead bodies, a fact she had learned from the nuns. A colossal cross hung at the front of the room, and there were no pews, only chairs. The shadows made more chairs, and darkened netherwalls made the chapel seem bigger than it was. The interior, she was surprised to see, was painted bright blue. A small pool, dank-smelling, rippled with air currents. He moved to the front of the church and sat down with his back to her. She loitered by the wall, waiting, she supposed, for instruction. He sat like he had that day in the lobby, deep in meditation, hands folded in his lap.

She expected him, when he shifted position, to turn around and speak to her. Her mind was too full, and she felt on the verge of epiphany. The things she could tell him—how bizarre they would sound! He could be her confessor, though she'd committed no sin. He could be her George, poring over the partial details as if they were X-rays.

There was no point in making small talk, not at this hour of the night. Nor was there room for big talk. She hesitated, wondered if she should walk out, scamper back to her hotel, whether that would bother him or whether he'd even notice. Then she walked down the aisle, every footfall a pronouncement, and sat behind him. Above her, beyond the ceiling, she knew that there were stars. In the distance she could hear the sea. The church was a conch shell, smooth and white and slumbering on the shore.

CHAPTER ELEVEN

"How was your Christmas?" Kamla picked an almond flake off the plate.

"Rubbish. Yours?"

She shrugged, then looked straight into him. "Lonely."

George gulped his coffee. "Get any good presents?"

The girl was here. Anisha. George had bought her her own croissant, which she accepted silently. Now she picked at it and trailed powdered sugar around her mouth. "Did you get any good pressies, Anisha?" She rolled her eyes at him. "Babygirl's getting a jewelry box."

"That's lovely," Kamla sighed. "Isn't that lovely, Anisha?"

The girl sized him up, then crossed her arms. She was obviously troubled and spoiled, but she made him nervous all the same.

Kamla studied the croissant. "Anisha wants to spend New Year's Eve with her father. He hasn't said anything about it, and he hasn't returned her calls." Smiling ruefully, "Who could have known it would turn into this?"

The café was open the day after Christmas. Unusual. If Viji were here, she'd say it was because the owners were Chinese, and the Chinese didn't care about Christmas. George smiled. Back home it was Boxing Day, meant for visiting relatives and watching television and eating even more than they'd eaten on Christmas. Originally it was the day when peasants went to their landlords' houses with empty boxes to be filled with coins and toys, whatever trinkets it took to distract them from the fact that they lived like pigs.

He hadn't been exaggerating. His Christmas was rubbish. He'd never loved the holiday, but spending it with Stan and Lupe had been nearly unbearable. The steaks from Super-Duper had been tough and fatty, and the worst of it was that they still had thirteen in the freezer, stacked to the top and spilling from the shelves. The potatoes had been potatoes, nothing better and nothing worse. The potato chips, at least, had been crispy and well salted. Stan and Lupe had held hands at the table, and after dinner they'd slunk up to Stan's bedroom. When the noises started, George left the house without his coat. He walked the streets of Maple Grove.

Through the squamous dark he roamed, skirting ditches, peering now and then into the bay windows of Winding Creek Road. When he hit Ladino, the leafless trees made way for the moonlight. His feet led him to Kamla's house, where the air was thick with the smell of damp grass. From halfway down the drive, he could see her empty kitchen window. She was there, rinsing plates, scrubbing at them with a sponge. She was talking, probably to the girl, or maybe singing. But no, he'd seen her sing before, in a distracted way, turning her head this way and that. She wasn't singing. She stopped, suddenly, and looked out the window.

He froze, terrified that she'd seen him. She turned and walked from the room. George ran down the drive, numb to his neck with cold. He ran all the way home, certain he'd been spotted, and arrived in his silent house, panting.

He lay awake. It was the second twilight, the milk-hued hush between night and dawn. He rose and wondered if he had to pee, but he didn't. So he moved to the bedroom window. At the other side of this sky, the bright afternoon side, his wife and children played. He imagined them with buckets in the sand, Viji in sunglasses, waving at a camera, her sari billowing like a sail in the wind. If he backed up a bit, retraced his steps to the next continent, he would find Victoria. In a leather office chair, probably, chewing on her cuticles, with her eyes crossed in concentration.

It was morning in England. He could call her now, if her number had stayed the same. He hadn't spoken to her since that last evening in Nottingham, and she wouldn't call him. She would never call him. She did send him something, an envelope with a small lump of tissue paper inside. No feces this time. He picked up the phone and dialed. It had been eight years.

"Hello?" a man's voice said.

"Hello. Hi, could I speak with Victoria Banks, please?"

"And who shall I say is calling?" He was what they called posh.

He heard the rustle of her before she picked up. "George?"

"Hi, Victoria?"

"Is that—who is this? Is that George?"

"George Armitage, yes, George." He paused. "How are you?"

"Well, George Armitage!" she gasped. "As I live and

breathe!" It was something someone's mother would say. Then, panic in her voice. "Is everything all right? Is Stan all right?"

"Yeah, we're fine here. Stan's visiting me, actually... well, living with me."

"Is he, now! Old Stan. Is he there?"

"He's sleeping, actually. It's late here."

"Is everything all right, George? You sound—so he's living with you? Just you?"

He scoffed at this. "Well, no, not just me. With me and Viji, of course, and the children."

"Oh. Right. So everything's all right?"

He wished she would stop asking that. "Sure, every-thing's great. Listen, Victoria, I've got to go."

"Of course you do, this must be costing you a packet. Happy Christmas!"

"It was good talking to you."

"Ring anytime, George."

"Bye, Victoria."

"Love you, George. Toodle-loo!"

He hung up on the false ring of her voice. In his chest, his slamming heart had slowed to a stutter. He didn't want to know any more about her, whether she was married or had two kids, or what they were called, or what she'd pub-lished, or where she'd bought a summer house. He feared that she had turned into one of those women, the sort who would call and assault him with the petty news of their lives for ten minutes without pause and then sign off by saying, *All right then I'll let you get on with it now, it was lovely talking to you bye! Bye bye bye....*It was enough, for those first few seconds, just to hear her.

When she'd lain with him that night in Nottingham, amid the mountains of his mother's clothing, neither of them had slept. They would have looked naked and laughable to anyone else. George had reached for his trousers and fished out the earrings.

"These would suit you, I think."

"No, George. I can't take those."

"Why not?"

"Your dad would want them."

"My dad doesn't want these."

"But they were hers; he would want to keep them."

"He wants *her* back, Victoria, not her earrings."

She let out a cavernous sigh. He worried he'd set her off again.

"What about your wife? Wouldn't she want them?" Her words were flat, monotone, but not bitter.

"I want you to have them, all right?" He pushed them into her thin fingers.

"All right."

She'd worn them the next morning at breakfast. Stan noticed them, or seemed to, staring at Victoria's ears but saying nothing. He had never, as far as George could tell, noticed them on Marla.

When the earrings came back to George a year later, without a letter, he didn't ask why. He never called her or wrote, but simply slipped the earrings in his drawer, amid the mess, and hoped they would go unnoticed.

Outside, next to the pool house, Stan sat alone. As if on cue, he stood and walked back across the yard and into the house. George got out of bed to go downstairs and close the sliding door.

✤ ✤ ✤

"I'm worried about my father." The line to Kamla's house was thick with static. He'd called her in the morning, hoping she'd be home. He had no idea what she did in the mornings.

"Is he all right?"

"Physically, yes. He has these…I guess you'd call them episodes."

"What kind of episodes?"

"Are you busy now? Do you want to go somewhere?"

"Everywhere's closed." It was New Year's Eve.

"Could we go for a drive?"

It was raining when they went. They drove around the park, this time in the same car. Two of them in the quiet front seat, fogging the windows as any two bodies would on a humid December day. Raindrops fell on the windshield like exploding marbles. Along the drive, weeping willows swung their leafy dreadlocks, lovely things dragged to the ground by their own weight. And the smell of warm wet earth seeped in through the air vents and edged past the windowpanes. It made George want to do something. It made him want to strip down and lie in the mud, to sling his leg around a willow tree and gnaw on its gray-white bark, to wrap those long limp branches around his neck and pull on them until he felt he could strangle himself.

He described to her what was happening to Stan. He told her about Marla's funeral, and what had happened with Victoria. He'd never told a soul about that night he spent with Victoria. He scarcely dared remember it himself. "It was a natural thing to happen," he said. "I mean, it didn't feel wrong."

"Of course not."

"I don't want you to think—"

"I don't."

He also told her about the earrings, how he'd been hiding them like a shameful secret when really, there was little to be ashamed of. Kamla had little to say in response. What could she say? She wasn't a psychologist. She hardly knew Stan. "Have you told Viji?" was all she asked. The name came breathlessly from her.

"About the earrings?"

"About Stan."

"No, I haven't."

"Why not?"

"It's hard to talk about that sort of thing. About Stan, I mean."

"You don't want to worry her."

"No."

"George."

"Yes."

"Are you and Viji happy?"

"Maybe you should ask her."

He looked at Kamla, and she looked back, not smiling this time. His breath seemed to echo through the car, drowning out any other words he might possibly try.

"Do you want to walk?" she asked.

Clumsy raindrops pelted his shirt, and he didn't have an umbrella. Kamla held a newspaper over her head. They wouldn't go too far. *This could be a Tamil film*, George thought ruefully, watching Kamla scurry for the shelter of a willow tree. Minus the singing, of course, and the rain-soaked sari.

The idea to walk had been a misguided one. Moments after they left the car, the steady drizzle swelled to an angry torrent. The rain was too loud to talk over, and they found themselves leaning pointlessly on a willow tree, with little to say.

He dripped onto his seat on the drive home, already regretting the wet-animal smell the rain would leave on his upholstery. He could feel Viji in the car, hissing and spraying like an agitated cat. Beside him, Kamla shivered.

He pulled into her driveway. "Do you want to come in?" she asked. How often he'd heard this question, always after dates, evenings at the movies, and late-night drinks.

"I'm quite wet," he said.

"I have clothes. Men's clothes."

"Probably shouldn't."

"George? Are you sure?" Her eyes were liquid, slack around the edges.

He paused. "I'm sure."

"Bugger," he said as he drove away. He sputtered the words again, "bugger bugger bugger," and they made him feel better. He spent that afternoon in his study, tracing a finger over freshman final papers that he had yet to grade, of which he had yet to read a single sentence. He was through more than half the stack of papers, all graded irritably, with lower marks than he was used to giving, when he heard a shuffling past his door.

"Dad?"

Stan's head. "What?"

"Have you been feeling all right lately?"

"Yep." He gazed slack-jawed at George's pile of papers.

"Getting enough sleep?"

"Yep. What is it you want, son?"

"Sit down, Dad." He kicked out the chair on the other side of his desk. To his surprise, Stan sat. "It's just that... well, I guess what I want to ask is, why are you here?"

"Why am I here? Well, that's a bit of a question, isn't it? Why are any of us"—he circled his arms in the air—"*here*?"

"What I mean is, why'd you pick up and come here after all this time?"

Stan was quiet for a long while, picking at the stubble on his chin. "If I'm not welcome, George, all you've got to do is say."

He sighed. "That's not what I mean. Don't be silly. I guess I'm just wondering—are you all right? Is everything all right, you know, with you?"

"Bloody hell, George."

"It's just that you seem to be...*sleepwalking*. Did you know you were sleepwalking?" His father had come to him for help, he was realizing. His father was not well.

"How d'you mean, exactly?"

George explained, in almost the same words he'd used with Kamla. He reminded Stan of the pine-tree incident. Stan eyed him incredulously as he spoke, as if George were the one behaving strangely. George finished, sighed, and waited for an answer.

The chair screeched. Stan stood. "If you think I'm touched, soft in the head, I'm not." The shake in his voice was surprising. "I've not gone soft in the head, George, and I'll thank you not to tell me I have. I may be an old bugger, but I've not gone soft yet!" Stan leaned on the desk. "What is it you want? Your inheritance? Well, there's not bloody much of that, I'll tell you now."

"Dad—"

"Don't interrupt me, you knob."

"Dad that's not what I want at all."

"Then you'd best not meddle."

George groaned, audibly exhausted. "As long as you're all right," he muttered.

"I'm all right." Stan tapped the desk absentmindedly. "Nothing else, then?"

"No," George replied. "Nothing."

CHAPTER TWELVE

He found her again that day.

"Happy New Year," he said.

"Same to you."

They sat side by side without saying anything. The sun was muted in the beige sky that afternoon. Rarely did she see a blue sky here. A skittish breeze lifted sand off the beach and made it hard to sit still without shielding her eyes. Viji pulled her sari around her to keep the flapping fabric from exposing her middle.

"You have a lovely church," she ventured.

"Thanks. They say it dates back to St. Thomas, but actually it's pretty new. Nineteenth century. Looks old, is all."

"Why would they say such a thing?" She turned to him. "Why would they say it was a church of St. Thomas if it wasn't?"

He shrugged. "I guess it makes it seem more credible."

"Older things are more credible." She wished this notion applied to humans as well.

"Do you have a husband?" he asked.

This startled Viji. She looked at him, shielding her eyes, which for some reason made him laugh. "Yes, I do."

He shrugged. "Just curious. You're wearing a ring. So where is he?"

"At home in California. He had teaching to do," she lied.

"So he's a teacher?"

"He's a college professor."

"Nice. This sand's kind of harsh on the eyes."

Silence.

"Do you have a swimsuit?"

She looked up, surprised again. What kind of question was this?

"Well, I mean, it's kind of a shame to be at a beach and not go in, right? It might be a good day for it, too, since sitting's a pain in the butt, with the sand and all."

"No thank you."

"No?"

"I don't swim." She did in fact have a swimsuit and she did technically know how to swim, though she rarely went in the pool, only dangled her legs in on the hottest evenings. She'd seen a science show once about a sea cow. She reminded herself of one whenever she swam, the way her bottom seemed to drag behind her. Eyes stinging, spitting into blue water, threads of saliva. These things were not for her. She hated the feel of water creeping up her nostrils.

"That's too bad. Do you body-surf?"

She thought of standing up and walking away and never speaking to him again. Why had he taken an interest in her, this young man? There were other ladies he could talk to, other ladies who, she assumed, knew how to "Body- surf." It was because they were both American, she told herself. Nothing more than two friendly Americans in a country far from home.

Never in her life had she so clearly been an American.

He lay back and let his arm fall over his eyes. His underarms sprouted like alfalfa. His nipples were precise, small, amid the hairless plain of his chest. He had the body of a prophet—lean, ascetic.

"Where's your walking stick?" she tried to joke. But he'd fallen asleep or was ignoring her, knitting his thoughts on some private beach. He said nothing, though his lips parted unconsciously.

Like a jagged nail, a longing drove through her. She would have to leave, quickly. But when she stood, a crown of vertigo spun around her head. She blinked hard into the afternoon sun and hoped the dizziness would pass. She would go to her room and watch the children from the balcony. As she stalked off, she thought he mumbled something to her. But it was too soft to hear, and too late to ask again.

A chill set in that evening, for which Kovalam Beach was not prepared. It was New Year's Eve, and she could hear the hushed beat of disco in the distance. At home, they would have watched the ball drop over Times Square, counting to midnight with the man with the square head. Two out of three triplets would have fallen asleep before midnight. George and Viji would have had to coax the children awake—they were too big now to carry.

She made her way to the STD office, which was open and crowded. "Yes, you can talk to Dad this time," she assured Kieran.

Several seconds of static, and then the phone rang.

"Hello?"

"Oh—hello? Hello, this is Viji."

"Hiya, duck. Calling from India?" Stan was practically shouting now.

"Yes, hello, how are you?" She tried to sound cheerful.

"Happy New Year!"

"Yes, Happy New Year. Is George there?"

"George?"

"Yes, is he there?"

"Naw, he's out. Gone down to your lady friend's house. Whatsername."

"Kamla?" She had only one lady friend.

"That's the one. He went down to hers about an hour ago. Should be back soon, I reckon."

"Okay," was all she could manage.

"Kids all right?"

Without a word, she dropped the phone into Kieran's waiting hands ("Hi, Grandad!") and stood by as the triplets wrested the phone from each other, ramming frantic words into the receiver. She couldn't help shivering, though the office was muggy and warm. She felt that something had gone, or was about to go, very very wrong.

And she was right.

George knocked on Kamla's door that afternoon. It was the natural end to a winter's walk that was meant to clear his head. The door opened, but he didn't enter until Kamla took a step back. There were no offers of tea this time. Kamla turned and proceeded down the hallway, into the back corridors of the house, where George had never been before. On the walls hung framed photographs of flowers, one of a swan. An Indian tapestry hung next to a door, and through this door Kamla passed, wordlessly, to her bedroom.

She had indeed brought a swimsuit. It was a reflex that she'd picked up somehow in America. Vacation equals swimsuit. Hers was brown, with yellow Hawaiian flowers, a one piece, nothing flashy. It hid her tummy and she didn't look foolish. This was all she asked of a swimsuit.

She put it on the next morning. And then took it off. She put it on again, standing before the bathroom mirror with a hand raised instinctively to cover a hint of cleavage. Between her breasts rested the pendant of her wedding necklace, its thick gold chain skimming her chest. She took it off. Avi's voice—*come on!*—impatient to run to the sun. She put it on again, and wrapped a towel high around her waist. Why was she doing this?

Because of the sun, of course. And the sand. And the sand dollars chipped by running feet. Frisbees, bonfires, and seaweed, splayed like dead, bulbous monsters on the shore. These, for Viji, were the sea. Shuffling through the sand, wearing only her swimsuit and towel, she would now be part of it. Resolutely she ignored the stares of the men around her. The hisses and clicks of the tongue she let ping off her invisible armor. They didn't do this to the white women, not as far as she could tell.

From the beach she stepped into the sea. Without a

word she'd dropped her towel next to Aaron, unable still to look him in the face. It was hot. She would go first to the water. Far off to her right, the children were digging. Another child, blond and pudgy, had joined them.

The waves settled around her feet and rushed back into the ocean, giving her the sensation of moving backward. On her back was the heat of the sun and a hundred eyes. Before her coursed the blind ocean. She saw herself, darkening in the day, hair wild with wind and salt. A spray of sand brushed her calves and the top of her thigh. She was aware of her buttocks, peeking from her suit as frankly as a child's.

Soon the water reached her knees. With a new wave it crept up her thighs and a tremor passed through her groin. She walked willfully farther, until the water reached her waist, and then with a leap she dove to the stony seabed, pushing back to the surface with her palms.

Behind her, through watery eyes, she saw him on the shore. He waded out. "Ready to get out there?" he called.

She furrowed her brows, shook her head. Soon he stood beside her, the breeze and water raising goose bumps on their skin. Unsure of what to do, she fingered the bicolored border of her arm, the upper part of it where the skin stayed pale, and the lower part, nearly black now from exposure to the sun. "Let's jump some waves," he coaxed. She was shivering and ready to get out of the water. "Come *on!*" His smile was so electric, so ludicrously happy, that she had to grin back. "Right on!"

"Okay," she said, "But I don't know how to do this."

"Easy." He pulled her deeper until the water braceleted her waist again. He showed her how he did it: how to wait for a wave to rise, then rise higher, and then higher, before ducking into its wall, tucking himself just beneath the crest. The wave scooped him up and lifted him to the sky, before handing him down again and rushing back into the sea. He held her hand.

With his fingers strong around hers, it was easy, and as the wave swept her into its arc she squealed. She saw herself, helpless as an infant, cradled in giddy, open air, then dropped gently to the shore. She hoped the triplets were watching.

It was important to be brave, to face a wave head-on. "If you trust the wave," he said, "it'll take you to heaven and back. If you run from it, you're toast."

Feeling brave, Viji shook her hand from his grip. She waded farther, until the water pooled around her chest. In the distance the ocean roiled, thrummed itself into a wave, and headed inland. And then it was there, towering above, rushing white noise, so much higher now that she stood alone.

This was when she turned. She tried to run, heavy-kneed, her feet leaden in the sea. And just like he said it would, the wave caught her.

From behind it bulldozed her, forced her underwater, and held her there. She flailed against it. The ocean roared back, filling her ears and eyes and nostrils. Once, she bobbed up like a seal but was pulled back under. She could see her own arms, stroking. Before her eyes, the pendant of her wedding necklace, slow-motion floating, first to the left, then to the right. For a moment, all was still. This was what he'd meant by "toast"

Then a kick and a splash, a sucking sound. She surged

to the surface and was out. Coughing, retching, she spat
water and wheezed in the open air. The fresh wind blew cold
against her eyeballs, and stung the inside of her nose. She
coughed, gagging, spitting a whip of saliva from her lips.

Her right breast hung from her swimsuit, flung from
its nylon casing. She rushed to cover it and looked
around—no one had seen. In the blurry distance, her children continued digging. They'd seen none of it. A blade
of pain sliced across her shoulder. She cried out and held
her arm.

Aaron was next to her now, his arm around her waist.
He was saying words to her and guiding her to the shore.

"My shoulder," she gasped. She let Aaron guide her up
the beach, past their towels that lay curled in the sand.
They moved, dripping, farther up the shore to where the
sand was dry. But once she caught her breath, a drum of
excitement beat in her chest. Only her legs were tired, ex-
tremely tired.

"Lie down," he ordered, and dipped her to the
ground. Her elbow still circled his neck. "Can you lift your
arm?" he asked. She whimpered when he lifted it for her.
With his thumbs he palpitated the flesh of her shoulder,
down to her elbow. "I think it's just a sprain," he said. "I
think you'll be okay." The pain began to fade, just slightly,
then more as he stroked her arm. She let him lie with her,
even as the sun bore down and she wished for water. She
didn't want to move, despite the piercing eyes of the fishermen, the shameless stares of the women passing by,
superior in their saris and their tightly braided hair. She
didn't want to lift her head to check on the children.
Aaron's eyes fixed on hers, and she didn't dare look away,

not even when he slipped from her shoulder the strap of her swimsuit and a trail of sand spilled into her hair, not even when he laid his mouth on hers and she tasted there the ocean's salty grit.

She awoke minutes later, or maybe hours. Behind her lay a misty memory of what she'd done. Aaron was nowhere.

She sat up. The children. They would be waiting for her, looking helplessly. She couldn't see them from where she sat, and she envisioned a floating body, two triplets on tiptoes looking out to sea, straining to find the third, a useless lifeguard chewing paan and spitting onto the sand.

She must have fallen asleep immediately on the warm ground. The sun was now high in the sky and she needed water. Her legs shook when she stood, and she felt sick with thirst. Bare-legged and without a towel, she ran across the beach and forgot about her shoulder. There they were, by their swimming pool. They had indeed been waiting.

"Where were you?"

"Where'd you go?"

"I'm hungry. Where were you?"

"I'm hungry too."

The wind whipped her hair into her mouth. "I'm sorry," she said.

"Where *were* you? We were waiting!"

"I said I'm sorry!" she snapped. The triplets fell silent. "I was here the whole time," she said, and paused.

A few seconds of quiet, filled by the roar of the sea.

"Where are we going to eat?"

Like baby birds abandoned in a nest, they demanded her attention now, so cocksure when they knew she was there, suddenly helpless in her absence. She ushered them to the hotel terrace, where they ordered jam sandwiches and veggie pakoras. The waiter gazed too long at her chest, then at her bare lap. The hotel balconies were caught in the midday glare. If Aaron was looking down at her, she couldn't tell. She felt exposed, completely, and wished she had picked up her towel from the beach. By now it would have curled into the shore and vanished, buried by a thin layer of sand, no more than a hushed memento of the morning.

That night, lest she forget what had happened, the pain returned to her shoulder. It kept her awake and coaxed her onto the balcony for fresh air. Below her the ocean surged and receded, calmly and without judgment. It didn't surprise her to see Aaron, planting his walking stick in the sand as he moved down the beach. He would have been at the church. He would have sat quietly, meditating, possibly thinking of her.

The corridor was close and humid. She waited for his footfall on the stairs before emerging from the shadows, startling him. "How are you?" he asked. One look back at her bedroom door to make sure it was closed, and she took his hand. She said nothing in response, not even when he asked her, for the hundredth time, if she was all right. Nor when he opened his door and the chill of the air- conditioning made her wince. His fingers slid around the buttons of her nightgown, and she let it drop to the floor, an ivory puddle at her feet. A fine column of sand had gathered in a fold of his bedsheet. This she brushed away with her hand before she sat on the bed, before she eased herself onto a pillow, lay back, and waited.

CHAPTER FOURTEEN

If I do this, George thought, *I will be changing things, perhaps forever. If I don't do this, I will have to face the endless stretch of days, and not regret my choice. Above all, I must not regret my choice.* George weighed the pros and cons of what he was about to do, or not do. The only fault in his process was that already Kamla had taken him by the hand, already she sat on her bed, and already he stood between her knees. He combed his fingers through her silken curtain of hair. Effectively, the decision had been made.

Her movements were hesitant. She'd lost her usual zest and now seemed thoroughly unsure of herself. He would help. He would lean down, kiss her on the mouth, and sink her onto the bed. He would unbutton his own shirt so that she would not have to.

There were no mirrors in this room and he was glad for it. It would have shamed him to see himself, clunky and pale, in the arms of a beautiful woman. The thought of Viji passed often through his mind during those few minutes. Something of her was in the room, a spirit imp that leapt from chest to dresser to headboard, hissing and scratching at the people on the bed. But it was easy not to listen, easier than George had guessed it would be. Their hesitancy swelled to urgency, they began to work with

hurried fingers, undoing, pulling, loud breaths punctu-
ating their movements, and thus it was easy to ignore the
girl in the doorway. An unwelcome mirage, nothing
more, a subconscious manifestation of his last dogged
tendon of morality.

"Mom!" This he couldn't ignore. Kamla whipped her
face from his and pushed him off of her.

The girl stood in the doorway. They hadn't even
closed the door. She held a sandwich low beside her hip,
and its contents slid individually to the floor.

Kamla clicked her tongue. "Anisha-beti, careful please.
You're spilling." George stared down at Kamla, propped
on her elbows on the bed, her skirt hiked above her knees,
lace bra half-exposed. He was aware that his own zipper
was open and that a flag of white cotton poked through
the opening. He sat up straight and hid his lap with his
hands.

The girl gazed at George as if he were a nuisance, a
disruption to her schedule and nothing more. She seemed
to focus on the white strip of his undershirt. With such a
flurry of hands, they'd hardly managed to undress.

"Can I watch *Three's Company*?" she asked.

Kamla sighed and assented, still propped on the bed,
her legs askew. They waited in silence as she turned and
exited, leaving a square of pink lunch meat on the rug.
Kamla turned back to George, slithered further along the
bed, fingering the buttons of her shirt. "I don't like her
watching that show."

"I—I should be going."

"What?"

"I shouldn't be here. You know…"

"Anisha doesn't mind. She's busy." Kamla bounced to her knees and made her way over to George, sliding her leg over his. She fingered the hair at his temples. She was incandescent, filled with a glowing, aching sort of need. Once again, he had the choice to make. To say no, and force himself into battle with regret. Or to say yes, to dive into the pool of warmth, if only for an afternoon.

But it wouldn't be just an afternoon. It couldn't be. He stood up now, and with liquid eyes, Kamla offered her hand. He could take it and pull her close. He nearly did. Her fingers lay gently in his. But then, instead, he dropped her hand and fled—from the room, down the hall, away from the stale television laughter, through the front door, down the drive, past the oleander bushes, up Ladino, left on Winding Creek. And in fleeing, he left behind afternoons of meeting away from the girl and the triplets, away from Viji. He left the innocent wanderings around bookstores (though these, he knew, had ended long before). He left behind the *he* he got to be with Kamla: the intellectual, the friend, the guide. He left the smell of hotel soap on Kamla's skin, on his skin too. The receipts thrown in distant trash cans, the constant showering. He was ending, before they began, the months or maybe years of this, pushed finally to an ultimatum, a threat to reveal all, a need for a decision. He jogged down Winding Creek Road, his head heavy and his feet light, just as a dappled rain began to fall.

The specter of Kamla wrapped itself around Viji in those few days. She tried to burrow away from it, to hide in the folds of sheets. She did not know why George had been to her friend's house for over an hour. What she did know lay deep within her, beyond the reach of reason. From this knowledge, Aaron was her only escape.

Her insides were like her outsides, like the world that coursed past the hotel entrance. The streets of Kovalam were a topple of everything, life spilling into itself, coursing out of windows and down the muddy lanes like the torrent of a flash flood. But the gush of it all stopped here. In this bed, soft against Aaron's back, she paused to breathe the warm salt. She let her lids drop, and slept.

And the thoughts of home that had weighed so heavily on her were sinking now between the sheets and pillows. The memory of George and Kamla, that Thanksgiving night, ran down the smooth groove in Aaron's back, dripped off him, off the bed, onto the floor, and away.

She remembered, though vaguely, her life in America, the daily business of moving from one place to the next—house, store, gas station, school. Each door was a full stop where the outside ended and the inside began. But here, the outside oozed in, the days careened into one another as if caught in a mudslide, like Aaron sliding over her now. The collisions couldn't be stopped. She opened her eyes. "You're not a very good missionary," she said.

He turned to gaze at her. "What makes you say that?"

She would go to him at night, once the children were asleep. He was awake, of course, every time. In the high heat of the afternoons, she and the triplets slept indoors, each exhausted for their own reasons. Sometimes when she couldn't sleep, she watched their sun-baked bellies rise and fall, at peace with the fact that on the shore, their man-made swimming pools were filling up and caving in. She had three days of this, though they seemed to stretch languorously into twelve.

On the third night, Aaron fell asleep right away. She watched as air swelled into his chest each time he inhaled. He was two different people: night Aaron, sage and tranquil, and day Aaron, young, splashing in the waves. Here in this room, she could catch him somewhere in between. He was nearly transparent when he stretched out like this. She traced the indigo veins that wound like rivers around his wrists. In his sleep he brushed her hand away. This was the last time she would see him. She tried to feel sorrow, but she couldn't. He was already of another world.

She left an envelope for him at the front desk. If she'd slipped it under his door he might have heard her and opened it before she could leave, standing tall in the filtered sunlight of his room. For days afterward, she would be sideswiped by flashes of their nights together—his fingers gripping her arm, his mouth on her breast, the startling force of him. A pleasant, faraway ache lingered in the dip of her back.

The old Viji, young Viji, would have stayed. She would have stayed in the hotel for as long as Aaron did, or moved into his room to soak up every night he had to offer. Without a second thought, young Viji would have risked everything for a man. But this Viji had other things to think about—dropping a key into the bellhop's waiting hand, herding the children outside to find a taxi, counting backpacks to make sure there were three, and taking a final, stolen glance back at the beach.

✤✤✤

It was her secret that when she'd first found out she was pregnant, she wanted to make it go away. She could barely discern the outlines of her own existence—to sustain another wholly dependent one was unthinkable. She discovered morning aerobics on the television, followed them vigorously, jumping against the unusual weight in her middle, hoping to jiggle it out, whatever it was, boy or girl. She imagined it as a small and tenacious spider, clinging to her insides in an earthquake, spinning webby reinforcements. If she'd known at that time that there were two little spiders, she would have felt sicker than she did. If she'd known there were three, she would have been horrified. She imagined all the worst possibilities—her father's chins, Stan's craggy nose.

The night before, she'd packed the triplets' luggage, flattening stacks of folded T-shirts with her palms. She placed their small sandals in the suitcase. For some reason, the sight of their shoes exhausted her. They were still petite children, still growing out of having shared a womb.

Now she watched them walk down the tunnel to the plane, and the same stubborn womb began to ache with fear. She was sending her children away, her drops of gold, perfectly spun. She was casting them deliberately from her sight, alone, breaking the first rule of motherhood. She'd done it for Shanta; she couldn't leave her sister now, not yet, and certainly not for another twelve-year span. She would have to make this worthwhile, this clench in her stomach, this sudden wave of revulsion.

When the children were very small, Viji had found a list of Indian names. On the list, defined at last, was Neha. The name didn't mean "air", as Viji had hoped. It didn't mean "freedom" either, or anything like it. The meaning was stated simply: "love, rain" Love or rain. Love and rain. She watched the back of Babygirl's head, a step behind her brothers, until it sank into the crowd. They would be suspended over an ocean until she saw them again.

Home again. She stood reluctantly in the doorway to her sister's house. The door had been unlocked, as always, despite Viji's warnings. This was Madras, not a village in the country where neighbors wandered in and out of each other's homes. Anyone at all could drift into this house full of women.

There was no one to welcome her this time, only the shriek of the dog in the distance. She could hear the usual sounds of the kitchen, and then a low shuffling from the puja room. Pushpa Athai inched across the floor, glanced at Viji, and made her way to the kitchen.

"There's a ghost in the sitting room," the old woman called. For several minutes, no one came out to greet her. Why should they? At last she made her own way upstairs, with just her one suitcase and a mild ache in her back.

She smoothed the covers on her bed, which had been pulled together sloppily, as if they'd expected her return. The only sounds were water running through the walls, and the dog, shrieking steadily to count off the seconds.

"It's good that you came back." Shanta stood at the threshold of the room.

"She called me a ghost," Viji said.

"Never mind her."

It must be easy to be mad. The aunts were accountable for nothing. No explanations, a backstage pass to do and say what they wanted. Briefly, Viji considered turning mad herself, but it wasn't as easy as rubbing turmeric on her face and squinting into the sun. Sanity was a demanding master.

Something occurred to her then. "How do we know they're mad?" she asked. "Have they been tested?"

Shanta scoffed at this. "Tested for what? No need for testing, sister. They're crazy and that's all." In English, "The proof is in the pudding!"

"The pudding is in their brains." The sisters giggled. Finally, Shanta sat down.

"Here's proof," she said, turning serious. Viji scooted closer to her. "Listen closely, you. I'll say this only once. Do you remember what Appa did to Old Krishnan?"

"He turned his face to pudding."

"Yes. Do you know why?"

"I assume—" Viji's voice faltered. Why Shanta should be talking about this, after weeks of silence, she couldn't fathom. "I assume because of Amma. Krishnan and Amma."

Shanta waved this away. "No. Yes, he might have known

of that, but that is not why." She tugged at a thread that sprang from the bedspread. "It's what they told him, those old hags. They would say anything, and Appa listened."

"What did they say?"

"It was about Krishnan. It was nonsense, really. I think." Shanta stared, then glanced away. "Did he...do anything?"

"What?"

"No. He mustn't have."

"What are you saying?"

"I heard them say it. Foul-minded old bitches. *See how he holds her on his lap,* they said to him, *why do you think he does that?*"

"W*hat?*"

Barely audibly, Shanta asked, "He didn't touch you, Viji, did he? He didn't do anything like that?"

"Is that why they sent Appa away? For what he did to Krishnan?"

"Yes. No. I was small too, remember."

"I remember."

Shanta's eyes snapped up at these words. "You do?"

"Krishnan did nothing to me," Viji said. "He was a good man."

Neither sister said it, but it drifted past them like incense, the thought of how it would be, in some other life, to have Krishnan as their father.

"Come with me," Shanta said. She led Viji by the hand to Shanta's puja room. Viji hadn't been here since that first time. "I want to show you."

Against the wall, chests made of teakwood stood in stacks of three and four. Clumsily, Shanta pulled one crashing to the floor.

"This was mine," she said. "This was for my wedding." She unlatched the chest. The lid was hard to budge, fastened tightly by time and neglect. At last it flung open and from it a flurry of moths spewed, hung like a cloud, and then scattered. They settled on the walls and idols, fanning their wings and waiting.

Shanta's wedding trousseau contained all the elements meant for a bride of a good family: heavy Kancheevaram silks, willowy chiffons, a bright pink Mysore silk, freckled now with holes. She pulled out a red sari that ran with rivers of gold thread, thick with embroidery that still hadn't faded. This could have been her wedding sari. The moths had chewed through the cloth but not the gold, so that in spots it looked like a weaver's loom.

"What's the use?" Shanta asked. "All this…"

"It's my fault," Viji said. "Shanta. It's my fault that you couldn't marry."

"Nonsense." But Viji saw it then—who would marry their son to this girl, whose sister had run around with a strange man, who'd carried on like a prostitute with a vellakaran, and yes, they knew—everyone knew about the girl with no respect for her family.

"Don't be silly, woman," Shanta said. "We wouldn't have married, either of us, no matter how many trousseaux they collected. People knew about Appa. And the aunts. Who wanted that?"

"But we were a good family. Appa was a magistrate."

"You really like to think that, don't you? Appa was a magistrate because we had money. We had enough money to buy a madman a title. Do you think they ever let him in a court?"

Viji ran her fingers along the threadbare silks, lost in the corners of what she did not know. "But he was smart. He was a reader, remember? Remember how he loved the library?"

Shanta sighed and fixed a stray hair on Viji's temple. "You think he was reading? I think he liked the quiet. I think he liked the dark." There were times, Viji recalled, when she'd found him alone at night on the veranda, or sitting on his own in the dining room, the candles blown out, the curtains drawn.

"Vijaya," Shanta began. "Viji," she smiled. "That's your American name, no? Viji. It sounds nice, it's a nice name." Her face fell. "When you say you remember that day with Krishnan and Appa—I don't think you do."

On the pillars, along the chests, the moths were still.

"What don't I remember?"

"No, I shouldn't say. It was nothing."

"Shanta, don't do this again."

Where the chest had been brought down, a banister of sunlight angled through the window and fell on the stack of saris—a highway of light, a million particles of dust traveling along it, too busy to notice the sisters or their silence.

"Okay," Shanta said. "I will tell you." She paused. "Close your eyes, and I will tell you."

Viji shut her eyes and yielded her hand to Shanta, who lifted it to her own face. First, beneath her fingertips, was something hard and thin, the bridge of Shanta's nose. Viji could feel how it leaned to the side. She knew the unappealing lump that divided the top of the nose from the bottom. She could see it with her eyes closed.

"Do you remember," Shanta asked, "when Appa found you?"

"When he found me? Krishnan was telling me a story. That's all, Shanta, he was only telling me a story." As if hypnotized, Viji spoke without knowing the words. "I remember I was sitting with Krishnan, then Appa was there, and he was so angry with me." She saw it now—she had always known this, but the vision rushed at her as if she were seeing it for the first time: Appa's great bear claws, the soft hands that had turned swift and strong, sweeping down on her. Words like poison spilling from her father, in a voice that wasn't his. *You are just the same, just the same as your mother, aren't you? Little scoundrel. You wanted him to do it to you.* She heard the crack of a hand against her head. The cold stone floor was a shock. She didn't cry because she couldn't breathe.

When she opened her eyes, Shanta nodded. "He was angry."

Viji saw blood. There was blood coursing from Appa's hand, like the nailed palms of the convent crucifix. It was Shanta.

"You—" Viji pointed into her sister's face. Shanta snatched her finger and brought it to her cheek, its slight depression, her half-closed eye.

"He was going to kill you," Shanta said. "I thought he was."

"He was so angry."

So Shanta had done what she felt was necessary. She had run to the kitchen, found Old Krishnan's chopper, the Saracen's sword, and brought it back. In it plunged, into Appa's raised hand, through the flesh between the fingers.

Viji remembered his screech, like a stricken wildcat's. And his hand, the other hand, coming down on Shanta, the blow to her head and the quick *snap* that followed.

"You were so small," Shanta said.

"So were you."

"And I tried to get him back. Remember the courthouse? I thought I could find him and convince him to come home."

"Of course I remember."

"To think I wanted him back after what he did. What was I thinking?"

"He was our father."

They were quiet for several minutes, sitting on opposite sides of the chest.

"I left you here, alone, with all of this," Viji said. She couldn't bring herself to say the other thing, that Shanta's face, her nose, her eye, her cheek, had been the lifelong price she'd paid for Viji. Who would want to marry the girl with the dented face? How happily Viji had flitted away to America, to her ranch house and rosebushes.

As if she could hear, Shanta clasped her hand. "What you did was good, sister. You did the right thing."

No one had ever said this to Viji.

"Come back with me, Shanta." She saw it with sudden clarity: Shanta in the kitchen on Winding Creek Road, grinding spices, tipping the teapot into a waiting cup. "Leave these women here and come home with me. There's no need for you to stay!"

Shanta laughed and brought the room to life again.

"Why do you keep them here?" Viji asked.

"Who, the aunts? Where else could we send them?

Where we sent Appa? They aren't a danger to anybody."

"We both know that's not true."

Shanta only shrugged.

"Do you think it will happen to us?" Viji asked. "The madness?"

"Maybe. Maybe not. Who knows?"

"But we could prevent it, no? We could get help before it happens."

"You think those big American doctors are going to help you? Mad is mad, Vijaya. It happens or it doesn't." Then Shanta gazed at the high, shadowy ceiling and said, "If I go mad, who in this world is going to know?"

⚘⚘⚘

The shrieking dog was out that night. With every shriek it counted the seconds to midnight. The sky was moonless, the house robbed of light. In the darkness the furniture turned into looming edifices, a maze of vast plains and sharp corners. She felt her way, following the snores of Kuttima in the kitchen. The woman had her own bed-room, but she chose to sleep in the kitchen.

It wasn't the dog that had kept her awake; it was her own thoughts, like off-key lullabies. She'd been picturing her children alone on a plane. Would they know where the bathrooms were? And what if Kieran got airsick? A stew-ardess was supposed to sit with them, but who knew if this would happen? And what if they were separated, what kinds of adults would they be put with? No one could be trusted. She hoped there wouldn't be turbulence. She didn't want them to be scared. She'd once seen a bolt of lightning from her airplane window and it had nearly stopped her heart.

To calm herself, she thought of the ocean, rolling forth, receding. She thought of the creek behind her uncle's old house in the country. She thought of warmth and sleep and love. Love: her sister's warm cheek resting on her shoulder; Krishnan's chapatis, kneaded into the waiting palms of her mother; George patting down the tall grass by the lake so she'd have a soft spot to rest her head; the triplets leaning into each other on the airplane, their arms transcending armrests, legs slung over knees; her own fingers tracing the valleys between Aaron's ribs; a chest of saris stored hopefully; the distant rhythmic creak of her parents' bed—yes, even this was love.

The puja room's doors were shut. She ran her fingers over their carvings to find the latch. Inside, the dark was thick as cloth. It filled her eyes-nose-mouth until, fumbling, her hands discovered a matchbox. A flame, scant at first and then steady and fat on its oil lamp. She didn't have to wait long.

"I'm glad you're back," her mother said.

That's what Shanta said.

"You had a good time at the beach."

I don't have to answer you.

"Up to the old mischief, always the same," Amma laughed. "This is why you came without your husband?"

No.

"A good-time holiday, isn't it?"

I had to get out of this house.

"Yes, it's such a terrible place, this house. Such gratitude."

That's not what I mean.

She knew now why there was no picture of Appa in this room. She and Shanta had been sent to the big house, away from him, and he'd been sent away the following week.

The osmosis of family living had taught her that Appa left the house. Viji knew the facts, though she hadn't seen them until now: he'd been sent to a place better suited to him. And at some point over the many, many years, he had died.

That night, the scenes flashed past again, like images on a looped projector: the yellow coloring pencil, that tip-toeing walk that she'd found funny at first, the blood like syrup that dripped from Krishnan's mouth, the shallow streams of it that coursed down Appa's hand, the dull ache at her temple, and the sense that the ceiling, at any second, would come crashing down. This was not love. She re-membered it all now. Most of all, she remembered Shanta, who kneeled thin and shaking on the sitting room floor, cupping her nose in her hand and watching helplessly as she covered the tile in a puddle of blood. She'd tried to wipe the blood away with her fingers, but there was nothing to be done for the floor, for her dress, or for the crimson tears that streamed down her face.

🌱🌱🌱

The next morning, Viji followed the sound of chopping to the kitchen. Shanta sat, legs splayed around a cutting board piled with plantains.

Viji sat down. "I know what happened."

"Right. This Kuttima left the batter too long in the

sun, didn't she? Now it's practically rotten!"

"No," Viji said. "I know what happened with Appa, and why we were sent away. I remember everything now."

"Congratulations." Shanta sent a plantain wedge flying across the floor. It was the same old knife she used, the rusting Saracen's sword. The morning after everything, the knife had been rinsed and returned to the kitchen. Krishnan had stayed away, only to return a week later. Where he'd been, no one knew, but he must have stayed close enough to know that Appa had left, carried off in a car, a doctor by his side. Viji had heard the rumors at the big house.

"So you knew all this time," Viji said. "You let me ask and ask. Why did you—"

"Enough, sister." Shanta put the knife down, reached up and retwisted her bun. "I said I'd tell you once, and that's it. The end." She sighed. "I have to live here, you know. If I don't keep things in their cupboards, they'll take over the house."

He'd worn a suit, they said. A three-piece suit on that hot day, seated straight and proud in the back of the automobile. With a white kerchief he'd dabbed at his forehead. He'd folded it in a triangle, the neighbors said, before tucking it into his breast pocket. When Viji came back from the big house, she'd found Krishnan in the kitchen. By the stove they had sat, the cook and the colossal chopper. Here they both resumed their daily duties. Life in the house continued.

CHAPTER SIXTEEN

George had difficulties with women. This much he already knew. What surprised him was that neither age nor marital experience had improved his ability to cope. Men like his father didn't have these problems—his father and James Bond. They did what they wanted and got on with it. Standing at the counter in his bathrobe and fishing hat, Stan chewed on a chicken bone with just his front teeth, pilfering some invisible bit of sinew.

James Bond, George was sure, would not have left Kamla half-clothed and stranded on her bed. He wouldn't have shrunk from the consequences that awaited him, or the guilt that promised to follow. *Now get those clothes off*, James Bond would have said, slamming the door shut with his foot, ignoring the muffled din of *Three's Company*. At the very least, he wouldn't have stood in the kitchen, as George stood now, his fingers trembling on the receiver, wondering feebly if he should call Kamla back. Maybe for a coffee, he thought. Or just to apologize? He wouldn't want awkwardness, after all. God forbid that anything should be awkward.

"What's gotten into you?" Stan asked.

"Nothing, Dad. Just a bit tired."

"Heading to work today?"

George looked at the calendar. It was indeed a weekday. It was Monday. Not only was it a weekday, but it was *the* weekday, marked in red capitals on the calendar: KIDS ARRIVE HOME 12:35 SFO.

"Holy shit."

"What?"

"What time is it?" What time was it? eleven-forty. He was still in his bathrobe.

George found himself honking through traffic at twelve p.m. He'd managed to pull some trousers on and shed his robe. Landing took twenty minutes. Immigration, thirty minutes. Baggage claim, fifteen minutes. Customs, zero minutes. The entire drive to San Francisco International, two and a quarter hours. He whimpered at the thought of his children standing fatherless in International Arrivals, searching among the unknown faces that would stare, raise an eyebrow, and then look past them. What was wrong with him? He pictured the airline employees who'd take charge of the triplets, waiting with them for their deadbeat father. Already he could see the disdain on their faces when he showed up, unshaven and uncombed, his breath rank with coffee and eggs.

He didn't crash. He wasn't pulled over for speeding.

He arrived at SFO exactly one and a half hours after the triplets landed, and found them sitting on their suitcases in a corner of the arrivals building. There were no adults looking after them, and for this, George was relieved.

"You took forever!"

"Where *were* you?"

"What happened to your face?"

George had gashed his jawbone while shaving a few

days earlier, and hadn't attempted to shave since. His mind
flashed to Anisha Mehta, the slovenly way she held her
sandwich. Then he dropped to the floor and pulled his
children to him, all three at once, holding them fiercely,
though they squirmed against the bristle of his cheek.

꽃꽃꽃

"So, what did you think of it?" George asked. The triplets
knelt on their chairs, their hands diving into the pizza box,
taking two pieces at a time, three.

They ignored him. He cleared his throat and waited,
glad that no one was there to witness him being ignored,
aware that for weeks the triplets had probably been
craving pizza, missing their hamburgers and chicken chow
mein and sugary cereals, the way he'd missed fish-finger
sandwiches and lager. He would surprise them tomorrow
after dinner with a trip to Leatherby's for sundaes—one
towering ice-cream sundae for each of them, no having to
share.

He waited for them to settle and tried again. "So,
how'd you like it?"

"Like what?" Babygirl asked through a mouthful of
cheese.

"India. Did you like India? What did you think of it?"
He remembered when they were babies, how he'd asked
questions two or three times, slowly and clearly, to help
them grasp the language, hoping that they might turn into
prodigies who started talking long before their peers. They
hadn't.

She shrugged. "Good."

"Good? And how was your aunty?"

"She was nice."

"She was nice?"

She shrugged again. There had been hundreds, thou-
sands, of treatises written on India, its paradoxes, its
unfathomable depths of tradition. "It was good," George
repeated. "It was good."

"I saw a man with no legs," Kieran offered.

"Interesting. And how did that make you feel?"

"Weird, I guess." With his finger Kieran pushed the
butt end of a crust into his mouth.

"I see. Did you two see this also?"

"No," Babygirl said. "I didn't. But we saw lots of beggars."

"Yeah," Avi confirmed, "there were beggars and bums,
like, everywhere. It was weird."

"Weird in what way?"

"Well, not like here. They don't have beggars here."

George wanted to tell them that they did, indeed, have
beggars here. Not in Maple Grove, but in San Francisco,
Chicago, New York, even as close as downtown Sacramento, there were people living in tunnels, sleeping on
burlap sacks, asking for spare change to make a phone call,
tying elastic bands around their arms and pulling them
tight with their teeth, spending the night in shelters and
abandoned buildings and subway bathrooms, sometimes
alone, sometimes hoping to God that their children
wouldn't remember too much of it. But the triplets were
showered now and dressed in pajamas, their hair still
damp and their cheeks tanned and clean, their eyelids
heavy with satisfaction. Before them sat cups of frothy

root beer, and cans that were still more than half full. Their Friday-night TV shows were starting in twenty minutes, and they chomped confidently on their pizza, so settled and secure with their place in the world that George didn't want them to have to know otherwise.

CHAPTER SEVENTEEN

The weight of Viji's thoughts bore down on her that day and night. Like a ratty bathrobe, they reeked of the past and turned the room gray—if only she could take a match to them and turn them into glorious flame. She wanted to call George. She wanted to know that somewhere in the world, things were ordinary.

"Hello, darling!" George sounded nervous.

"What happened?"

"Sorry? Well, nothing."

"Are the children back?"

"Sure, I picked them up yesterday," he chuckled.

She could tell something was wrong. "You know," Viji said, "I was thinking. I want to come home."

She heard him inhale and then his voice, as if untwining, relaxed. "Really? You do?"

"But not yet. I need to be here longer." A flash of Aaron, which she pushed away. "Just to spend some time here."

"Um, okay. What, a week or two?"

"Mm. A week or two. I'll look for tickets." And she would find one. The tourist season was drawing to a close.

"I'm glad, Viji. I'm glad you're coming back."

Through the streets of the city a fresh wind sprinted, lifting Viji's sari off her shoulders. The sky above was no longer colorless. It was an empty white canvas, ready for the spill of possibility.

She caught an auto rickshaw and took it to the nearest shopping complex. No more memories. She'd had them all. She wanted fresh things now, she wanted armfuls of beauty.

First, a sari shop. No more rifling through moth-eaten trousseaux. She would buy her sister something new and beautiful, to be worn every day, not stored away for some special occasion that was never to arrive. The shop boys climbed the high shelves, tossinging down the tight parcels like monkeys throw down fruit. The salesman unfolded the saris and billowed them out in three swift moves. He asked her to sit, sensing she had money to spend, and when he snapped his fingers a tumbler of tea appeared at her elbow. He had a remarkable talent for choosing the ugliest saris to show her, but she knew to be bossy with these men, and soon she had what she wanted: five saris for Shanta, two for Kuttima, and one for each of the old crones. The cashier slid them to her, wrapped in brown paper and tied with string, cradled in a cloth bag that bore the store's logo.

This was the city she knew. She'd missed it more than she realized. Back on the street, she bought a strand of jasmine for her hair and another for Shanta's. The lady selling them rolled the fat, fragrant bulbs in newspaper and wound them round with string. From the next cart she bought a paper cone that steamed with chili peanuts, too hot to touch. She blew on them.

Last of all, she bought a phone. It was a red one with touch-tone buttons. No more STD offices, no more months and years of transoceanic silence. She caught an auto rickshaw. It wound through traffic like an ant, touching noses with other rickshaws as it made its way home.

Viji spent six more days in her sister's home. She made Shanta try on all of the saris, not just by holding the fabric up to her chest, but by unraveling all six yards and wrapping them around herself. She knew how easy it was to let a perfectly folded sari stay perfectly folded. "All of them are red," Shanta said.

"I know they are. You'll be a bride every day."

Twice, Viji picked up the telephone and dialed the operator, asking for the number of the Sea Rock Inn at Kovalam Beach. There were plenty of hotels in Madras. Aaron could book a room in one—but she stopped herself from calling him every time. Instead, she filled her days doing as she pleased, taking afternoon naps on the sofa, wearing only her petticoat and a cotton blouse. There were only women in the house, so why get dressed at all? On the fifth day, she hired a car and took Shanta to the Marriott, where they ate a lavish Chinese meal. On the sixth day, she found a salon and the sisters got their eyebrows threaded. This was what sisters did.

And on the seventh day, the new red phone rang for the very first time. Shanta shied away from it. Viji picked it up.

"Viji?" George's voice was shaking. "Viji, you have to come home." The line was poor, the seconds between them chipped by static.

CHAPTER EIGHTEEN

Anisha Mehta stood squarely in the kitchen. She'd rung the doorbell and stalked past George without a word. He wondered if she was angry with him, too. On the driveway, on the street, there was no sign of Kamla. "I walked here alone," the girl said, as if reading his thoughts.

"Babygirl's in her room." George found his keys and left.

It wasn't his fault that the route to work took him past Kamla's house. Nor could he be blamed for the stop sign that allowed him to slow, peer past the bushes at the front of the drive, and watch her needlessly water her lawn. He drove on.

✤✤✤

Leaves gathered like floating scabs on the surface of the swimming pool. The cleaner came only once a month in the winter, and the water had turned soupy from the rain. Around the perimeter, the automatic pool sweeper darted, a sea serpent whipping its long-hosed tentacles.

Babygirl liked being outside in the winter, when the backyard turned into a secret world of silent grass and frost-powdered branches, where at any second bushes with dripping black leaves could morph into gargoyles. When she pressed her ear to the ground she could hear the wet worlds that moved beneath, the whisper of insects that sounded like an ocean. When she looked closely without blinking, she could see the grass blades quiver.

"I can do a handstand on the balance beam," Anisha Mehta announced. She demonstrated on the diving board, which, Babygirl noted, was clearly wider than a balance beam. "Now you do it," Anisha ordered.

"I don't want to."

"Come on."

Babygirl was quite happy where she was, digging her nails into the thick, mulchy soil.

"You're a baby," Anisha Mehta said. "But I guess you can't help it."

Slowly, the earth began to freeze her fingers. It was a satisfying feeling.

"How come you guys came back without your mom?"

"I dunno. We had to start school."

"But how come your mom didn't come back with you?"

"I don't *know*."

"My mom said your mom had some things to figure out."

Babygirl shrugged.

"Anyway, my mom said the same thing when my dad and her got divorced."

"So? That doesn't mean my parents are." Babygirl crammed more mud beneath her nails.

"I bet you they are. Everybody's parents are doing it. Almost everybody I know. And now yours, too."

"You don't know anything."

"I do too. You know what?"

"What?"

"I know a secret."

"What?"

"Can't tell, it's a secret." She stretched like a cat on the diving board, her body as long as a grownup's. "I know something you don't know," she sang.

Babygirl couldn't help sitting up. "What do you know? Tell me!"

"Come here and I'll tell you." She sat up to make room for Babygirl. Babygirl sat beside her on the diving board, her feet dangling above the lifeless pool.

Anisha Mehta leaned in close, her breath like dragon-fire in the icy afternoon. "Do you know what fucking is?"

༒༒༒

Stan lay in his grandson's bed and watched as Lupe got dressed. She strapped her bra like a harness around her back, forming new hills of flesh, warm and fresh as hot cobs.

You're a right bacon butty, he was tempted to say. Normally he would have, but he was tired, and he suspected she wouldn't know what he meant. She might even have taken offense. They didn't do much talking, and for this he was thankful. Time not chatting was better spent with his face pressed into her neck, his fingers kneading her ripe handfuls. He was one of the lucky ones, he knew. Now and then he thought ruefully of his mates back in Nottingham, the men at the pub his age and even younger who hadn't touched a woman in years, not even their own wives. He knew that age brought with it an intense longing the young could never imagine. It enraged him to see the young wasters in his pub, men in their twenties and thirties with worlds before them—riches and places to go and women and women and more women. They could have all the women they wanted, and what did they do? They met their useless mates in the pub every night and wasted their time staring into pints of lager, talking shite for hours on end.

The young ached with desire. For the old, desire was a knife blade. Stan felt as if every woman he'd ever been with had gathered to wait for him here, at the end of his life, an army of skin and hair and lips. They'd found him at his weakest. His skin sagged everywhere—*everywhere*—but this only meant he had more surface area that needed to be touched. The copper spots on his hands and arms and face were no more than a trail map that whispered to the world, *Here's where I want you to touch me, here and here and here and here.*

At the sound of Lupe's zipper, he closed his eyes and thought of England, as the English always did once they managed to escape. He remembered the perfect summers, his memory splashed with make-believe because no English summer was perfect. But like he did with his women, he stacked all the lovely days together, squeezed out the clouds and heavy mists, and made for himself one long legendary summer, an uninterrupted trail of beauty. WHAT SUMMER MEANS IN A COLD COUNTRY HOW TO PLAY CROQUET THAT THERE ARE PEOPLE IN THE WORLD WHO DON'T OWN SWIMMING POOLS HOW TO JUDGE A MUSHROOM THE DIFFER-

ENCE BETWEEN WATCHING THE FOOTY AND WATCHING RUGBY
DAYS THAT LAST UNTIL MIDNIGHT HOW TO GET YOURSELF OUT-
SIDE BEFORE THE SUNSHINE GOES. All seasons were half
invention, anyway.

But this was real, this he remembered clearly: the
fields of rapeseed that stretched outside the city. Once,
when he'd been driving Marla to her mother's house, he'd
stopped the car and parked off the A35. The heat was intense that day, the air perfectly still. He'd grabbed Marla's
hand and marched her to the center of the field, where,
without a word, he'd laid her down, vanishing into the tall
grass. Beneath the roar of the highway, they had made the
buds tremble, almost as if their yellow tips had been
caught in a passing breeze.

ψ ψ ψ

The word rose like gunsmoke in the cold air. Babygirl
knew what fucking was. She knew it was what people did,
and animals. It was a terrible word. Anisha Mehta edged
closer until their knees were touching.

"Your dad? Your dad fucks my mom."

"Shut up, Anisha."

"It's true. I saw it with my very own eyes." Anisha
Mehta's fat fingers clamped down on Babygirl's wrist. "My
mom, she was on the bed, and your dad had his hands all
over her shirt—"

"Let go of me!" Babygirl yanked at her wrist, but Anisha Mehta was strong.

"Listen to me. Your parents are getting divorced and
someone's got to tell you!"

Babygirl leapt to her feet, but Anisha grabbed her around the shoulders. "They meet all the time! When you were in India, they met every day almost!"

"I said, *let me go*." She pushed Anisha to the diving board. Anisha, on instant rebound, pushed her back. The push sent Babygirl into a spin, reeling and then teetering, arms flailing at the swimming pool's stony edge.

"Wake up!" Anisha commanded, and with a final push she tipped Babygirl into the pool. It was an odd sound: a splash in January, followed by silence.

Like a polished rock, Babygirl dropped smoothly to the bottom of the pool, her legs cycling weakly, her arms drifting and useless above her head. Below her, black leaves made a mosaic on the deep-end floor.

In the summers they played dibble-dabble, a game where a twig was thrown somewhere in the deep end, and the first to find it and capture it was the winner. Babygirl never won, because secretly she thought there were snakes waiting on the deep-end floor, obese black serpents that slithered around the drain. She would dive as far as she could, then charge back to the surface when she felt something brush her foot. But not this time. This time she twirled calmly to the floor. Around her, the underwater world flashed from blue to black and back to blue. Her hair floated around her in thick brown tentacles. She was an octopus. She wasn't frightened. Her eyes opened wide in the chlorinated water.

Inside the house, something jolted in Kieran. He ran to the bathroom and sat on the toilet. But no, this wasn't the problem. In the family room, Avi was watching television. When Kieran found him, Avi was holding his chest, peering at the ground. Whatever psychic tendon had pulled Kieran to Avi now tugged both boys to the sliding glass door.

Outside, Anisha Mehta stood stiff as a scarecrow. Her arms stuck out from her sides. She was in another world, like a sleepwalker. Her eyes were turned down, deep into the pool. Kieran ran upstairs. Avi ran outside, shouting his sister's name.

The chubby one burst through the door while Lupe was pulling up her stockings. She wore only her bra on top, and she gasped and turned away. The boy was shouting something and pointing to the ground. He was flapping his hands like he'd touched something hot. Stan could make nothing of this wall of words, but like the children on that *Lassie* show, he knew he had to follow.

The cold slapped his belly and his bare thighs. He was wearing his underwear and nothing else. Avi wielded a pool net. Its pole rose high above the boy's head, and he was fishing something out of the water. He was prodding something—a hand. A hand lay limply on the surface of the pool. They were playing a game. A pool game. When she saw him, the neighbor girl ran.

Children didn't play pool games in January. Attached to the hand was the arm, the shoulder, the head with long willowy hair now floating—his granddaughter. Stan dove in. In the water, he was young and strong. He grabbed the girl around the waist, and with a single kick he shuttled her to the pavement. Hair stuck like webs to her face; he had to sift through them to get to her mouth. What he'd learned so long ago came back in an instant. He'd done this once, to a cadet who'd fallen overboard off the coast of Norway. They said anyone who fell into that sea died instantly, that there was no point in rescue. But the boy was fished out, and Stan had brought him, half-frozen, back to life.

Babygirl spouted water like a fountain, gagging. Her chest convulsed and her mouth grew wide in a silent sob. But her eyes were open. "All right, chick?" Stan said. She looked straight back at him with brown eyes and ebony lashes. He saw it then, clear as day: these were Marla's eyes. Here she was, sitting upright and looking around her like she'd been in a dream. *And you were there*, Stan thought, *and you were there, and you and you and you*….His chest exploded. He fell to the frozen ground.

CHAPTER NINETEEN

Turbulence didn't bother Viji. It was no more than bumps in the road, which felt like a natural part of traveling. She didn't mind the way people's heads bobbed and rattled, like eggs in a crate. What did worry her was smooth, motionless flight—this did not feel natural. This could lead to anything.

A stewardess was leaning on a seat a few rows up, talking to a man with a crown of white hair. She was Asian, wrapped in a long printed dress that clung like skin to her fairy-tale waist. A smile lilted across her face, and she never once took her eyes off the man. In one hand she held a pitcher of water, in the other a tower of plastic cups. Viji was thirsty.

"Excuse me," she called. "Excuse me!" The eyes snapped up. "Can I have some water, please?" With the gloom of a mistreated servant, the stewardess straightened and made her way to Viji, pouring as she walked, spilling water down the side of her hand. She did something that was not a smile but a stretching of her lips, and handed Viji the cup.

Stan had had a heart attack. George found out from Mrs. Bauer, after Lupe ran half-clothed to their home and begged her to find Mr. Armitage's number at work. Mrs. Bauer had called an ambulance and then called George. Viji couldn't help smirking to herself. All this hanky-pankying like a young bachelor—a man his age should have known better. If he were a devout Hindu, he'd have been spending these last years in prayer and meditation, preparing himself for the next life. She thought of her father, his last years spent who-knows-where—in a chair, most likely, staring out of a window until the last day of his life and the final, soundless slump.

They'd been in the air for eleven hours. She had to use the bathroom, but she knew it would stink by now.

"I need you to come home," George had said. She closed her eyes and sat back, bathing in the words. George had never needed her for anything before.

The man next to her had fat hands and a walrus-like pinky that hung over the armrest, only inches above her thigh. He smacked his lips, eyes closed, oozing into her personal space. From the corner of her eye, she could sense a colossal wart that stuck from the thick brown bark of his face. As if he sensed her sensing him, he sat up straighter, though his eyes stayed closed. The pinky flexed and curled above her thigh, a caterpillar escaping its cocoon. There was a smaller wart lodged next to the fingernail, and soil-colored age spots sprinkled over the hand. To think, this hand had once belonged to an infant, had once been as silken and fine as her own children's hands. She thought of George's hands, the dry skin at the knuckles, the elegant line from bone to joint and the square nails, pillowed in cuticles that he used to chew until, eventually, she had made him stop.

The man sputtered a sigh of fetid breath. She had to lift her hand to her nose. This was why they gave out mints on airplanes. She looked for the stewardess, who had rejoined her gentleman friend a few rows forward. Surely the woman had better things to do; Viji strained to see the man's face, but she couldn't. Never mind. She'd heard about stewardesses.

By the last hour of the flight, the air had grown thick with collective breath. A sediment of thought had built up on the plane, the imaginings of so many people over so many hours, peaking with every inhalation, rushing through the air with every exiting breath. Freed from dark nose tunnels, the ideas hurried along the aisles, past beverage carts, and into Viji's nostrils as she slept.

She thought then of Krishnan's hands, her memory of them as unobstructed as the sunshine that streamed through her airplane window. How thin and weathered they'd been, every centimeter covered with star-shaped wrinkles that he said had been there since birth, an omen of luck in life. A track of shiny welts had run down his left forefinger, where he'd cut himself with the chopping knife, repeatedly over the years. He'd said it was like falling in love: no matter how many times he nicked himself, he never seemed to learn. How different his hands were from Appa's great paws, soft and untraced, the hands of a magistrate. She'd left Krishnan's picture behind where it belonged, in the house's puja room.

When she pressed her face to the airplane window, the cold felt good against her forehead. She ran a hand over her belly, between her legs, where all was normal again. There was no telling why the pain had gone, or where. She rolled her thoughts away, the crinkled remembrances, scrunched them into balls, and dropped them from the airplane. Through the clouds they plunged, down into the death-freeze of the ocean.

CHAPTER TWENTY

George couldn't remember if socks were allowed. Surely
Viji had worn socks in here on cold days—or was there
something holier about bare feet—the humility of toes,
the honesty of the heel? He balled his socks and tossed
them to the hallway. Flowers lay ashen on the shelves,
falling away to dust. He sniffed: oil and smoke and a rosy
trail of incense. They'd been gathering here for twelve
years. He hadn't been in the puja room for three years, not
since he and Kieran and Avi had painted the walls blue.
Kieran had painted the top half of each wall, on tiptoe on
a ladder as George held his calves. The deities, framed and
carved in stone, gazed out at him blankly now, like in-laws
unimpressed with both his looks and his credentials. So
he did what he felt was right, and sat on the floor.

His body stuck out at surrealist angles into the room,
his knees at his ears, his elbows rising to meet his temples.
When he crossed his ankles, they trembled and ached. He
managed to stay in this position and even brought his
palms together in prayer, like he'd seen Viji do. It gave him
something to do with his hands. When he lowered his
forehead, a drop of sweat ran down his finger.

It resembled praying, though he didn't know exactly
how to pray. It had to involve more than just asking for

things. And he couldn't do what Viji did, string together line after line of Sanskrit mantras in a sad harmonica monotone. All George could do was close his eyes and feel very, very worried. For a moment he thought he saw a light, but this too faded to darkness.

They pressed against his eyelids, the years of muttered prayers. They towered to the ceiling, crowded the walls, and made it hard to breathe. Lingering in the room was the smell of palms pressed together, the damp that gathered between them. Around him hung the steady aroma of daily devotion, the milky smell of hope.

He opened his eyes when he felt he had finished. When he noticed his mother's picture on the wall, he took it down and picked away the sticky residue that had built up in the corners of the frame. Without planning to, he brought the frame to his forehead, his own nose smashed against Marla's, and he began to ask for things. Two things.

When he looked up again, he saw a white square where the picture had hung. It was bright white, covered over for years by the frame. When they'd painted, they hadn't bothered taking anything off the walls. He pulled down another frame and found another white square. Then he found two more, and three more. The newer photographs were backed by blue, but the old ones left a spray of white shapes across the wall. In the lightless room, they glowed like the shadow of a prism.

Babygirl had been given a bed in the children's unit after arriving in the same ambulance as Stan. George imagined her sitting upright in the large transport section of the vehicle, strapped into a fold-down seat, unable to take her eyes off the old man stretched on a gurney with medics buzzing around him, machines bleeping. (In reality, Babygirl had ridden in the backseat, wrapped in a thermal blanket, and Lupe had held her hand.) Her vital signs checked, she was given a bed, hot chocolate, and warming blankets. When George found her, she was still shivering, though he sensed with relief that she enjoyed the shivering, that the clacking of teeth entertained her in some way. There were rainbows painted on the walls. She finished one hot chocolate and asked for another, leaving only a few coagulated clumps of cocoa powder to rest at the bottom of the mug. She fell asleep, and in case she was indeed still cold, he climbed onto the child-size bed. He wrapped his legs around her and pulled her to his chest so that her head rested just below his neck. It was the closest he could come to carrying her inside him.

If only his children could have stayed in the womb, protected by its liquid cushion, where nutrition was a given, and safety as natural as breath. In the uterine world, water didn't kill. It didn't fill his daughter's lungs or seize her small body in its frozen fist. When his children had been inside Viji, he'd never had to feel the guilt of not being around when he was needed. He'd never had to think about what he'd been doing when his child had almost died, whether he was already at the office, or whether it happened, by spiteful coincidence, in those moments when he'd sat in his car and peered down a driveway to watch Kamla water her lawn. But that place, where all was safe, that was a mother's world, closed off to the likes of him. He hadn't been able to touch his children then, or smell the chlorine in their hair. This place, with its frigid air and metal hospital beds and shatter proof windows and rainbows painted on the wall, this place was his.

   He'd always imagined heartbreak to be a sudden thing, like a vase shattering on a marble floor. His own heart cowered somewhere in a corner of his chest. It had been pinched and bullied. It was covered in stress fractures, tiny enough to go unnoticed but large enough to leak away all that he'd once thought was his. His father's heart, on the other hand, was whole and beating weakly, a few floors up, in the intensive-care unit. The doctors—he imagined a crew of them standing white-coated in a dark room that glowed with X-rays—were deciding whether an operation would be too risky.

   Meanwhile, he realized, he'd have to corral the events of the next few days into some sort of manageability. He had a talk with the children.

   "I'd like you to do something for me," he said to them. He stood blocking the television. They craned their necks to see around him. "I think we should keep quiet about the swimming pool around Mum. All right?"

   "Why?" Babygirl had been looking forward to spreading the tale of her brush with death.

   "I don't think she'd take it very well. She's been through a lot lately." They'd all been through a lot. Even the triplets, whether or not they knew it. He could see, in their screen-addled eyes, a sort of gravity that hadn't been there before. Yes, they must have known it. He spent the rest of the afternoon waiting for the phone to ring. It would be Viji or the doctor.

   His father could die. Correction: his father would die—if not now, then soon enough. George gathered his disparate trinkets of emotion and tried to whip them into a foam of sadness, something he'd be able to feel. But he couldn't do it. He was unable to feel a thing that hadn't happened yet. It would be practical to think now about this death, before the reality of it made him useless. If Stan died now—today or tomorrow, say—would George send him back to England, fly back with him on the plane, the coffin thrumming and sliding in storage below? He had no idea how bodies were transported—in coffins, metal cases, or maybe nylon sacks: black, with zippers going all around the edges, like the protective bag he got when he bought a new suit. And if he did take Stan home, he'd have to arrange a funeral—for whom? Barney from the taxi firm, the men at the pub, the obese landlady, rough as bricks, Victoria? No, he would keep Stan here. He would bury him in the dry ground, in the January sun.

He went through his father's closet that morning to look for a suit. Of course Stan hadn't brought a suit with him. George found a shirt with buttons and a decent pair of trousers. These would do, if the need arose. Into the pocket of the decent trousers he slipped the blue crystal earrings. He spent the rest of the day reading every article in the newspaper, standing at the window, and watching the phone. He longed to leave but knew that he'd miss the call if he did. He made several pots of tea and let most of them go cold. These could be the last hours of his father's life. Stan could be slipping off at that very moment. And where was George? At the kitchen window, waiting for a phone call and burning his lips with tea.

CHAPTER TWENTY-ONE

Viji stood at the foot of the drive, her suitcase at her feet.
The taxi left only fumes. She couldn't believe how large
her lawn was. The way her house sprawled, it was a foreign
thing, alien to her. The bushes around the entrance were
lush and green after the winter rains. The eucalyptus trees
looked sullen, impatient for summer—this was not their
season. From where she stood, the house looked unnatu-
rally still. She hoped someone was home. She didn't have
a key.

For the first time in twelve years, she rang the bell and
waited at her own door.

Eight notes, one missing in the middle, where Avi had
pulled down a chime. Inside the house, the bells would
echo for seconds after the ring had finished.

George opened the door. His movements were unreal
and stilted, as if he were stuck in a dream. When she
handed him her suitcase, it felt empty, like a stage prop.
He took it from her, and she stepped in.

"I wasn't sure when you'd arrive," he said. And between them, the seconds froze. How real he suddenly
looked, here in the light and shadow of their home. She
could see the heat in his face, she could smell his wheati-
ness from where she stood. It was a scent like baked bread,

and it would fade as she got used to him again. She breathed deeply. "Viji," he said, and took her hand. She couldn't stop the shaking in her wrist. They stood this way for several seconds or maybe minutes, until the final echo of the doorbell faded and they were left in silence.

The next morning, George woke early. He'd heard Viji get up in the middle of the night and pad out of the bedroom. They'd slept in the same bed. They had not made love. Nor had they kissed goodnight. He felt almost as if they'd never touched each other before. A kiss now would feel like their first, with all the accompanying uncertainty, the negotiation of space and force, the placement of lips and nose, the skirting of the tongue. When she came back to bed he placed his hand over hers. And that, for the moment, was enough.

Ten o'clock, and she was still in bed. They were going to see Stan that day, the doctors had decided to send him home. George stood at the window with his tea. He stood at the window with his tea and watched, as if on a movie screen, as a figure turned the corner and headed for the drive. She was brisk. Her legs moved like pistons.

The pavement sent spikes of cold through his socks, but he didn't have time for shoes. He jogged clumsily to the mailbox at the end of the drive.

"What are you doing?" she grinned, pointing to his feet.

"What are you doing here, Kamla?" He didn't smile back.

"I heard that Viji's back."

How had she known? He scanned the surrounding houses.

"She's in bed."

"Hmm. Jet lag, it must be. She must be so tired."

They hadn't seen each other since the day on the bed. Kamla hadn't asked after Babygirl, nor had she said anything about her daughter or what her daughter had done to his daughter.

"You probably shouldn't be here."

"Nonsense, George." Kamla patted his chest. "Bygones, all right? I just want to see how Viji is."

"You shouldn't be here, Kamla." At the other end of his drive, his family hung together precariously. Their pieces had floated back somehow, and rejoined.

"You should go," he said. His words were final.

Viji was not asleep. Viji was awake, standing and looking out the bathroom window when she saw George in socks running down the driveway. She saw him speak with Kamla, his hands on his hips. She saw Kamla smile, then not smile, and at last she saw her walk away. None of this made sense to her—it might have, if she'd thought about it and come up with various scenarios of what could have happened between George, her husband, and Kamla, her only friend. But after everything, she decided not to think but to let the matter go. What a lesson to learn in the end.

The first shower after a twelve-hour flight is like a new birth. Viji closed her eyes and smiled into the torrent of water. The door opened. It was George, standing in the bathroom, watching her. She didn't mind. After twelve years she could move freely before him, attending to the business of washing, cleaning her ears, soaping her breasts. But she couldn't keep the shyness from her voice. "Do you want to come in?" she asked.

"Really?"

She pointed to the other showerhead, the one they'd never used.

"It would save time," George mused, "if not water." Soon his clothes lay in a pile and he was in, as naked as she was, his back turning pink from the pinging spray of her shower. In the steam, he looked like an apparition. Moving to the other end of the large cubicle, he began to fiddle with the tap.

Out shot a jet of cold water that made George squeal and Viji laugh. The shower gurgled and sputtered and petered into a trickle, the faucet head blocked by rust and neglect. A single runtish stream dripped down on him, making bird tracks in his chest hair. He reached for the soap and began to wash.

"Don't be silly," Viji said. And with this, George crossed to her side. There was plenty of shower for two. When they turned the water off, the room was cushioned in steam and the ceiling dripped down on them. George kissed Viji. It was hesitant at first, and then permitted and, as it turned out, nothing like their first kiss. That one had meant almost nothing, it had been fueled by gin, planted firmly in a first meeting. This kiss held in it everything that had come before. It teetered at the summit of twelve years.

That evening, the triplets looked up to see a man in the hallway with a shock of white hair. This was Grandad Stan and this was not Grandad Stan. He nodded to them and made his way slowly to his room. Avi got up and followed.

"He's wearing a towel on his head," Avi said.

"Why?"

"I don't know. He looks smaller, too." To Avi, Grandad

Stan looked as if the hospital had vacuumed something out of him.

Babygirl stayed away from Stan's room. She didn't understand why he looked at her the way he did now, peering into her eyes as if trying to hunt something down. He did it at the kitchen table, he called to her from his bed whenever she passed his door. Each time he called her she scurried away from him, pretending she hadn't heard.

"I wonder if it hurt," Kieran said. "I wonder what it felt like." To Kieran, a heart attack sounded like a bludgeoning, like a surprise machete out of nowhere.

"Let's leave Grandad to rest," George said. "Let's save the questions for later."

Stan would be with them for five more days. George spent much of this time stationed at his father's door, just out of sight. He'd had a dog when he was in school. The dog was hit one day by a car speeding on the Sneinton main road. He hadn't died immediately. When George found him, he was lying on a neighbor's lawn, mewling weakly. He didn't seem to be in terrible pain, but he couldn't be moved. More than anything, he seemed a bit miffed to have been run down, annoyed at the bother of it. There was nothing for George to do but stroke the dog and wait for him to either get up or die. Animals could be stroked, children could be held. Stan sat upright in bed with a towel over his head, draped from shoulder to shoulder. It made him look like a Monty Python woman.

Sick man, injured dog. It was a cruddy, obvious metaphor and George tried to push it from his mind. All he wanted was to touch his father without being told to sod off, but that was impossible. So George watched from the other side of his door as his father stared at the wall, as he let his head fall to the side for a doze, as he picked the tobacco packet from his bedside table, pinched a bit of the dried mulch, and placed it on his tongue. He spent a good deal of time gazing at the walls, as if the room were new and foreign to him. The heart attack had left him stunned in a way George had never seen, as if he'd awoken to a wrecking ball crashing through his home. George did get to bring Stan to the kitchen for meals. At those times, he could touch his back and hold him by the elbow. When he raised and lowered him from his chair, he held Stan firmly around the shoulder, in a disguised sort of hug. It was a comfort to feel his bulk.

Only Viji could sit with Stan. She brought him his tea in the afternoons. When she tried to get up from his bed, he pulled her back down by the wrist. She had to wait until every drop was drunk, and then she could leave. Not even Lupe was allowed in with him. She spent the first afternoon in Viji's kitchen, waiting at the table for Stan to summon her. When he didn't, Viji sent George to remind Stan of his visitor. When George came back, shaking his head, Lupe went back to the Bauers' and never returned.

On the third day, Stan refused his tea. He didn't eat breakfast that morning and he tried to avoid lunch. On the fourth day, he skipped both breakfast and lunch. He had little interest in food and could think of nothing that he wanted to eat, not even when Viji offered to make a roast. But Viji didn't mind—Stan made sense to her now. He was, at last, an old man.

On the fifth day, dinner was quiet. Stan ate boiled po-tatoes and peas, and the children watched him cautiously,

still awed by this new and brittle version of their grandfather. "Couldn't get their potatoes right in that bloody
hospital" was all he said. Viji took this as a compliment to
her cooking. He went to bed early that night and, somewhere in the middle of it, he died.

༄ ༄ ༄

"George," she said. Viji called him to come and see: his father, chilled and gray, his eyes closed and mouth wide
open. George shuddered and turned to leave, but Viji held
his wrist and kept him in the room. This was death, empty
and rattling. Viji wanted him to see. She sat next to Stan on
the bed and, cupping his jaw in her hand, she closed it.
This didn't bother her; she would have done it for her own
father. George sat next to Viji and placed a hand on his father's forehead. Then he leaned over and rested his head
on his chest. There was no heartbeat there, just a silent
rush, the sound of the ocean. George sat up. He began to
suck in heaving breaths, shaking his head. What he felt was
rarefied fear. Because he couldn't look away, he stared at
his father's corpse, stared and stared. He felt the skin had
been peeled from his own body, that it was left flapping
and raw in the wind.

Death had turned him into a small boy. Not Stan, but
George. George fell asleep that night with his head on
Viji's chest, his arms twined around her waist. His hold on
her was fierce, even after his face had gone slack with sleep.
Again, it was five in the morning and she was awake. She
pried his hands from her, rose, and walked straight to the
hallway closet. There would be a new photo for the puja

room. She couldn't deny that she was pleased in some way. She was a collector at heart.

She knew the right one when she found it in a shoe-box at the back of the cupboard. How handsome he looked in his navy uniform with the white sailor hat. His small smile said, *I'm going to war now, but I don't want any trouble.* He had George's eyebrows, the same shallow divot at the side of his mouth. She'd had this young sailor in her home. She had hated him and fed him and found him dead one morning. From the closet she chose a frame and, kneeling on the carpet, she put it all together.

In the puja room, she hung him next to Marla. She lit an oil lamp, straightened the frame. The scant light left the other photos in shadow. As far as she could see, Stan and Marla hung on her wall—Stan and Marla and nobody else. She stroked her belly. The pains were gone for good. Now, for a few weightless moments, she felt what it was to be a girl: a purity of limbs and hair and fresh white teeth. She dabbed her finger in the oil lamp, dabbed it again in the small pot of vermillion, and smudged it onto Stan's forehead. She touched some to her own forehead, blew out the lamp, and left.

Avi and Kieran were in their sleeping bags, Babygirl in her bed. The children wouldn't go near their grandfather's room—now it was the death room—and she couldn't blame them. Even she had begun to hurry past its door after she'd found him that morning, staring past her, past the wall, all the way to England or into eternity. Never mind. A fresh coat of paint would help.

She sat on Babygirl's bed, just on the edge of it so as not to shake the mattress. She used to do this. She used to watch her children sleep, back when they all fit into one bed or within the bars of a single crib. These days they didn't like to sleep. In a few years they would want nothing else. She noticed a pink bracelet on Babygirl's nightstand. It was the kind they used in hospitals, made of semiclear plastic that had to be cut off with scissors, with a name typewritten and taped onto the surface. Stan had one also. Viji smiled at the thought of a nurse making this for Babygirl, probably to humor her while the children were visiting Stan. Children loved these knickknacks that meant nothing to adults.

From their window she could see the swimming pool. Someone had left the pool light on and it glowed in the night like a warm wound. The switch was outside. She cherished this hour, just before morning, when she could be alone with the ceiling and the windows and the walls of her home. As she crossed the dark well of the living room she thought of Aaron, how he'd kept his jet lag. What a thing to do.

Outside, the night was warm for January, and windless. Light from the pool scattered like gems over the rosebushes. They were bare, waiting for spring, hung with a few sluggish leaves. She crossed to the pool house, where spiderwebs gave in to her, spreading themselves over her hair and shoulders as she reached in to turn off the pool light. There was only the moonlight now. In its wan mist she could see the lawn, crystal-frosted. Through her feet she could feel the dark buzzing soil, its coursing underworld. In one swift move, she swept off her nightgown. She wasn't cold. She slipped off her panties and stifled a laugh, afraid someone might hear. A breeze brought her

skin to life; the night licked her with its scratchy tongue.
She lay down in the grass, naked. It tickled her bare back
and she began to laugh again. This time she didn't stop
herself. Let them come, the triplets and George, the Bauers
and Fromms and Attenboroughs. Let them go home to
their kitchens to talk about the crazy lady, the barenaked
one laughing here, her arms splayed on the grass,
wreathed in cobwebs, the green ants losing themselves in
her hair and in the crannies of her thighs. She could smell
it all when she turned her head to the ground—the ants
and the grass, the frost and ice and eucalyptus resin, roses
and cherries and the warm cement of summer, dandelions
and dog shit, the slime-coated frogs who swam up
through the pool drains from the nearby creek, tree bark
and bees and clouds of gnats, sunscreen and slippers and
the dirt that clung to her garden shears, barbecues and
woodsmoke and parting clouds, the rain, the wind, the
valley fog, and, somewhere in the middle of it, the faintest
trace of spring. She grabbed a handful of grass and yanked
it from the ground. Soil crumbs hung from the roots. She
shook a few blades, placed them on her tongue, and kept
them there, chewing, just to see how they tasted.